D0557022

The Thirteen

The Thirteen

A Novel By

James Patterson

Copyright © 1995 James Patterson

All rights reserved. No part of this book may be reproduced, stored in a retrieval system, or transmitted by any means, electronic, mechanical, photocopying, recording, or otherwise, without written permission from the author

ISBN 1-58500-478-2

About the Book

Five Lowrey's passage from the center of his universe — Hockingport, Ohio — to nearby Ohio University is more than just a coming of age journey. If Thomsen Lowrey V had a middle initial it would be "N" for naive. Five's choice of going college seems his only alternative to following the family tradition of life on Ohio River towboats, as his father and three previous generations had done.

With only one hometown friend on campus — Denzel "The Bear" Duerhof — Five is thrown into the turmoil of university life without a clue of a goal. That changes rapidly as his penchant for drawing brings him early notoriety and that rarity among freshmen, campus recognition. He finds classes, especially art courses, can be fun. He discovers beer drinking, pizza, an unique money-making scheme, and above all, a wonderful variety of girls.

His love affair with a town girl, Darcy Robinette, leads to even greater campus recognition and his first conflict between life and love. When fraternity rush rolls around, Five goes along with the crowd and finds himself a pledge to Alpha Chi Epsilon.

The Thirteen, as the ACE pledge class is known, move from early euphoria to the depths of despair as their pledgeship reveals some of the harsher aspects of brotherhood. When tragedy occurs, the Thirteen maintain their unity to prevail against a sadistic element within the ACE membership.

Five's role in this story of changing college life in the Fifties brings him into the realms of Korean War veterans, secret society intrigue, modern art and ultimately, vengeance for a murder which he and his pledge brothers seemingly cannot prove.

Chapter 1

The Center Of The Universe Shifts

My eighteen years of life have been spent at the center of the universe: Hockingport, Ohio.

My life is history now and my future is as formless as the morning fog that floats above the Ohio River below our house on the bluff.

Choices. Oh, I have choices. My father, Thomsen Lowrey V, — we call him the Captain — would like to see me follow him, my grandpa, my great-grandpa and my great-great-grandpa onto the river and life on the towboats. The Captain's not really a captain right now but a first mate on Valley Barge Line's *Point Princess*, demoted after a tow broke loose last Christmas Eve and crashed into the rain-swept piers of the Silver Bridge in Gallipolis.

My mom, Ellie Lowrey, still has fond memories of her two years at Bethany College and urges me to think about college as the next step in my life.

My best buddy, Jack Gestner, wants me to join the Navy with him and "see the world." More boats.

My little sister is an interested observer. Sissie Eileen wants me to go — go anywhere — so she can move her growing collection of stuffed animals and posters into my larger room.

My last choice would be to do nothing, stay in Hockingport after graduation sorting out overripe tomatoes and lettering signs for Emmit's produce stand on Route 7.

My indecision has cast a cloud of tension over our little family. The Captain, when he's home, talks about the glories of life on the river. But I've seen the split thumbs and broken legs of the bargehands who work the river tows and am pretty sure it's not the life for me.

Although Mom's reminiscences about college life make that

sound interesting, after twelve years of school it's all I can do to stay awake until graduation. I'm not much of a jock but have gone out for basketball and track, Hockingport High's two sports, just to escape the excruciating boredom of sixth period study all.

The war stories I've heard from veterans in Shorty Decker's barbershop make me think that joining the Navy would be something more than just "seeing the world." I harbor a nagging suspicion about the joys of a military career, swabbing decks, peeling spuds and losing my belongings to the "slickie boys" of the world's ports.

• • •

The epiphany comes to me in Shorty's barbershop. With a wink and nod, he indicates that I can take a magazine from the racy top shelf, forbidden to everyone except adults.

Reveling in my newly-appointed adulthood, I grab the raciest of the bunch — *Esquire:* "the magazine for men" — and leaf through its pages while awaiting my customary flattop. I ogle the Vargas and Petty girls, their unbelievable boobs swathed in the flimsiest of gauze. Some of the cartoons are funny. Many of them I flat don't get.

But it's a page entitled "Back To Campus" that grabs my attention. There in a color picture is a guy who could be me, clad in chinos and dirty bucks, and surrounded by luscious-looking coed babes. Maybe college life wouldn't be so bad after all.

• • •

It's nearly dawn and Mom and I have driven our old Chevy up to Lock 19 with a laundry box and bag full of goodies for the Captain whose towboat is bound upstream with a load of empties.

As the tow is locked through, Mom and the Captain will exchange a hug, a kiss, laundry boxes and a few brief words. This is a four-generation tradition in the Lowrey family and one I'm just not willing to continue.

As we sit on the bench above the lock wall, waiting for the *Princess* to round the downriver bend, I put words to the thoughts rampaging through my mind.

"Mom, I've been thinking a lot." Pause. "Y'know, what I want to do after graduation." This discussion has been circling around my indecision for so long that I'm almost afraid of her reaction.

"What's that, Five?" she asks with a catch in her voice. My name is Thomsen Lowrey V but everyone just calls me Five.

"Well, you know, it'll probably make the Captain unhappy... if I didn't go on the boats... you know."

Her expression is grim. "It's not a really matter of making the Captain happy, Five." Her lip quivers. "You'll be here long after the Captain is dead and gone. What matters..." Tears well up. "...is whether you'll be happy."

I gulp and stammer on. "But y'know, I've been here around boats all my life. I know the captain loves the river..." God, why won't words come out where you really need 'em? "...but it's just a river to me. And I think... well, I think I'd like to try somethin' different."

"Like?"

"Like... goin' to college?"

"Oh, hon," she says giving me a big squeeze, "that's terrific... and the Captain won't be displeased. He'll huff a little but down deep, he'll be happy. He just wants you to do what's best for you."

We sit there in silence for a minute or so. Mom wipes the corners of her eyes. "Where do you think you'd like to go?"

"Oh gosh, I haven't given it *that* much thought. I don't think I want to go too far from home, though."

"Well, there's Rio Grand for sure. It's so close you could probably buy a car and live at home, if you'd want to."

I flash back to our senior class field trip to Rio Grande last fall... this little cow college just a few miles from Gallipolis where a big geek named Bevo Francis and his coach Newt Oliver have put the school on the big-time basketball map. First, we went to chapel in the biggest of the four brick buildings on the campus. Long, hot and boring with the high point being

Denzel Duerhoff letting a loud fart during one of the many prayers.

Then we toured the classrooms which were right up there with ours at WPA-built Hockingport High. Lunch was in a termite-eaten barrack building with white bread sandwiches of bologna and sandwich spread.

The gymnasium was a depressing box and I couldn't blame Bevo and Newt for escaping for big money to the pros, even if it was playing the sacrificial white guys against the Harlem Globetrotters.

After a thoughtful pause, I respond, "Jeez, Mom. Rio Grande's maybe a little *too* close to home. I'll have to give it some more thought."

We stand as the *Princess* blows for the lock and wave to the distant pilothouse. "I think I'll just not tell the Captain about our talk 'til he gets home for a couple of days," Mom says. "He's always in a better mood after a home-cooked meal."

On the drive back to Hockingport, Mom bubbles on about college life, how exciting it will be for me. Just before she lets me out at Hockingport High, she leans over and gives me a kiss on the cheek.

"It's Monday, Five, and the stores in Parkersburg will be open tonight. After school, you take the Chevy and drive up to Dils and get some college clothes. You simply can't go off to college with only blue jeans and tee-shirts."

• • •

I kind of like Parkersburg, the nearest big town to Hockingport. Although the kids at Parkersburg High are sort of snobbish to us "river rats," the town has four movie theaters and lots of stores.

Monday nights are a big deal in Parkersburg with the stores open and the Market-Julianna Street "loop" crowded with teenagers cruising their cars looking to pick someone up. I circle the loop a couple of times, then park right in front of Sterns, the "store for men."

Mom shops at Dils but it's too much of a lady's store for

4

me. The twenty dollars I had from produce stand wages has been augmented by a fortune from Mom — five twenty dollar bills. Though I've never really enjoyed shopping for clothes, this time is a little different. Almost fun.

I pick up two pairs of chinos, some sports shirts and a dress shirt and what the salesman calls a "rep" tie. Then I pick out a brown tweed sportcoat and finally, a pair of white bucks with bright red soles.

Driving across the bridge into the little Ohio town of Belpre, I even has enough change left for a cheeseburger at the Blue Moon drive-in. As I cruise on down Route 7 toward home, I realize that Hockingport is no longer the center of my universe. I don't know where it is yet but I do know it's shifted to somewhere.

Chapter 2

Rum 'N Coke On Death Row

It's a glorious spring afternoon. Glorious because it's nearly over. The week. The school year. The whole high school experience.

We're jogging our long mile for the last time, keeping to the outside of the HHS cinder track. Coach Robbins has always made his teams warm up in the outside lane. "The extra distance won't hurt you. And you won't rut up the inside where the running takes place."

Just one more lap around the outside. We're loafing along. Our last track practice. Our last high school class period.

"Shit! Slow! Down! Shit!" Behind us, Denzil Duerhoff puffs his plea to his barely moving fellow seniors. None of the lower classmen would think of passing a senior on the Last Mile but at the speed Dense moves along, the temptation has to be back there.

"C'mon Densley," I call over my shoulder. "For once in your life, see if you can run the entire way."

"Shit. No! Way!"

Actually, Dense does belong on this track running his senior Last Mile. Of all the HHS Falcons, he's the most likely to qualify Saturday for the state meet. Indeed, he'll probably go to State in both of his events. Shot put. And discus.

After years of work on the farm, Dense is considered one of the best heavers of heavy objects in southeastern Ohio.

Coach Robbins hollers something muffled away by the spring breeze as we slog by the sixth turn and slow the pace even more. We're going to force Dense into the honor of leading the seniors home on the last lap. If he can survive the distance at a run.

"OhhhhhhsonofabitchI'mgonnadie," Dense lets go in one big exhale as he breaks for the finish line just 20 yards away. He also breaks a giant fart in the process and we seniors whoop and dance in his fetid wake.

As Dense pukes in the background, Coach Robbins gathers us around. "I know everyone will be at practice tomorrow afternoon. In case you *shouldn't* make it," he smiles at our nervous senior grins, "we'll leave here Saturday morning at 7:30. And we're taking the bus to Athens so we don't have to mess with lashing down the vaulting poles.

"Should, for any reason, you not be able to practice tomorrow, I am sure you will behave yourselves and not do anything that might affect your performance in the district meet Saturday. Have a good time."

We whoop in unison and break up to run our last track practice ever. Well, maybe not exactly. If any of us *should* qualify for the state meet. But, except for our hairy, barfing, farting over-muscled buddy, fat freakin' chance!

Tomorrow is Skip Day and Coach Robbins' little speech tells us that the faculty knows we're planning to cut out. But what're they gonna do? Keep us for another year?

Senior Skip Day has a bad rep as a tradition at HHS since five members of the class of '52 drove their car off the river bank and one of them drowned. Why, last year's class didn't even skip. But '54 is determined to renew the tradition and the plan is to drive over Lake Hope, west of Athens. It's supposed to be a neat place although only a couple of us have ever seen it.

• • •

My Skip Day was uneventful. Except for the money, six bucks in salary and another two in tips for bagging beans and carrying cukes at Emmit's market, I might as well have stayed in school. During the drudgery, I contemplated the colleges I knew of. Marietta College, just 30 miles upriver, was private and would cost more. At Morris Harvey or Marshall in West Virginia, I would be an out-of-state student and that too would cost more.

Rio Grande was out of the question 'cause it seemed too much like four more years of high school. Ohio University, just 40 miles up the Hocking River, was a state school and I could get a look at it tomorrow during the district track meet.

On the ride to the district meet, we six seniors huddle in the back of the bus and the others regale me with their adventures at Lake Hope.

"Man Five, you shouldda been there," Pinhead Wellersmirks. "I never seen such quiff in all my life. Most of 'em college girls too. Two piece suits. Boobs hanging out all over."

"Marylou Suter got her ass just blasted," Gestner chimes in. "She must've chugged three beers. And barfed all over Doc Suter's new Chrysler all the way home."

"And what about Dense?" This comes from Toad Shaffer. "You had to see him, Five. Makin' out with this college chick under the divin' board."

My farmer friend turns a deep red in response. "You guys just have a case of the ass 'cause you had to play with the high school girls."

"That was a college chick?" Shaffer says with great wide gestures. "We thought she'd walked out of some farmer's pasture."

"I got a good look at Suter's ass," Toad giggles. "As much as she was bendin' over to puke, that's about all anyone saw of her."

"Five," Gestner brings the subject back to important matters, "this woman Dense was playin' kissy-face with was unbelievable. She was bigger than he was."

"But not as hairy."

"But not as ugly."

"But she must've been blind to see anything in Dense."

"Perhaps she has Superman X-ray vision," Dense replies, "and caught a glimpse of the famed Duerhoff Dong."

Hoot. Hoot.

Coach Robbins shoots us a glance but I can tell he's happy we're having fun. Not keyed-up and tense about the district meet.

For all but Dense, a ride in the yellow-orange school bus is a treat. We enjoy the comradeship of Skip Day memories except for me but I'm eight dollars richer.

···

The ride home is happy. Marietta High's Jeep Davis won the meet all by himself: first in both hurdles, the 220, high jump and second in the half-mile relay.

But our big story was Dense. He fouled out in the discus but put one of his foul throws out over 160 feet.

Then he put the shot 48 feet, seven inches for a gold medal and a district record. Toad finished third in the 220 and the mile relay team finished third. So… as a team we finished fourth behind Chillicothe and Coolville and Dense gets a trip to Columbus next week.

···

Walking across the parking lot from the bus yard, Dense drops another surprise on me.

"Y'know, Five. I've been thinkin' some more about what I'm gonna do."

"Yeah, and…"

"Well, my ole man says he can swing it. If I want to go to college, that is."

"God Denzel, that's terrific. I didn't even know you were thinkin' about it."

He shrugs, grins and gives the twelve-pound shot in its sock bag a little flip in the air. "Well hell. To tell the truth, I hadn't been much. Til' Friday, that is."

"Does this have anything to do with Lake Hope?"

"Well, that ole' girl is pretty fine. And she was nice to me. They were all nice. Don't know if I can find anyone that nice shoveling cowshit for the rest of my life."

I can't disagree. "It's a hard decision. I know I've had second thoughts several times since I told mom I was thinkin' about going."

Dense shrugs again and gives the shot another flip in the air. "Maybe not so hard. At least for me. One of the guys judging the field events today was Coach Widdoes. He introduced me to

10

Coach Street."

"Coach Street?"

"Yeah. He's the OU track coach. Said if I wanted to come, he might be able to find me some help."

"Well Dense, your grades should get you in. I wish to God someone could find me some help. But I did like the looks of OU. Since it's a state school, I think they have to take me if I apply. I think I'll try to get in"

"Terrific Five," my huge buddy exclaims. "We're gonna be classmates for four, five, maybe ten more years.

• • •

The thrum of a far-off towboat and the tinny whisper of a nearby car radio are all the sounds we hear as five of us gather at The Point. Six members of the Class of '54 — me, Dense, Toad, Gestner, Marylou Suter and Tina Shivley — sit on the big rock where the Hocking flows into the Ohio and rehash the events of the evening. Graduation evening.

Most of our classmates went somewhere with the steadies or parents but later, we six pile into and onto Dense's pickup and drive down to The Point.

None of us has much to say. The other five pass one of the two quarts of Miller's that Marylou swiped from her dad's Sohio station. I try a taste of the icy stuff and nearly gag. Great entertainment for my companions as I spit it into the river. I'm sipping a warm Coke that was rolling around the bed of the pickup.

"Christ Five, you'll never be a college man if you don't drink beer," Dense observes.

"Don't take the Lord's name, Denzel," Tina chides.

"Ohhh right, Teens. And you didn't misuse His name on the way home from Lake Hope? Driving Doc's Chrysler without a license while Miz Suter here barfed her lungs out on the dashboard?"

We can't see her blush in the dark but we all know she's doing it. Tina is a pretty neat ole' girl. Big shiny front teeth. Little bitty boobs. And a brain as big as her teeth. That brain got her through HHS with straight A's and made us listen to her surprisingly good valedictory speech at graduation.

"Bullshit, Dense," Toad chimes in. "Teens performed admirably on the way home from Lake Hope. I should know because I was trying to look down her suit the whole way and she never once noticed."

Another invisible blush in the dark.

"Do you guys really think I did OK with my speech? Really?"

For all her accomplishments, Tina's a pretty insecure girl, even though she is going off to Marietta on a full academic scholarship.

"You *were* great, Teens," I hasten to reassure her. "I 'specially liked the line about 'setting our sights for loftier targets.'"

"I got that out of *Bartlett's*," she says, "so it wasn't really my idea. But I did change it a little." She scoots over a bit closer to me on the rock. "Also... I have a little bitty graduation present to share with y'all but it won't mix with beer." Against the reflections on the river, we can see a half-pint bottle she holds up.

"Five? Did you ever try rum and Coke?"

"I just heard of it. The song, y'know. Never tried it."

"Well there's a first time for everything, the Bard or someone said," Tina declares, "and this is the time."

"Where'd you get that baby bottle of rum, Teens?" Dense belches, taking a big drag of the last of Marylou's first quart of beer.

"I'm not sure. It was lying beneath my mortarboard when I got ready tonight. I think it's probably a graduation present from Leslie." Leslie is Tina's hell-raising big sister, a teller at the Bank of Pomeroy and Hockingport's acknowledged *loose woman.*

She empties the rum into my half bottle of warm Coke. I thumb the sucker and give it a shake, squirting the mixture right across her chest.

"Shit, Five. You're wasting it all," Toad screeches. "Now you have to go last, if there's any left at all."

12

After Tina, the Coke bottle makes the rounds with everyone taking a big slug. Dense declares his preference for beer. Marylou allows as it might make her barf. Toad and Gestner smack their lips.

I'm last and empty the dregs. The taste is pretty good and a warm finger slides down my chest. I can't tell if it's the rum or Tina.

"See, Five," she murmurs, "now aren't you sorry you wasted so much"

I'm inclined to agree, especially when she whispers in my ear "Wanna feel my breasts? Kind of a little off-to-college present from ole' Teens?"

Who can say our graduation night was uneventful?

Chapter 3

A Through M and Two Number Twos

"All right folks. A through M to the left. N through Z to the right. Have your information cards and two number two pencils ready. That's your ticket of admission to Ohio U."

I display my index cards and pencils as I file past the proctor with the rest of the A through Ms, none of whom I recognize. We're in a big old building called Ellis Hall.

Dense should be in this crowd somewhere but I lost him just before lunch. He went off with a couple of older guys I thought might be Coach Street and one of his assistants.

It's a hot July afternoon in Athens and although the windows are all raised high, a miasma of chalk dust and old cigarette smoke seems to hang over the big classroom. Through the windows I can see the lawn which we learned this morning is called the College Green. Out there, birds tug at worms, some people lie on the rich grass reading books or napping, others walk purposefully across the campus.

Another proctor raps a pencil against her podium. "O.K. Listen up folks." The murmur in the room hushes. "As you heard this morning in orientation, each of you is qualified to attend OU this fall because of your high school grades and your Senior Scholarship test scores.

"This test this afternoon is to help your counselors and the university decide in which English, math and sciences classes, to place you according to your current knowledge. It is not a test that will prevent you from registering at Ohio University."

A few audible sighs of relief can be heard, although we got the same lecture from different people in the morning orientation.

"There are 150 questions on the test. They are broken up into the Humanities, Mathematics and Science. Forty of them are multiple choice. The rest are true-false.

"You'll have 50 minutes to complete the questions. Then

15

we'll take a ten minute break. Then you will come back and have another hour to write a simple essay on one of several subjects that will be provided. Any questions?"

Of course there are some questions.

"How many true-false questions will there be?"

"What do I need to pass the test?"

I feel less dumb with each question that is asked, although several of them *have* passed through my mind.

"OK now. Let's begin. I'll start the timer and will give you time signals at 30 minutes and then each ten minutes until time is up. Turn to page one of the test booklet and fill out all the blanks. Use your information card if you have any problems."

Our information card is a mimeographed form that we filled out carefully under the guidance of another tedious proctor in the morning orientation. It contains such vital data as name, address, date of birth, high school. Christ! A cheat sheet for an entrance exam!

· · ·

I rode up to Athens this morning with Dense, not too thrilled about going to college orientation in a rusting yellow International Harvester pickup. Still, it was better than the Trailways or catching either of the B&O locals that stop in Coolville.

"Shit, Five, but I am scared," Dense mutters, death-gripping the skinny steering wheel with his massive paws. "Coach Street says I got nothing to worry about but I am still scared."

"So am I but not as much as thinking about going to work for the Captain as a barge hand. Or lettering cantaloupe signs for Emmit for the rest of my life."

"But I've never done well in tests," he replies. "What if I can't pass this one?"

This is true. Since I've known him, Dense seems to soak up facts and learning in the classroom and from books. Then he freezes up when tests are taken. He was lucky to graduate with the C average that I had to sortof coast to achieve.

"You'll do just fine," I assure him. "College can't be much

more than kinda super high school. Just more tail there to look at and chase."

We pass a John Deere pulling a farm wagon along the berm of Highway 50. Dense honks and waves at the stranger farmer.

"So long sucker. I'm a farmer too. But not for loooooooonnnnnnng," he chortles.

• • •

"Ten minutes." The proctor's call.

I'm down to my last few multiple choices in the math section. 'If Train A leaves City B at 10 a.m. and travels west at 45 miles per hour…' Oh if there's a God, please let Him find something for me to take at Ohio University that doesn't involve mathematics.

The minutes scamper by with spikes on their soles. "Time folks. Please put down your pencils. Be sure your page ones are filled in completely. That includes your name. Verrrrry important. Now a ten minute break and then back here when the bell rings."

A through M mills out the doors and spreads like a slow liquid down the steps and around the sunken brick courtyard. Dozens of kids, girls and boys, light cigarettes. Nervous chatter breaks out.

"Hey Five, man. Here I am. How'd you do?" Dense comes through the crowd like a bowling ball, elbowing smokers aside right and left.

"Where you been man? You missed the test?"

"Nosireee. Coach Street and Coach Widdoes took a bunch of us over to Men's Gym and we took the test in a smaller group. Less distraction, they said. I met some neat guys too."

"Neat guys? Thought you came here to meet neat girls?"

"In time. In time. They got one big Negro kid down here from Cleveland… that big stud from East Tech? He's the only weight guy they're talkin' to besides me."

"That's great Dense. Did they say anything about your major."

"Phys Ed, Five. Phys Ed. Can you imagine me back at HHS

17

teaching gym to eighth graders?"

"Sure beats shovelin' shit," I respond, thinking I sure can't imagine me back at HHS teaching anything. The bells in Ellis Hall begin to clang and I turn to go back across the brick courtyard.

"Where'you goin' now?" Dense asks.

"We have to write an essay on some damn thing."

"Awww, we don't," he says with obvious glee. "We're going back to the gym and shoot some baskets, maybe lift some weights 'n stuff."

Deep in my soul I realize that my friend has made the move from life on the farm to college man in a single 25-mile drive of his battered pickup truck.

"I'll see you at the wheels about four o'clock," he shouts over his shoulder as he wades against the tide of kids milling into Ellis.

• • •

From the slip I was handed when I returned to the classroom, I choose 'The Role Of Transportation Technology In Western Settlement' as my subject and open the blank blue book lying on the empty desk.

"Settle down folks," the male proctor calls. "You have 60 minutes to write your essays. They can be as long as you wish. If you need another bluebook, just raise your hand."

Loud giggle from the herd of would-be essayists.

"Be sure to put the first five lines from your information card on the cover of your blue book and your name at the top of each right-hand page. Any questions?"

A few questions. None any brighter than before.

"OK," he says, pulling down the arm on the timer clock, "let's begin."

• • •

Slippery pencil in sweaty hand, I ask myself, 'what in hell do I know about transportation and western settlement?'. As usual when I'm confronted with a mental quandary, I doodlea sketch on the bottom of the page and before I realize it, Captain's towboat materializes.

I begin to write. About what I know. Towboats. Riverboats. Flatboats. Western settlement. River pirates. Somehow the words flow out.

• • •

There are about twenty of us in Ellis 316. At the end of the essay, we were handed random appointment slips as we left the big classroom.

"Folks, my name is Trish Spotswood. I'm a grad assistant in the registrar's office and unless you lose your information card, I'll be the one who helps you September 17th at registration. Unless you decide to go somewhere else. Or decide not to go at all."

This proctor, or grad assistant, is a pretty great looking girl… or woman, I guess. Must be 25 or so. Red hair. I pay attention. She starts reading names from the slips and asking for hands to be raised.

"Lowrey. Thomsen the Fifth?" I raise my hand. "Were there really four Thomsen Lowreys before you?"

"Yes maam, but it's not Lowrey. It's Lo-ree like 'low man on the totem pole." For some reason, this information seems funny to my fellow pre-college classmates.

"All right, Thomsen. That's an interesting name. I hope I'll see you at Men's Gym for registration on the 17th. Do you know where you'll be living?"

"On something called 'East Green' and we saw it this morning from the top of that hill over there."

"Indeed. How many others of you are going to live on East Green?"

All the guys' hands go up. No girls.

"Well, as you could see, East Green is still under construction. It used to be Vet's Village but most of those old barracks buildings have been moved out to the airport."

A pretty thing holds up her hand. "How come it's just guys

living down there?"

Trish puzzles this for a second, a charming frown on her smooth face. "I don't really have an answer for that. Maybe it has something to do with keeping male hormones as far away from the rest of the campus as possible."

I decide to ask a question of my own.

"Yes, Mr. Low-ree?"

"Aaaah, Miss... Trish? Aaaah, will those buildings be finished by September? Some of 'em looked like they're just started."

"They're supposed to, and you don't need to call me 'Miss' or 'Maam.' I'm just a grad student and you can all call me Trish. Any more questions."

Silence.

"Allllright, then. See you in September!"

• • •

"Jeeeez Five, what a day! What a big assed wonderful day!"

Dense pounds the wheel in glee as we head home, east on Route 7 with a planned stop at the Idle Hour Tower outside Coolville for a burger.

"My gal from Lake Hope dropped by the gym. Imagine that?"

"Dense. It staggers my imagination. How'd that happen?"

"Her name is Page Dobrowski and she just happens to be smart and beautiful. Smart enough to realize the Dense One and his magnificent equipment are in town."

Since I haven't met Page Dumbrowski or whateverhernameis, I decide to reserve comment.

"And Coach Widdoes and Coach Richey had a long talk with me about playing football. Football Five! Football! Kick heads in without some asshole blowing a whistle and fouling you out of the game.

"They say if I can get in shape and have a good freshman year, I might get a scholarship. And Coach Street said he's sure he can swing a partial scholarship for shot put and discus.

"Scholarships Five! Kick heads in! Get paid for it! Page

20

Dobrowski!"

We hoot and honk all the way to the Idle Hour Tower near Coolville where Dense devours two burgers and a beer.

"It's my second beer today, Five. All us big college athletes drink a beer now and then to keep our strength up."

Chapter 4

My Life Begins In Athens

"Should be hearin' her blow for Porter's any minute now," Mr. Steffins says as he checks his railroad watch.

Sure enough, a distant whistle sounds a few seconds later. "Right on time," the Coolville stationmaster pronounces.

I've known Mr. Steffins since I was a little kid. One of Captain's pleasures is a drive up to Coolville on his days off to hang around the B&O station, chat with Mr. Steffins and savor the sounds and smells of the trains as they mostly pass through.

Mr. Steffins is venerable. He's seemed old to me for years but today he appears to exude an aura of wisdom that only centuries of experience can pass on to those younger. He stuffs the big watch back into the pocket of his shiny black vest and leans his frail weight into the tongue of the baggage wagon.

"No, no. Company policy," he chides as I offer to help move the wagon, heavy on its steel-clad wheels although its load is only my two articles of baggage. "I can do'er myself just like I been doin' for 36 years."

He positions the wagon adjacent to the westbound track just as number 23 appears around the curve and slows for the Hocking River bridge. As it coasts through the truss span, the engineer blows his steam in a hair-raising hiss and walks the nearly silent locomotive past us and the baggage cart.

Twenty three is a simple train, one of two passenger trains that call each weekday at Coolville. Two mail storage cars and a coach-baggage combination make up the consist pulled by one of the B&O's aging steam locomotives. Its water pump pants like a patient hound on this hot September morning and faint wisps of steam leak from its boiler jacket. I wonder if this engine will still be around when I finish college.

Mr. Steffins slides my bags across the wagon's surface and into the wide maw of the combine's baggage compartment. The conductor, perhaps Mr. Steffins' twin, leans from the passenger steps and calls "Boooooaaarrrrd!" beckoning to me, the sole Coolville trade for the day.

I climb aboard and begin the 22-minute ride to my destiny.

• • •

I'm riding the train to college because Captain is on the river and mom didn't realize she had an important appointment in Pomeroy on this first day that freshmen could move into their dormitory rooms. Freshman orientation begins tonight and I felt it important to be there.

"Ah darlin', I am so sorry but I just didn't put two and three together to come up with today," she repeats for the fifth time as we drive up to Coolville. She's clearly upset and I'm a little hard-pressed to understand. It's not as if I'm off to college in Nome or New York.

• • •

Twenty three makes a quick stop in Guysville and then chuffs on toward the west and knowledge. We're in the Hocking River flood plain now and the railroad runs like an arrow paralleling Highway 50 and the river. Pretty quickly the Athens airport flashes by and then I can hear the whistles as the engineer blows for the first of Athens' many grade crossings.

I catch a glimpse of some red and white buildings and lots of people walking around, unloading cars and carrying luggage as we round a curve and slow for the Athens station.

"Athens. Athens. And Ohioooooo University. Next stop," the conductor calls with a smile for me, the only occupant of the coach section of the car. "Good luck son," as he hands me down the steps and onto the platform.

Sure enough, I'm the only Athens passenger on the brick platform as number 23 chuffs off to the west with its grimy blue-gray cars in trail. The stationmaster comes out and gives me my first words of welcome. "Guess these are yours, eh? Where'd you come from?"

"Coolville. Hockingport, really."

"Almost a townie, then," he says. "You want a taxi? Or is someone pickin' you up?"

I decline, pretending great familiarity with the place, and hoist my luggage: a graduation present gladstone bag and a slightly scuffed steamer trunk that weighs in at about 40 pounds.

Starting off down the platform, I am interrupted by the station agent. "You goin' to the University, ain't you?"

"Yessir."

"Well take Depot Street then," he advised with a jerk of his thumb in the opposite direction. "When y'get to Union, take a right and that'll lead y'right up to the campus."

So off I trudge toward Depot Street, looking back as I hear laughter. The agent and one of his depot buddies were sharing some kind of joke.

• • •

Union does lead right *up* to campus as I realize while passing the State Liquor Store, the steam plant, and a couple of run-down bars. The 40-pound steamer trunk, my mother's pride and victory, gains 10 pounds in the first quarter mile.

• • •

"Five. You cannot, can not, go off to Athens with your clothes stuffed in that ratty duffel bag. I would die of shame if you do," she declares with dramatic flourishes. "We shall find you something suitable.

"Plus, I think you should wear your nice sport coat and that black knit tie. You'll look really collegiate," she finished. College will teach me a phrase that describes the way a woman can dominate a man's thinking but that's in the future. Plus, it's not an appropriate phrase to use in terms of one's mother.

The only good thought I have about the cursed trunk is it does make a convenient seat when I want to rest. Which is soon about every 10 steps. Off comes the knit tie. I cram it between the stiff lips of the gladstone.

25

Sitting on my trunk in front of the *Athens Messenger*, I ponder the Bataan Death March and wonder if its survivors made it in tweed sport coats. Several passing cars honk and their riders lean out to yell derisively. I pay no attention.

Nine steps and rest. Eight steps and rest. The sweat is pouring now and my collegiate three-button collar is a limp appendage to the rest of my once-collegiate shirt. If only I could ditch this goddamn coat!

Another honk which I ignore. A persistent honk. "Hey you. Lo-ree The Fifth." I look around at the battered, dogshit colored convertible. "You look like you could use a ride."

It's Trish Spotswood, the grad student from the placement tests. And she's at the wheel of my chariot of salvation. With great joy I heave the 300-pound trunk into the back seat, then the shiny gladstone, finally myself into the front.

"Welcome to OU," she smiles, "but where in God's name did you come from? You look as if you'd walked from Nelsonville."

"Oh thank God for you," I pant. "Just from the train station but that thing weighs a ton. I don't think I'd have made it."

"And where are you going with that load? I'll take you there if we can get close."

"Biddle Hall?"

"East Green? Oh shit. That'll be a madhouse but let's see how close I can get this rolling disaster. You could've walked back around the railroad tracks and saved the hike up the hill, y'know?"

"No. I didn't realize," I say lamely, thinking revenge against the sadistic station master. "Are these your wheels?" I inquire, dignifying the conveyance with the popular term of the day.

"No. It belongs to a… friend. But I had to get in to campus and didn't want to ride my bike. Can you believe it's this hot in September?"

As we roll past Court Street, I begin to appreciate the former gravity of my situation and how much Trish has saved me, even though we are now in a long line of barely moving cars.

"Jesus, what a mess!" Trish waves a languid hand toward the windshield. I can't tell whether she's referring to the several stars of shattered glass or the general congestion in the street ahead.

"We've got sororities and freshmen coming back on College Avenue, more on University Terrace, and then every freshman stud in the universe going down the hill to East Green.

"That's where Biddle is. If I can get you to the top of the hill, you can slide that coffin down the steps."

I shoot her a raised eyebrow. "Just kidding Lo-ree The Fifth. I'll get you there."

Finally we achieve the crest of the hill and can see the line of cars stretching below us. Students are slowly trudging up and down steep concrete steps on each side of the hill.

"Biddle's a lucky shot for you," Trish waves again. "It's finished and it's right at the foot of the stairs that go up by Bryan Hall."

"Are they as steep as these? At least I won't have to drag the trunk to class every day."

Her laugh is the second good thing that's happened today. "Keep your sense of humor, Lo-ree The Fifth. It'll be hard to drown in all the shit that'll drop on you here if you keep laughing."

At the bottom, we turn on East Green and creep by a group of one-story frame buildings that rival Trish's car for decrepitude.

"Those are temps. Most of 'em have been moved out to Vet's Village but they've saved a few to house the freshies until all the dorms are finished."

"They look like army barracks," I observe.

"Right you are. World War I, II or Korea? Who knows? But they're better than getting rained upon. At least the roaches'll have dry feet."

She points. "That's Biddle over there. I'll just pull this junker up over the curb and hope we don't bottom out or run over an upperclassman."

And she does. Across new squares of brown sod and right to the front door of Biddle Hall.

"Your home away from whatever, Lo-Ree," she proclaims and gives my bicep a punch. "You owe me one, don't forget that. I won't."

In a cloud of exhaust and dust, like some red-haired genie on a rusty rug, she tears across the rapidly dying sod. I have arrived.

• • •

All around me activity swirls. Hundreds of young men are carrying luggage, hugging parents and girlfriends, talking with each other, smoking and generally milling up a huge confusion.

One guy adroitly walks across the lawn on his hands. I'll never see him again in four years at OU. I'm reassured by the number of faces which appear to be as lost and confused as I feel.

I park the steamer trunk beside a huge pile of luggage and tentatively open the door to Biddle Hall. Inside, a large lounge or lobby is filled with people. It's noisy but a little more orderly than the mob scene outside. Spotting a couple of desks with signs above them, I head for A through M.

A guy with a sandy flattop looks up as I approach the desk. "Hey! Welcome to Biddle. I'm Art Long and a floor advisor." He reaches out a hand. "Who're you?"

"Thomsen Lowrey. From Hockingport."

"No shit? I'm from Racine. Don't see too many river rats up here."

Art Long leafs through a clipboard and gives me an "ah-ha" in triumph. "Here you are. 205. You're gonna be one of my guys. Nice room, too. On the corner in the back. Little ways from the stairs but just a few steps to the latrine."

"Latrine?" I ask.

"Bathroom. John. Shitter. Kaibo. You're gonna be sharing it with about forty other guys."

I nod in dumb comprehension. Sharing a bathroom at home with Sissie Eileen hasn't prepared me for the shock of shaving and shitting with forty other guys.

"OK, let's get you fixed up." Art reaches beneath the desk and slides a long cardboard box filled with manila envelopes. "Do you know if you've paid room and board in advance."

Embarrassment. "My er, ah, mom sent a check."

28

"All right then, you'll be in the other box. Yesssir. Here y'are. Thomsen Lowrey the Fifth? Man!"

"It's Lo-ree," I respond automatically, "and most people call me Five."

"Five it is then. Here's your envelope, Five. Open it right now and I'll go through all this stuff with you."

I dump a collection of folders and other stuff out of the envelope. Art begins his explanation.

"Room key, only one. Not allowed to get dupes made and no locksmith in town'll make one unless you have a form signed by me. Pale green card's your East Green cafeteria meal ticket. You've paid for the full plan so you'll have a total of 320 meals on your punch card. Your entrance is the door closest to Biddle and they'll punch your card out each time you go in.

"Don't try to go in any other door or they'll send you around and to the back of the line. Meal ticket's pale green so it'll match your skin after you've eaten." Pause. "Little joke there. It's not so bad. No lunches on Sundays... just breakfast and dinner. Serving times're on the back of your meal ticket.

"This thing," he holds up a crude green and white badge with a bobcat's likeness on it, "is your ticket to all Freshman Orientation events. Wear it everywhere so you don't forget it and have to climb back down the hill.

"Some upperclass assholes may tell you to buy a beanie. Ignore 'em. Beanies went out when the first Korean veterans arrived but there's always some weenie whose daddy went to school here... wants to uphold the traditions... bullshit.

"This is your pre-registration advisory appointment card. You've got a grad student as an orientation advisor. Probably better than getting confused by some faculty boob. Name's T. Spotswood and you'll meet him Friday morning, Room 240 in Ewing Hall. Don't be late or your whole registration process can get fouled up.

"Rest of this stuff is compliments of the many folks around Athens who'd like for you to spend some money with 'em. Real ball-point pen from The College Book Store. First time they've ever given out ball-points. Free pass to the Varsity Theater. Sample packets of Chesterfield Kings and Camels. Coupons for free Coke or whatever at several of the bars. You can check it out.

"My room's 114 right off the lobby here. Check with me any time you've got any questions. Hall meeting tonight at 7 p.m. Any questions?"

I feel hypnotized by this recitation. "Nope. No questions. Where're the stairs?"

"Through that door, down the hall and right. Stairs on both ends of the wings."

"I've got another bag outside. Will it be safe til' I dump this stuff?"

Art gives me a slow grin. "Five. This is college. These are your classmates around you. In short, nothing's safe if it's not too heavy to carry off. Keep that in mind."

I head for the stairs. Screw 'em if they can drag off that friggin' footlocker.

• • •

I drop the gladstone on the shiny vinyl tiled floor and paw through the envelope to find my room key. Before I can dig it out, the door swings open and I'm facing this stocky guy with gray hair and a brush cut.

"Whoinhell are you and whatinhell are'ya doin' outside my door?"

"I'm Thom Lowrey and I'm supposed to be in this room. It is 205, isn't it?"

"My roomie!" This boob gives me a big hug around the shoulders. "Welcome to the premiere, primo room in Biddle!" He gestures grandly for me to enter.

It is a pretty primo looking room. Gray walls. Matching green steel desks and bunks. A single chest of drawers in the same green steel. Curtains in a red, gray and black plaid are matched by spreads on each of the single bunks.

"My ma made the curtains and spreads. We got a look at the place when we came down for summer tests and she decided the gray plaid would go good with the floor. You like 'em?"

I nod numbly. The bed by the corner with two windows is

rumpled so I assume it's been claimed by this gray plaid momma's boy. I motion toward the other bunk, hard against a blank wall. "That mine?"

"Yeah. Hope you don't mind. I like to have the windows open at night so I took this bed. And that desk, since it's close to the bed." The desk he indicates takes up the remaining space beneath the window. My desk — apparently — is at the foot of my bunk, slightly hiding behind the open door.

"Listen," I say, "it's OK for now. And, ah... do you have a name?"

"Jezzzzzzzus, I'm sorry. Yep. Toby Wolfe. Everyone calls me Grey Wolfe. From Ashtabula. Gray, red and black. Ashtabula High. Yeah!"

I introduce myself. We shake hands. He repeats my name, incorrectly just like everyone does. "Lo-ree," I correct. "Call me Five."

The Grey Wolfe seems overly delighted to have me in his lair. "Christ, a roommate at last! You got any brothers, sisters? I'm an only kid and I've always wanted a brother."

"Yep. A little sister. Just barely a teenager and a mature pain in the butt. But if we're going to be brotherly about this roommate thing, why don't you come downstairs with me and help get the rest of my stuff up here."

With one on each end handle, the unstolen footlocker doesn't give us a problem. "Luggage room's in there," he nods, "under the stairs. I've already stored all my bags."

Toby sits on his bed and watches with great interest as I open the locker. I pull out my carefully packed suit, nice gray flannel pants, crew neck sweater, dress shirts, sport shirts. At the bottom is my pair of dress shoes and the precious white bucks. Nooks and crannies are wadded with socks, underwear, tee shirts.

"I guess it's a good thing you don't have too much stuff," Toby observes. "Unless, your folks are bringin' more over this weekend, or shipping another locker, or somethin?"

"No, this is it. My mom even made me bring clothes hangers."

"Damn good thing. There were only about ten in the closet.

Mamma had to go buy three more packages so we could my get stuff in there." Toby slides one of the doors back from the closet alcove that makes up the other wing wall of our room.

My allotted space is obvious. About a foot of depth along the pipe rack from the back wall. The rest of the rack is stuffed with a glorious treasure of black, charcoal, light gray, pink and powder blue... sport coats, shirts, pants, a revolving tie hanger with thin knits in matching colors and shades. The closet floor is solid with a wardrobe of shoes that would handled my entire senior class. Suede shoes in black, dark and light blue, shades of gray, and several saddle oxford patterns. Three pairs of white bucks. Several pairs of saddle oxfords in black/white and brown/white combinations.

"Ma was sorta' pissed that we had to cram my stuff in there so tight," Toby seems to be giving me a half-assed apology. "And it's good you've only got the three pairs of shoes. They can go under your bed. It's a damn good thing they didn't try to put a third into this room."

"A third?" I ask. "A third person?"

"Ohhhh, yeah. Mamma was really strong about this being a double. My allergies 'n everything. I think she'd have thrown a third bunk out the window if they had tried it."

In the few minutes of knowing her son, I was growing a strong conviction that I will not like Mamma Wolfe when I meet her.

Under Grey Wolfe's supervision, I finish unpacking the footlocker, discovering in the process a five dollar bill pressed beneath the sheets, pillowcase and blanket at the bottom. A going-away present from mom.

Following sport shirts and jeans out of the gladstone are my smaller treasures... many of them graduation presents. A new Dopp kit. A jewelry case holding three pairs of cufflinks and two tie-bars. A new Waterman fountain pen with my name engraved in gold. My new Parker fountain pen in stainless steel. A double frame with mom and Captain's pictures. My old high school dictionary and thesaurus, each a pitifully thin little volume.

Toby shows me his first offering of roomie compassion. "I

hated to have to take up four of the six drawers like that. But as you can see…"

Three drawers on his side of the chest are filled with underwear, socks, tee shirts and sport shirts. The top drawer of my three is filled with puffy dress shirts, their curved Mr. B. collars extending like wings. This is the final straw. I pull the drawer out and dump it on the bed.

"Fuck this!" I holler at him. "You and your mamma can just pile your stuff somewhere else but I'm gettin' all three of my damn drawers. You're just damn lucky I don't have more clothes or I'd throw some of that ugly zoot suit crap out of the closet, too!" Grey Wolfe's face is a stricken mask of horror. Mamma should've told him there might be days like this.

"God Five, I'm sorry. Sure, take the drawer. Man, I am sorry. Take more room in the closet. Jeez. I'll have mamma come down and take some of that stuff home."

"Never mind, Toby. I can't use any more of the closet. I don't have anything to put in it anyway. But shit, man. You *have* taken over the room pretty well. I don't even have to buy a bedspread!"

My little flare-up seems to have solidified our budding friendship. Toby — to this day I can't think of him as The Grey Wolfe — helps me decide to tilt the footlocker on its side to create a bedside table. He writes down items for my *need to get* list… study lamp, notebooks, shaving cream, a pillow, after shave I've forgotten at home. With its stiff top and handles crushed down, the gladstone slides under the bed. Quickly, my new base in this strange land of Biddle 205 is established.

• • •

I accompany Toby downstairs to visit "some guys I know from home." His friend Don Massman is crammed into a single window room with two other roommates: Jeremy Winkler from Cleveland, Len Stolski from Martins Ferry.

"Hey, I heard your name before," Stolski says to me. "From this guy on the frosh team wit' me. Big hairy guy. All the time goin' on about his buddy Five."

"Gotta be Dense, Denzel Duerhoff," I respond. "Sure sounds like him. Big? Hairy?"

"He's a strong motha," Stolski goes on. "Doesn't know shit but he can sure dig in and hold his ground on blockin' drills."

None of them has ever heard of Hockingport, so we talk a little about our home towns. "My ole' man works in the mills," Stolski tells us "and so have I for the last five years. Damn good thing too. Helped me put on thirty pounds."

Massman's father is on the boats on the Great Lakes so we have a common interest. He seems impressed that my father was a towboat captain. "Dad's never been higher than first mate," he says. "He usually drinks himself down to his own level every trip out."

Noise outside draws the four of us into the hall where we find three guys taunting an obviously angry, very wet and naked victim. His black skin glistens as he growls "You mo'fucks think it's funny. Give a guy a heart attack doin' that shit."

Stolski wades right in muttering "C'mon, knock it off. What'sa matter? Who's givin' who a heart attack?"

Another voice. "Who you callin' mothafucka, jungle bunny?"

The black kid clinches his jaw, both fists and strains toward his tormentors. By this time, Stolski has him in a bear hug.

"You, you jive-ass shithead. You motha' too ugly to have somethin' as sad as you the regula way."

Just then, a muscular guy with a blond flattop comes tearing out of his room and wades into Stolski and the black kid. "Christ, you guys inna fight again? I told you both to watch this shit last week. Now you got civilized people here and I do not want you messin' around this way."

"Yassuh, Mas' Scales," the black kid grins, "we just be jivin', showin the greenies how the Bobcats gon' kick Bowlin' Green's butt next week."

Stolski grins sheepishly and releases his dripping companion. "Wesley here was just showin' us some broken field stuff, Mr. Scales."

"Ohhhh, right. Drippin' wet with his big high school All American schlong hangin' down, I suppose?"

The three guys who had surrounded Wesley are sort of blending down the hall, obviously not wanting to mix it up with Scales. Scales says, "Nuff this shit. Wes. Get dressed. Stolski, you go over to Perkins and pick up that hairball farmer. Coach wants you guys on the field by three p.m."

Stolski introduces us to Watt Scales, OU's hope for a running attack this season, and Wesley DeVon, who seems to have a lock on taking Scales' place after graduation.

"What got you so riled, Wes?" Scales asks the well-built black kid as he dries off in the hallway.

"In there takin a shower, shavin' my handsome chin, and those assholes throw a trashcan'a cold water on my ass. Coulda cut my lovely throat and nevah made All 'Merican."

"Good thing you weren't shavin' your pubic hair," Stolski grunts. "Would kept your friend there from makin All 'Merican at the Kay A A house. And those ladies would've been in big mournin'.

Toby and I say so long and promise to meet Massman and Winkler in the lobby to go to supper. Stolski tells me he'll bring Dense over after football practice.

Chapter 5

Rubber Pie And Rules

It's hard to describe our first meal in the East Green Cafeteria. It takes the longest time just to get near the food as the guys at the ticket counter have to search for each meal ticket by alphabet. As the year goes on, they'll learn most of our faces and names, but on this first night, it's slow.

Loud, noisy, smoky. That's the line that winds around the wall of the huge barracks-like structure. Those already served eat at long tables in the middle, enduring the critical comments from the waiting circle. Since East Green is nearly all male, the comments are barbaric.

"What is that brown runny stuff on top of the slice of shit?"

"Liquidized shit, you fool? What did you get at home?"

"Look at the pie. That is pie, isn't it?"

"Just like my baby brother's diapers."

Many of the waiting diners attempt to distract their minds and appetites by smoking. I've seen more cigarettes smoked this afternoon that are consumed at home in a week.

Finally we're to the tray pile and the cafeteria workers are urging us on to our culinary fate. Meat loaf. Meat loaf gravy. Hash brown potatoes extra heavily browned on one side of the tray. Green beans swimming around an enormous island of ham fat. Rolls. Butter. Stoke up on them. Coffee. Black, bitter, awful. The baby shit-colored pie wobbles on its own plate.

Just as we sit, Dense and Stolski make their entrance, slamming through the screen door.

"Make way for the bear," Stolski cries. "The bear is hungry. Famished. Stand in his way at your risk."

Dense, 'the bear' in question, grins broadly at the attention as they amble past the line of waiting diners.

Served, they slam their trays down at our table.

"Dense, man, way to go," I greet him. "Piss everyone in this

37

place off and then sit at my table. Two weeks in Athens hasn't civilized you."

"I am The Bear now, Five," he returns, "so please refrain from using that childish high school stuff. Either call me by my Christian name or my proper nickname..." he pauses, then grabs a roll from my tray and flings it across the cafeteria, "Theeeeeee Beaaaaaaaarrrrrrrrrrr! Raaaahhhhrrrrr!"

Perhaps no one would've known where the airborne roll originated except for Dense's dramatic declaration. Instantly, a little guy in big brown horn rims is there with his bird-like claw in the shoulder of Dense's tee shirt.

"On your way, buddy. We don't throw food in here. Out. Right now. Out!"

Dense turns slowly at looks up the skinny arm that's clutching him. "Christ, it's a Martian. Look guys, a real Martian!" To the Martian, "I thought you guys were green."

Realizing that he's grabbed the biggest living thing in the cafeteria, the Martian lets an uneasy grin wipe across his face. With horrifying effect. Dozens of tiny, square teeth appear, each separated from the next by a half millimeter gap.

"Tell you what, Martian. The Bear's gonna let you off easy this time. I was just tryin' to eat one of my buddy here's rolls." He picks up my remaining roll and pops it whole into his huge maw, grinding his jaws dramatically. "See. Goddamn fings ah too hahd to chew." Dense mimics a giant gulp. "Even with teeth like yours. No one can chew 'em. That other one just sorta flew right outta my hand."

"Well," the Martian responds. "Don't let it happen again. It's my job on the line, y'know. I don't wanna lose my job."

Dense shrugs the Martian's claw away and gives him a huge slap on the arm sending him staggering down the aisle. "Good boy, Martian. You'n me's gonna be buddies, I can tell."

We finish our meal with Dense snatching my yellowish slice of pie and a spoon. "Goodgodamighty, Five. You're not gonna' try to eat this, are ya?" He smashes the spoon on the pie and we all watch in amazement as the pie resists with a bounce.

"Rubber pie. Hot damn. They're feedin' us rubber pie," Toby chimes in. Dense holds the pie between two fingers and waggles it in the air.

"Gotta do somethin' about this shit. Can't play football with a gut full of rubber pie."

We leave our table with Dense waving the pie in the Martian's direction. "Where do we file our complaints, Martian, ole' buddy?"

At the door, Dense stops to remove a notice from the cafeteria bulletin board. He then mashes the thumbtack through the pie and affixes it to the bulletin board.

In its first night of operation, the great East Green Cafeteria Revolt is born.

• • •

"OK, guys, quiet it down. I'm Don Daniels, resident manager and I'd like to welcome you all to Biddle Hall. And this is my wife, Kaye, and our son, or daughter. We'll all know in a month or so."

Cute little Kaye Daniels, a living pixie with a huge stomach, gives us a shy wave. Someone claps and quickly, the Biddle lounge is filled with applause. She gets up and gives us little bows which emphasize her gravid belly.

Daniels continues. "You guys are lucky to be living in Biddle. Biddle and Perkins are the first East Green dorms to be finished. Actually, they were all supposed to be finished.

"As you've seen, we've got guys living over in Gamersfelder with no windows on their rooms. And people will be moving into Jefferson next month but right now, they're doubling up in the old Vet's Village temporaries.

He stops to light a cigarette, then continues. "Further, Biddle is closest to the cafeteria." Boos and hisses of response. "And closest to the Bryan steps." More boos, hisses. "As you'll discover, the Union Street steps number 127 with five landings. The Bryan Hall steps, right out our east wing door, number 122 with three landings. Whatta deal you guys got." Applause and laughter.

"As a resident of Biddle, you have become a member of a new community — the East Green. Next week, we'll be electing a Biddle dorm council and the week after, the East Green Council will be formed with your elected representatives as a part.

"In any community, even a dormitory, there have to be some rules." This is met by more derisive response. "But here, we don't have many ways to enforce those rules." Cheers. "We can't send you to your room. And if we could, we can't guard you there. This is a residence hall, not a jail.

"And we can't fine you, if you break a rule. All we can do is send you to the East Green Council's student court and there... if you screw up bad enough... they can recommend you be dismissed from the university."

Thunderous mixed applause and jeers from the audience greet this statement.

"But the rules aren't tough. And they make sense. If we all follow them, we'll live here in Biddle as a peaceful community, have some fun, and get the most out of the college experience.

"Rule one. No drinking in the dorm. In the lounge. In your rooms. Anywhere. This is a university rule and the penalty is dismissal.

"Number two. As soon as the last parent has come and gone tomorrow, no women in your rooms." Prolonged boos and hisses. "Like you learned today, if someone's mother comes up on the floor, you call out 'woman on the floor.' And that doesn't mean that you all leap out of your rooms naked to see what she looks like."

We laugh loudly, each of us with the vision of a hundred naked guys confronting our own moms.

"We'll have our Christmas Dance and our Spring Formal and both of those will be events where women can see your rooms... and, God forbid... how you live. But those'll be held with some special rules.

"Next. Kaye and I live in the east wing apartment number 100. Our front door opens into the hall. So we'll appreciate it if you guys on the ground floor of east wing will all wear bathrobes when you go to the john.

"And everywhere else in the dorm. Try to wrap up in something when you move from your room to the john. You probably don't go around nude at home," he grins as several wisecracks echo around the room, "so be considerate of your dorm mates.

"Noise. Noise is always a problem in a dormitory. OU women have to be in at 10 p.m. weeknights, 11 p.m. on weekends, so those will be our quiet hours also. Turn your music down. Keep down the loud talk and shouting.

"We can't have private phones in the dorm rooms. That's a university rule. A pay phone is located at the end of each wing. If a phone rings as you walk by, be a buddy and answer it. Then go down to that person's room and tell him he has a call. He'll do the same for you.

"That's about it. Any questions?"

As usual, there are several dumb ass questions. Then someone asks, "What about jobs? I was told I could get a job but most of 'em already seem to be taken."

"Student jobs are available. Most of the board jobs, like holding down the dorm phone desk, working as waiters or checkers in the cafeteria, so on, were awarded to freshman applicants based on need.

"Now I know we all need some extra money. If you want a student job, check in with the Student Employment Office in Cutler basement starting tomorrow. It'll be open after the Freshman Convocation at ten a.m. at Mem Aud... Memorial Auditorium. The big building on your left as you get to the top of the Union Street steps."

Don then introduces the floor advisors. Art Long, Watt Scales and the others. And the meeting breaks up.

The Grey Wolfe and I return to our room and my stomach rumbles as we unlock the door. "Damn, but I'm starved already Toby. You have anything to eat?"

"Nope. But we can walk up to the Sundry and get a candy bar or something."

Before we can decide, a cry rings down the hall outside. "Sandwich man. Sandwiccccccccch mannnnnnnnn." We join the rush down the stairs and into the lobby.

There an older guy in an army shirt is opening a big wooden box and displaying his wares. "Got tuna fish, bologna, egg salad, ham, just like at home. Everything's a quarter except ham, that's thirty cents.

"Got milk, pop and juice. Everything's a dime. Be here every night at 10:30. Be here fifteen minutes. You have ten minutes to get your money. Come on, young men, get your money right now. We got wives and kids to feed."

We take our sandwiches and pop bottles down to Massman's room on the west wing. Winkler and Stolski are there, also chomping sandwiches.

"Almost like home," Winkler says, "cept I like mayonnaise on my bologna. Who is that guy? The Sandwich Man?"

"He's a vet," Stolski contributes. "One of the guys on the varsity is an old fart. Twenty six, twenty seven years old. I heard him talkin' about the Sandwich Man thing. Something they do out in Vet's Village. The wives make sandwiches all day and the husbands peddle them around at night.

"Well, if they're gonna keep my trade, they'd better add peanut butter and jelly," Massman says. "And none of this stuff would be a good hamburger.

The Grey Wolfe and I lie there in our dorm beds. Mine feels pretty comfortable even though I haven't bought a pillow. In the dark, we discuss the day's events.

"Y'know, Five, that egg salad was better than the ones my momma makes. But Mass is right. None of that stuff beats a good hamburger."

Day is done.

Chapter 6

Excerpts From Freshman Orientation

"Green as the grass grows, white as the driven snow, where we have da, da, dum, our Oooo-hi-ooooo."

We da da dum along with the green and white clad cheerleaders on the Mem Aud stage. Toby, Mass, Winkler, Stolski, Dense and his newly discovered roommate, none other than Chris Cobb The Martian.

Already we, the Class of '58, have bungled through *Stand Up And Cheer* three times and now we're doing this green snow thingie. But the girl cheerleaders are cute. And the guy cheerleaders don't look too much like fags.

"OK gang, let's have another *Stand Up And Cheer* and this time really hit it," a little blonde booms at us through her megaphone. The pep band strikes up and we really hit it.

"Now freshmen, let's hear a chain Ohio. Let the rest of this great university hear how much spirit you've got. Give me an Oooooooooh!"

"Oooooooooh!" we roar.

"Give me an Aaaaaaitchhhhhh!"

"Aaaaaaitchhhhhh!"

"Give me an Eyyyyyyyyyye!"

"Eyyyyyyyyyye!"

"Give me an Oooooooooh!"

"Oooooooooh!"

"What've we got?"

"OooooooooHiiiiiiOoooooh!"

"Louder!"

"OooooooooHiiiiiiOoooooh!"

"One more time! Hit it now!"

"OOOOOOOOOHIIIIIIIOOOOOOOH!!!!!!!!!"

• • •

"…and now, it gives me great pleasure to introduce to you a man I greatly admire, and a man whom you will learn to admire and respect, the president of Ohio University, Dr. John C. Baker."

We greet President Baker with great applause. Anyone would be an improvement over boring Dean Whatsis who has droned on for nearly a half hour on the academic challenge ahead of us.

"Welcome to you, the Class of 1958. I know that title may sound strange, perhaps a bit beyond attainment, to you. But that seemingly endless stretch of time will, as time does, fly by faster than you can imagine.

"Now, take a moment and look at the person to your right, then to your left. Remember those faces. Remember this time.

"Of the three of you, only one will be here on this College Green in four years and some months as a member of the graduating Class of 1958."

We do look, Toby on my right. A tall, thin girl with dark hair and glasses on my left. She stares at me as if I'm an obvious candidate for not being here. President Baker continues.

"We know, the faculty and administration of this institution of learning, that your best intentions will not carry you through four years of a degree. As graduates of Ohio high schools with at least a C average, you have earned the right to attend this university.

"You students from other states, other countries, have qualified equally. Yet," pause, "will you qualify in the years to come?

"The answer is flatly, sadly, no. Two out of three of you will not graduate in four years. Some of you *may* graduate in time. And some of you *may* be here, as my friend and neighbor Mr. Ferguson here," Baker nods to a student leader sharing the platform, "for perpetuity. Or at least it seems. Right Mr. Ferguson?" A titter ripples through the audience as Ferguson acknowledges with a blush and grin.

"But in four years, sixty some percent of you will be somewhere else.

"Many will fail academically. Many of you will discover other interests.

"Many of you will change your goals. Your ambitions for life. And you too will be gone from our number.

"So today, I ask you to pledge to yourself that you become one of that thirty percent that shall meet with me again on the College Green in the spring of 1958." Polite applause and he too drones on...

• • •

Outside the auditorium, we gather in a knot to watch the girls go by. "Dense, how in hell did you get linked up with the Martian?" I ask.

"Five man, I tell ya. It's the weirdest thing. I got home from practice last night and his stuff's there in the room but no roommate. Then we meet him at the cafeteria, right?

"Last night, we have this dorm meeting and then I hit the sack 'cause they are runnin' my ass off at practice every day. I'm sound asleep and then the lights come on and there's this awful scream."

I try to imagine the scene.

"There's the Martian, standin' there in his little white jacket, lookin' like he's about to piss himself. Guess he thought he was Goldilocks and found The Bear sleepin' in his room." He roars with laughter.

"God Bear, he's really your roomie, though?" Massman interjects. "He's such a twerp!"

"Naah, Mass. He actually seems like a pretty neat ole' guy. Got me into breakfast twenty minutes early this morning. Made sure I got seconds on cakes 'n eggs. And he sounds pretty smart, too. We oughta get along just fine."

We look at the Martian who is in deep conversation with one of the most gorgeous creatures we've seen. Tall, shiny long brown hair, perfectly placed equipment and supports. Well-filled sweater. We sidle over to join Dense's new roommate and his friend.

"Hey guys. Bear. This is Jackie Adamson," he beams, "and

Jackie, this is my roommate, The Bear." The lovely Jackie bestows a joint-melting smile on Dense and us. The Martian continues, "and these are my buddies. 'Though I don't know all their names yet."

We rush to introduce ourselves and warm in the reflected glow of Jackie's smile.

"Jackie, how do you come to ah, know, er...?" I ask hesitantly, suddenly realizing I don't know the Martian's name.

"Chris?" Dense interjects. "Yeah, how do you two know each other?"

"We're from the same home town," Jackie's voice goes right with the rest of her issue.

"And where's that?" Stolski asks.

"Blue Ball!" she tinkles with laughter.

• • •

Back at Biddle, the subject is Jackie. Mass is on the pay phone at the end of the hall, dialing each of the women's dorms to try to reach her for a date. To think none of these romeos was bright enough to ask where she lives.

"Blue Balls!" Toby exclaims. "She gives me blue balls just thinking about her."

"Definitely not anything like her in Hockingport," I add.

"I think I'll see if the phone on the west wing is free," Stolski says. "Maybe I can beat Mass'es time."

After the convocation, we ran out of clever conversation and let Jackie get away in a cluster of other freshman coeds. I don't have the guts to try to call her for a date. But I do hope she'll show up at the East Green Mixer, the only social event on tomorrow night's campus calendar.

Dense had left us to go to practice but the Martian, Chris Cobb we've discovered, accompanies us down the Bryan steps toward East Green.

"Honest to God guys, our home town's really named Blue Ball. It's too small to have its own high school 'n stuff, but that's its name." He shrugs and grins his tombstone smile. "Jackie and I went to Middletown High School. That's where

46

Jerry Lucas plays."

"Jackie was a cheerleader and prom queen but just runner-up for homecoming queen 'cause everyone was so jealous over her," Martian continues, "but she never went steady within anyone at home."

A joyous screech sounds down the hall. "I got her. I got her!" Mass bursts into the room. "I got a coffee date for Monday."

Toby has a blank look. "What the hell's a coffee date?"

"We're meeting at 12:15 at the Frontier Room for coffee."

I chip in. "Damned if that doesn't sound exciting. And then what?"

"Then things just… go… from there. I guess."

Another scream from the hall. Stolski this time.

"Yahooooo. I got through! And she's miiiiiiiiiiine!"

From the Gray Wolfe, now a statue of doubt. "Let me guess. You have a coffee date?"

"How'd you know?" Stolski looks amazed at the quartet of clairvoyants.

"Just a good guess," Mass mutters and leaves for his room.

• • •

"Well, Lo-Ree the Fifth, you're lookin' good for the third day of Orientation Week. How's life in Biddle Hall?" Trish Spotswood — the 'P. Spotswood' on my counseling card — is looking pretty good herself. White sweater. Green plaid skirt. Red hair in a ponytail.

"Great, Trish. I've met some terrific guys already."

"Guys? How 'bout girls?"

"Just a couple," I reply uneasily, "but tonight's the East Green Mixer."

"Ahhh yes. The East Green Mixer. Should get everyone's blood stirring. Where's it being held?"

"East Green Cafeteria. I hope they can mop up the barf before the girls arrive."

"And how's your roommate? That's usually the biggest gripe I hear in these first counseling sessions."

47

"He seems OK. A little weird. He has gray hair and likes to call himself the Grey Wolfe. But we're getting along OK, so far."

"OK for roommate. Now let's get down to business." I lean forward. "Have you given any thought to your major?"

My blank look seems enough of a response.

"You know! What you want to study? The field in which you'll major? What you want to do with your life?"

"God, Trish. I haven't given it much thought. I want to stay away from the towboats… don't want to be a river hand and end up as a first mate forty years later.

"And I sure don't want to take math if I can help it."

"Your test scores would indicate that."

"And I didn't do too well in science in high school."

"They indicate that as well. But your intelligence tests bump you right up to the top. What was the matter in high school? Big jock? Girls on the mind?"

"Naw. I guess I just didn't like studying that much. I got good grades in biology 'cause I liked to draw leaves and bugs. But the rest of the science stuff left me cold."

She picks up my placement essay blue book. "I noticed this drawing of a boat on your essay. It's quite good. But I don't see any art grades on your high school transcript."

"Ha, har. You obviously have never been to H'port. No art classes. Boys took shop every year. Girls took typing or home ec. Other than English, history, science, math 'n stuff, that was the only choice you had."

"Still," Trish persists, "you have some skill. Have you thought about art as a major?"

Art as a major? "Never thought about it period. What would I have to take?"

Trish opens the thick OU catalog. "First, you don't have to declare your major until your junior year… after you've completed University College requirements.

"But you can take a lot of your electives as courses that would help you fulfill your major. Introduction to drawing. Art appreciation. Introduction to painting."

I'm astounded. "You mean I can take these courses and

they'll count for a degree?"

Trish looks astounded. "Lo-ree! Can you really be as naive as you sound? Didn't you read the catalog before you applied here?"

I admitted I had not.

"Listen, I don't have an appointment after this one. Let's go over to the Frontier Room, get a cup of coffee and talk about you, art and life."

• • •

Just before lunch time, the Frontier Room is hazed with a mix of cigarette smoke and the aroma of frying hamburgers. I grab a recently vacated table while Trish goes to the counter for our coffees.

Even before noon, a group of kids is on the dance floor, swaying to the rhythms from the big square jukebox.

This is my first visit to the Frontier Room, other than glancing through the door on campus tours. The official campus snack bar, it occupies two windowed walls of the Center overlooking Union and College Avenues.

Trish arrives with our coffees and hands the tray to a waiting busboy. She opens a leather case and extracts a long filtered cigarette, pausing to look at me.

I look back. Then she finally reaches over for the matchbook that sits beside a foil Camel ashtray. "You don't smoke?"

"No m'am. Never really liked 'em."

"Don't maam me, Lo-ree. You'll smoke. Believe me, this place runs on coffee and smoke."

Just then I spot Stolski grinning and waving, then walking across the dance floor toward us. "What say, Five? How's it going?"

"Hi Stolski. What'y doing?"

"Just got finished with my pre-reg counseling." He smiles at Trish. "Hi, I'm Len Stolski."

"Hey Len, I'm Trish. Trish Spotswood."

Seeing I'm not about to offer him a seat, Stolski shuffles, then leans toward the door. "Well, gotta get on the move. See y'for lunch, Five?"

"Probably. See y'later."

Trish smiles at me, then plays with the matchbook. "Look, Lo-ree. On the face of it, college's pretty simple. You need 120 hours to graduate, so many of them in your major field... whatever it might be.

"That's fifteen hours a semester. Two semesters a year. Four years. Right?"

I nod agreement with her arithmetic.

She continues. "But it gets complicated right off the bat. You have to complete University College... that's your first two years. Either catching up on courses you didn't take in high school, or got poor grades in. And taking the required courses the university feels you need to be a well-rounded scholar when you receive your degree. Clear?"

"Yep," I reply. "And I suppose these required courses include math and science and a lot of crap I'll never want to use?"

"Well, not exactly," she says. "Different colleges have different requirements. Take journalism, for instance. Almost no math requirements other than high school. No hard sciences if you had biology and chemistry in high school."

"You mentioned art."

She leafs through her worn OU catalog. "Art's pretty much the same. Actually more major requirements, fewer electives. But most of them are in the humanities."

Another new term. "Humanities?"

"You know. History. Speech. English Lit. Those kinds of classes." She turns a page. "And a lot of your art pre-requisites can be included in your University College electives. Art Appreciation, for instance."

"Jeez, Trish. You keep losing me with all these terms. Pre-requisites. Humanities."

"Lo-ree! Quit trying to be dense." She holds up the matchbook, her pencil and a small pad. "Try this for me."

This inside of the matchbook has a "Can You Draw Me?" cartoon of a pretty girl's head. It's the *Famous Artists School* test. I take the pad and in a few seconds hand my copy back to

50

Trish.

"Damn, Lo-ree. That's fast. And pretty good too! Maybe you do want to think about art as a major."

"But Trish, what would I do for a living?"

"Teach. Be a graphic designer. Maybe become a famous artist. But only if you'll give me a good deal on one of your first paintings."

"Well... al'right, I guess. What do I have to take? How do I get started?"

"OK, Lo-ree. Perhaps, you've made a decision. Now here is your registration form. These are the courses you're required to take according to your test scores and these..."

Chapter 7

A Through M — One From Column A

I join Mass, Stolski and Winkler — each in sport coats and ties — in the lobby. I have my sport coat, black knit tie, and charcoal gray pants on... my "casual dress-up" as mom put it.

"Where's the Wolfe?" Winkler asks me.

"Just got out of the shower. Said he'd be here really quick 'n for us to wait for him."

The first chords of *Be Bop A Lula* clank across the lawn from the cafeteria. Some of our dorm mates shuffle toward the door, anxious for the first big social event of Orientation Week — the East Green Mixer.

"Sound the trumpets. Ta-daaaaaaa," calls the Grey Wolfe as he enters the lounge.

"Jesus H. Christ, Wolfe! What in hell are you supposed to be?" Winkler snickers.

Toby is dressed! *Really dressed!* Blue suede shoes are topped by black flannel trousers with pegged legs that appear to grow from the shoes. A pink shirt with the biggest *Mr. B.* collar I've ever seen blossoms from beneath the light gray sport coat. Its lapels run from shoulder blade in a roll down to the single button nearly at the hem. A light blue knit tie completes the ensemble.

"God Wolfe, you look like fuckin' Billy Eckstine," Stolski comments, "cept for the hair and skin tone. A little shoe polish would fix that."

"You bastards are just jealous," Toby responds. "Big story in the *Plain Dealer's* fashion section will back me up too. You just don't recognize fashion when you see it."

Doubled with laughter, the four of us accompany *Mister B* off to the East Green Mixer.

• • •

Some green and white crepe streamers and about half the bulbs unscrewed have transformed the East Green cafeteria into a romantic cave with just a slight hint of odor from the grease pit.

On the shadowy sidelines, the men of East Green huddle in small knots. After six so-called meals in the cafeteria, many of the faces are familiar but few have names attached yet.

Like their East Green counterparts, the freshmen women of OU come in all sizes and shapes. Our little school of would-be predators concentrates on shapes.

"Look't the tits on that one in the red sweater!" Toby hisses in a whisper that reverberates around the hall.

"Christ, Wolfe! Why didn't you bring a microphone?" I ask.

Still, the comments we can hear from our fellow predators basically concentrate on anatomical characteristics.

The band strikes up a discordant version of Big Bopper's *Chantilly Lace* and one of the first girls on the floor is our dream, Jackie Adamson.

"Look't that. There she is," Winkler screams above the music. "And she's dancin' with the Martian."

Sure enough, the Chris and Jackie are shagging through *Chantilly Lace* like they had practiced it for years at slumber parties.

Behind me, a bass growl announces the presence of The Bear. "Little fucker can sure move those skinny legs, can't he?"

"I'm gonna cut in," Len announces.

"Nah, give 'em a couple minutes," Dense cautions. "Maybe she'll throw him over her head."

• • •

"Christine Jordan," the blonde responds, "and what's yours?"

We go through the name game pretty quickly and she smiles in approval of a cool nickname like Five.

"That's neat. Five," she pronounces it as if a thought aloud. "Wanna dance, Five?"

We take to the floor with dozens of other couples. The grease pit odor is being overtaken by the smell of heated mixed deodorants. Thank god for mom's dance lessons at home. I hold my own and twirl this pretty blonde in and out of the shadows. Then Winkler cuts in and I'm alone on the floor.

"I'll give him two minutes," Toby says in my ear, "then the Grey Wolfe takes over. What's her name?"

"Er, Christine… something." I spot Jackie Adamson kind of bopping in place with some short guy in shirtsleeves and move in myself.

"Can I cut in?"

"Beat it, clown," the short guy snarls as he puts a tighter grip on Jackie's lovely waist.

"Oh hi," she smiles at me. "Bruce, you'll just have to wait another turn," she says to the stump. And I'm dancing with the dream from Blue Ball. But the interlude is brief as Winkler makes his cut and I look around for other prey.

Seconds later. "Jesus, I didn't even get a sniff." It's Winkler who nods toward Jackie spinning off with Stolski. Toby is sidling through the dancers toward Jackie, cut-in written on his face.

"Hope I get the last dance with her," Winkler says. "She'll be too tired to resist."

• • •

The subject is women. We're back in the "Wolf's Lair," as Toby has dubbed 205.

"Man, that Jackie is hot," Toby proclaims. "And I, too, have a coffee date with her. Monday." His shirt is soaked and wrinkled. The bowed collar now droops like a Thursday handkerchief in flu season.

Disbelief shades the faces of our group. Perhaps pegged pants do have an effect!

"I liked that blonde babe from Kentucky," Stolski announces. "Nice bod. Cute face. Great accent. What was her name?"

"Christine. Christine…? Shit!" I am angry. "I forgot her

name."

"Jordan. Christine Jordan. From Ashland, Kentucky." Toby looks up from the palm of his hand. "Lives in Lindley Hall."

"Right! That's great, Wolfe. How'd you ever remember?"

"The Wolfe has many secrets," he proclaims, "but I'll let you poor fools in on one of them." He holds up a tiny book. "Does anyone remember Angela Watts?"

Silence. Blank faces.

Toby refers to his black book. "Angela Watts? Cleveland? Had a plaid skirt, black sweater? Awful bow in her hair?"

"Yeah, I remember," Winkler adds. "Heavy-set chick. Danced like a cement block." We all nod in agreement.

"Well," she happens to be the first entry in the Grey Wolfe's Black Book. "And she happens to be the only daughter of Watts Paints. Fifteen stores in Cleveland and up and down the lake shore."

"Ah yes, the beautiful Angela Watts," Stolski sighs. "I think I could be in love with her."

• • •

Once more I'm flushed through A through M and into the cavern of Men's Gym. The gym floor is a maze of tables manned by busy looking people and attended by relatively short lines of would-be students. Trish made sure I got an early appointment.

Two quick checks at tables lead me on to the L through M where only three people are ahead of me. So far, the horror of registration has been a breeze.

Soon I'm at the head of a growing line where a bespectacled woman looks up, frowns and holds out her hand. I present my carefully filled-out pre-registration card.

"Hmmmm. Lowrey, Thomsen. No middle initial?"

"No maam, and it's Lo-ree, not Lowrey, if you don't mind."

"OK Thomsen, let's see if we can get you into some classes."

She scans my card and refers to a large binder filled with pages. Her frown doesn't change.

"English composition, you're OK there with a Monday nine

o'clock. And Western Civilization? Monday-Wednesday would conflict with your English comp. How about a Tuesday at nine?

"And Introduction to Fine Arts. Your advisor did a pretty good job of getting you nine hours of pre-requisites. Mondays at ten? All right with you?"

Again I nod my assent, not quite sure what I'm agreeing to.

"Now then. Introduction to Speech. That's a humanities prerequisite. We can work you in Mondays at two p.m." She shoots me a quizzical frown.

"That sounds fine, maam."

"That leaves Introduction to Drawing. Are you going to be a Fine Arts major?"

"Yes'm. I guess so."

"In that case, speech will qualify for another degree pre-req and the drawing course will, of course, count toward your major. Excellent."

"Yes, maam."

Her lips move as she scans my card again. "With ROTC, that will give you fourteen hours. Physical education is a two-hour prerequisite. One hour per semester. Want to start getting that out of the way?"

"Sure. I mean. I think so."

"Fine. One hour of Seasonal Sports. That'll be Tuesdays and Thursdays. No Saturdays. And you're set for a fifteen hour load." She stamps my card and directs me to the next table where a tall black man sits beside an adding machine.

"Thomsen Lowrey. Fifteen hours," he chants. "That's $115.50. Plus the $10.50 Student Activity Fee. Plus $21 Student Health Service. Mr. Lowrey, you owe Ohio University $147 and no cents. You can use this table over here to make out your check. They'll have a stamp at the cashier's window." He cranks the machine hands me a tape from its whirring mouth.

With check number one in hand, duly made out to blank for $147 and no cents, I stand in line with others at the cashier's desk. A small cage transforms the desk into a semblance of a bank teller's cage.

My check is stamped and I'm handed a receipt by someone's nice grandmother. "There you are, Mr. Lowrey. Take your

57

receipt and this form to one of the girls at those tables. They'll type in your Student Activity card."

As I stand in another line, a guy next to me nudges and whispers, "Thirty three."

I raise puzzled eyebrows. "Thirty three?"

"Your birthday. Makes you legal."

I nod sagely, not sure what he's talking about. Then it's my turn. A vaguely familiar-looking brunette takes my card form and begins typing on it.

"Residence? Date of birth?"

"Biddle Hall." Type, type. "Uh, March 18, uh. Nineteen, er... thirty three?"

She looks up and smiles. "Sure. And I'll bet you were the Hero of Inchon Harbor, too?"

"Yes maam. Aw, no, I mean." Type, type.

"There you are, Mr. Veteran Lowrey. Hand your card to the girl over by the lights and pose for your mug shot. Good luck."

In fifteen quick minutes, I am nearly $150 poorer and an official college student.

Chapter 8

The Three C's: Coffee Dates, Classes and Confusion

"Good morning, ladies and gentlemen. I am Mark Tharp, professor of English. This class is English Composition, section six. We shall meet at this hour each Monday, Wednesday and Friday.

Professor Tharp surveys us with a sweeping gaze beneath bushy gray eyebrows. His hair is nearly silver, lighter than Toby's. It is combed back in what might be termed an elderly duck's ass, ending in a pile above the collar of his blue work shirt.

He is ancient. Must be nearly 45 or so. Several girls at nearby desks squirm beneath his gaze.

"You will need two texts to meet the reading requirements of this class. A third, of which I have the pleasure of being the author, will be most helpful. Julia, my teaching assistant will pass out the syllabus.

• • •

"I swear to god. No shit. The guy gave us four books for his stinkin' econ class. And two of them 'he has the honor of having written himself'." Toby was purple with indignation when we ran into each other in front of Cutler Hall. Now, sitting on the Cutler wall, his anger seems to be boiling toward a higher degree.

"Plus. The asshole had the nerve to single me out. Out of 90 or some people. Wants to know if I'm 'related to someone in show business?'."

"Same for me, Tob," I try to cool him off. "I have three English books to read, one of them by the prof. I can't wait to see what comes next. Intro to Fine Arts in Mem Aud." Bells ring and we depart in our separate funks.

· · ·

The ubiquitous A through M signs have been moved to Memorial Auditorium where proctors are herding kids into lines according to their names.

"Sorry, babe. Only way we can take roll," one apologizes to a whining girl holding hands with a geeky looking guy. They break their grips and follow their separate letters.

I fall into my directed line and then move up as my name is called. Once in a proper line, we follow our proctor into Mem Aud, dark and gloomy compared to my first visit at Freshman Convocation.

"Good morning, students," a woman's voice booms through the PA system. "Please take your seats quickly. We have a lot to cover."

The girl to my left is good-looking. Longish blonde hair. Nice figure. Seems friendly as she smiles and leans down toward my leg. *Friendly? Is she going to grab my leg?*

No! She pulls up a flat desk top between the seats and rotates it in front of her. "Hi! I'm Andy Logan. Been taking notes in this place since I was a little kid."

"Hey Andy. I'm Five Lowrey. Since you were a little kid? I thought this was a freshman course."

She giggles. Neat giggle. "Yep. I'm a townie. A teacher's brat."

Just then the lights dim and the ghostly voice booms. "Good morning. I am Pat Trevayne. Welcome to Introduction to the Fine Arts." A single spotlight shines on the podium where it becomes obvious a tall, thin woman with tightly pulled-back blonde hair and gold glasses is the speaker.

"Miss Trevayne. Biggest ass-kisser in the department," Andy nudges me with another giggle.

Trevayne the ass kisser continues. "Doctor Logan will be here Friday for his first lecture. As you can see, this is a very large class." We can't see because it's so dark but the murmur of hundreds of voices confirms her estimate of the crowd. "So it's very important that you make note of your row and seat number.

Each class the proctors will take roll by checking the seats. You don't want to sit in the wrong seat and give someone else credit for your presence, do you?"

A mirthless chuckle echoes across the vast hall.

"There are no required publications for this course. But I would advise you to strongly consider purchasing the three books listed in your syllabus. They are available at the library but will usually be checked out as there are more than 600 students registered in the three sections of this class this semester."

Trevayne rambles on for a few minutes and then signals for the lights to come up. "That's it for today. We'll see you Friday morning." The mob begins to disperse.

I turn to Andy Logan. "Doctor Logan?"

"Yep," she responds. "Dear old dad. But keep in mind that he is a dear, old dad, regardless of what you think when you see him Friday." She spins and heads down the row. Over her shoulder, "See ya Friday, Five."

• • •

Seventy one dollars and forty cents. I make out check number two to the College Book Store, shocked by the impact three days of college have had upon my bank account.

My book pile weighs an easy thirty pounds but for forty cents more, the clerk supplied me with a canvas bag. The load includes books for Western Civ, English, Speech and one of the three Fine Arts books recommended by Ass Kisser Trevayne. It's a big paperback with hundreds of stamp-sized black and white photos of paintings and sculptures.

The clerk carefully places the long bag of charcoal sticks on the top of the load and hands me the newsprint sketchpad. "This won't fit and you won't want it bent, will you?"

Five charcoal sticks. A chisel tip pencil. Newsprint sketchpad. No books. The only required purchases for Introduction to Drawing. I haven't drawn a lick and already it's my favorite class.

• • •

Stolski and Mass slump on the study chairs as we gather in the Wolfe's Den, as our room has become known. The Bear's Lair. The Wolfe's Den. *Are we really becoming sophisticated?*

Once again the subject is women. Specifically, Jackie Adamson.

"Two coffee dates and then she brushes me right off," Toby complains.

"Well, shit. That's better than having me standing outside the Frontier Room while she's having her *second* coffee date of the day with Mass," Stolski says. "Goddamn woman must have kidneys like a hot water bottle."

"I really would like to go to the MIA movie, Donald," Massman mimics a girlish voice, "but I've been asked to a fraternity party. What a bunch of crap! Do you suppose fraternities really have parties on Wednesday nights?"

A knock at the door is followed by its opening and the entry of the Bear and the Martian. "Hey guys," Dense greets us, "guess who has a date for Saturday night?"

"If you say Jackie Adamson, I'll shoot your big bear ass," Toby retorts.

"No, maannnnn, Page Dobrowski."

"She's a big girl Dense met last spring at Lake Hope," I add. "And I do mean big.

"Betcherass she's big. And she's a big woman on campus, too. Reason I haven't seen her is she's a rush party chairman for the Alpha Gams." Dense pauses. "That's the sorority right at the top of the hill here and she's going to live in the house next semester."

We assure our big friend that his social life is on track. Mass turns to the Martian. "We were just bitchin' about your friend Jackie, Chris. What's with her?"

"Whaddya mean?"

"Well, the Wolfe, Stolski and I all had coffee dates with her. Then she dumps us for a fraternity guy."

The Martian grins his wonderful tombstone smile. "Well, guys, I can only tell you one thing. She's a nice girl and she's been my best friend in high school forever. Even though I wasn't popular.

"But some of the jealous kids in high school nicknamed her "The Caboose" because she always hooked onto whatever guy was popular at the time."

"Well, right now she's coupled onto some guy with a Phi Delt pin on his sweater," Toby says.

"How do you know what a Phi Delt pin looks like," I ask Toby.

"Easy. I'm a legacy."

What in hell is a legacy?

Chapter 9

Let The Games Begin

The simple vase with dried flowers sits there, challenging me to do something with the charcoal stick between my fingers. A vast expanse of virgin newsprint spreads before me.

"One minute," calls the instructor. We're doing our first Intro to Drawing exercise, a three minute speed sketch of the vase. Two-thirds of my exercise time has vanished while I stare fixedly at the piece of pottery.

Around me, kids are busily sketching. Reluctantly, I put charcoal to newsprint.

"Are you going to sign that before you start?" a voice over my shoulder startles me. It's the instructor, Professor Dabny. She leans over my arm and grasps my wrist with one hand, snapping my long charcoal stick into two pieces with the other. "First, hold the charcoal thusly, between forefinger and thumb.

"Second. Use a shorter piece of charcoal." The sound of charcoal sticks snapping clatters across the studio. "This isn't a Chinese restaurant. These," she says waving another of my charcoals in the air, "are not chopsticks."

She leans back into me, her ample breast on my arm helping gain my full attention. "You've never had art instruction before, have you?"

"No maam. Our school was too small."

"Well, first of all, I want you to draw with your feelings, not your fingers." Roughly and quickly she runs her hand from my fingers up my arm and across my shoulder to my chest. "Draw from here. The heart. And here. The head. And here." She grabs my buttock. "Draw from the ass. Draw from the soul. Draw what you feel. Not what you see."

Someone giggles behind one of the bench easels.

"You think it's funny?" Dabny yells. "Not funny if you *want* to become an artist. You'll see funnier things than this, this poor thin buttock," poking my butt again, "if you really work to become an artist."

She moves on to another easel. With a sweeping stroke of the charcoal stub, I begin to draw from the ass.

• • •

Pooooosh 'em back. Pooooosh 'em back. Pooooosh 'em back in the boooooshes. Let's go Bobcats. Deeeeeee-fense!

OU's mighty Bobcats dig in as we urge them to smother the Youngstown Penguins on their first play from scrimmage. The red and black-clad Penguins come out of their huddle and line up on the six yard line.

Get 'im, get him! the crowd screams as the Penguin tailback takes the direct snap and goes into a spinner move in the backfield. Penguin backs swirl right and left. Then suddenly one of them is alone at the 15. With the ball. ***Get 'im, get him!***

The Youngstown halfback runs 94 yards for a touchdown on the first play from scrimmage and the crowd descends into silent despair. Below us, blocks of guys with their dates set about passing wax cups of drink down the rows. If this is college football, maybe studying will be a better way to spend Saturday afternoons.

• • •

Stand up and cheer, cheer loud and long for old Ohio.
For today we raise, the Green and White above the rest...

We march happily up President Street toward town, following the marching band as they play the fight song over and over. Their green plumed hats are turned backwards, traditional symbol that the Bobcats have prevailed at Ohio Stadium.

Prevailed? If beating Youngstown State in the first game by one extra point can be called prevailing. Crossing the bridge over the Hocking and the railroad, I notice a gang of guys and girls on the porch of a big brick house with white pillars.

"Delts!" Toby observes. "They're one of the coolest frats on campus. Not as good as Phi Delt, but good just the same."

66

The Delts seem to be having a good time. Except for one guy who's holding his date by the shoulders as she barfs over the porch railing.

Go Bobcats. Go big green. "Stand up and cheer, cheer loud and long for old Ohio...

• • •

We pack in with the rest of the crowd at Begorra, a tiny hamburger joint where equally tiny burgers sell for nine cents apiece, 11 for a dollar. Dollar bills wave madly as football fans try to get attention at the counter. The place is a madhouse.

"Gimme ten. Gimme ten. No cheese today. Whattareya, crazy? This is a football day."

The seven of us — Toby, Mass, Stolski, the Martian, Dense, his date Page Dobrowski and me — walk across campus munching the juicy, greasy burgers.

The Bear and Page leave us at University Terrace for Scott Quadrangle, where Page lives. "Bye guys. It was great meeting you all," she waves.

"See ya' tonight, guys. I oughta be back in time for the Sandwich Man," Bear mumbles through his mouthful of Begorra. "Should be good 'n hungry by then."

"God, is the Bear never full?" the Martian asks as we wind down the Bryan steps. "He eats three meals a day, at least ten candy bars, and's first in line for the Sandwich Man every night."

"He's just a growing boy," I respond. "How else can he keep up his playing weight? Can you believe anyone eating twenty-two of these greaseballs?"

"Do you think he'll get to start against West Virginia?" Mass says. The Bobkittens are playing WVU Thursday afternoon, their first game of the freshman season.

"He says he thinks he might," the Martian answers. "Says Coach Richey think he's doing great, especially since he never played football before."

We agree to go to the freshman game as a group, all except for Toby who has a coffee date.

67

· · ·

We're in the Bear's Den in Perkins Hall, eating soggy Sandwich Man products and drinking sodas.

"Jeeeeeesus guys, you shoulda seen what goes on at Squat Cod just before the lights go on. Couples makin' out everywhere." Dense has a smear of lipstick on his chin, a badge of accomplishment in the Scott Quadrangle courtyard.

"Same thing at Lindley," Toby chimes in. "I'm just standin' there, saying goodnight to Stacy and all around me, people are playin' kissy face and grinding up against those big pillars. I didn't know what to do. Shit or go blind?"

"You? The big stud Wolfe from Ashtabula?" I ask. "Wasn't Stacy, er, responsive?"

"Responsive enough," he answers. "I just didn't want to make my move too fast, spoil a good thing in case I want to ask her out again."

"How was she, Wolfe?" Mass asks. "A good date? Big tits? Nice ass?"

"I'll bet she has a *great* personality," Winkler contributes.

"And *beautiful* handwriting," Stolski says in a falsetto. Already we're picking up on campus jokes.

"Screw you guys," Toby growls. "Just wait. I may turn her over to one of you if she doesn't make the Grey Wolfe's A List."

"Anyone got a fag?" This from the Martian. "I'm all out." So far, the Martian is the only one of us who smokes and he claims he's been smoking for years.

"There's some of those little sample things in my top drawer," Dense says. "I sure don't want 'em."

The Martian produces a dozen of the four-packs of sample cigarettes that are given away everywhere on campus. "So... we've got Pall Malls, Chesterfields, Camels. Anyone wanna try one?"

"What the hell? I will," Stolski says. "I felt like a big dumbass on that coffee date with Jackie when she lit up. Gimme one of those Chesterfield Kings. That's what she was smoking."

"Me too," Winkler adds. "Might as well get with the plan

68

here."

"How bout you, Five?" The Martian spreads a deck of sample packs before me.

"Mom'll kick my ass, but... sure." I take the box of Pall Malls and extract one of the long cigarettes. The Martian passes a pack of matches with the "Draw Me" girl on it and we light up.

Sounds of coughing. Hacking. Gagging.

"Not bad," Stolski muses.

"Shit, Ski. You're just blowing it around. Try inhaling," the pro smoker from Blue Ball advises. "Take a big drag, then just sorta swallow it."

Stolski does. We follow his lead. More coughing. My head swims.

"Ohhhhh, I'm gonna barf," Toby moans. He flops back on the Bear's bed. "Ohhhh, shit. That's even worse. The whole room's spinning."

"Take it slow. You'll get used to it," the Martian counsels.

Dizzily, I take it slow. Inhaling again. The second time's not quite so bad. The room is filling with a cloud of gray. Winkler stubs his cigarette out in the Bear's coffee cup.

"C'mon Winky, don't give up so fast," Toby says. "If we're gonna be sick, we're *all* gonna be sick. Winkler lights up another Chesterfield.

"Now guys, lesson two." The Martian lets some smoke ooze out between his wide lips, then snuffs it up through his nostrils. "We'll learn how to French inhale."

• • •

The September rain creates a drumbeat on the window of my Western Civ class. Dr. Stansfield drones on and I find my eyelids growing heavier.

"As you can see, the Dark Ages were aptly named. The wealthy lived within their enclaves of privilege, fearful of the populace that supported their life styles, yet threatened their very existence."

My head snaps back violently after my forehead tells my brain it's made contact with the desk surface.

"Superstition ruled the land," Stansfield drones on. "Literacy was the key to success and very few, even among the royals and the wealthy, held those keys."

I vow never to register for another nine o'clock class again.

• • •

A sooty sunbeam pours through the skylight of the drawing studio. Today, the model stand is bare. The rustle of sketch pads being set against the easel stools is broken by Professor Dabny's entrance. She's followed by a middle-aged woman in a Japanesey-looking robe and bare feet. A cigarette droops from her lower lip.

"Today, class, we begin figure studies. Our model today is Anique, one of our most experienced models."

Anique butts the cigarette in one of the ubiquitous tin Camel ashtrays and with a fluid motion, whips the robe from her shoulders.

She's stark naked!

Dabny announces "A three-minute warm-up. Remember. Draw from your feelings, from your soul." We sit there, slack-jawed. I feel the warnings of an erection.

"Ready Anique? Ready, pose."

Trying to draw from the soul, my fingers snap the already stubby charcoal in two. My first totally naked woman. I concentrate on her features. Her hair. Eyebrows. Eyes. Ears. The long braid that hangs across her shoulder down to her…

"Two minutes."

I sketch in her nose. Anique's nostrils. The thin lips of her wide mouth.

"One minute."

Her chin appears on my pad and then… *Oh God. Less than a minute for the rest of her!*

My soul takes over. Two sweeping lines across her chest. The drooped arm is a single stroke that joins her straightened leg. Another stroke delineates her protruding, slightly square stomach. The cocked leg is another swoop ending in an approximated foot.

"Time. Rest Anique." A sigh of relief sweeps the gray room. Nearly everyone lights up, including Anique who exposes her ample buttocks and other equipment to us as she bends to her robe for cigarettes.

Dabny tours the room, *ah-heming* and *uh-huhing* over the artists' shoulders. My erectile condition subsides as she nears my easel.

"Ahhh, Mr. Lowrey. A very interesting portrait. Pretty good detail but... perhaps you should save that for portraiture class." She pats my shoulder and moves on. I French inhale my Pall Mall and steal another glance at Anique, now in her open robe and touring the easels herself.

At my drawing, she giggles and asks, "Is my nose really that long?"

• • •

"No shit? Totally naked? No shit?" Dense is amazed at my drawing class experience. "I've got to drop intro to public health and get into that sucker."

Page smiles to herself at the Bear's apparent new enthusiasm for academic matters. I realize her smile is that of a really pretty woman but can't bring myself to look beneath her chin, even though she's fully clothed.

"Ahhh, but it gets better," I continue. Toby shifts in his chair and leans forward.

"Dabny brings Anique back to the posing stand and says, 'Ladies and gentlemen, let me call your attention to a few things. This is a woman. A nude woman. I am sure that for a few of you, this was your first encounter with a nude body.'"

"Then she puts her hand right under Anique's boob, cups it and says, 'And this is a woman's breast. You'll notice she has two of them. You young ladies have, in the privacy of your bath, probably noticed that you also have breasts. Breasts are common among human beings. Turn please, Anique.'"

"She points to Anique's big square ass and continues, 'These are Anique's buttocks. Anique has born children, isn't that right my dear? And her buttocks... and her abdomen...

show the results of that experience.'"

"Finally... and I swear to God this is true, she spins Anique around and points to her, her... ah, and says, 'And finally this is a woman's pubis. As you can see, Anique is a fully mature woman and has an abundance of pubic hair. This too is natural and common. Let me assure you, as you progress as artists, you will understand these attributes of the human body and appreciate their importance to your art.'"

All three of my listeners are now forward, rapt. "So we run through three more poses, doing as many sketches as we can," I tell, "and by the time the bell rings, Anique is about as familiar as the vase of dried flowers that we sketched last week."

"Can we see your sketches, Five?" Page asks with a grin.

"I only kept one. And I'm not too proud of it. But..." I display the sheet of newsprint.

"Christ, she looks like a giant pear," Toby exclaims. "Is that a front or back view."

"Five, I think it's very good," Page comments softly. "Perhaps you can draw me sometime." The Bear muffles a growl.

• • •

After days of beautiful weather, Athens unleashes its famed drizzle on the OU-WVU freshman game. Play signals echo from the walls of the nearly empty stadium and are muffled by the misty rain.

Huddled together for warmth, our little knot of fans emits an occasional faint cheer but on this gloomy Thursday afternoon, there's little to cheer about. The Little Mountaineers recover two straight Bobkitten fumbles and march for a touchdown and a field goal. OU has not run a successful play.

Dense stands among the substitutes on the OU bench, his shoulder pads adding to his bulky number 52 jersey, an ugly leather helmet from the forties dangling from his sausage fingers. *We want the Bear. We want the Bear.* Winkler, Toby, Mass, Page and I throw this chant toward the bench and grin when Dense turns and gives us a grin and wave.

72

We cheer lustily when Stolski bobbles, then holds onto a pass to give the 'Kittens their first success on offense, a first down. More cheers as Wes DeVon takes a hand-off, breaks a tackle and dances down the sideline for a big gain and another first down.

Groans when DeVon is smacked by a giant West Virginia tackle and the ball spirals into the dense air. Another OU fumble. Another West Virginia recovery. *We want the Bear.*

Suddenly Dense jerks, jams on his helmet, and dashes onto the field. We cheer for our Bear.

On his first play following the fumble, Dense sidesteps the opposing tackle and gets a hand on the WVU quarterback… just enough to throw him off balance and cause an incomplete pass. We cheer and cheer.

On the next play, number 52 is again in the West Virginia backfield. Then smash. His white leather helmet goes flying and his huge body vanishes beneath a pair of giant gold jerseys. Time is called. Trainers run onto the field to tend to the recumbent Bear. West Virginia ran a trap on the Bear and it worked to perfection.

• • •

"Jeeeezus! Did you see what this big hunkie did to me?" The Bear's grin has a gap where a tooth used to be. His green jersey is smeared with muddied blood. One cheekbone is a mass of purple. His huge arm is draped over the even broader form of the giant from West Virginia.

"These're my friends… Five, from my home town, my girl Page Dobrowski, Mass, and Winkler. This's Gornochek."

Gornochek is equally muddy and bloody. He has all his teeth but blood drips from his chin down his mustard-colored jersey. "I cain't believe this is the first game this big sombitch ever played," he drawls. "Surrrrre, we trapped his big ass that first time but sheeeeeit, he learnt fast."

West Virginia beat the Bobkittens 18-12 but we're not blue. Biddle Hall's Stolski caught five passes and nearly scored a touchdown. Biddle Hall's Wes DeVon scored both of OU's touchdowns. And our friend the Bear got to kick some heads in, getting his own severely bruised in the process.

"Well, I gotta get goin," Gornochek says, "nice meetin' y'all. If you get up to Morgantown, come see me."

"Take care o'yourself, Gorno," Dense says, warmly clasping the big West Virginian's paw. "And thanks a lot for the lesson. Wish I could get together with you guys again but probably'll not happen." West Virginia and OU don't play each other at the varsity level.

He gives Page a muddy peck on the cheek and flashes his gapped smile at us. "Sheeeeeit, that was great. Sheeeeeit." My friend has learned a new game and a new word. *Sheeeit.*

• • •

I puff up the steps to the barracks building near the stadium and open the door just as class bells clang around the campus. I'm greeted by an older man in uniform who looks up and declares, "Well, young warrior! Where are you coming from, the Olympic Games?"

"Seasonal sports, sir." I hand him my class card. He glances at it.

"Don't sir me, Mister Lowrey. I am a sergeant. Gym class? Then Military Science?" He glares at the sweat-soaked card as if I had just handed him the Asian Flu virus.

"Yesssir, er, sergeant."

"Goddamn, those women up in the registrar's office have got their heads so far up their butts they need glass stomachs to see where they're goin'."

For what seems like an hour he gives me a visual inspection. Cold, steely eyes. Looking me up and down. Taking in my orange and white HHS shorts. The gray OU Phys Ed shirt.

"Do you realize, young man, that from Seasonal Sports, you will have to appear at Military Science in full Class A uniform? Clean? Smelling reasonably good, which you do not at this time?"

"No sergeant."

"Come out here, Lowrey." He rises from his desk and

74

beckons me toward the entrance door. I follow him to the small wooden porch where he extracts a stubby Camel and lights up. "Tell me, Lowrey. Do you really want to be in the Army?"

"Eeeehr, I haven't really... really given it much thought, sarge."

"Do you really have a desire to lead your fellow man in combat? As a commissioned officer in the United States Army?"

"God sarge, I don't know. The lady at registration just told me Rotcee is required."

"Well, Lowrey. It is, kind of. But if you want some advice, well-meant, heart-felt advice..."

"I'm listening sergeant."

"If you try to make it from gym class to R.O.T.C., that is, this Military Science class, and expect to pass inspection... Well... You. Just. Will. Not. Make. It." Each word is punctuated by the cold eyes and thin-lipped smile.

"So my advice to you is to hie your ass up to the registrar's office and drop Military Science. Pick up something you can go to in sweaty clothes."

"But it's required, sarge!"

"Tell those bags at the registrar's office that classes in Army Military Science are full. Tell them you're a conchie. Don't tell 'em you're queer. They'll gossip about that and you'll never get a date. Don't worry about it being required." He gives me a genuine smile and for the first time I notice his name tag says "Waller."

"That's my advice to you."

"It sure sounds like good advice to me, sir. Er, Sergeant Waller."

"It is Sergeant, Lowrey. Sir was for when I was a major... at the 38th Parallel. I'm just a riffed lifer now, putting in my time and hopin' for thirty. You're just damned lucky, Mr. Lowrey, that I wasn't sitting in a recruiting office. Your ass would'a been mine."

Stunned. I don't know quite what to do. This forbidding soldier with the friendly advice doesn't look like the hand-shaking sort. So I click my Keds heels together and throw him my snappiest movie salute.

75

"Thanks sarge. I really mean it. Thank you." And that's how I escaped from Saturday morning drill.

• • •

I'd never given much thought to the word *sundry* until my life at Biddle began. The OU Sundry sits on hilly Mulberry Street and is the only outpost of commerce convenient to the East Green. The Sundry lives up to its name: bits and pieces of everything from cigarettes and gum to deodorant and overshoes.

"Y'know, you can save fifty cents if you buy these by the carton," the gum-chewing Wanda tells me as I fork over another quarter for a pack of Pall Malls.

"Well, yeah, but I really don't smoke that much," I return.

"Oh sure, right! And you'll be back in here in the morning on your way to class, too."

Wanda is right. An astute judge of all things student and sundry, she knows well that I'll be buying my cigarettes by the carton before October.

The bell over the door tinkles and in come Winkler and Mass from the drizzle of Mulberry Street.

"What say, Five?" Winkler greets me, "y'gonna buy another pack of those to make up for all the ones you've bummed from me?"

I smile sheepishly and plunk down another quarter. As Wanda reaches for the Pall Malls, Winkler interrupts. "Make that Chesterfields, Wanda, if y'please. They seem to have a richer flavor."

"What're you two up to?" I ask the dripping pair.

"Gotta get some poster stuff," Mass responds. "Wink here's gonna run for Biddle president. Wanna help? You know anything about posters?"

"A little. Anything'll beat studying English."

We pick a dozen huge sheets of poster board, a jar of red tempera paint, several lettering brushes. I suggest a couple bottles of Fisher's India Black ink and a Speedball pen set with three nibs.

"What're those for?" Winkler asks.

"You'll see. But believe me, they'll come in handy." I promise to meet them at the dorm after my speech class and leave the Sundry to trudge up Mulberry Street.

• • •

Winkler and Massman's room looks like a murder scene. Red splotches — tempera I realize with relief — are everywhere including across the candidate's forehead and his campaign manager's new OU sweatshirt.

"Holy shit, guys! What in the world are you doing?" I haven't seen such a mess since Sissie Eileen was three and fingerpainted our dining room walls.

"Well," Massman says ruefully, "these damn posters are a little more work than we'd figured. But we've got this one done." He holds up a grotesque piece of poster board that proclaims *Vote Winkler For Biddle President.*

"Nice. I especially like the accent blotches. Kinda like someone threw blood at the poster. And it's big," I add. "Probably read that sucker all the way to Perkins.

"OK wiseass. Can you do it better?"

"As a matter of fact... I can... help you do it better. First, let's cut down on the words. How about 'Wink For Pres' since they'll just be going up around the dorm?"

"That's OK but the words'll have to be huge," Winkler says.

"Nope. We'll cut the boards into fours and have that many more posters. More exposure."

They nod agreement and immediately attack the boards with scissors.

I open the Speedball set and take one of the smaller boards and begin to ink the campaign slogan on with open, cartoony letters, just like at Emmit's market.

"Shit, Five. That's good. And you're fast, too." Massman seems impressed.

"Right, Mass. Now this is India ink and when it's dry, it'll be permanent. But don't smear it while it's wet.

"When I've done 'em all, you guys can use these two lettering brushes to fill in the open parts of the letters. And I'll go study."

"Wink For Prez" seems a lot more creative than "Cukes 25¢ Ea." and I finish the signs in less than an hour. Winkler's entry into politics is rolling.

Chapter 10

College Life: The Passing Parade

My eyes are drooping over lines of type rapidly turning gray . How can I be tired of studying? I've only been at it for twenty minutes. From his desk Toby groans in mock agony upon discovering that turning a page in his Western Civ book only leads to another pair of pages.

Our door bangs open and Ted Brewer bursts in. "No studying tonight, guys. You'll miss the *big parade.*" We follow Brewer, a sophomore who lives on the third floor, into the hall and meet a swarm of fellow Biddleites. "C'mon," he urges, "only happens once a year and believe me, it's worth flunkin' a class to see."

As we puff up the Bryan Hill steps, I can see other groups of East Greeners heading for the main campus. And on the College Green, an air of festivity prevails, even on this Tuesday night.

Brewer leads us to a perch on the wall in front of WOUB on College Avenue. The *big parade* is something to see. Hundreds of coeds in their finest dresses are converging on College Avenue from all directions.

"It's the first night of sorority rush," Brewer chortles, "and every chick on campus is out to make a great impression. That's Alpha Xi Delta over there," he points out the first house past Howard Hall. "And beside it is Chi Omega. That's where I wait tables. And next to Chi O is Pi Beta Phi.

"They're all great groups," he continues in a professorial tone, "but you should see 'em when they come down for breakfast. At least the Chi O's. It's just disgusting. Enough to put ya' off sex forever."

The march of girls diminishes and the sounds of singing, screams and laughter trickle out of the three sorority houses.

"This'll go on for an hour." Brewer obviously relishes his role as guide. "Then they'll move on up the street to Phi Mu and Kappa Sig. And more'll come around the corner from Zeta and Alpha Gam."

One of the guys in our group chimes up. "Do you belong to a fraternity, Brew? Isn't that a fraternity pin you've got on?"

Brewer points to a white shield on his sweater with some gold stars. "I'm a pledge. Beta Theta Pi. So this is a pledge pin."

"What's a pledge do?" I ask.

"Well, it's the way a fraternity has you join, sortof on probation. While you're a pledge, you get to do lots of neat stuff and you have to learn a lot about the fraternity."

"Like what?" someone else asks.

"Oh, its history. And lore. And lots of it is secret. I guess I'll know it all when I go active."

"Go active?"

"Yeah... after you kindof prove yourself to the fraternity brothers, they put you through Hell Week and then you go active. It's like the fraternity initiations you had in high school."

Several of us laugh and contribute that our high schools didn't have fraternities.

"Is that it? You just party, do neat stuff, learn lore and go active?" This from Winkler.

"Well, not exactly." Brewer is more measured in his response. "You have to do some work... clean up after parties... help build floats and displays... shine the brothers' shoes. It's all part of proving yourself to the brothers."

"Sounds sorta like slavery," someone muses. "What's there to prove? I thought they wanted you to be in their club?"

Brewer pauses to think before he responds. "Well." Pause. "If you pledge the right house, you keep going with the feeling that it's all worth it. That all the pledge stuff is only temporary."

"When can *we* pledge?" a voice from the crowd asks.

Brewer's more comfortable with this question. "OU has deferred rush for freshmen men. In the second semester. IFC... that's Interfraternity Council... felt that freshmen men would be better off waiting a semester before going through rush."

"We have to wait a whole semester before we can join a frat?" the voice persists.

"First of all, you don't call them frats. They're fraternities. Or houses. Secondly, you don't join. You're asked to pledge, if they want you."

"Aw shit," another voice chimes in, "what if they don't want you?"

"Oh, your chances are pretty good," Brewer smiles. "There're nineteen fraternities on campus and they pledge anywhere from fifteen to thirty guys per pledge class. That's say, about 300 hundred out of 800 freshmen men.

"Ace only takes thirteen, but they're different," he says with a shrug.

"What's Ace? And why only thirteen?"

"Alpha Chi Epsilon. I'm not sure about the thirteen but it's something to do with their lore, I'd guess. And not everyone wants to be in a fraternity. Lot's of guys like being GDI."

"GDI?"

"Goddam Independent," Brewer responds. "Especially with all the vets on campus. The vets have changed a lot of things with the G.I. Bill and that stuff. They cuss a lot more. And dirtier too. And they're making more people think it's not so bad to be an independent. We've only got one vet in our chapter and one in my pledge class."

"So we're GDI's?" I ask. I'm not sure why but I kind of like the sound of it.

"Well, not exactly. You're freshmen. Of course, anyone can be just as GDI as he wants. GDI's just a term Greeks use to describe anyone who's not a Greek."

"Greeks?" the querulous voice in the back asks.

"Fraternities and sororities are referred to as Greek organizations. Because most of 'em have Greek letter names. Like mine. Beta Theta Pi."

"And Chi Omega? That's Greek too."

"You got it. One of the first things any pledge learns is the Greek alphabet. Alpha. Beta. Gamma. Delta…" and he rambles quickly through a bunch of words that certainly sound Greek to all of us.

• • •

A new wave of rushees floods College Avenue and our interest picks up in the passing charms of OU woman flesh.

Unlike the conversations in the gloom of a dorm mixer, our comments about various individual coeds are reserved, almost respectful.

Occasionally, small groups of coeds will walk by in every-day clothes: skirts, sweaters, rolled bobby socks and saddle oxfords. Books cradled in their arms.

"GDI's?" someone asks as a particularly charming set passes us.

"Perhaps?" Brewer responds. "Probably. But again, not every coed wants to be in a sorority."

As the second wave of freshmen women vanish into the three houses across College, Brewer stands and asks the assembled Biddle group, "Anyone wanna go get a beer? Maybe a slice of pizza?"

"I've never had pizza," I blurt before I realize what a farmer I sound. "But it sounds good. I'll go."

A number of the group decline and head back across campus toward Biddle. Mass, Winkler and I are among those who walk along College with Brewer.

"We'll swing by Phi Mu and Kappa Sig and then hop over to the Tavern. They've got the best pizza in town."

• • •

The Tavern is dim and grungy. A gray fog of smoke tones down the hanging light fixtures.

"Jesus! What's that smell?" I ask as we enter the main room. "Just like someone's old tennis shoes."

"That's pizza, Five ole' buddy. Cheese." Massman seems perplexed. "You've *really* never had pizza? What do you guys eat in Hockersville?"

"Hockingport, fool. Burgers mostly. I don't even like cheese that much except the little slices that mom puts on her homemade burgers."

"Well Five, you've never had real cheese until you've had the Tavern's pizza." Brewer leads us to a pair of booths. The Tavern may be a great but it's not too busy. "Everyone have an ID?" he asks. We all nod.

The waiter is obviously a college guy, dressed in khakis and a Big Mac workshirt protected by a long, semi-white apron. "What'll it be guys?"

"Strohs for me, Frank" Brewer says, "Up?"

"Right Brew," Frank winks at our host. "And you guys?"

"Strohs up. Strohs up." I assent. *What in hell is Strohs up?*

"I'll have to see some ID cards," Frank says to the rest of us. We all pull out our wallets and display our student activity cards to the skeptical waiter.

"Down. Down. Down. Up?" He looks at my card, then at me. "You got any other ID, driver's license?" Brewer gives me a slight but negative nod.

"Uh, no. I don't drive."

"OK, I guess," he shrugs. "But don't ever let me find out any different."

As the waiter walks away, one of the other guys asks, "What's this up and down stuff."

Brewer looks astonished. "Haven't you guys ever bought beer before? Up's six percent beer. You have to be twenty-one to drink that... like our friend here," he nods at me, "who was obviously born in... when, Five?"

"Uhhh. 1933?" Suddenly the advice I received from the weird guy at registration is making sense.

"Thirty-three, right! And you guys were all born later, right? So you get down beer or three point two."

"Three point two?"

"Percent alcohol," Brewer continues. "It's just weaker. Idea is to protect young men and especially young women from the evils of drink."

"Right," says another voice. "That's all they serve in West Virginia and you can't even get legally drunk there if you can prove that's all you've been drinking."

Frank returns with a tray full of tall, glistening brown bottles, each topped with a tiny narrow glass. Brewer's and my Strohs are delivered first. "Quarter each, guys." Our bottles have intact labels on their long necks. The others have had their labels torn with a thumbnail. We ante up for the bar bill and as soon as Frank turns his back, everyone grabs for my beer to do a taste comparison.

When we order pizzas, Brewer orders another round. My beer has been OK, better than swilling it out of a quart bottle with the gang back home. The narrow glasses seem to capture the yeasty smell and tantalizing bubbles pop to the foamy surface.

Across the room, a few cheers accompany a syncopated crash from a booth. "Chugging contest," Brewer observes. Indeed, two drinkers have their glasses filled again and someone counts to three. They grab their glasses to their mouths and in one swift motion, beer disappears and the glasses are slammed to the table, almost simultaneously. The loser reaches in his pocket, extracts a bill and waves to Frank for more beer.

The pizzas arrive with our third round of beer. The beer certainly *does* taste better but my precious supply of Pall Mall money is dwindling. Brewer assures us we'll split the costs of the pizzas.

"Now tell me, Five. Does *that* smell like someone's feet?" Mass asks pointedly as the steaming pizza, a sea of yellow-orange cheese steaming on what looks like a pie crust is set before us.

Not as much as it did when we came in," I admit. "But then, all this beer's made me hungry."

We divvy the pizza slices onto paper plates and someone immediately screams as he burns the roof of his mouth. I let mine cool, swig some more Strohs, then take a tentative bite. *From the gods.* I look around the booth. Two pieces for everyone. But Winkler doesn't seem to be eating as fast and he has ordered one more beer than the rest of us.

We drink some more. Brewer teaches a song about a little mouse on the barroom floor. Some guys come in, pause by our booth, and give Brewer a strange look. The evening gets more jolly. Then it's time to go home.

Going home starts off as a pleasant experience. The streetlights of Court Street give off a wonderful, orange fuzzy glow. And the brick surface of the street looks soft and undulating, like a patterned mattress.

Massman stops at a storefront. *What's he looking at in*

there? Mass barfs on the window of Steppe's Beauty Salon. Winkler makes it another half block and vomits into the gutter in front of the Athena. Toby joins him. Suddenly my pizza doesn't taste as good and I wobble toward the intersection of Court and Union.

Across the street and up the steps onto the College Green where pizza and beer all come up in an ungodly fountain. "Not bad for a first-timer, Five," Brewer says, "slapping me on the back as I bend over for the next heave. Not many first-timers can make it all the way back here from the Tavern. I think you have a future ahead of you."

• • •

I fumble for my dorm key but my pocket doesn't seem to be where it was. Toby somehow produces his. We open the door and he grabs his mouth and spins. I dry-heave right on the spot as he spews down the hall toward the john.

Lying down is worse than standing up or walking around. I reach over and drag my wastebasket to me just in time. Now I know why they're called wastebaskets.

• • •

"And the new president, the first president of Biddle Hall, and our representative to East Green Council, and to student government is... Jeremy Winkler!" Cheers from around the lounge as Don Daniels leads the applause for Winkler who gives us the champ signal and makes his way to the front. Kaye Davis leans over her big tummy to plant a kiss on Winkler's cheek.

"Thanks everybody. I appreciate your votes. And I want to thank, Mass, my campaign manager, and Five, the best damn sign painting artist that ever came out of Hooterport." Laughs and cheers. Mass and I stand and take mock bows.

"We have some exciting things to work on coming up. Homecoming in just over a month. And the first annual Biddle Christmas dance. So I'll do the best job I can and my door is always open."

· · ·

"My door is always open. Har, har," jeers Stolski. He's the only one of us not smoking in the presidential triple with its tightly locked door and the blinds pulled down. Massman the campaign manager produces a church key to open the first of six Strohs the Bear has brought for the celebration.

"Well, it surely will be open for someone if Davis comes down here and catches us," the new prexy groans.

"Don't worry, Wink. He and Kaye went to the MIA movie and Watt's at a Varsity O meeting," Stolski says. "No one here but the president and his cabinet."

"Where'd you get the Strohs, Bear?" The memories of our Monday night pizza party have dimmed and the beer tastes pretty good.

"One of the guys on the varsity lives down by the footbridge and keeps a big cooler full of six-packs. Another privilege of being a jock," he smirks.

"At least we won't barf all over the room with just a six-pack," Toby observes.

"Speak for yourself, Wolfe," Winkler says. "But seriously fellow Strohs lovers, now that I've got this thing, what am I gonna do with it?"

"What thing, pres?" Massman asks.

"Biddle. The dormitory. I need help. Suggestions. A program?"

"How about a free beer ration instead of the Sandwich Man?" I throw in.

"Yeah, right! And coed visitation rights before curfew?"

"Well," Stolski says, "you mentioned homecoming and a Christmas dance. Seems to me that should be enough for a semester. Especially if anyone wants to study on the side."

"You're right, Len," Winkler responds, "We've got to think about homecoming. Davis says we can budget $100 to do something. Maybe a little more if we come up with something great."

"A hundred bucks to do what?" I ask.

"Brewer was talkin' about the Betas building a homecoming float. And the Delts always build a house decoration," Wink says. "I saw homecoming floats at Ohio State a couple of years ago. They're big monsters."

"What's a house decoration look like?" I ask.

"Big sign thing," Stolski says. "Says something clever, nasty about the team we play."

"Who we play?" Toby wants to know.

"Bowling Green. They're the Falcons. We go up there next week to play their freshman team," Bear says.

"OK," Winkler says firmly, "Five will design a house decoration. And Toby and Mass will be his committee and round up whoever we need to get the job done."

"So what do I design? I mean, just draw a dumb falcon gettin' his ass kicked? Or something like that?"

"Don't worry, Five. We'll come up with a theme," Wink says. "We've got a whole month."

• • •

"Five, I've got somethin' to ask you," Bear says as we leave the presidential suite. "You interested in a date?"

"A date? Shit yes."

"Well, Page has a girl on her floor that she thinks you would like. I met her last night and she's not bad."

"Whattya mean 'not bad?' Like in, not bad, stark raving ugly?"

"Naw. She's cute. Tall, sortof blonde. Fairly good build. And she's from some farmer town upstate."

"What's her name?"

"Judy Graham."

"Doesn't sound bad. But a date? Shit, Dense. That costs money and, to tell the truth, I haven't got a whole lot."

"It doesn't have to cost a lot. Meet her after a class for a coffee date. Then take her to an MIA movie. That's only thirty cents."

"OK. But if she's one of these babes like Connie Corson who wants a cherry coke and ends up with burgers, fries and a shake, you'll owe me one, Ace."

"No sweat, Five. It's kind of a favor to Page. She's rushing this girl for Alpha Gam and the kid hasn't had a date since she's been here. She thinks getting her a date might help her think about going Alpha Gam."

"She's that great, uh? She and I must be the only two people at OU that haven't had a date yet!"

• • •

I call Judy Graham at Scott Quadrangle, my first experience using the hall phone and navigating the shoals of dormitory phone desks and locating a girl somewhere. She seems pleased that I called and agrees to meet me for coffee at the Frontier Room after our Friday ten o'clocks.

It's nearly 11:15 by the time I get to the Frontier Room. Dr. Logan really went on about some Italian painters in Fine Arts, even after the class bell rang. He's the kind of prof that you just don't pick up and haul ass on when the bell says it's over. Besides, sitting next to his daughter and in the middle of a huge row, doing such a thing is impossible.

The Frontier Room is hopping as usual. Black kids and greasers from Cleveland doing *The Stroll* to the jukebox, lots of people sitting around the uncomfortable tables drinking coffee and smoking. The pine-paneled walls are nearly invisible through the haze.

"Hey Five! Five, over here." A pretty girl is waves at me from a table near one of the big windows.

"Are you Judy?" She nods yes and puts out a hand. "And how did you know who I am?"

"Easy. The Bear loaned Page your high school yearbook and Page showed me your picture. Hockingport looks about as lively as where I come from."

"Which is?"

"Enon. Up by Lima. Near Toledo. That's the stock answer. Actually, it's Nowhere, USA. and am I glad to be away from there. Do you feel the same about Hockingport?"

"Yeah, I guess I do. There's sure a lot to do here. I just got stuck with designing a homecoming decoration and I don't even know what one is."

She smiles. "Me neither. We didn't have a homecoming at Enon. Who wants to come home to a dump like that?"

"Are you rushing a sorority?"

"I'm rushing all of them. Whoever named it *rush* had the right idea."

"How's it going? Is it fun?"

"It's hectic. And nervous. I got invited back everywhere I want for the second round. And got invitations for four parties for tonight. That's pretty good, I guess."

"Four parties? They have parties?"

"The whole thing's like a big party. You troop from house to house, drink lots of ice water, put on this big smile, which gets awfully painful after a while, and meet beautiful girl after beautiful girl. It's kinda depressing, in a way.

"They sing. And put on skits. And get you off by yourself and ask the dumbest questions."

"Like what?"

"Oh! Was I a homecoming queen? How could I be one if we didn't have a homecoming? Was I a cheerleader? Yes to that. What does my dad do? Page says I should tell them he's in the meat industry instead of a hog farmer.

"I just have the feeling that whatever answer I give isn't the right one." She smiles wanly and tilts her head. *Reassurance needed?*

"Aww, you'll be just fine. You're pretty... and obviously smart... you'll be OK," Doctor Five says. *What the hell do I know about sorority rush?*

For a coffee date, it seems to be going pretty good. Our conversation has been so steady since I sat down that I forget to get coffee for us. One of the Frontier Room's rare waiters comes over and we each order a cup. Thankfully, Judy doesn't pile on a burger, fries, shake and the works.

She's planning to major in education. Wants to teach. Maybe at the college level. She seems to think my thinking about art is interesting and we talk about that some. We finish our coffee and I offer to walk her back to Scott Quad... easy

89

enough since it's just down the hill from Mulberry and I need a pack of smokes from the Sundry.

As we near Scott, I get up my nerve for the big question. "Say, Judy. How'd you like to catch an MIA movie sometime? Maybe Saturday night?"

"Oh, Five, I'd love to. But I can't Saturday night. That's the last round of rush parties and I may get an invitation back to some house."

"Oh yeah. Well, what about Sunday night?"

"Wellllll. I better not. Bids go out Sunday morning and… well, you understand, don't you? But I really would like to go out. Would next Wednesday be OK? Do you go out on study nights?"

"Sure, I do," I respond. "Wednesday'll be great. I'll call you before then." Lamely, I reach out and shake her hand. "See you Wednesday, and good luck with rush."

• • •

It's early Sunday evening and I'm at my desk, laboring over an English composition. Toby is away somewhere and although he's a pretty good study companion, I'm thankful for the solitude to concentrate. The hall phone rings and once again, I'm thankful for our room so far away from that constantly ringing instrument.

A knock at the door. "Hey Lowrey, you gotta phone call." I go to the door. It's Norman, one of the unfortunates who lives in a room by the phone. "Why don't you bastards ever come down and answer your own calls?" he chides me.

"Hello?"

"Hello, Five?" Pause. "This is Judy Graham."

"Hi, Judy! How's it going? Is rush over?"

"Yes. It is. I was just wondering…" her voice sounds strange, "if you were busy or anything? Got time to get a coke?"

"Sure. Now?"

"Yeah. I'll wait for you in the quadrangle, if that's OK."

"OK. See you in about ten minutes."

• • •

I walk through the entry hall at Scott and find Judy leaning against one of the pillars that surround the quadrangle that gives the big boxy dorm its name.

"Hi Five. Thanks for coming over."

"Glad to. Sorry it's too late to go to the MIA. Want to get a drink somewhere?"

"Oh, let's just go for a walk if you don't mind."

We head down University Terrace toward the river and the footbridge that leads to the stadium. Judy seems withdrawn and after a couple of attempts, I decide to hold back conversation. We stop at the middle of the footbridge and look at the lights reflecting on the Hocking.

She breaks the silence with a sob. "I didn't get a bid."

"You didn't? Why not?"

"I don't know," she whimpers, turning into my shoulder. I put my arms around her gently. "I asked Page and she just seems angry. She won't even talk to me."

"That doesn't sound like Page," I say. "Something must've gone wrong."

"I'll sayyyy…" she sobs even louder. "Saturday night was just perfect. I got invitations back to three houses. Pi Phis, Fuzzies and Alpha Gams.

A long moan. "Ohhhhh, Five. I really wanted Alpha Gam. Page is so nice. And so was everyone else. I waited all morning and… never got a single envelope."

"Aw, Judy. Please don't cry." With that statement, I have exhausted my entire collection of comfort for crying women. After all, my mom and sister are the only two crying women I've ever known. "It's gonna be all right. Sororities aren't everything."

"Whooooooooooooooo." Her sobs echo up and down the river. She clings even tighter and I can feel my shoulder becoming extremely damp.

"Just think," I'm winging it now, "now you're a member of an even greater organization."

"Smmmmmf, I ammm?"

"Yep. GDI. And you've got me, and a whole bunch of other great guys on East Green, as a sorority brother."

A little smile appears on her tear-stained face. "Awww, Five, that's nice." Pause. "You're nice, too. Thanks for being a friend." She leans up and kisses me softly. I respond. Softly.

"Perhaps you should blow your nose," I suggest. Then realize I didn't bring a handkerchief. She produces a wad of Kleenex. And blows. And wipes.

Slowly, we walk back up the hill to Scott Quad, holding hands and murmuring platitudes about the importance of life and the vanity of sororities. We kiss softly again in the gloom of the quadrangle. Then a little more firmly. Finally, she pulls away.

"Thanks a lot, Five. And don't forget. We've got a movie date Wednesday. Nite." One final kiss and she's gone.

• • •

Dense is lying on my bed, eating one of my apples and reading the half page of English composition I've finished. "This is a piece of shit, Five. Whoever told you you could write?"

"Well, come to think of it, no one. I just happen to have this silly professor who wants me to write something."

"I just talked to Page on the horn. She said you were with Judy. Page's really pissed."

"At Judy? About what? I mean, what's Page mad at Judy for?"

"Not at Judy dumbass. At her stupid sorority. One of those bitches dropped the ball on Judy."

"Dropped the ball?"

"Blackball. That's how they vote. Someone calls for a box vote and they pass this box around. Everyone has a white ball and a black ball. A rushee gets a black ball in the box and she's out. No arguments."

I'm dumbfounded. "Does Page know who did it?"

"No. That's what's got her so pissed. Evidently, they'd cut a deal with a couple of other houses and Judy was supposed to be theirs. Then some asshole pulls this blackball stuff and Judy's out in the cold."

"Man, that really eats it," I contribute. "I mean Judy could've maybe gone Pi Phi or Fuzzy. I should call Judy. She thinks Page is angry with her."

"Naw, I wouldn't bother. Page said she was gonna talk to her when you brought her back. Page is so mad, though, she may just quit the sorority. Say, though. Is that lipstick on your chin?"

Chapter 11

Life Goes On

Dear Five,

Thanks for your nice letter. Captain and I are both so proud of you and glad to hear you're doing so well at OU. He seemed a little surprised about you taking a drawing class. Not me. Will you send me one of your drawings? I'll frame it and put it up in the Herald office. You didn't mention money, except for how much books cost. Is your money holding out? I've slipped something in here just to help. Captain is very set about $20 a week being enough spending $$. I don't agree. But you know how he is.

Your roommate and your other friends sound nice. I'm glad you've made friends so fast. OU's so much bigger than Bethany was and I remember how lost I felt when I first went there. And your advisor. Miss Spotswood. What's she like? Would you like to bring Toby down here for a weekend? It would be nice to meet him.
Have you met any nice girls? Don't forget that studying and getting good grades aren't everything. Take a little time for your social life.

I talked with Mrs. Duerhoff at the post office and she said Denzel lost a tooth playing football. She seems worried that he'll be hurt. I assured her that Denzel is big enough to keep from being hurt. You take care of him for her, will you?

Got to close for now. It's Wednesday noon and I should be getting a bunch of last-minute ads in for the paper. Take care of yourself and write. Love, Mom

• • •

Life goes on. Dense gets to start for the Bobkittens against Bowling Green and doesn't get another tooth knocked out. Judy and I have had several dates and I'm not broke yet, but hovering at the edge of it. She seems to be getting over sorority rush. I don't know what Page told her but she can walk by the Alpha Gam house — which she has to every day on her way to class — without bursting into tears.

Thayer gives me a C+ on my first English composition plus margins filled with dozens of tiny notes. For such a stuffy ass, he seems to spend a lot of time on his students when he grades papers.

Andy Logan becomes more friendly with each Art Appreciation class. Her dad, a bald, round gnome of a guy, has a commanding voice and really knows his art. Andy's mom is upset with her because she pledged Pi Phi, even though she was a Chi O legacy. Jackie Adamson is one of her Pi Phi pledge sisters.

On the Monday after rush, bosoms all over campus sprouted tiny enamel pledge pins and the larger, more ornate badges of active sorority women. This adornment attracts more of my attention to coed breasts.

Don Daniels gives me $110 in cash from the Biddle treasury to finance the homecoming display. The "committee" promptly blows $10 of it on beer and Begorras for a planning session. Since the homecoming theme is "Great Works," Judy has suggested "Nevermore" as a theme, something to do with Edgar Allan Poe and a big blackbird. I'm not sure how to handle it artistically. She offers a couple more ideas from Poe stories and we settle upon one of them for our theme.

The $5 bill which accompanies each letter from mom keeps me in smokes and Captain is just barely right, $20 a month *should* get me by if it weren't for beer, cigarettes and my burgeoning social life.

• • •

What say Five?

I'm heer on the steel beach as they call it and though I'd drop you a line or two. How do you like my fancy stationary? That's my ship on it — the USS Kestrel. Neat, huh? She's a destroyer escort and we're somewhere in the Pacific, headed for Japan.

I am sure glad I had to wait for boot camp for a couple months. It wasn't bad at Great Lakes but I guess it was really hot there during July and August. Then the day we graduated from boot, the temp went down to 22 which would've froze our konies off.

Yeoman school was reely easy and Dago is a great town. Lots of pusy and once you out of boot, weekend passes every week. Lots of ways to spend your pay. Im usully broke a week before payday.

How's OU? Have you got laid yet? And how's Dense doing? My ma said she heard he's playing football up there. Is he any good? He is big enuf. Write me a line or two when you take a break from gettin your ashes hawled and gettin shitfaced. Yur friend, Gestner (Yeoman3)

• • •

Riding on the back of Dense's truck is tricky enough, since its bed is a sheet of plywood bolted to the frame. So we make our way from Athens Lumber slowly, me driving, Mass, Wink and Stolski on the truck bed holding down the plywood, two by fours, paint buckets and tools for Biddle's decoration . I stay on the side streets since the Bearmobile, as Dense has dubbed his vehicle, tends to attract attention. Attention from the Athens cops we don't need.

"Slow down Five." Winkler pounds on the cab roof and

shouts into the open back window. "Babe alert. Check it out up there on the right."

Sure enough, there is a babe ahead. Short shorts. Blue t-shirt. Blonde hair pulled into a pony tail. Pushing a lawn mower. I slow for us all to get a better look, then recognize the babe.

"Hey Andy, how'ya doing?" Andy Logan brushes her sweat-soaked hair back from her forehead and looks up.

"Hi, Five. What are you guys up to?" We've pulled up beside the curb. Even covered with perspiration, Andy Logan is a knockout.

"On our way back from Athens Lumber. We're going to build Biddle's homecoming decoration.

"Andy Logan, these are my buddies. Mass. Winkler. Stolski." My friends hop down and say hello, obviously wanting a closer look at this lawn-mowing vision. "Andy and I sit together in Fine Arts Appreciation."

"What's your decoration going to be, Five?" she asks.

"It's based on a story by Poe. *The Cask of Amontillado*," I reply. "You wanna see my drawing?"

"Sure," she says with a smile. I produce the sheet from my sketchpad where I've roughed out the display. Andy holds it for a second, then out at arm's length. "God, that's great. Are the eyes going to be looking out this hole in the bricks?"

"Yep. And then we'll have the bobcat with a trowel and a smug look on his face standing out in front."

"That's going to be a lot of work," she says with a frown. "How're you gonna cut out the bobcat? And the brick wall?"

"We bought a coping saw at the hardware," Mass replies, holding up the shiny new tool.

"Jeez, that'll take forever... with that little saw. Do any of you know how to use a jigsaw."

"I sure do," I say. "Took four years of wood shop in high school."

"Wait a second. I'll ask my dad if you can use his jigsaw. He's working in the back yard." Andy trots around the side of the big frame house and vanishes.

"Damn, Five. She's a real winner. Haven't you asked her out yet?" Massman wants to know.

"Naw, she's just a nice gal that happens to sit by me in class. I have noticed her, of course. But her dad teaches the class and I didn't wanna seem like a brownnoser."

"Well, if you don't, I sure will," Mass says. "You don't see too many of her kind around this place."

Andy returns with Professor Logan, who's dressed in khaki shorts, a Cleveland Browns t-shirt and a silly navy hat rolled down to cover his balding head.

"Dad, this is my friend Five Lowrey. This is my father, Gordon Logan." I shake hands with Professor Logan. "Five sits beside me in your lecture class. He's going to major in art."

"How do you do, Five?" Dr. Logan says. "I'm always glad to meet one of my victims of the mass art lecture."

"How are you, sir? These are my friends. Len Stolski. Don Massman. Jeremy Winkler. Jeremy's president of Biddle Hall." Each of my cohorts shakes hands with the round little Cleveland Brown.

"Andrea tells me you have a project that might require more than a coping saw."

"Yesssir. Here's a sketch of what we're planning to do."

He examines the sketch, then glances at the pile of plywood and two by fours. "That's very interesting. Original. You're going to cut out the wall and bobcat with a coping saw. That's pretty ambitious." I nod in agreement.

"I don't think we could handle these sheets of plywood in my shop on the jigsaw. But... I do have one of those new electric saber saws we could use in the back yard."

"Gosh, sir. That would be great."

"But you'll have to do an outline on the plywood. We'll have to do it today as Mrs. Logan and I are driving up to Columbus this afternoon for a meeting and dinner."

"I can draw the outlines on right now, sir. We'll unload the plywood and I'll drive over to the dorm to get a pencil."

"Nonsense," he says. "We've got plenty of drawing tools around this house. Bring your plywood around back and I'll find something."

We carry the plywood around to a backyard festooned with bird houses, an elaborate martin village on a pole, a beautiful yard swing on a scrolled stand. "Gosh, Professor Logan. This is really beautiful. Did you make these things?" I ask in genuine admiration.

"Why thank you, Five. Yes, I did. I got interested in woodworking when I decided I'd never be a successful sculptor."

Andy comes out of the house with some contè crayons. "These are OK, aren't they dad? Take your choice, Five. Black or red?"

"Aw, Andy, these things are expensive. Forty cents apiece. I'll take the black and be sure to get another one."

"Nonsense, Five," Professor Logan booms. "Let's get to work." He walks to a shed at the back of the yard and brings out a pair of sawhorses. "Outline the wall first and we'll start cutting."

We lay out two four by eight sheets of plywood and I sketch in the ragged top of the wall, an uneven step of bricks. Dr. Logan looks on and says, "This is from Poe's *The Cask of Amontillado,* isn't it?"

"Yes sir. Here, I'm going to have a sortof window in the bricks. Then we'll put the falcon's big eyes on a separate piece of plywood behind the window." I draw in a rough window with uneven sides where several bricks will remain to be pushed in. Professor Logan helps the guys settle the finished wall piece on the sawhorses, then disappears down his outside cellar steps. Shortly, he returns with an extension cord, the saber saw and a brace and bit.

"You start drawing the bobcat, Five," he directs, "and we'll cut these outlines in no time." He uses the brace and bit to drill two starter holes in the window area.

Against the whine of the saber saw, I start a tentative shape of the bobcat on the last four by eight sheet. Andy watches attentively, then offers to hold my design sketch while I work. I just rough in the outline of the character, drawing rough ovals where his eyes will be and a large curve for his smug grin. The plywood surface eats up the contè crayon quickly as the bobcat takes shape.

"That's very impressive, Five," Professor Logan says.

"You've a good eye. And a good hand. Have you been cartooning long?"

"Errrr, no sir. Just lettering signs at a produce market down home in Hockingport. Emmit's Market."

"Ah yes, we've been down there a number of times. Best sweet corn in the valley, out of Hockingport."

I finish the bobcat and step back. "He's great, Five," Andy says with a smile. "Better than that thing they had on the College Green at Freshman Week."

I add a few adjustment lines to the bobcat's hip and the trowel he holds. Mass, Wink and Stolski smile in approval.

"Let's cut 'im out, Professor Logan," Winkler says in an invocation of his presidential personality.

"No. Let us give the artist that honor. Ever used one of these gadgets, Five?"

"No, sir. But I can always paint over little mistakes and I'll hope I don't make any big ones." The saber saw is a joy to use. Quickly I work around the bobcat's tail and feet and follow the outline toward his torso and head.

"If you don't mind a suggestion, why not cut out his eyes and then give them some dimension on another piece of plywood." Professor Logan is throwing himself into our project. "And... I have another idea or two. Go ahead and drill some starter holes there where his tail will be. And his eyes. And the curve of the arm. I'll be back in a few minutes."

Without the professor there to supervise, I cut with more caution and the work goes slowly. But the bobcat shape steadily materializes from the plywood sheet. Professor Logan returns with some smaller pieces of plywood.

"Here's my thought," he says with a grin, "if you don't mind my intruding upon your creative processes."

"No sir. Not at all. I mean, it's not like I'm working for a grade on this project."

"Hmmm, Five. Never can tell. You just never can tell," he says. "But here's what I'm thinking. If you made the eyes behind the wall as separate eyeballs and connected them with a simple cam and crank, you could have them rolling in fright." He takes my sketchpad and draws a rounded triangle, connected to two round pieces which represent the eyes.

"Make the axis of each eyeball slightly off center and I believe you could obtain a very comical effect."

"Man, professor, that's terrific," Massman says, sliding a step closer to Andy. "We could probably do the same thing with the bobcat, couldn't we?"

"I don't see why not. His eyes could be coupled on an on-center axis so they would roll in the ecstasy of victory."

We agree enthusiastically.

"You could even control these with a small electric motor, make a belt and pulley arrangement," he suggests.

"We only have a hundred bucks and we've blown about forty of it on supplies," Stolski volunteers.

"Oh, I'm sure I have a motor I could loan you in the cellar somewhere," he responds. "Just don't let the word get out that you have a department chairman working on your display. I might never hear the end of it."

We finish the cutting in short order and Professor Logan promises he'll have pieces cut for the cam and eye rig by Tuesday night.

"Thanks so much, Professor Logan," I say with great sincerity. "You've been terrific to help us." The others add their thanks.

"Well, you're quite welcome, young men. And Five, it's been a pleasure watching one of my students in real life, as it were. Not just a frantic pencil scratching out there in the darkness."

We carry the parts back to the Bearmobile, Massman walking a bit behind with Andy. I overhear her say, "Gosh Don, that's nice. But I really can't. My big sister has already fixed me up with someone from the Phi Delt house."

• • •

By Wednesday night, our Biddle display is pretty well assembled and I'm supervising my painting crew behind the dorm. The "committee," plus the Bear and Page, Judy and Andy Logan are among the onlookers.

"OK, guys, that coat of gray should be dry," I advise, testing the flat gray paint that covers the entire wall structure. "Now, I'll put on the masking tape to make the mortar stripes, then we'll paint the whole thing with the red."

The painters groan. "We just finished painting this bitch gray. Now you're gonna have us paint it red. Why didn't you decide upon red in the first place?" They watch as I line up the horizontal stripes of masking tape to line up with the cutouts at the top and the window. Eyeballing the job, I quickly apply horizontal stripes all the way down.

"Hey Five," Toby yells, "I've got the green on the bobcat's sweater done. The bobcat, painted in a base of white, now has gray fur around his chops and legs and sports a turtleneck sweater that, when I'm done with the details, should look just like a Varsity O garment.

Judy cuts short strips of masking tape as I apply the vertical lines that will finish the mortar. "Now I'm beginning to see what you're doing," one of the bitching painters notes. With the striping done, they rapidly apply the quick-drying red enamel with broad brushes. When it's dry, I strip off the tape to admiring oohs and aahs. It looks just like a brick wall.

• • •

On Thursday night, we work on finishing the details. Big letters spelling out "Brick Up B.G." across the wall beneath the window. Some cracks in the bricks and mortar. A few splotches of gray and green to simulate moss.

With a fine brush, Toby paints in the black details on the bobcat. His upraised eyebrows, the curled, sardonic upper lip, the finger lines on his white cartoony gloves.

At the base of the wall, I've drawn in a large, open book, its white pages still blank.

"Exactly how do you spell this 'cask' thing?" I ask in general. No one seems to know. "I'll go call Judy at Scott and have her look it up," Massman volunteers. "I know it's 'The Cask of...' but I'll get the exact spelling.

As the dorm door slams behind Massman, Andy pulls up in

her dad's Plymouth coupe in the alley behind the cafeteria. "Here're the eye cams, fellas. Dad and I just ran the last test and they work pretty good." She produces a cardboard box full of wooden parts, pulleys, belts and a small motor. "He put a gear train on it so the eyes will roll in slow motion."

One of the Biddleites looks at Andy questioningly. It's nearly 11 o'clock and women's curfew isn't extended until tomorrow night. She laughs and says, "Don't worry. I'm not in trouble. I live in town and my parents happen to believe I'm a big girl now."

We screw the eye pieces for the falcon onto their driving rod, then connect the rod to the cam and assemble the whole works onto the back of the wall. Professor Logan's done a great job as everything fits perfectly. The bobcat eyes also fit into place and we test the entire effect by turning the drive rods by hand.

"Amazing. Terrific." A small round of applause.

"Can you guys handle the motor and pulleys by yourself?" Andy asks. "I've got a quiz in English in the morning and have to do some studying."

We assure her that we'll do our best and wave her off in the green Plymouth. Massman returns just as she drives away. He is crestfallen that he's missed his dream girl but says to me with a smile, "Here's the correct spelling, Five. I didn't realize it was two words."

• • •

A big crowd is gathered in front of Biddle on homecoming morning. Clearly, "Brick Up B.G." is a big hit from the crowd reaction. The orange, bloodshot eyes of the Falcon roll in realistic terror. The bobcat's eyes give him just the perfect touch in fiendish delight. His trowel drips still-wet cement. The big book at the bottom attributes the proper literary reference in keeping with the homecoming 'Great Works" theme.

We've walked around the East Green, checking out the other displays. Perkins has a pathetic pile of crepe-papered chicken wire that is supposed to resemble a bobcat shoveling a falcon into a sewer. Its closest resemblance is to a pile of chicken wire covered with crepe-paper.

Gamertsfelder's display says something about 'GAM'bling With Bobcat Luck,' an approach that, to us, doesn't seem to quite make the theme. At Read Hall, a sheet is hung from a third-floor room that says 'Beat B.G.' *The Minimalist Approach,* as I've learned from my Art Appreciation class.

Back at Biddle, the crowd is bigger and as we approach, I realize that the judging committee is viewing our display. Five or six students, men and women, peer at the wall and clutch their clipboards. There are smiles. Then laughter. Someone says something and they all laugh even harder. Notations made on clipboards, they move on with broad smiles on their faces.

• • •

Except for a three-touchdown Bowling Green lead, it's a beautiful afternoon at Ohio Stadium as half-time nears. At the west end-zone, the floats from this morning's homecoming parade are lined up for one last review before winners are announced.

The Biddle gang is sitting in a group high above the forty yard line. Good seats are never a challenge at OU football games. Judy looks great, wearing a pale green sweater set against her green plaid skirt. The white mum with dark green ribbons I'd bought her on the street near the footbridge looks perfect.

Next to me sits Stacy Gordine, the Grey Wolfe's date. My roomie is decked out in a pink one-button roll sport coat, dark charcoal slacks and matching charcoal and pink suede saddle oxfords, all of which fight the green and white ribbon in his lapel.

Winkler and Massman sit in the row below us. Winkler's date is named Susan something and Massman's last-minute fix-up has a name but we've promptly nicknamed her "O-Two" for her strong resemblance to Olive Oil. Page Dobrowski's knees dig into my back as she sits beside the Bear... the only non-Biddle spectator in our group.

With seconds to play in the half, the Bobcats score on a wobbly field goal after failing to convert a third and inches play. The band hits the opening notes and we rise to...

"Stand up and cheer, cheer loud and long for old Ohio.

For today we raise the Green and White above the rest..."

• • •

"And now... now... now... now..." the PA announcer's voice echoes back from across the river. "The winners of the homecoming decoration competition." We tense a little, although none of us has given much thought to actually winning.

"In third place, with its terrific theme of 'Workin' on the Chain Gang,'" a cheer goes up from down the stadium a few sections, "Sigmaaaaa/ Alphaaaa. Epsilonnnnnnn! SAE!!!!!" The SAE's jump up, hop around and generally raise hell in celebration of their third place finish.

"In second place... place... place... 'Milk of Bobcatesia. It Always Works! From the women of Lindley Hall!" All over the stadium, individual girls jump up and scream. Coeds don't sit in blocks from their dorms but with their dates. O-Two is among the screamers. I guess she lives in Lindley.

"And in first place. Ladies and gentlemen, this display is really an eye-opener..." Judy nudges me and grins. "...as well as an eye-roller. With a very imaginative interpretation of Edgar Allen Poe's..."

We all leap to our feet. Dense grabs me from behind and lifts me to stand on the bleacher seat. Everyone is holding breath. Can it be?

"'Brick Up B.G.!' from the men of Biddle Hall." Pandemonium in our section. The announcer continues, "Will a representative from Biddle please come down to accept the trophy. And... if you haven't seen this display folks, be sure to go by the East Green on your way home from the game. American literature will never be the same after this

106

interpretation from Poe's..."

"The Cask Of... *Monty Dildo!*"

• • •

When I get back from my MIA movie date with Judy Sunday night, I discover a note taped to 205's door. It reads:

Five. The Dean of Men's office would like for you to stop by tomorrow morning before your ten o'clock. I hope you have an idea of what it's about. Don Davis.

P.S. We've left for Athens General. I think Kaye's labor is here.

• • •

After consulting with Toby and the rest of the committee, I decide not to dress up for my visit to the Dean of Men's office. No coat, no tie. Just look like a harmless, ordinary student.

A kindly, motherly-looking secretary smiles at me and motions me to a waiting chair. In a few minutes, she looks up and says, "The Dean will see you now."

The Dean looks like a bloodhound. High, hairless forehead. Pouches below mournful eyes. Jowls that hang from below his drooping earlobes.

"Good morning, Mr. Lowrey."

"Good morning, sir."

"Have you any idea why you're here in this office, Mr. Lowrey?"

"Well. No, sir. I don't."

"Am I to understand correctly that you are the, uhh... author... creator, of the Biddle Hall homecoming display?" I brighten up.

"Why yessir, I am. Yes sir."

"And... Mr. Lowrey. Am I to understand that you're proud of your, er, display?"

"Yes sir, although I didn't do it all by myself. Lots of people

107

helped. We even had some advice from one of the faculty members."

"One of the *faculty* members? Who, man? For God's sake, who?"

"Oh, I can't say sir. I promised I wouldn't. But I know he, er, perhaps she, is also very proud."

"Proud? Of that? Of that… obscenity?"

"Obscenity, sir?"

"Obscenity, Mr. Lowrey. Don't give me that dumb act. You knew what you were doing. Admit it!"

"I am sorry, Dean. I *really* don't know what you're getting at. What's obscene about bricking up Bowling Green? We almost did it Saturday afternoon?"

"Come on, Mr. Lowrey. And I suppose you have not read Poe?"

"Well, no. Sir. Perhaps we did in senior English in high school but I don't recall it."

"And I suppose you don't know what that implement is which you've referred to in your bastardization of Poe's story?"

"Implement, sir?"

"Dildo, Lowrey. Dildo!"

"Uhhh, no. Sir. Ahhhhh. Is a dildo something I should know about?"

The Dean sighs, leans back in his chair. Looks at me with those basset eyes over church-steepled fingers. "Perhaps not, Mr. Lowrey. Perhaps not. We shall see."

• • •

Relieved and slightly puzzled, I walk from Cutler Hall across the College Green, reflecting upon The Dean's mysterious ending to my interview and the whole tilt the axis of my life has taken since half-time of Saturday's game.

I'd been honest with The Dean. I *did not* know what a dildo was when Massman played his little joke and I inscribed those two fateful words on the bottom of Biddle's display. By being honest — painfully honest — and by telling the truth as it existed then, I have evaded telling the truth as it exists this morning to The Dean.

At half-time, Winkler and I had accepted the trophy on the field and held it above our heads as if we had won an important athletic event. Back in the stands, a halo of good will surrounded us for several rows of seats. Someone handed me a brimming Coke cup which, when I tasted it, seemed half full of whiskey. We — Wink, Mass and I — shared it with our dates. O-Two made a face.

When I got back to Biddle to change for the homecoming dance, my mailbox contained a fat pile of yellow envelopes. Telegrams of congratulations. From fraternities and sororities. Many were addressed to me personally.

There was even one there from a familiar name: *"Congrats Five. You've started making name for self at OU. Had a feeling you would. Keep in touch. Trish."*

Judy and I had planned to go to an MIA movie — staying within my budget — but the homecoming chairman had insisted we come to the dance to accept the trophy one more time and that tickets wouldn't be a problem. Ralph Marterie's orchestra was terrific and Men's Gym was a sea of happy homecoming celebrants, even though the Bobcats had missed beating BG by a single point.

On Sunday, Judy and I had a study date at Chubb Library and on our way across campus, it seemed that everyone had a smile and greeting for me.

And this morning's English class! "It pains me to announce that my syllabus for this course has been altered by one of your class members," Professor Thayer announced with his usual aloof snootiness. "But I shall suffer the pain and in a few weeks, we shall read Poe's *now famous* story regarding the unfortunate Fortunato and "The Cask of...? What was it again, Mr. Lowrey?" The class breaks up.

Now, as I enter the drawing studio, Dabny grins and says to me and the class loudly, "I had hoped to begin studies with a male model this morning... but thanks to Mr. Lowrey here — the most famous freshman artist on campus — we'll have no need. We shall just draw from our imaginations." I can feel extreme warmth on every square inch of my skin.

"Just pick up your red contè crayons," she continues, "and we'll do some exercises to match Mr. Lowrey's present complexion."

• • •

Page and the Bear have captured a table already for our eleven o'clock coffee meeting in the Frontier Room. The Bear has this strange leer on his face as he rises and claps his big hands. People all around him look up, then in my direction, then slowly join in the applause as I make my way to their table.

"Look at this, Five!" Page hands me a copy of the *OU Post,* the campus newspaper. "I've never known anyone so famous." On the front page, Wink and I are pictured holding our trophy in front of the display. The photographer has managed to include the letters "D.I.L.D." in the lower right corner of the photo.

"And you're on the inside, too," Bear adds. "Check out *The Hells of Ivy.* Leafing through the inside pages, I find the column and scan it quickly. At the bottom of the column, these lines pop out:

"And can there possibly be a town so small, so provincial, as Hockingport? Where one of its finest products, truly a talented artist in the making, has never heard of a d - - - o? We owe a debt of thanks to Thomsen 'Five' Lowrey V for bringing us the most light-hearted moment of the homecoming weekend. Five, we hope you'll still be in school this week to continue your career and share more of your sophistication with us."

I just thank my stars that the *OU Post* isn't delivered to Hockingport. *Wouldn't the folks be pleased to discover one of the first things I've learned at college is the nature of a dildo?*

Chapter 12

Routine Matters of Collegiate Importance

"Aw, the guy's a flamin' asshole. Everyone knows that," Winkler declares, "all you gotta do is read that crap he writes every week."

"Don't talk like that in front of a lady," Mass admonishes. "She's got delicate ears."

The four of us are watching month-old Melody Davis while Dense walks Page home for curfew. They have been baby-sitting Melody for Dan and Kaye's first night out and we're substituting while Bear goes to play kissyface in Scott Quad. The 'asshole' Winkler's discussing is Rog Gorton, author of *The Hells of Ivy* column in *The Post*.

"No one takes that stuff seriously, Wink," I say, "least of all, me." Gorton has kept our 'Dildo Display" a running joke in his column ever since homecoming. If anything, it has helped me make some new friends and acquaintances.

"Well, I do," Winkler continues. "He's made Biddle into a laughing stock. And anyone who insults Biddle..."

"Insults me!" we three chant. Wink's pride in his leadership of the dormitory has grown to the point of being obnoxious.

"You're just pissed because Gorton just writes about Five and never mentions your name," Stolski says, once again sticking the needle to Wink's thin skin.

"And how come I've never gotten any credit?" Massman whines. "It was my joke. My idea in the first place."

"Right, dickhead," I turn on him. "And your big idea... your big joke just about got me kicked out of school."

"God, Five. Really. I didn't' have any idea you wouldn't know what a dildo is!"

"The only reason you know," Winkler comes back with a sharp needle of his own, "is 'cause you found one in your mother's medicine cabinet and asked her what it was." Massman shoots Winkler a really dirty look but doesn't respond.

The discussion ebbs and each returns to his books or notes. Studying has begun to play a vital role in our lives after mid-term grades give us a look at academic reality.

Someone's stomach rumbles to break the studious silence.

"Wonder where the hell the Sandwich Man is?" Massman asks in general. "It's 10:45 already. And I'm about to die of hunger."

"I'd offer up my left nut for a bag of Begorras," Toby says.

"Both of 'em," Stolski agrees. "Screw the Sandwich Man. Let's go to Begorra as soon as Bear gets back."

"Bullshit, man. Haven't you seen what it's doin' outside? No way I'm gonna tromp up the hill in this rain and all the way across campus," Toby declares.

A light bulb flashes in my nearly penniless mind. "I will."

"You will what?" Toby returns.

"Go to Begorra! For you guys. But I don't have any money so I'll need your money up front. And it's gonna cost you."

"Cost us what?" Stolski wants to know. But I can tell from his expression that he's hungry enough to be interested.

"I'm hungry too. So I'll charge you fifteen cents apiece for the burgers. That way, I'll make a nickel a burger and can afford my own."

"Fifteen cents," Winkler snorts, "that's fuckin' robbery. But count me in 'cause I've got to study and there's no way I'm goin' out in that rain." We all raise eyebrows at Winkler's language.

A soaked Bear knocks and enters the Davis' apartment. "God, but it's pissin' out there. Thanks a lot guys. Is Melody OK? Did she cry?"

We assure him that the baby has slept through our deliberations. "You want some Begorraburgers, Bear?" Wink asks. "Five's selling them for fifteen cents apiece, delivered to you hot and steaming." Dense's face lights up.

"Sheeeeit, yes. Bring me twenty-two, Five. Here's three dollars." The others contribute their money and I make note of my orders on a notebook page, then leave for my raincoat.

• • •

The Begorra diner is a gleaming beacon through the sheets of rain that sweep across deserted President Street. Duff Noonan, known to most as 'Gruff Duff,' peers through the cook's window of his domain as I come through the front door.

"What say, kid? You must be starvin' to come out on a night like this. Or are you a pledge?"

"Hey, Mr. Noonan. Pledge, no. A starving artist, yes. I need some Begorras."

"All right! I know you. You're the dildo kid, aren't ya?" I admit I am with a sheepish grin as he wipes his hands on his apron and comes out to the counter. "How many you need? I'll even throw a couple in on the house for the laughs I got about that dildo deal."

"Well, actually, I'll need eighty-eight Begorras to go. Then, let's see. That'll give me $4.40... so I'll have a dollar's worth too, but I'll eat those here while they're hot."

"What're ya doin? Sellin' back at the dorm? I've had guys do that before."

"Well, I just took a bunch of orders cause we were all hungry and I'm nearly broke. I'm chargin a nickel a burger for the delivery service."

He slides a plate in front of me and heaps a stack of the steaming little burgers — redolent with fried onions, pickles and mustard — on it. "There's your dollar's worth and a few to grow on."

"Gee thanks, Mr. Noonan. That's great!"

"You want to pick up some change, huh?" He looks at me carefully. "Tell ya what. If you call me, say at ten thirty with a big order, I can have 'em ready for pick up by eleven."

"D'ya mean regularly?"

"If you want? Whatever. No skin off my ass but you can make some real change sellin' these little guys at a nickel or more profit."

"Or more?"

"Yeah. I'll give ya' up to a hundred burgers for eight cents apiece. A hundred to hundred fifty, I'll make it seven cents

113

apiece. Any order over hundred fifty, you'll bottom out at six cents apiece. Sell hundred fifty at six cents and charge fifteen for them and what'ya got?"

I do the math, as usual, poorly. "Twenty two dollars?"

"To be exact, $22.50. And you pay me nine. I sell a bunch of burgers and still make some profit. You pick up some change. Sound like a deal?"

"Sounds like a deal, Mr. Noonan."

"Duff, dildo kid, Duff."

"All right. I'll call you Duff if you don't call me *dildo kid.* My name's Five. Five Lowrey."

"Gotcha, Five. I'll put these in a double bag to keep 'em dry and warm. But you gotta figure out something better to carry a buncha burgers in, dildo kid."

• • •

In the weeks that follow, our lives seem to follow a pre-determined course. Professor Logan invites the four of us — Stolski, Winkler, Massman and me — to Sunday dinner, an event which Mass interprets as a personal come-on from Andy. Once again, his advances are gently rebuffed.

Mrs. Logan, an older and rounder version of Andy in looks, kids her husband about his role in "l'affair Biddle," as she terms it with a suppressed giggle. For his part, Professor Logan expresses gratitude that we have kept his participation a secret. We share small snifters of brandy and some elegant cigars with him in his study after dinner.

Constance Prendergast, my pretentious speech instructor, seems pleased with the progress I make from the first disastrous three-minute presentation to my latest effort, four minutes on "The Fleeting Comforts of Fame." By mid-terms, my grade average in speech has climbed to a B minus.

The Begorra Express, as it's become known at Biddle, has grown to a regular feature of dorm life, with me making four runs a week: Sundays, Mondays, Tuesdays and Thursdays. Wednesdays I've saved for weeknight dates with Judy. Some nights, I've cleared more than twenty dollars with orders for

114

more than two hundred hamburgers. Judy's and my social life has been picked up financially by Duff and his Begorraburgers to the point where we've even gone to the Athena to see *On The Waterfront* at full price.

• • •

Old Man's Cave is a fairyland. The deep, twisted canyon is draped in new snow and at its bottom, the creek splashes and leaps among the boulders. Judy holds my hand as we slide along the snow-covered walkway.

The day began as a winter picnic for eight of us. Bear drives the Bearmobile with Page in the middle and Judy sitting on my lap. Huddled on the back with my Begorraburger orange crate which we're using as a picnic basket are Toby and his date, Stacy Gordine, and Mass with O-Two, whose name is unforgettably Alice Swindoos.

Despite her tall, thin frame, Alice has a great sense of humor and has proven herself capable of drinking great quantities of beer in short spans of time. She's the unofficial chugging champion of our informal gang.

"Avalaaannnnnche," comes a cry from above us. I pull Judy beneath an overhang just as a huge pile of snow slides past us with a roar to splash in the rapids below.

"Nice going, Grey Wolfe, you silly asshole," Massman calls from somewhere above and out of sight. "You damn near wiped out Judy and Five."

"You've got a cold nose," I whisper to Judy as we hug and I give her a gentle kiss.

"Mmmmm, like a healthy puppy dog," she whispers. We continue on our untrodden trail, somehow separated from the rest of the group whose shouts and squeals we can hear echoing through the cave's canyon.

"Judy, y'know. I've been meaning to get around to this and… guess this is as good a time as ever. Y'know we're having our Biddle Christmas Dance on the eighteenth of next month and I just wondered if you'd like to go."

She turns and snuggles into my encircling arms again, lifting her chin and giving me another soft, warm kiss. "Ohhh, Five. I've been dreading this… 'cause I just knew you were going to ask me."

"Dreading it, why?"

"Well, Scott's Christmas Dance's the same night. You must know that, the way Bear and Page have been going on about it?"

"Yeahhh, guess I do. Well, couldn't we go to both?" I ask. It sounds like a reasonably enjoyable way to spend a Saturday night.

"Uh, huh. We could. But I can't." My face must betray my puzzled reaction.

"Months ago. Ages ago. Before I met you. I asked this guy I know. He goes to Ohio State. I asked him if he'd like to come down for the Scott Christmas dance." A tear forms at the edge of her eye and I wipe it away with a gloved finger. Are all our *serious* moments going to be accompanied by tears?

"I just can't back out on him, Five. He's a really nice guy. Used to be my boyfriend in high school… but we don't go steady or anything. And… awwww, I feel so bad."

"Awww, that's OK, Jude. I understand." I *guess* I understand but I really don't want to. "There'll be other dances. And it's just one night." I pause. "*It is* just one night, isn't it?"

"Oh yes, of course. He'll drive down from Columbus. Probably go back the same night or the next morning. I *said* we don't go steady any more."

The voices of our companions seem fainter, more distant. "I guess we'd better find the others. I'm getting hungry," I add. Actually, the feeling in my stomach isn't really hunger, just a gnawing sensation.

"Yeah," she responds glumly, "I guess we'd better."

● ● ●

"What say, Five? Colder'n hell out there, huh?" Duff Noonan peers through the steamy grill window at me. "Have a cuppa' coffee. I'll have your burgers ready in a couple minutes.

"Darcy, this is the guy I was tellin' you about. The one who orders all the burgers for Biddle Hall."

A tiny girl pops up from behind the counter where she was kneeling, stacking paper bags. "Hi. I'm Darcy Robinette." She has dark hair in a pixie cut around her ears. Big brown eyes with long lashes. A great smile.

"Hey Darcy. Five Lowrey. How long've you been working here?"

"Just a couple days and this is my first full one, now that I'm moved in."

"Darcy's from Nelsonville," Gruff Duff contributes. "She's moved to the big city to make her fortune in the kingdom of Begorra. Darcy, pour Five a cup of joe."

I get a better look as she turns to the coffee urn. She has a maroon sweater on and the tightest blue jeans I've ever seen on a great little ass. And the jeans aren't rolled up to her calves, like the few coeds you see who wear them on campus.

"Black, Five?"

"Black's fine, Darcy. So where are you living? One of the dorms?"

"Ah no, I don't go to OU. I'm just a working girl. Got a place over the Wonder Bar on Union."

"Burgers're ready, Five. Hand me your crate," Duff calls. I sling the foil-filled crate across the counter and shove it through the serving window. Hundred eighty-six burgers, Five. Make it eleven bucks even, Darcy, and ring 'em up."

"Gosh, thanks Duff, I appreciate it." Duff seems to always round off the price and I've picked up an extra sixteen cents.

"No big deal, kid. You'll probably find a couple extra burgers in there, too."

I slurp the dregs of my coffee and shoulder the strap on the Begorra crate. "Thanks again. Good to meet'ya, Darcy. I'll be seeing you guys."

Another interesting night. Sixteen dollars profit and a cute little ass in the tightest jeans I've ever seen.

• • •

"As you can see, ladies and gentlemen, the work of Sandro Botticelli displays his keen instinct for drama... his mastery of

117

expressive gesture…" Professor Logan's voice is hazy and muffled, suddenly sharp and clear as a pain jolts through my side.

"My father does not like sleeping in his lectures," Andy whispers, withdrawing her sharp little elbow, "but he is absolutely tyrannical about snoring. Stay up too late, last night?"

On the screen, a willowy redhead stands on a big seashell, one hand holding her long tresses before her crotch, the other gracefully draped across an ample breast. "Yeah, was," I grunt. "Where are we?"

"Botticelli. That's Venus up there. Botticelli's *Birth of Venus*. He painted it for Lorenzo de' Medici around 1486," she whispers in my ear. Her soft blonde hair tickles the rim of my ear. "Better make a note of it," she breaths, "daddy's hell on Botticelli and thinks the *Venus* is hot shit."

"Pretty nice boobs for an old babe," I whisper back. "Botticelli know how to pick 'em."

• • •

For mid-November, it's a surprisingly mild night. Darcy looks up from the counter as I enter Begorra. "Hello, Five. How are ya' tonight?"

"Fine, Darce. Where's Duff?"

"Just back there takin' a leak," she says, "but your burgers are on and I'm sure he'll wash his hands."

"Say, Darce. Do you get any nights off from this grease bucket?"

"Wednesdays and Saturday nights unless I want the overtime," she answers. "Why you ask?"

"Ohh, I just wondered if, ah maybe you'd like to take in a movie sometime? With me?"

"I don't see why not. Duff's said he thinks you'd be safe enough to be around."

"He did? You asked him about me?"

"Sure. I ask him about a lot of guys that come in."

"Huh! Well… how 'bout Saturday night?"

"That's great. Give me a ring here, say Friday . OK?"

"Terrific. I'll call you then. See ya!"

"Hey, Five?"

"Yes?"

"One thing. Don't forget your burgers."

• • •

The subject is, once again, women. The scene is once again the smoke-filled 205 where we gather to bullshit... anything but study.

"Goin' steady has its advantages," Toby states. "Like you don't have to sweat getting a date..."

"Or gettin' a little," Mass breaks in.

"Or gettin' your balls busted when you look at someone else," Winkler chuckles.

"Well, I think it's pretty nice," the Bear declares. "I've never really gone steady before."

"With a girl? With a sheep?" Mass is really in great form.

"Really," I interrupt, "we just didn't date much at home. Not that many things to do at night."

"Well shit, Five. What'ya do for sex," Toby wants to know.

"Probably the same thing you did in your hometown," Dense throws in, "seein' the skanks you're going out with now."

"Who's a skank?" Toby snaps. "Stacy's a great kid."

"Yeah," Winkler adds, "so's a baby goat and it doesn't wear a girdle."

• • •

A light rain begins falling just as I start down the Mulberry Street hill. Below me, the lights from the Sundry flick out, meaning it's past eleven o'clock. I'm running a little late with my biggest Begorra order ever. More than two hundred forty burgers lying in their warm little bed of foil.

Halfway down the hill, I hear a scraping noise and turn toward the dark wall that holds back the hill. From a set of recessed steps, a figure appears.

"Where you goin' ole buddy?" The voice is familiar but I

119

can't see his face in the shadows.

"Just headin' home," I reply.

"Oh yeah? With what? In the big box there? What's in the box?"

"Just hamburgers."

"Ahhhh yes, the Begorra boy." Now I recognize the voice. It's the Sandwich Man. He takes a closer step forward, stops, and flicks a lighter to the cigarette in his mouth. "You know, Begorra boy? You're makin' some women and little children very unhappy?"

"I am? How?"

"You're taking food out of their mouths, Begorra boy. And you're makin' their husbands very unhappy, too!"

"Hey, I'm sorry. But it's a free country. I've got a right…" He snaps his arm out and knocks the strap of my burger crate from my shoulder. "What the hell! You can't…"

Smash! It's not so much pain as this white light in my head. I feel the crate slide away from my thigh and down my leg, which suddenly doesn't seem to work.

"You little shit fucker, civilian asshole. It's a free country, all right. But you've got to learn *some* people fought to make it free. Not to make your chickenshit mommy's kid…" all this is an indistinct background to the cold wetness of the Mulberry bricks on my cheek. I can sense a pair of feet right beside my open eye.

"So why don't you just find something else to play at and leave the…" A split second pause, then a great gasp. Then. "Aiiiiiiiiieeeeeeeeeuffffffffffff!"

"Whatthefuckya doin', you big bastard?" a strange voice asks.

"Back off cocksucker," Bear's familiar growl is welcome. "Pick up this asshole before I break his shitty head off his scrawny neck and make you eat it."

"Easy, big fella. Let me get closer to him."

"No first, you get closer to that crate over there. Any of those hamburgers that are on the street, pick 'em up and put 'em back in the crate. And do it fast! Before I finish this cowardly whore off and start on you." I can hear Bear's feet slide across

120

the wet bricks.

"Noooo, wait. I'll get 'em," the panicked voice says.

"You'd better. I saw you clip my buddy from behind. That's real brave. Did you fight for your country, too?"

"Ease up, buddy."

"I'm not your buddy, you olive drab pus-snuffer." I must be coming to because I think *where in hell did Denzel Duerhoff learn all these interesting words?*

"All picked up. A couple of them came unwrapped. We'll pay for them."

"You'll pay for them, OK, you asshole. And here's how. Get the hell outta my sight right now, and take this slime with you. And the next time you see me, or him, you stand to attention and keep your fuckin' eyes straight ahead until we say 'at ease.' Got that, asswipe?"

"Yes… sir!" As Bear rolls me over, both eyes come into focus and I can see a shadowy form trying to pick up the recumbent Sandwich Man. He is face down on the bricks. He's not moving much, but then, I guess I wasn't either.

"Y'OK, Five?" Bear holds me under both arms.

"Yeah, I guess. Head hurts like hell."

"It will for awhile, I'd reckon. Skinny peckerhead over there hit you with his fist right behind the ear. Take a good look at 'em, Five. Both of these assholes fought to protect our country. And now they're blindsidin' their fellow students who're just tryin… Ahhh, what the fuck? We've got hamburgers to deliver. C'mon, Five. Let's go home."

• • •

In the dorm everyone is great. Stolski, Toby and Mass are delivering the cold Begorras with my promise to pay back anyone who wants a refund. Winkler, Bear and Don Davis look at me solemnly as I rub the growing knot on the side of my head.

"Now Denzel, tell me exactly what you saw," Davis says.

"Well, I was coming home from Scott. Page had a late permission and we'd just said goodnight.

"As I turned to go down Mulberry, I could see Five with his

121

crate. This guy steps out and they seem to be talkin'. Then the guy lights a smoke and I recognize him. The Sandwich man." I nod in confirmation of what I can remember.

"I get closer and see this scrawny little fucker jump out behind Five…"

"Uh, Bear," Winkler interrupts, "to you, everyone's a 'scrawny little fucker.' Do you know who he is?"

"Oh yeah, he's the turd who drives around with the Sandwich Man every night. Comes into Perkins every once in a while."

"Go on, Denzel," Dan urges.

"Well, the Sandwich Man gives a slap at Five's burger crate. Five makes a grab for the crate and the other asshole clips him one on the side of the head. Five goes down like a rock.

"The Sandwich Man's standin' over Five and ranting about kids and wives," Bear says, then pauses to reflect. "Then it looks like he's gonna kick Five in the head, kind of has his foot drawn back so I return the favor. Thump him right in the side of the head with my fist."

"And he goes down?" Davis asks.

"Betcher ass he does," Bear says proudly. "Stayed down, too. Then I make the scrawny guy pick up the burgers and tell 'em to haul ass. And I help Five on down here and then… well, you know the rest."

"Think we should call the cops?" Winkler wonders aloud. Bear shakes his head no emphatically.

"I don't know," Davis muses. "The Sandwich Man made a point of talkin' to me last night. His name's Bertone, by the way. Bitched about how Five's Begorra business was cutting into their profits."

"What did'ya tell him," I ask.

"Just that the vets don't have any exclusive franchise here. And that you're not breaking any University rules by going after Begorras. Not much I can do about it even if I wanted to."

He pauses, then steps closer to examine my lump. "I didn't really take anything he said as a threat. Five, I'm sorry. I should've mentioned it to you, I guess."

"That's OK. But do you think I should drop the Begorra

business? It's really helped me with finances."

"That's up to you," Davis responds. "Personally, I wouldn't. I don't think we'll have any more problems with them. And... if we do... then we'll call the cops."

Sure enough, though, there's a new Sandwich Man in the Biddle Lounge the next night.

• • •

The smooth stone steps of Chubb Library are frigid, sending waves of cold through my butt as I sit there smoking. Judy sits between my knees on the next step down, leaning back and sharing drags on my cigarette. You can smoke in the library's study carrels but not in the reading room, so on our library study dates, we usually come out on the steps for a break.

"Are you mad at me, Five?" she asks softly, exhaling a long cloud out against the dark campus setting. It's not quite nine o'clock and the College Green is quiet, almost empty save for the occasional student hurrying along the brick walks.

"Mad at you, Jude? Well no, why?"

"Ahh, you know. The Scott dance and all. Don's coming down? You're just so quiet."

"No, I'm not mad. You explained it all. I understand."

"You do?"

"Yep."

"Well... you know? You haven't said anything about Saturday night?"

Ohmygod. "Saturday night? Well, errr, I can't go out Saturday night, Jude. I've got something else to do."

"Something? Else?" Her unspoken question hangs there among the tendrils of our smoke.

"Uh huh. That's why I haven't asked you out."

"I see." Pause. A long pause. "Well, I guess I'd probably finish studying at home, then."

"OK," I respond lamely. "If you think so. I'll walk you home."

"If you want to." We go back into the library and gather up our books from the reading room. I'm amazed at how long a

123

short, familiar walk can be when it's made in total silence.

• • •

"C'mon Five, let's go up town," Toby urges. "It's Friday. TGIF!"

"TGIF?" Where Wolfe comes up with these things is beyond me. How can anyone be so hip and still dress like a refugee from a zoot suit gang?

Thank God It's Friday. Where'n hell have you been? It's a campus tradition.

"No thanks, Tobe. I've got to finish studying. And I've got some sketches due for class Tuesday. And a phone call to make. So I'll pass. See ya' later."

A few minutes later, I check the hall and see that the phone is vacant. I dial the now familiar Begorra number and hear Darcy answer.

"Hey Darcy, it's Five."

"Hi Five. How are you? I heard you had a problem. And you weren't in last night. I was worried. Are you OK?"

"Ahhh, no big deal. But I had to study last night and then didn't feel too good. Are we still on for tomorrow night?"

"Surrrre, if you want to," she says. *Do I detect enthusiasm there? I hope so.*

She gives me directions to find her place and I hang up. Back to the room. Study and sketches. Thank God It's Friday.

Chapter 13

Behind The Green Door

Saturday's a strange day. I study quietly in the morning, careful not to disturb the sleeping Grey Wolfe whose hangover is guaranteed if he ever comes to. I refused to help Mass and Winkler hold his head when they brought him home from TGIFing the night before. So Toby 'drove the China bus' by himself for most of the night.

I call to ask Andy Logan some questions about Art Appreciation but she's at a sorority tea or something. Mrs. Logan chats with me amiably and mentions she's sure "Gordon would be happy to answer your questions." I thank her a lot but decline the Professor's help.

For lunch, I grab a hot dog and cup of coffee at Goodie's on Mulberry Street, then wander on up the hill with sketchbook in hand. On the College Green, I sit on a wall and make the first of the sketches I'm supposed to have done by next week. Campus scenes. Athens scenes. My sketchbook and mechanical pencil have become constant companions as the semester wears on.

Devoid of leaves, the tall elms reach for each other in graceful arches above the brick walks. I doodle in bundled-up figures scurrying across the chilled November campus.

Past Park Street, I discover an empty lot near the Sigma Chi house that provides an excellent view of the President Street bridge and two fraternity houses beyond. One I recognize as the Delt house. The other is a huge brick structure with curved windows and tall rounded towers overlooking the river .

Perch on a stone bench, I quickly line in the bridge's arches, the empty branches below the cliff, the sweep of the B&O's tracks along the gray river and the shapes of the buildings.

The chill gets to me so I head back across campus for the Center and the warmth of the Frontier Room. There's an empty chair at a table where Sandy Feltner, a guy in my speech class, and some others are smoking and listening to the OU-Kent State game over the loudspeaker. I join them with a cup of coffee, light up a Pall Mall and pull out the sketchpad.

"Y'all mind if I make some sketches?" I ask the table in general. They give me some strange looks but nod their assent.

Except for one girl with this incredible mop of curly, orange hair and pale blue eyes. "No sketches! No pictures!" she cries in exaggerated alarm. "My agent would kill me." Then she grins and says, "sure, go ahead. But I get to keep one if they're any good. What's your name, artist?"

"I'm Five Lowrey," I respond. Sandy names the others including the redhead with the electric curls.

"And this is Ann Oxburn. She's gonna be a great actress some day."

Roughing in figures around the table, I find my attention being drawn to the loud broadcast where it seems the Bobcats may be on their way to a rare victory. A big cheer erupts as the announcer screams a description of Watt Scales breaking loose from the twenty and scoring for OU.

Several of my companions gather around as I shove back in my chair, indicating my rough sketch is done. "Damn, Five. That's pretty good. And quick, too," Feltner says.

"Pretty good, nothing!" Ann exclaims, "it's terrific. Can I have it, Five?"

"It's not finished," I protest. "Besides, I've got to turn in five sketches for class next week. Maybe after I get them back?"

"OK, but I mean it. I really want one. You should see my room. We've got nothing on the walls, except a stupid pledge paddle covered with brassieres," she laughs.

"When can I see your room, Ann?" someone asks. "And did you get a paddle for being a stupid pledge?"

A great cheer erupts as the game ends with the 'Cats victorious over the Golden Flashes. One and seven now, with Morris Harvey, Miami and Marshall to go. The jukebox cranks up and the *strollers* take their accustomed places on the dance floor. I reach for the sketchpad again.

• • •

126

Other than my torturous climb up its grade back in September, I'm not very familiar with Union Street. I find the Towne House Grill, just like Darcy said I would, and beside it, the grimy exterior of the Wonder Bar. And... just west of the Wonder Bar, the plain green door that guards the steps to her place.

It's nearly six as I climb the dimly lit, narrow steps to the first landing. Beyond the landing, another set of steps leads down in the opposite direction. I turn on the landing and peer through the gloom at the hall of doors, seeking number three. Her door is at the end of the hall.

Darcy answers my first knock, standing there all in black except for her bare feet. "Hi Five, c'mon in. I'm almost ready." She twirls and swings the door further open to reveal a most amazing room.

Two tall windows on the far wall reach from floor to the high ceiling. The other two walls I can see are covered with posters. Movie posters. Concert posters. Dance posters.

"Have a seat, if you can find one," she calls out from an unseen area, "I'll just be a jif." I take a seat on a flat couch covered with magazines: *Life, Look, Saturday Evening Post.* On the other side of the room, a small kitchen table and two skinny chairs sit beside an alcove. The hall? The bedroom? Darcy emerges from the alcove with a dramatic twirl.

"Ta, da. Like it?"

"Yeah. Yes, indeed. You look great." She gives me an upraised eyebrow of doubt. "No really. I mean it." She has on a black sweater and form-fitting black pants and sleek black shoes that look like ballet slippers.

"Duff slipped an extra five in my paycheck today so I went down to Belk-Simpson's and splurged," she beamed. "New dance slacks. New Capezios. The sweater's not new, though." She plops down on the couch beside me, sending magazines skittering. "Want a drink? I've got some cold beer in the fridge."

"Sure. That'd be great," I say. *Cold beer in the fridge. A private apartment. A tiny beautiful girl. I've died and gone to heaven.* Darcy hops up and over to one of the windows, raising its lower sash with a grunt. Cold air swirls in.

"This is the fridge," she says proudly, producing a pair of Budweisers from somewhere beyond the sill. I get up to peer out. "Later on in spring, it'll probably be a porch, if the sign doesn't fall down. But right now it's definitely the fridge" The windows open onto the flat surface of the top of the Wonder Bar sign and Union Street beyond. "Sorry it's just three-two. There's a church key on the nail over by the table," she directs. "You do the honors. And I've got some jelly glasses somewhere."

We toast each other with Bud-filled jelly glasses decorated with bright yellow and blue flowers. Darcy leans back against the wall and pulls her knees up against her chest.

"So what's this big secret you've got?"

"Big secret? I'm not sure I know what…"

"Sure you do. Duff says he won't tell me but it has something to do with his nickname for you."

"Five? Just that I've got my dad and three grandpas before him with the same name."

"That doesn't sound like much of a secret. Sure doesn't sound like what Duff was kidding me about." I realize what Duff's kidding about and feel the bloom of embarrassment all over my face.

"Oh. *That* big secret! Maybe… just maybe when we get to know each other a little better… I'll let you in on the big secret."

"And there's the lump on your poor head," she pouts, softly reaching over to touch my swollen scalp. "I've heard several people talking about what happened. Those damn vets. They've got their nerve."

"Ah, I sort of understand their point. But jeez, that was a damned hard way to make a point."

"That's a buncha crap, Five. There are several vets living in this place and they all seem like nice guys. They kind of treat me like a little sister, when I see 'em in the hall or outside. But you should hear 'em talk when they don't know I'm around. The guys that hit you must just be a couple of sadists."

"Nuff about me," I plead, "tell me a little about yourself."

• • •

128

We're in a cozy booth at the Campus Pizza. So far, the date's gone well but what can go wrong after one beer and with a pizza place a half block away?

"So I went to Jackson-Trimble til' my junior year. And you really played basketball for Hockingport? I thought I'd seen you somewhere before."

"I was just a sub. Not very good," I mumble through a mouthful of pepperoni and cheese. I've never had pepperoni before and it's great!

"Then when my dad left my mom, she got in a car accident and died. I didn't know where dad had gone so I was left by myself with this little rental house in Trimble and his old junker of a car.

"My Aunt Ida, she's not really my aunt, but my mom's best friend, asked me if I'd like to come to live with her in Nelsonville. So's I had nowhere else to go so I said what the hell and moved down there and finished my senior year."

"So how was a year at Nelsonville?"

"Ahhh, just OK. I was pretty blue about mom. Then Aunt Ida found out dad was dead too. Got smashed up in an accident the same week mom had hers and died out in New Mexico somewhere. That was really the low point."

"Geez, Darcy, that's terrible. So you're a real orphan, then?"

"Bona fide, gold plated, real orphan," she said with a wistful grin. "Not even an heiress, either, unless you can count an ancient Ford as an estate. Duff's offered to buy it from me but so far, I've decided to hold on to it. What if I want to take off for somewhere?"

"Like where?"

"Like New York! Hollywood! Somewhere were I can get a job acting."

"You're an actress?"

"Not really. But I'd like to be."

"God, you are the second aspiring actress I've met today."

• • •

129

Pizza dinner is followed by a walk over to Mem Aud where we watch *Lili* with Mel Ferrar and Leslie Caron. The MIA movie finishes about ten and it's kind of fun to watch guys and their dates rushing for a quick cup of coffee or a beer before make-out time at the eleven o'clock curfew.

We stroll slowly back in the general direction of Union Street. "I just love this campus," Darcy sighs. "It's so pretty, any time of year." I hum *Green as the grass grows...* to accompany her rhapsodizing. "I've just got to hustle enough, earn enough, to be able to get in here."

"You think you can save enough working at Begorra, paying rent on that place, to make tuition and stuff?" I ask. "I know I'm having a time. Without Duff and the Begorra run, we wouldn't be out here together right now. At least we wouldn't have had a pizza and a movie."

"Oh, we both owe a lot to Duff," she says with a wistful smile beneath the lamplight. "Duff pays me a lot more than I'm worth at Begorra. And he says if I can get a second job, he'll keep paying me my full salary."

"Why's he so nice to you?" I'm not suspicious but interested. Duff is one hell of a nice guy.

"Oh, didn't I mention it? Well, if my mom's friend in Nelsonville is my Aunt Ida, then he's my Uncle Duff." Giggle.

"I don't get it."

"He and Aunt Ida are... you know... a thing?"

"You mean?..."

"Yeah. Sleeping together. He was up there about three times a week. Probably there a lot more now since I moved to Athens."

"Is Aunt Ida, er, married?"

"Well, she was. Maybe still is. But her husband's been long gone for years."

We near her apartment block and I ask, "How 'bout another beer? Want to stop for a beer? Or cup of coffee?"

"That'd be nice," she answers. "Not the Wonder Bar, though. It's a hole. Let's go in the Towne House."

• • •

The Towne House has pretty much emptied as curfew nears. We're in a booth facing the big front windows, each nursing a Strohs and sharing a plate of fries.

"Are you really twenty-one, Five? How'd you get a high-test beer?"

"I was born March 18, 1933, and I have the official Ohio University student identification card to prove it."

She giggles. "So? A smart guy, uh? And when *were* you born? And how did you get that card?"

"1936," I reply, "and the card's the damnedest thing. Some weirdo in registration sidled up to me and whispered 'thirty three' just before my turn to give the girl my card information."

"So..." she studies, "I'm really a year older than you are. Hmm. But not a year smarter, cause I'm still drinkin' three-two beer."

The Towne House crowd is growing again, this time mostly guys smeared with lipstick and bubbling with brotherhood.

"Frat guys," Darcy sneers. "This is the worst time of night at Begorra. They come in and think they're big studs just 'cause they got a quick feel on some dorm porch or in a sorority house living room."

"They give you a bad time at work?"

"Nope. Most of 'em behave, especially after they've gotten a hot spatula across their grabby hand." I grimace at the image.

We split another beer. It's nearly midnight. Are there any other women loose in Athens at this time of night? Is Darcy loose? Does she keep a spatula in her apartment?

• • •

Sunday morning's dim light peeps through the gray plaid curtains of Biddle 205. Evidently Toby has slept the Saturday through for he's in the same basic position, same basic clothes as yesterday morning.

I throw open the curtains and raise a window to clear the air. He shudders in the icy blast and pulls his smelly blanket closer over his ears. I dance in bare feet across the cold tiles to answer the knock at my door.

"I've got an *Athens Messenger* little buddy." Bear beams at me, fully dressed, shaved. "Been to church already with Page. Got a paper and I'm ready for you and me to go over to the barfeteria and drink some coffee. I'll read you the account of our glorious victory yesterday."

"No thanks, Dense, I just got up. It's too damn early."

"Too early? It's nearly ten, Five. The cafeteria opens in five minutes. Brush your teeth. Scrub your face. Hurry up. I have news!!"

In rumpled khakis, OU sweatshirt, tennis shoes and no socks, I trudge beside the Bear as we head for the East Green Cafeteria. Inside the wind lock, the lack of patrons tells us how early we are. But they'll serve brunch from now until 2 p.m., the only meal on Sunday.

With our coffees on the table and me lit up with the first drag of the day, the Bear plops his *Messenger* down and pronounces, "Five, my boy. You are in deep, deep shit!"

"I'm what? Now what's happened? Did the Sandwich Man call the cops?"

"Sheeeit, no, Five. That Sandwich Man crap's behind us now. I'm talking about real deep shit. Genuwine deep shit."

"OK, Dense. Whatever it is. Let me have it?"

"Judy came home last night madder than hell and jumped all over Page for being my girlfriend." He smirks broadly.

"So what in hell did you do to Judy? To Page? How's that affect me?"

"I didn't do anything… except be acquainted with you, you Don Juan sucker, you." *I'm beginning to sense where this thing is headed.*

"More details, Bear. More details."

"It seems, according to Page, you dumped ole' Judy and lied to her about your big romantic date last night."

"I didn't dump her! I didn't lie to her. I just told her I had something else to do."

"Well, yes. There it is. She saw you with 'something else' in the window of the Towne House. Something else looks like a perky chipmunk in a tight black sweater."

I grin sheepishly. "The description is sort of accurate. I

132

wouldn't exactly say 'chipmunk,' though."

"Ah, ha!" he exclaims. "So it's true? You're two-timing ole' Jude and she's got you on her shit list now."

"C'mon Bear. You're enjoying this entirely too much." I blow a rude stream of smoke into his grinning fool face. "Besides, two-timing is sort of a two-way street. She's the one who wouldn't go to the Biddle Christmas dance because she's got her old boyfriend coming down for the Squat Cod dance.

"And wait just a minute?" I have a sudden thought. "How in hell did Judy see me in the Towne House anyway. It was after 11 o'clock! And what was she doing up there?"

"Well, Five my friend, that shall become clear. Judy's roomie was so sad for her when you dumped her Thursday night that she got her fixed up with a Beta pledge. So she was on her way home from the Beta Basement. And there you were. You and your chipmunk. Lovin' it up in a fishbowl like the Towne House."

I smash my empty coffee cup down on the table. "I'm two-timing her," I screech. "Well, she's three-timing me. Goin' out with some Beta pledge behind my back. I don't have to take that shit."

"Tell you what, Five. I think we have the makings of an interesting situation here."

• • •

That evening I try a phone call to Judy but get her roommate, Donna Caruso. "I don't think you want to talk to her right now, Five," Caruso tells me. "I think your friend Denzel was right about you being on her list."

"OK, Donna. Just give her this message for me," I say, trying subtle sarcasm. "Just tell her I hope she had a really great time at the Beta Basement Saturday night."

"Oh, I don't think you want me to give her that message either, Five. You see, she came home from the Beta house by herself. Her date got sick and passed out."

• • •

133

Darcy is busy with two or three customers down the counter. Duff grins out at me from the steamy frame of his griddle window. "Hey, Five. Got 'em ready for you in a few minutes. Get yourself a cup of joe," he calls. I've become almost a fixture in the Begorra.

Darcy flashes me a smile as she hustles past with the Begorras for her counter customers. "Hey, Five. Be with you in a second, OK?" I smile back and wait, content to watch her behind the counter. "Five, I had a nice time last night. Thanks a lot. Again."

"Me too, Darce. Does that mean you'd like to do it again?" She shakes her head in agreement. *Enthusiasm. Hot damn!* "How about Wednesday night? Can you get off? They're showing *Shane* at the MIA."

"That'd be great. I'll see you before then?"

"Tomorrow night. For another load of these little greasy jewels."

"Hey, kid! Watch whose jewels you're calling greasy," Duff snarls as he hands me the burger crate. "I'll tell her your real nickname if you don't be careful."

• • •

"Mr. Lowrey, these sketches show a certain degree of achievement upon your part. I'm quite pleased with your progress," Professor Blockhart says, holding my sheath of drawings in his long thin fingers. Blockhart, my Intro to Sketching professor, talks just like Professor Logan. Come to think of it, everyone in the art department talks like Professor Logan except for Dabny.

"Your lines show a spare sophistication. You don't overdraw where details aren't needed. These figures, for instance…"

I leave the Sketching Class on the smooth ride of a B-plus sketch assignment.

• • •

After three dates, Darcy and I are very comfortable together. Luckily, I haven't seen Judy on campus and have avoided the library on our *traditional* study date nights. After his initial burst of harassment, Dense has backed off from continued observations on the saga of Judy and Five.

Although the room and bathroom alcove that also houses Darcy's hot plate have become familiar to me, none of her other physical properties have. We've smooched a little. And she's curled up close at the movies. But so far, she's been warm but aloof.

On the first night I took her home, she asked me up and we stared in admiration at the light show out her windows. "I love the pink glow of the Wonder Bar sign," she says to me, "and then seeing it reflected backwards in Quick's windows, that's really neat. And stand here, Five." I stand to the left two steps. "Now you can see the Towne House sign reflected. And the Wonder Bar sign reflected in it! Isn't that great? It's like one of those halls of mirrors."

On our second date, I am again invited up. This time to listen to records on her little 45 rpm player. The soundtrack from *Lili* was followed by the theme from *Ruby Gentry*. I find the harmonica solo haunting. But after couple of friendly kisses I'm gently shown the door.

Tonight, the third date, she surprises me by showing up in high school jeans, rolled up to the calves, and a t-shirt. Then another surprise.

"C'mon Five. No movie tonight. I've got something to show you."

We walk down Union to High Street, then turn left toward the railroad tracks and the river. This is new country to me. Darcy stops at a garage apartment that appears to teeter on the edge of the cliff over the tracks and river.

"Close your eyes. And keep 'em closed." I follow orders and listen to the scrape and rattle of a key in a padlock. "Now, give me your hand but keep your eyes closed." She leads me in shuffling steps. I try the tiniest squint but it's pitch dark inside.

"Ta, da!" Darcy pulls a light cord and the garage is flooded

135

with sixty watts of yellow light. Squatting there, its chrome reflecting the light bulb in dozens of places, is a gleaming black roadster.

"Damn Darcy. It's a thirty-five Ford!" *My dream car.* "It's beautiful!" And indeed it is. Black paint job that shimmers like a deep pool. Shining chrome. Brown leather seat and a matching brown top folded tightly down.

"It's the entire Robinette inheritance, Five. This is the junky old car my dad left me when he left my mom, rest his soul."

"Jeez, Darce. It's gorgeous." I find my reactions somewhat limited. "You could get a thousand dollars for this baby. That'd put you through school!"

"Not on your life, bub. This is *my* baby. And no one gets to ride in it unless they're really my friends." She pauses and grins slyly. "And *they* don't keep any secrets from me."

"Ohhh no you don't," I say, edging toward the running board. "Ride first. Then I tell you the Big Secret."

"Forget it, Five." Darcy pokes a finger in my chest. "You tell me right now… or you walk home… forever!"

"Well? Can we at least sit in the rumble seat?

• • •

"Go on, Five! I cannot believe that!" Darcy shrieks with laughter and curls up against me in the rumble seat. "Hoooo! That is hilarious!" She wriggles around, near tears she's laughing so hard.

"C'mon Darce. It's not *that* funny!"

"Yes. It. Is! It's hilarious. You really didn't know what a dildo is and you just painted that sucker right out there for the whole university, and God, and everyone to see. Hooooeee!" For a little girl, she sure does laugh hard. At least we're getting a little more physical.

"Ohhh God. That's great. Hop up in front, Five. You've earned a ride. Hooo! Don't scrape the paint."

The Ford cranks right up, its distinctive chuckle echoing off the retaining wall above High Street. She pulls out of the garage, then hops out to close the door and snap the lock.

136

"Where to? How far is Hockingport? I'd like to see your home town."

"Whoa. It's Wednesday night and I've got class tomorrow."

"Oh come on. Don't be such a poop. Anywhere you want to see?"

"Nope. Surprise me."

"OK, you asked for it." She drives straight up hilly High Street toward another new part of the town. "This's 550. Goes over the hill to Marietta. But we won't go that far. Dildo! Whoooeee. Dildo!" She screams into the cold wind.

Darcy's a skilled driver. We fly along the narrow curving highway but she never oversteers, never lets the Ford's tires lose their grip with the road. We roar through a darkened little town. "Amesville," Darcy shouts, "you probably played them in basketball. Ames-Bern?"

"No!" I shout back. "Never been here before."

Past Amesville, the road climbs out of the Hocking Valley and we follow it up the winding hill. A few minutes later we crest the hill, drop down for a mile or so and then attack a new hill. As we round a bend, the few dim lights of another hamlet appear far away. The valley between us and the lights appears to be shrouded in fog. Darcy slows and pulls over to a wide berm.

"That's Sharpsburg over there. Those lights. Ever been here before?"

"Nope. Not to my memory. Why's it so foggy."

"Not fog. Smoke. That's why we're here. You'll see in a few minutes."

Darcy lets out the clutch and the Ford chugs back onto the highway. Tapping the brake and riding in second gear, she eases us down the curving hill and into the smoke. Again she slows. "Look over there, Five. See that light?"

"Not a light, really. A glow. Is there a fire?"

She doesn't answer, just lets the car drift on down the road slowly. Some trees ghost by and then another, brighter glow is revealed.

"Damn!" I gasp. "What *is* that?" Gingerly, she pulls the Ford off the road onto the gravel shoulder aiming right at a bright orange fissure that looks exactly like pictures I've seen of erupting volcanoes.

"Coal mine, Five. *The Sharpsburg Hell.* That thing exploded back at the turn of the century and has been burning like this ever since. No one knows how big it is."

We get out of the car and walk with careful steps toward the hellish cracks in the earth. Sulfur fumes, smoke and steam billow from the fissure.

"Not too close," Darcy grabs my elbow. "I think that stuff can be poisonous."

We stand there, arms around each other's waist, and stare at the hypnotic scene. As our eyes become more accustomed to the darkness, other fissures grow in their intensity. *It is* a landscape out of hell.

"Look at that, Five. Isn't that the damnedest thing you've ever seen? The goddamnedest thing?"

• • •

Thanksgiving vacation is a cold and rainy week in Hockingport, perhaps the most dreary place on earth when it's cold and rainy. Captain makes it home for two days, coming in on the bus from Portsmouth where the *Princess* has tied up for the holiday.

Although home feels familiar and I feel welcome, our Thanksgiving dinner is quiet and reserved. They ask me polite questions about school. I respond with polite evasions. I'm truthful when I say that my money situation is OK but don't elaborate on my Begorra enterprise.

Although she quizzes me about college life, what the coeds are wearing, who I'm dating... I see little of Sissie Eileen. A full-blown teenager, she's running with a pack of goose-like girls who totally disrupt the house with their shrieks and squeals every time they appear. She makes a point of having moved most of her stuff back to "my tiny little garret of a room" when I first arrived home to reclaim my space.

On Saturday, mom drives Captain down river to Portsmouth and I walk over to The Point at Hockingport with my sketchpad. I notice Mary Lou's rusty Oldsmobile at Suter's Sohio and decide to stop in and say hi. The station's interior is a warm mixture of grease, tobacco and the stale nickel pies and cakes we used to buy when we had the money.

"Hello there, Five. How's the college boy?" Doc Suter looks up from his stool behind the register.

"Hi, Doc. Fine. Just fine. How's business? Hey, Mary Lou, how are you doin'?"

Mary Lou looks up from the metal porch chair in the corner where she's reading a fat book. "Hi, Five. Just studying my accounting. I cannot believe my fool prof scheduled a test for right after Thanksgiving."

"Yeah. I think they get a kick out of stuff like that. At OU, you get your grade dropped a letter if you miss the class before or after a vacation break. Like that at Marshall?"

"You got it," she says, "they all read from the same book on student torture. Have you seen Teens? She was just in here."

"Nope. Haven't really seen anyone but you. I was just takin' a walk. Wanna go along?"

"No. Can't do it. I've got to keep after this accounting." I make my good-byes and leave the warm station, heading toward the river. Walking through the trees of the little park by The Point, I see Tina sitting on the flat rock where we partied on graduation night.

"Pretty isn't it? Peaceful." She looks around.

"Hi, Five. How are you? Yes, it is peaceful. Even pretty, gray and brown and cold as it is." I sit beside her on the rock and give her arm a squeeze.

"S'good to see you Teens. How's life at Marietta? You getting along OK?"

"I guess so, Five. It's all so... just so different. I can't believe it was just a few months ago we were all together here on graduation night. So happy."

"You're not happy now?" She doesn't look unhappy but I've learned it's hard to tell when talking with girls.

"Oh, sure. I was just thinking though how different things can become in such a short time." She pauses and gives me a long stare. "I just saw Mary Lou a while ago and she's studying, of all things."

139

"Yeah. I just left their place." I grin and shrug. "But believe it or not, even I study some these days."

"Oh, I believe it. College is harder than we thought it'd be, isn't it? But Mary Lou studying!?" She laughs. "What's that you've got there?"

"My sketch book. I thought I'd try to get some sketching done while I was home."

"You're still at your drawing, uh? Do you still doodle on your homework."

"Teens, this *is* my homework. I'm going to major in art."

"You are?" she squeals. "Really? That's so neat. Do you have any sketches in there?" We scoot close together, much like last June, and I leaf through some of my rough sketches. "They look pretty good to me, Five. How're you doing with grades?"

"Straight B's in my two art classes, maybe a B in Fine Art Appreciation, another B in speech right now, and C's in English comp and history. And you?"

"Same old thing. I find it hard to concentrate, to study. Still, I'm getting a four point. You have a girlfriend at OU?"

"Oh, I've dated a couple girls. Nothing serious, though. How 'bout you?"

"I've been going out with an awfully nice guy. He's a sophomore. And an Alpha Chi Epsilon. There's an Ace house at OU, isn't there? Are you going to rush?"

"I don't know. Yeah, I think there's an Ace house in Athens. But I don't know much about fraternities, how much they cost. All that. We can't rush 'til second semester so I haven't thought much about it."

"Well, the Ace's are really nice guys. They've had some neat parties. If you rush, take a good look at them."

I scoot back a bit and look at her, hunched in her peacoat, hands in pockets, legs pulled up under its short hem. "Would you pose for a sketch, Teens? This would make a nice drawing, I think."

"Sure, Five. That would be fun. Will it take long? I don't want to freeze my butt off on this rock."

• • •

140

Mom and I are finishing our coffees and smokes. For some reason, I didn't smoke while Captain was home. But now, mom seems to take my smoking for granted.

"Five, I'm just awfully sorry I can't drive you up to Athens. But that damned Chevy started wobbling just after I got through Pomeroy last night and I'm afraid to drive it until Doc takes a look at it."

"Ahh, that's OK mom. Trailways is only two bucks and I'll be there by three. Besides, it's an easier walk from the bus station to the dorm than it is from the train station.

"I'm just glad the Chevy didn't die on you on the road. Course, we might've seen you on our way home from Pomeroy last night." Mary Lou, Tina and I drove into Pomeroy for burgers and cokes and a look at the bright lights.

"Yeah, but I was looking forward to seeing your dorm. Your room."

"Well, you'll get to see it. Right now, you wouldn't want to. Toby and I left it pretty much in a mess." I stub out my cigarette and carry the coffee cup to the sink. "Guess I'd better go pack my stuff. One of the nice things 'bout being at OU is I don't need to bring much home." What I really mean, but don't say, is one of the bad things about Hockingport is you don't need to bring much home.

I fill the gladstone. Clean socks and underwear. A new Valley Barge Line sweatshirt that Captain brought me. Two cartons of Pall Malls which mysteriously appeared on my bedspread. I hear a distinctive oooo-gah noise and start.

"Five! There's the cutest little car out front. Are you expecting someone?" I hurry from my room to the living room. There on the driveway is the black '35 Ford roadster.

"Hey, that's my friend from Athens. Darcy Robinette. What's she doing here?"

"Well, go bring her in," mom says, beaming.

As I approach the Ford, Darcy's smiling pixie face appears as the window cranks down. "Hey, Darce. What are you doing here?"

"I told you I'd like to see your home town, Five. Just

thought you'd maybe like a ride back to school?"

"Great. Come on in. I want you to meet my mom." She hops out of the car, dressed in wool slacks and a car coat. In a way I'm glad she doesn't have her slinky black outfit on.

"Darcy, this is my mom, Ellie Lowrey. Mom, this is Darcy Robinette."

"How'd you do, Darcy? It's nice to meet you." Mom's appraisal of my little friend seems favorable. I think her response is genuine.

"Hi, Mrs. Lowrey. I've heard so much about Hockingport, I just thought I drive down and see it for myself."

"Well… if you drove out here from 144 through downtown, you've seen about all there is to see."

• • •

We're buttoned up in the Ford with its heater whirring out a toasty breeze. "Gosh, Darce. This is nice. How'd you find the house, anyway?"

"Oh, I saw a girl by the post office and asked if she knew you. She said she did and told me where you lived." *Sissie Eileen? Teens? Whoever it was, Darcy's existence will be all over town before mom can get to the Herald.*

"How was Thanksgiving? How was Athens? Quiet, I'll bet."

"Pretty quiet. Duff closed the Begorra and I went up to Nelsonville for Thanksgiving dinner with Aunt Ida. Other'n that, it was kind of lonesome. That's one of the reasons I came down to pick you up. I'm glad you hadn't left already."

We chug on up 144, chatting and enjoying being back together again. As we hit Route 50 in Coolville, some snowflakes begin to fly across the Ford's flat windshield. "I hope it doesn't snow hard," Darcy frets. "Putting chains on this thing's a real chore."

The snow does pick up and begin to stick. But traffic is light on the highway and we make pretty good time. "Say Darce, I've been thinking… and meaning to ask you…"

"Yes, Five?"

"Well, Biddle has its Christmas Dance on the eighteenth and

142

I wonder if you'd like to go? I mean, I don't think it's gonna be anything really big, but… I'd like for you to go with me."

"Why Five! That'll be fun. I'd love to go."

By the time we reach Athens, the snow is about two inches thick and the roads are starting to become slick. Darcy insists she'll drive me down to Biddle. I insist she won't, afraid the Ford'll never make it back up from the East Green. We compromise and she lets me off at the Bryan steps, down which I slip and slide back into academia.

• • •

I discover the college days between Thanksgiving and Christmas vacation are compressed into a hectic whirl of classes, projects, papers, tests, work and a little socializing.

Winkler works us like slaves getting ready for the Christmas dance. I draw a very sophisticated-looking Santa Claus in red tux and tails preparing to come down the Biddle chimney. His face is a cut-out hole so people can pose for pictures as Santa.

Massman is overjoyed because Andy Logan has finally said yes to one of his dozens of requests for a date. She'll be at the Christmas dance with him. Stolski has, upon my recommendation, made a blind date with Ann Oxburn, the aspiring actress. This worked out well and he's asked her to the Dance, nicknaming her "O-Annie" for *Orphan Annie,* because of her pale blue eyes and giant mop of curly red hair.

The dance promises to be interesting with O-Annie and Winkler's date, O-Two of Lindley Hall fame. Plus my "Pixie Chipmunk" as Dense has described her. Actually, of our crowd, Judy is the only one who *really* knows what Darcy looks like and Judy will be busy on the night of the eighteenth. *I hope.*

Winkler and the Bear have announced a surprise for the dance but as of *the* Saturday morning, we have no idea what it is. "You'll find out in due time," Dense says mysteriously.

Now I'm nervously standing in line at the State Store on Union Street. In my pocket is a flat wad of various bills. In my hand is the carefully filled out form for my "milk run," as Stolski described it. Behind me, Dense fidgets in line even

143

though his only role is to keep me company.

"OK son, need to see some ID here," the clerk says in a bored tone. I hand him my OU student card which he glances at, then my face, and hands it back. "Let's see now. One pint Old Crow. Eighty proof? Or hundred?"

"Hundred will be fine, sir." *What the hell is proof? If eighty is good, hundred must be better.*

"Two pints Gilby's vodka. It'd be cheaper by the fifth, son. Want a fifth?"

"Err, nossir. Better make it two pints. We might not use it all."

"Oh, you'll use it all, son. Believe me, you'll use it all." Wink!

"And a quart of Hiram Walker sloe gin. Looks as if you boys are gonna make a Christmas punch, huh?" I nod affirmatively. The sloe gin is Dense's idea… something he's had at some jock party. We're going to buy flasks and split the bottle.

"And two pints of Seagram's Seven. That's it, right?" With my nod, he turns and vanishes into the library of tall shelves that make up the back of the liquor store. Quickly, he returns with our booty and starts tapping into an adding machine. "Thirteen dollars and… forty-seven cents. That includes the governor's share."

I pull out my wad of dollar bills and count out fourteen of them. I have one left over. Profit for the messenger?

• • •

"Gosh, Darcy. You look wonderful." She's standing in her darkened apartment, washed in the magentas and golds of the reflected lights outside. Her dress is black, tight around the waist and flaring a little to a skirt that comes to mid-calf. The top is some kind of sparkly stuff that clings to her bosom and ends just beneath her armpits. It has no straps.

"You think so, Five? Really like it?" I try not to drool. "You'd better. I worked my fingers off to get it finished."

"You made that dress? By hand?"

"Of course, fool. You think I could afford something like

144

this? You think I took four years of home ec for nothing?"

I help her on with a black, open sweater. "I hate to wear the sweater but I'd look like a derelict in the car coat. It's not *that* cold outside, is it? Besides... it'll be warm in the Ford pretty quick."

"We're going to drive?"

"God, Five. You are out of it. Of course we're going to drive. You think I want to walk all the way across campus in these darling little shoes? People'll think I'm nuts."

When we unlock the Ford's garage, Darcy hands me the keys and says "Here, you're driving. I'll lock the door behind you."

"I'm driving? You're gonna let me drive this beauty?"

"Of course. You're my escort aren't you? How would it look for us to pull up to the grand entrance of Biddle Hall with me behind the wheel?"

Actually, I pull up behind the east wing entrance on the empty cafeteria driveway. We walk the long way around to the front door so Darcy won't have to walk in the damp grass in her "darling little shoes."

The *big surprise* is playing full blast in the lounge. "Chris the Martian and the Spacemen." Actually, the sounds coming from Chris Cobb's clarinet plus his piano, bass and trumpet men are pretty good. The Martian winks and gives me a wave as he bobs behind the clarinet.

"It's really pretty, Five," Darcy coos at the usually spartan lounge in its Christmas finery. "The tree's beautiful. And look at the Santa Claus. Isn't he neat?" The lounge does look pretty fine. Red and blue lights in the ceiling spots. The floor lamps turned low. The chairs and couches pushed back to create a pretty sizable dance floor.

I introduce Darcy to the Davises as we head for the hall doorway. Kaye has Baby Melody dressed in a green and white elf suit. Darcy coos at the baby. "Remember the rules, Five," Dan chides me with a smile, "one foot on the floor at all time and the doors stay open."

"Sounds like a pool room to me," Darce comments as we climb the stairs to Biddle's second floor. "Is that the john? Can I see?"

"Do you have to go?" I ask. "I'll make sure it's empty if you do."

"No. Maybe later. Though I'm so nervous, maybe I should go right now."

"Don't be nervous. They're just my weird friends... weird just like me."

All down the hall, room doors are open an inch or so, the Biddle residents' interpretation of the university rules about having members of the opposite sex in their rooms.

"The really big party's in 205," I say proudly, "cause we've only got two beds and more room than anyone else." Sure enough as we near 205, the sounds of partying grow louder. We enter and discover a smoky den of would-be evil. Toby's study lamp and the nearly empty closet offer the only illumination, each sporting a fifteen watt blue bulb.

"Five's here!" Toby shouts from his bed where Stacy Gordine is semi-draped over his pale-blue torso. "What say, Five? Welcome to the Wolfe's Lair, lovely little lady."

"Quiet everyone," Winkler calls out. "Five's gonna introduce the mysterious woman we've been hearing so little about."

"Everyone. This Darcy Robinette. Darcy... that's Toby, my roomie, and Stacy. And Wink, he's the president of Biddle, and his date, er, O-Two, and that's Massman... and my friend and his date Andy Logan... hey Andy... and this is Stolski, and his date, Ann... uh Ann... I'm sorry Ann, I can't remember."

"Oxburn, Five. Ann Oxburn. You did fine. And I guess you can call me O-Annie, like everyone else is."

"Don't tell. Let me guess," Darcy says with a grin at O-Annie. "Those pale eyes. That hair. Little Orphan Annie?" The crowd cheers.

We've scrubbed one of the wastebaskets several times, then lined it with foil to hold the crushed ice. I make Darcy and myself a drink from my flask of sloe gin hidden in the inside pocket of one of Toby's few remaining sport coats hanging in the closet. Most of Toby's clothes have been moved to the presidential suite so we could construct a makeshift bar in our

146

closet.

"Watch out for the booze, everyone," Winkler warns. "Dan said he'd take a couple of tours of the dorm but I have a feeling he'll make lots of noise when he gets on the floor. Just keep it out of sight."

"Love your Capezios," Stacy says to Darcy. "But wasn't it a bitch walking across campus in them? I thought I'd freeze!" Darcy turns her head and flicks me a wink and smile.

"And where did you get that dress?" O-Annie wants to know. "I haven't seen anything that cute in any store in Athens."

"What about that Martian, Five?" Winkler hugs me over the shoulder. "Is that a great surprise, or what? I didn't even know the skinny fucker... er, scuse me maams... er, character, could play til Bear told me. Is Bear comin' down?"

"He said they'd try to get down from Scott later on," I return, hoping the evil Bear doesn't decide to bring Judy and her date along.

"C'mon everyone," Massman calls. "Fortify yourselves. We've gotta be in the lounge by eight o'clock and can't come back up here 'til intermission." There's a rush to the closet for fortification.

• • •

The Spacemen are really rocking the lounge and everyone seems to be having a great time. Different girls squeal as they take turns posing beside my cut-out Santa Claus. Their dates can stand behind his trim, red-suited figure. My project is an obvious hit.

Stacy and Toby are jitterbugging up a storm. Stacy's tight purple dress is accented by one of Toby's sport coats, a long pink number that comes to her knees. I realize from their actions that it's probably the one with my flask in it.

I dance with Darcy every chance I get and she proves to be a popular partner, a good dancer. We get cut lots of times. "She's really cute, Five," Andy Logan says as we dance a slow number, "where did you find her? I didn't see her during rush."

"Uhh, she didn't rush, Andy. She doesn't go to OU?"

147

"Oh, you imported someone for the big Biddle dance?"

"Not exactly. She works here in town."

"She's a townie. I don't know her. Did she go to AHS?"

"Nah, she's from Nelsonville. We kind of, well, ah knew each other from high school," I evade, remembering Darcy's remark about seeing me play basketball.

Just before intermission, the lobby doors burst open to the cry of "The Christmas Bearrrrrr is here! Merry Christmas from the Christmas Bear!"

Dense and Page enter, Dense in a white tux jacket that does make him resemble a polar bear. I heave a sigh of relief that they're by themselves. Everyone gathers round them to say hello. The Bear is as much a fixture in Biddle as if he actually lived here.

"So this is the PC, eh?" Bear says to me with a wink. Darcy stares at this giant white apparition, then gives me a puzzled look.

"PC?' Obviously she believes I haven't shared *all* my secrets with her.

"Pretty Child," Dense responds with a cunning grin, "and he's absolutely right. You *are* a beautiful child."

"Hardly a child," Page says, sort of archly. "Nice to meet you Darcy. Where do you live? A dorm? A house?"

"Oh, I'm really lucky," Darcy flips back, deciding to play into the game, "I got a single and I just love it. Terrific view. C'mon Five, let's dance this one. See you guys later."

Intermission comes and Dan and Kaye make a big deal of announcing they'll take Baby Melody for a quick tour of the dorm to see the room decorations. Everyone scurries to their rooms to ensure that bottles are out of sight. Windows are thrown open to dispel the odor of booze.

The Davises pop into 205 and Kaye admires my soap drawings of a snow scene across the two windows. Then they move on down the hall and our party resumes.

"So this is your bed? Just about as big as mine," Darcy says as we lean against the wall and nurse our third sloe gins and sodas. It dawns on me that the couch in her apartment is also her bed.

148

"Yeah," I respond, "but mine's got these neat little legs with the metal caps so they can be used as ashtrays." I demonstrate by removing a cap and flicking ashes down the hollow leg nearest us.

"You're not supposed to smoke in bed, you boob. You could ruin this pretty bedspread if it all burned up."

"Lay off the bedspread, Robinette," I growl. "It's the work of Mamma Wolfe, who thank God has slightly better taste than her son does."

"Oh, Five, I wanna see the rest of Toby's clothes. That wardrobe is too much. Can we look in Wink's room? That's the wing where the ladies' john is, isn't it?"

"Sure, on the way back, I'll get their key and you can see the entire Wolfe blue suede, one-button roll collection."

She giggles and snuggles into my arm. "This's fun, Five. Thanks for asking me." A long kiss and a tighter snuggle. "Now... what's the PC stand for."

• • •

"Good God, look at this stuff! Doesn't he have any normal clothes?" Darcy sways a little in front of the pile that constitutes Toby's wardrobe, stacked on Massman's lower bunk. "Those colors. They're awful. But I'll bet everything cost a ton." She leans back against me. I slip my arms around her waist.

"That sloe gin stuff is good, but it makes me so sleepy," she murmurs. I trying moving my locked hands a little higher. "And warm, too." Hands a bit higher just to where her waist begins to be her... Then she spins in my arms and we have another long kiss. "Now Five, show me where the john is before I embarrass myself."

• • •

As the dance nears its end, the success of Biddle's first big social event is obvious. Either Dan Davis is a very understanding dorm manager or he doesn't have the slightest idea of the effects of booze upon young people. Stacy and Toby

149

are wildly gyrating on the floor; she's still in his sport coat buttoned down around her crotch. Everyone gets an eyeful of Stacy's attributes as the Grey Wolfe swings her around. The top of her dress hangs down beneath the sport coat like an apron.

"Damn, Five. But you've just got to see what's outside." Bear and Page have been outside rearranging her makeup a little. "Talk about beautiful." We follow them out into the darkened front yard. "Over there, by the barfeteria. Look at that little beauty." The little beauty, of course, is Darcy's Ford, shining beneath the cafeteria's security spotlight.

"Denzel, you're right. That is a beauty," Darcy giggles. "This Purty Child sure would like to own one of those."

"I wonder whose it is?" Page slurs. "Wouldn't it be fun to ride in the rumble seat of that, Bear?" We all agree how much fun it would be and bid them goodnight as they totter off toward Mulberry and Scott Quad's dance.

• • •

"Can you drive? Can you walk? Not sure I can do either," Darcy says as we leave the dance. Behind us in the smoky lounge, the Martian is bowing and grinning, accepting congratulations.

"I'll drive slowly… and carefully." Actually, we still have an inch of sloe gin in my flask, hidden in a gray, one-button roll sport coat that Darcy has slipped over her shoulders. "You can return it someday," she said when she slipped it out of the closet. "I don't think Toby'll ever notice it's missing… and even if he does, we're doing him a favor."

"What're you gonna do with it?"

"Bathrobe, silly. Look how long it is. Don't you think I'll look good in it?"

• • •

She's grinning wildly as she swings open the garage door. I ease the Ford into the garage, thankful to have made it up the hill without a mishap. She locks the door, then looks around. At the

150

apartment above. "Pretty quiet on South High tonight. Duff must be in Nelsonville."

"Duff lives up there?"

"Sure! How'd you think I got the garage? He parks his car behind the Begorra and walks over." Down the street, a bottle clanks against something hard, bounces once, then shatters in the gloom.

"What's that down there?" I point to the big brick pile that sits on the curve.

"That's the ACE house. Spooky lookin' isn't it?" The huge brick mansion looms against the dark sky and a few streetlights that show behind it. A brick wall curves in and out toward the property line near us. "Street dead ends down there," Darcy adds, "but there's a walkway that goes between that wall and the Delt House, over to President Street."

Back at Darcy's place, she turns the light in the alcove on and takes the flask from her "robe."

"Les' finish this baby up, Five. It's Christmas." She pours the contents into a jelly glass, then lifts it and takes a big swig. "Want some?" she giggles.

"Save me a sip, Darce."

"Sure thing, Five ole' buddy. Here!" She takes another swig and hands the nearly empty glass to me. The purple sloe gin swirls inside its yellow-flowered container. I finish it. Almost a good dose of cough syrup. "Gotta go't john, Five. Don't go 'way." She lurches to the tiny bathroom and pulls the door closed. "Uuuh, it's dark in here," she giggles. "Where's the light cord?" I hear the click of the light switch being pulled down.

In the neon glow of the Wonder Bar sign, I sit on the edge of her couch… her bed… and enjoy the effects of the straight sloe gin. The commode flushes and seconds later, Darcy reappears in the lighted doorway.

"Wanna see how I look in my new robe?" She slinks across the room and sits beside me, tossing her dress on one of the kitchen chairs. "How I look? Look in my new robe? Huh?" She reaches her arms up to me and in the same motion, slowly falls backward onto the bed. I pull her legs up onto the bed and the bedspread from beneath her. Covering her with the spread, I tuck her in with a soft kiss.

"Night, Five," she giggles. And she's gone.

• • •

Darcy isn't the only naked girl in one of Toby's sport coats I tuck in that night. Arriving back in 205, I discover Toby curled up in *his* bed and snoring loudly. Matching him snore for snore on *my* bed is Stacy, flat on her back with her headlights full on, as they say.

Risking the smallest of glimpses, I try to adjust the top of her dress back to its proper position, then pull the lapels of the sport coat together and work its single button. Finally, I pull my bedspread out from beneath her and drape it across her snoring form.

Toby won't waken. He snuffs and snorts but just rolls into a tighter ball when I try. I give up and head for Winkler's room. There I discover the presidential trio, smoking and finishing off a pint of something clear.

"Wanna shot, Five?" Mass looks up. "Great dance wasn't it? Really liked your date. Did she like us?"

"Ah, guys, I hate to mention this but… Toby's date is ah, asleep on my bed, ah, passed out."

"Still half naked?" Stolski wants to know. "Let's go have a gang bang." We glare at him.

"Just kiddin'," he shrugs with a grin. "I don't think I could get up off this bed, much less get anything else up."

"But what's she doin' there?" I want to know. "If Davis finds out, Toby'll get kicked out of school. They both will."

"She took an overnight permission," Mass mumbles, "told 'em she was staying with a girlfriend in Columbus. So she's not in any trouble… unless she goes wanderin' around in the middle of the night."

"Well, shit! And where'n hell am I gonna sleep?" I grab a blanket from Winkler's bed and plop on Toby's wardrobe pile which is now in the corner by a desk. "This isn't too bad. Maybe I will have a swig of that stuff. What is it? Vodka?" Biddle's Christmas dance is officially ended.

Chapter 14

A Semester Of Innocence Ends

Monday, January 3, 1995. The new year dawns with blinding clarity. Temperature near freezing. Sun bright and cold in an utterly transparent sky. We students trudge across the snow-covered campus, blobs of gray and black trying to shed the fuzzy memories of Christmas vacation past.

Some vacation! Captain surprises me upon my arrival home with the news that I have a substitute berth on the *Ernie M.* for the week, if I want the work. I surprise him by accepting it and a week later, I'm fifty dollars richer for the experience.

The *Ernie M.* is a smaller, older boat berthed in Hockingport and working the local pool between Parkersburg and Pomeroy. Captain Scullen is a nice guy who likes his Christmas vacation as much as anyone so we put in very few hours on the river during that week.

My social life is virtually nil. Dense is with Page in Westerville. Tina is spending most of Christmas week with her boyfriend somewhere. Mary Lou is holed up with her accounting and economics texts. After not reaching Darcy at the Begorra, I settle for spending Christmas Eve with the family and going to church.

I'm awarded the Chevy for New Year's Eve and call Darcy to meet her in Athens. She's spent Christmas in Nelsonville with Aunt Ida and is ready to party. Except that she has a terrible case of flu and we spend a quiet New Year's Eve holding hands and listening to the *Student Prince* album I gave her for Christmas. And listening to her blow her nose into a ton of Kleenexes. I'm home by one a.m.

Now the semester has but a week to run with final exams to study for and course projects to complete. As I trudge to Western Civ, I detect an itching sniffle growing in my nose. *Well, maybe we did just a little more than hold hands.*

• • •

"In my opinion, Lowrey, you've made a good choice of art as your major. Your sketches have improved immensely, considering you had no high school training," Professor Blockhart says in a serious tone, leaning over his steepled fingers. "And the word I get from Professor Dabny is that you're one of her best introductory figure drawing students."

Blockhart is my official faculty advisor now. He's not nearly as much fun to look at as Trish Spotswood but he does seem to have a sincere interest in my education. "Before you seek a particular niche for your talents," he continues, "you must continue to acquire elementary skills.

"I would recommend Advanced Figure Drawing, Theory of Color and Light, and Introduction to Wet Media, if you can work those into your prerequisite schedule." He pauses and leafs through my manila portfolio. "The way you've used the pen to ink in parts of these pencil sketches is particularly intriguing. Crow quill?"

"Yessir," I respond. "I really… ahhh, I'm quite taken with the finite detail the smaller nib gives my lines." *Shit! Is that me speaking? Perhaps I'm learning the jargon.*

• • •

"All right, Austin. End pose." Jan Dabny hands Austin, a lithe young black man, the figure drawing kimono as we hustle to put finishing touches on our sketches. Austin replaced Anique halfway through the semester and provided some entertainment for the male segment of the class, vast amounts of blushing for the females, as Professor Dabny repeated her graphic lecture on anatomical features.

"How in hell can you do that, man?" Barrett Chumley asked Austin one day during a smoke break.

"Do what, man?" Austin grins. His smile betrays that he knows exactly what's on Chumley's mind.

"You know. Stand there in a pose like that. Without… I

154

mean, in front of all those broads?"

"Ahhh, Barrett," Austin says dramatically, "there are times when one must perform. And then there are times when one must perform in another manner. Anyone who says our brains are all down here," he gestures, "has never posed nude before a group of young women."

Of all the classes I take, figure drawing is the most informal... and in many ways my favorite. Unlike most other faculty members I've met, Professor Dabny is totally down to earth, insisting everyone calls her Jan. Bumming smokes from anyone with a visible pack.

"OK, gang. That wraps it up for the semester. Your best two sketches in my office by next Tuesday. For those of you who'll join us next semester for the advanced class, you can beat the rush by picking up a Strathmore six fifty pad and a set of basic Prisma pencils.

"If you're not rejoining us, thank you very much for behaving as professionals. I know this is sometimes difficult in this class. Don't forget Tuesday noon."

• • •

"And we'll resume next semester with the beginnings of the Industrial Revolution, wherein we'll discover that the impact of machine can be as great as the impact of written communication... but in a different way..."

Ohmygod, I cannot wait until next semester to resume Western Civ. If I were Catholic, I would say my rosary in hopes of not getting Doctor Stansfield again.

• • •

"Five, I'm very pleased with your progress," Professor Buehler tells me as the rest of our speech class files out of her classroom. "You've done a lot to conquer your shyness. If you continue in speech, I would hope you will broaden your subject horizons a bit. Not that I've found your discourses upon life on the river and riverboats dull, understand..."

• • •

The campus is like an empty battlefield the day after the fighting. Flu has swept OU clean. The Bobcats-Western Reserve basketball game has been canceled. Toby's in bed with an ice pack on his head and mustard plasters from momma on his chest. Having shed my fever and sniffles, I avoid room 205 like the plague it contains.

I spend my afternoons at Chubb, occupying a study carrel that gives me a view down President Street and of the Begorra. Occasionally, I catch a glimpse of Darcy going in or out of the diner.

• • •

"Four hundred! A new record, Five!" Duff beams at me from behind the mound of steaming burgers. "We don't get much action in here during finals week but studying must make 'em hungry on East Green?"

Darcy and I pile the cartons of burgers into the rumble seat of the Ford. "Don't get any ideas about this being a permanent delivery service, bub," she admonishes me, "but I'd hate to see you have to pay refunds on that many cold Begorras."

As I drive down Mulberry toward East Green, Darcy turns sideways in the seat and faces me. "Got a secret, Five!"

"No secrets, Darce. You know the rules. What is it?"

"Won't tell. But it's exciting news."

"A new job?"

"Duff told you! And he said he wouldn't."

"Nope. Just guessed. What is it?"

"Not tellin' yet. But it really pays good and I don't have to quit Begorra." She helps me unload the three cartons of burgers and then chugs off into the night with a quick kiss, a wave and hoot of the klaxon.

• • •

My pre-addressed postcards come rolling in with grades. Western Civ: B-. English comp: C+. Speech: B-. That's one I didn't expect. Figure Drawing: B+. Intro to Sketching: A. Fine Art Appreciation: B+ (thanks to Andy Logan and her sharp elbow). With Seasonal Sports still to report in, I'm finishing the semester with what looks like a three point something grade average!

• • •

Second semester registration seems a breeze. In and out with another check written to OU in twenty minutes. Now I'm observing our *traditional* post-registration coffee date with Trish Spotswood at Quick's.

"I'll have a toasted roll, coffee with cream," Trish orders. "Have you ever had a toasted roll, Five? They're great."

"Nope, sounds good. Trish. Same for me."

"So, Five… bring me up to date since Operation Dildo. What else good has happened to you? How's your love life?"

I briefly synopsize the first semester, leaving out certain parts, emphasizing my grades and the success of the Begorra service.

"God, that's some real money? Are you going to keep it up next year?"

"Guess so, unless someone else cuts me out. I don't think Duff would sell to someone in the same dorm, though."

"Where are you going to live next year? Biddle? Maybe a fraternity house?"

"Dan Davis is moving over to Tiffin — the new dorm on the corner of Mulberry and East Green — and said he can get me on as a floor counselor over there next year. That'd mean a single room which would be nice after a year with Toby."

She smiles at Toby's name. "Yeah. Roommates can be a real drag. Did he get under your skin?"

"A little," I admit. "Shouldn't this semester, though. He TGIFed his way to barely a two point and Mamma Wolfe has come down on him big time. But it'll be nice to have a quiet place to study when I want to. Don't know about fraternities. I guess I'll rush. But don't know much about it.

"How 'bout you, Trish? Your car still running?"

"Maybe," she frowns, "but it wasn't my car and I don't really know any more. I split up with the car and its owner. Moved out on him a couple of weeks ago."

"You were livin' with a guy?" This is a new side to my graduate advisor.

"Oh, yeah. Maybe in love at one time. Just a big pain in the butt the last six months. I've got an apartment right over there." She nods across her shoulder but I pay little attention as the toasted rolls are served. The ordinary sweet roll has been transformed by being split, toasted on the grill and served oozing with butter. One more delicacy discovered. I vow to make Quick's a frequent stop.

• • •

I arrive a few minutes late to my new sociology class to discover a crowd around the classroom door in Ellis. A tall, thin man calls for our attention. "Sorry… people. We've got a scheduling conflict here. Why don't we go down to the courtyard and I'll pass out the syllabi and give you the word on where we'll meet."

In the familiar sunken courtyard, we all light up and accept the mimeographed forms.

"I'm Thurmond Gessler, your sociology instructor," the skinny guy tells us. "I'm afraid that all of the classrooms open for my afternoon schedule are not available, so… we shall meet in 221 at 8 a.m., Tuesdays, Thursdays… and Saturdays." This announcement is met with a groan of despair. Several guys on the edge of the crowd start up the sidewalk on the run for the registrar's office.

"I'm sorry," Gessler pleads in a whine, "just as sorry as you are. I cherish my Saturday mornings also, you know." Pause. "Any questions? I thought not. Well, I'll see you Thursday morning."

As the class disperses, I see Andy Logan across the courtyard. "Is that a big crock of horseshit, or what, Five? Eight

158

o'clocks... and Saturday, too! At least it isn't during football season. That would really be a loser."

We walk together toward the Union and I offer a cup of coffee. "Can't do it. Should be up to the house if I don't have class. We're starting Harpy Week."

"Harpy Week?" This is another new one to me.

"Hell Week. Harpy Week. Makes no difference. For the next four days, all my Pi Phi sisters are going to treat us like bitches. But by Saturday, it'll be over and I'll be an active. See you Thursday at eight."

• • •

I return to the drawing studio for my first advanced figure drawing. Lots of familiar faces including Jan Dabny and our old friend, Anique, blowing smoke rings down the arm of the now-familiar kimono.

"Well Five, welcome back. Are you ready for some foreshortening?" Dabny asks. Since this sounds something like circumcision, a subject I know little about, I just grin and take my place at an easel.

"Ready Anique?" Anique disrobes, revealing a few extra pounds from the Christmas break. By now, we veteran figure drawers are also familiar with Anique in clothes from her job at the reference desk of the library. "Today, we're going to start some exercises in depicting the limbs and body from particular views. To start, Anique will strike a pose and each of you will come up here and take a look from several angles."

Anique lowers her big butt on the posing stage and draws one leg up in an exaggerated fashion. The other leg dangles at a slight angle outward. My buddies in Biddle would call this a *crotch shot.* Following Dabny's instruction, we line up and then hunker down, bend over, lean one way and the other, all to get a new perspective of Anique's haunch and parts connected thereto.

"Notice now that you're back at your easels, that the appearance of Anique's leg is considerably different from your present vantage point than it was upon closer inspection. What you've experienced is called perspective." *From whose perspective? I still think it was a crotch shot.*

Professor Dabny picks up a pad and charcoal and quickly lines in what looks like the short end of a Virginia ham. "Expressing perspective in this manner is called foreshortening. And that is what we will begin to learn today. Rest Anique."

Anique rises but doesn't make for her smokes and kimono. Dabny places her hand on Anique's knee and slowly runs it up her thigh toward… "As you can see, the distance from Anique's knee to her torso is approximately fifteen inches. But, by establishing lines that exaggerate the normal shape of the leg as a shorter distance…" *I wonder if Professor Dabny is one of those 'strange' ladies?*

• • •

After a semester of boring dorm meetings — orientation, homecoming program, Migration Week, the dangers of mononucleosis (which according to the infirmary nurse who spoke, leads to even worse things; all we can do is hope), new rules concerning panty raids — the one we've been waiting for is about to begin.

Biddle lounge is packed and so abuzz with speculation that the usual smoke cloud swirls around near the ceiling. Dan Davis whistles for attention and introduces the speakers… "Mike Jewell, Rick Satterwhite, and Ron Rosen, are all members of fraternities but more important, they are Biddle's representatives from the IFC Rush Committee. Without further ado, I'll turn it over to them."

Rosen, a short man in gray slacks, dark blue crew sweater over a dress shirt, wears enormous horn-rims and has black, curly hair. His compatriots are in sort of uniform: tweed sport coats, dress shirts and narrow knit ties, khaki trousers and white bucks. None of the three has a fraternity pin showing.

"Good evening, gentlemen, and thanks for coming out for the first official event of fraternity rush…" Rosen seems to be the spokesman. He folds his hands before his waist and paces back and forth as he speaks.

"As you're probably aware by now, fraternity rush will begin with house visits next Monday at 7 p.m. We're here tonight to provide you with some information that IFC feels is important for you to know... in order for you to have a successful rush experience. Please ask questions anyt..." Hands shoot up.

"What's IFC?" someone beneath a raised hand answers.

"Interfraternity Council, I.F.C. It's the formal organization that each fraternity belongs to and it supervises rush activities, enforces rush rules, and serves as a governing board for fraternity matters on campus." *This seems like more than I wish to know about IFC.*

Rosen continues, "There are nineteen fraternities on campus and you are invited to visit each of them. Unlike the sororities, you are not required to visit each house... nor will you receive a formal invitation to return to a house as the sororities do.

"House visits will run from seven to ten, Monday, Tuesday and Wednesday. Thursday night's an off night for you... and us. Then on Friday and Saturday, the houses will be open for return visits."

Another question from the floor. "How will we know where to go back to which house?" *Keep asking questions like that and it won't be a problem.*

"OU's fraternity rush works upon the principal of sensibility from both rushee and the rushing fraternity. I'm sure each of you will receive indications from an individual member that you'll be welcome back to a particular house. Mike, Rick and I will be here Sunday night and each night, including Thursday, after rush hours to answer your questions, handle your complaints... of which I'm sure there will be none..."

• • •

So I said I was a morning person? So perhaps I lied. The Bryan steps seem steeper than usual this Thursday at 7:55 a.m. Although Toby seems dedicated to a new pursuit of academic excellence, he was still careful to schedule no class before 10 a.m. and I overslept.

The door is still open to Ellis 221 but I discover a packed classroom when I enter. A hand waves from the rear of the room and Andy Logan half-rises from her seat to indicate a space. Gessler shuffles his lecture notes. "Thanks for savin' me a seat," I whisper to Andy, sliding into the lecture desk. Andy scoots her desk closer to mine until its writing arm is almost against the edge of mine. She hands me her notebook on which is scribbled:

Can't talk. Will tell you about it Monday. XXX

Gessler clears his throat a couple of times, peers at us through the gray morning light and begins our adventure in sociology, "If you must smoke in class, please observe the university rule and provide your own ashtray." There's an immediate scuffle as we search for tin Camel ashtrays and cigarette packs. Gessler lights up himself.

"Sociology, as you may know, is the scientific study of collective human behavior. The term was coined in the late 1830s by Auguste Comte, who attempted to identify the unifying principles of society at different stages of human social development." Andy's notebook reappears before me.

May I copy your notes later?

I nod yes and she blinks and smiles wanly. Gessler seems to be warming up. "It may shock and surprise you to discover that major contributions to nineteenth-century sociology were made by Karl Marx, who emphasized the economic basis of the organization of society and identified the concept of class struggle as a major agent in social progress. Yes indeed, the same Karl Marx who has been at the root of all things evil according to Senator McCarthy…"

Scribbling notes, I'm pleased to recognize Senator McCarthy's name and to have a basic knowledge of who Karl Marx was. *Perhaps this sosh stuff won't be so bad after all?* There's a sudden pressure on my shoulder. There, just inches away, is the sweet face of Andy Logan, sound asleep. After sitting by her for a semester in Mem Aud, I am used to her odor of *White Shoulders* and *Dentyne,* but today she carries a slightly different scent. *Onions?*

• • •

Short. A few pounds overweight. A big ole' Pi Phi pin on her round left boob. My new seat mate in Fine Arts Appreciation showers me with an austere look and turns to her notebook.

"Hi," I say, "I'm Thom Lowrey." She looks at me again. *Is there something hanging out of my nose?*

"Hello. I'm Andrea Logan. How are you?" *What in hell is going on?*

"Not *the* Andy Logan?" Pause. "The one I came to know so well in this class last semester?"

She cracks the slightest of smiles. "Ohh, you must be Five. Why didn't you say so? Andy's err, indisposed. I'm Pris Pitts, just came to get her on the seating chart. She'll probably be back on Monday."

"Is she OK? I'm mean, she's not sick, is she?"

"Well, not exactly. She'll be fine on Monday. Will you let her use your notes?"

• • •

I don't have to worry about notes for the absent Andy on Saturday morning because Gessler doesn't bother to show up. In fact, I'm only one of five students in the sosh class who does. The five of us agree to go over to the Frontier Room and call Gessler rude things.

On Saturday night, I sneak Darcy into Men's Gym for the OU-Xavier basketball game. We sit packed in with Dense and Page while Toby and Stacy poke their knees into us from the row behind. After the game, the six of us squeeze into a booth at the Esquire Grill for some beer.

Darcy and I leave when the others do, although nothing has been said about Darcy's "curfew" or place of residence.

"I think your friends are pretty nice, Five," she says softly, blowing a perfect smoke ring toward the frosted magenta windows of her room. "Even Page. I thought she didn't like me at first…"

"Page's OK, Darce. She's really been a good influence on Dense. You wouldn't recognize him from the farmer he was a year ago."

"I think Page knows that I'm not a student," she continues with a giggle. "Toby and Stacy are so out to lunch that they may never know."

There's a long thoughtful pause. She makes another perfect smoke ring. Try as I do, I can't create that kind of perfection. My smoke rings always look like a little invisible guy is hanging onto the bottom.

"Five? Are you going to rush a fraternity?"

"I guess I am. At least go through rush." My turn to think and pause. "I don't really know how much it would cost to belong. We've got guys at the dorm to help with rush but they don't tell us anything specific."

"If you join a fraternity, do you think it would change?"

"Change what?"

"You know. Things? You? Everything. Us?"

"I sure can't imagine why," I reply earnestly, "but it's probably not likely to happen anyway."

• • •

Andy's holding our seats in the back of the sosh room on Monday morning, looking bright and chipper. As I sit, she leans over and gives me a quick peck on the cheek. We're back to *White Shoulders* and *Dentyne* again. "Thanks for the notes, Five. And thanks for the soft shoulder. Lookie here!" She turns so I can see the sparkling gold jeweled arrow dangling right on the tip of her left breast. "Isn't it beautiful?"

"Congratulations, Andy. You made it!" The Pi Phi arrow seems enormous and the jewels wink in the rays of early sun. "That's really a nice pin but it looks sort of different."

"Oh Five, it is. Mom's best friend, Ceil Windom, was a Pi Phi national officer and she gave me her pin at initiation. Isn't that just the neatest thing? She hasn't any girls of her own and I think she got a kick out of having me with this big ole' arrow on instead of Mom's X and O."

"That's really nice. Are you going to wear it all the time? It looks expensive."

164

"Oh, no. Just the next few days and special occasions. But I'm *so* proud of it." She pauses. "Are you going to start rush tonight?'

"I guess so. Don't know much about it…" Gessler begins with something sociological. We bend to our notebooks. I notice Andy's head nod sharply.

• • •

"Shit, guys, doesn't look like anyone's in there. I don't wanna be the first," Bear grumbles in general. It's five past seven and we're standing in front of the Acacia house — Dense, Toby, Mass, Winkler, Stolski and me. All dressed in our best "casual" wardrobes — sport coats and ties — according to our IFC advisors.

The Grey Wolfe is resplendent as usual . Light gray one-button roll sport coat on charcoal trousers. Black suede shoes. Black knit tie over the pale pink shirt with its ballooning Mr. B collar. "You're lookin' great, Wolfe," Winkler says in a stage whisper. "C'mon guys, let's go. Someone's gotta be first.

We're welcomed by a door that opens before anyone could knock. "Welcome to the Acacia house, gentlemen." Inside, a small receiving line of Acacians greets us, each introducing himself and beginning the chain of questions we'll grow to recognize by heart.

After a fifteen minute tour of the house, I catch Bear giving me a nod. We pick up Wink and Mass, then Stolski. Toby is in another room, engrossed in conversation with a couple of Acacians. We all nod toward the door but he stays put. "Just a sec, guys," he says, "I'll be right with you."

"We'll meet your outside, Tobe," I say in a stage whisper and make for the door. Our departure isn't too noticeable as other rushees are coming in at the same time.

"Jesus. We could've spent the night there," Massman says. "Those guys are really friendly."

"Wonder if we'll ever get the Wolfe outta there?" Bear asks. "I've got to get going. Maybe we should split up."

Just then, Toby appears through the door, shaking hands and

gripping shoulders as if he's running for governor or something. "Why'd you guys cut out so early? They were sort of disappointed to see you leave."

• • •

As we work our way around the College Green, it's pretty much the same experience. Lots of names, faces, handshakes and questions. At Sigma Chi, Toby is instantly separated from our group and becomes the center of a laughing, joking knot of Sigs and other rushees. He gets the same treatment at Phi Delta Theta. While we're being treated politely and with mild interest from the brothers, Toby is the hub of a great deal of jolly good fellowship.

I'm the first out of the Delt house and stand on their porch overlooking the river to light a cigarette. Way up President Street a group of rushees makes its way toward us but except for me, the porch is empty. I hear some voices beneath the porch railing.

"God! Did you get a load of that geek in there in the high school outfit? Thought I'd pee myself right on the spot when he came in."

"Glad you could hold it 'til now, Brother Durban. That would've made a poor impression on the rushees." I can now see two guys standing at the edge of the embankment, relieving themselves onto the dark tracks below.

"I don't think negroes wear Mr. B collars that big," the first voice chortles. I lean closer. "It'll be just our luck that asshole's a Delt legacy." I move back toward the center of the porch as the rest of my group comes out the door, meeting the next mob of rushees coming up the steps.

"God, those Delts are great guys," Toby says to the world. "What a terrific bunch! So far, I feel like I could go with any of these houses and be welcome."

I change the subject. "Where next, guys? The Alpha Chi Epsilon house is back this walkway so that's close."

"I want to get to the Beta house and Sigma Nu," Bear says. "Several varsity guys there said to be sure and get there the first

166

night. Make a fresh first impression."

"That sounds good to me," Mass agrees. Toby is ready for anything. Stolski and Winkler start along the sidewalk.

"Think I'll just go over to the ACE house while we're here," I say, not really understanding why. Perhaps I've had my fill of fraternities. And rush. Maybe I just want to stop at the Begorra on my way home to the room. So I part from my friends and turn down the narrow darkened path past the Delt house.

• • •

Unlike the other times I've seen it, ACE is lit up brightly. But there doesn't seem to be quite as much activity as at the houses on the main streets. A couple of guys sitting on the front steps stand as I approach and introduce myself. They welcome me with handshakes and tell me their names. Galen Curtis. Chet Lee.

"Don't see too many rushees making the rounds by themselves," Galen Curtis observes. "What's your name again? Lo-Ree?" he asks.

"That's how you pronounce it," I respond. "But everyone calls me Five."

"Five? Hmm, Five. Oh yeah," the fellow named Lee says as his face lights up, "you're the homecoming dildo guy!" I blushingly admit that I am. "Shit! That's terrific. That's one of the best ones that's been pulled around here in a long time. C'mon in and meet the brothers."

I follow Lee through the big double doors that are flanked by stained glass animals and knights. "Hey, Brother Simmons, look who I've got here." I'm led to a tall, severe looking man with a thin black crew cut. "This is Five Lowrey. He's the dildo artist from homecoming."

A smile breaks Simmons' severe expression. "Five Lowrey!" he exclaims and extends a big hand. "Welcome to Alpha Chi Epsilon. So you're the dog who pulled the wool over The Dean's eyes with that stunt? Glad to meet you. I'm J.L. Simmons."

J.L. seems to take over and leads me from the entry hall into a huge living room. A big bay window looks out over the river and the asylum grounds, its panes held together with black frames. At the other end of the room, the biggest fireplace I've ever seen squats beneath a long mantle covered with trophies and strange objects.

"Gunner, Brother Jake, want you to meet Five Lowrey. He's the artist who created The Dean's dildo." I shake hands with Gunther Schmidt and Jake somethingorother. *How'm I going to remember all these names.*

My progress through the room is slow but steady. This is the first house all evening where I haven't had some wisecrack made about Hockingport. One of the brothers, Doak Phipps, comes closest. "Hockingport. I know that place. I'm from Fly. Probably only town on the river as small or smaller than Hockingport, right?"

"Say, have you met our housemother yet, Five? Mom? This is Thomsen Lowrey the Fifth. Five, this is Mom Holmquist." Mom Holmquist is certainly an ace among housemothers… about the age of anyone's mom but with a beehive of blond hair accenting a very un-motherly figure.

"How do you do, Five?" she asks in a mellow voice. "Are you enjoying rush?"

• • •

Now on my lonesome, I walk up Congress Street toward the Beta house. I've spent more time than I'd planned at ACE, but as Toby has proclaimed, 'those guys were so damned friendly.' My reception at Beta Theta Pi also seems more genuine that at some of the earlier stops. Again, someone comments upon how unusual it is for a rushee to come in alone.

"Well, I kinda got lost from my buddies," I say. "Has the Bear Duerhoff been by here? I'm sure someone would remember him."

"Hey," someone says, "you know the Bear? C'mon in here and let me introduce you…"

• • •

Begorra is pretty quiet. The sizzle of burgers on the grill. I sit at the counter and sip my coffee, content to watch Duff fry the little hamburgers and wait for Darcy to return from some errand.

"Did you find any houses you really liked, Five?" Duff asks through the smoke and steam. "The Delts and Phi Delt guys who come in here all seem pretty nice."

"Oh yeah, Duff. Everyone's pretty nice. But I get a feeling that it's some kind of show. Not real, maybe? And... I heard something at the Delt house that I didn't think much of."

"What's that?"

"Nothing important. Just something that made an impression. The IFC guys in the dorm told us to be alert for things that make a real impression. This one did.

"I guess the Beta house was pretty nice," I continue, "and the guys at ACE. I spent a while there, met a lot of guys."

"Betas. They're a great bunch of party guys," Duff observes. "And the Aces, now that's a strange group. Not too many of 'em come in and the ones who do are pretty different." Just then, Darcy bursts through the back door with a big bundle in her arms.

"Hi, Five. Why aren't you out there greekin' it up?" she grins. "Couldn't make it from house to house without a grease fix? Or a moment in the presence of my charms?"

• • •

Biddle's lounge is crowded with three knots of rushees gathered around the IFC advisors. I join Bear and the rest of my gang where Rick Satterwhite is answering their questions.

The first question immediately got everyone's attention. "I don't understand the names of these outfits. For instance, there's that ACE house but when I go up their steps, the sign over the door says AXE. What gives?"

Rick smiles. "Remember guys, these are Greek organizations. Back in the last century when the first fraternities were started, everyone studied classic Greek. The founders gave their new clubs Greek initials… I suppose to make them sound classy and exclusive.

"So what you see on the ACE house are the three Greek letters for 'Alpha Chi Epsilon. The 'X' is the Greek letter for Chi." He pauses. "When you see ACE in all capital letters, say in the *OU Post,* that's the abbreviation for the full name 'cause the *Post* doesn't have any Greek typesetting."

Another question. "What about that 'OX' house? Are they any good?"

Rick responds, "That's Theta Chi. The 'O' with a hyphen in the middle is the Greek for Theta and you already know what the 'X' stands for.

"But guys, I can't comment on any of these houses specifically," he says with a broad gesture of helplessness, "it's against IFC rush rules. Remember what Ron said about sensitivity. It's something you've got to watch for in each house you visit. How do they respond to you? How do you react to them."

"OK, then…" one of the rushees says, "I was at this place and the next thing I knew, three guys had me in this room with the door closed. Really giving me a pitch. I thought I was shopping for a used car. What do you do in a situation like that?"

Satterwhite frowns. "That's called 'hotboxing' and, if you want to make a formal complaint about it, it's a violation of rush rules."

"Naw, they're nice guys in that house. I wouldn't want to get 'em in trouble."

"Then your best response is to politely but firmly tell them you have some other places you want to go and it's time for you to leave."

• • •

Without the IFC advisors, our rush bull session in 205 is much more frank.

"That one house," Massman observes, "I think those guys were all… *Jewish.*"

"Of course, you asshole," Winkler responds, "that's a Jewish fraternity! What'd you think they were, a-rabs?"

Bear hoots at this. "And what about that Alpha Phi whatsis, Mass? I suppose you thought those guys were putting on a minstrel show?"

"I liked those guys," I chime in. "I wouldn't want to join a negro fraternity but I thought they were neat guys. Treated me all right but I doubt they'll offer me a bid."

"They treated Tobe like he was hot shit," Winkler tells me. "Five, you missed some good houses when we lost you."

"Oh, I think I did all right," I shrug. "Time to hit the books. We've got two more nights of this stuff before a break."

• • •

Alone in our room, I ponder how to bring up the subject that's bothering me. "Tobe. You really seemed to have a great time while I was with you. Do you think these fraternity guys are… sincere about this stuff?"

"Shit no, Five. No way! Most of those bastards are phony as some professor's Ph.D. thesis that sells for forty dollars. Can't you see how they're treating me, even in my high school clothes?"

"What? You mean…?"

"Five, get with it. I know I've been a big joke in these outfits. I mean, I thought I was hot shit when I got here from high school. Didn't take long to see charcoal and titty pink aren't exactly Ivy League," Toby says with a rueful smile.

"And I wanna go Phi Delt and I'm gonna go Phi Delt cause my ole' man's a Phi Delt. It's a simple as that. But right now, I'm havin' a great time parading around in these be-bop outfits and watchin' these jokers fall all over themselves trying to be sincere."

"Well, I did overhear a couple of guys at the Delt house talkin' about you."

"Fuck 'em all. And I don't even want to hear what they said. Just think of the looks on those Phi Delt guys' faces on Friday night when I turn up in real clothes and tell 'em I'm a legacy."

171

He chortles at the thought. "Joke's on you, brothers! Here I am."

· · ·

On Tuesday night, we head for the houses out on State Street: Theta Chi, SAE, Phi Tau, with plans to work our way back toward the campus. It's just Dense, Toby and me. The other three of our gang wanted to go back to some houses they'd been impressed with. The Grey Wolfe hits the second night of rush with the same glad-handing enthusiasm as the night before. While the pastel shades of his outfit have changed, they don't seem any more subdued.

On this second night of rush, I'm a bit more observant. Not so overwhelmed by the welcomes we receive at each house. And indeed, I can detect a certain air about the people I meet. More jokes about Hockingport... none of them really funny and a couple of times I worry that Dense might coldcock someone.

"C'mon Five, I'll take you up to the Sigma Nu house," Dense urges, "they're really super and you didn't get there last night. Remember what a good time you had there, Toby?"

"Yeah, Bear, but I think I'll slide on down to the Phi Delt house. See how the guys are doing. Maybe cadge a free beer from one of 'em." Toby gives me an evil grin over the stiff color of his pale blue shirt. *Are those really flecks of silver in his maroon knit tie?*

The Sigma Nu's *are* really great. Dense is welcomed like he'd just chased the North Koreans beyond the 38th Parallel. Bobbing in his wake, I meet brother after brother and here, the welcome seems more honest, more warm. Then Dense vanishes somewhere with a couple of the Sigma Nus and I'm left scanning book titles in their library. After a few minutes, I slip toward the door and no one really makes a move to halt my progress. Quickly I'm on the sidewalk of Congress Street.

· · ·

Walking down Congress, I approach the Beta house where the porch is lighted up and packed with brothers and rushees. At

172

their sidewalk, I hesitate and then, for some strange reason, keep on going down the hill.

At the Ace house, J.L. Simmons greets me in the hall with a big grin and welcome. "Five, glad you came back tonight. Have you hit all the houses so far?"

"I think so," I reply. "Not keeping count, really, but it sure seems like nineteen… maybe twenty five or so." J.L. guffaws at my little jest.

"C'mon Five, there's a guy I want you to meet." He leads me down the hall and we turn left into a big room with rounded, windowed walls. "There he is. Hey, Mark?" Mark is a short, thin guy whose face is plastered with freckles, what you can see of it beneath his mop of blond hair. "Mark Husted, this is Five Lowrey, the guy I was telling you about last night."

"Hi, Five. I'm hearing some good things about you. Let's have a seat over here." He gives me a warm handshake and leads me to a long, red leather couch facing the curving windows.

"This is a great room, Mark. What exactly is it?"

"We call it the sun porch. These windows come out and screens go up in the spring. It's really a comfortable room. I guess that's what guy who built this place had in mind. As you've probably noticed, the ACE house is pretty unusual."

"Sure is. Who did build it?"

"Man named Horner. Owned lots of land up around New Marshfield and New Straitsville, more over east of Athens. Rich old bastard and made even more with coal mines… 'til it all exploded out from under him."

"How so? What happened?"

"Well, he built this big old mansion. They called it 'Horner's Castle' back around the turn of the century. Story goes that he liked to sit here and watch his coal go by in the railroad cars down there.

"Then, one of his mines exploded and killed a bunch of people. Mine caught fire, burned 'em all up, a terrible thing. Still burning today, they say."

"I've been there! Over at Sharpsburg. It's called The Sharpsburg Hell."

"That's it. Really something, eh? Well anyway, ole' Horner

173

was a real gentleman, I guess for a rich guy. He tried to repay the families of those who were killed, sold his mines and land. Finally went broke and killed himself just before World War I. Shot himself right here in this very room."

"Damn," I respond, "that's an interesting story."

"Ahh, this old house has got lots of interesting stories. But tell me a little about yourself. I understand you're going to major in art…"

• • •

Wednesday morning's beautiful and unseasonably warm. So warm that several students can be seen on the College Green sunning themselves in shorts and t-shirts. In January! Even so, the steps of Mem Aud are cold under our fannies as Andy Logan and I sit smoking after Fine Arts Appreciation.

"Betas were pretty nice. And Sigma Nu," I add, recounting my impressions of rush so far, "but I think they were nice to me because I was with the Bear."

"Sigma Nu's are big jocks. They'll probably really go after the Bear," she says. "Any others you like?"

"Ahh, Andy, it's really hard to pin down, y'know. I think I feel most welcome — most comfortable — at the Ace house. I'm not sure why, I just do."

"Well my dad will certainly be glad to hear that," she smiles. "He's an Ace you know. Although he doesn't go by the house much any more. But I understand what you're saying about being comfortable." She pauses. "Don't ever tell mom this but… well, the Chi O's are great people and I like a lot of them. But they kind of treated me like a sure thing during rush. Just because I was a legacy."

"You mean you got to look at the books in the library a lot?"

"Oh Five, you've been there! Exactly right. They just seemed to spend more time and… more effort on other girls." Another pause for reflection. "I didn't feel that way at the Pi Phi house. Like you, I felt more comfortable. More at home."

I find this encouraging. "I met a nice guy at ACE last night. He told me a lot about their old house. It's a neat place."

"I've never been in it," she responds. "What's his name?"

"Mark Husted."

"I know Mark Husted! Of course I do. And you don't? He's got some work hanging over in the Center gallery right now. Come on! Let's go take a look at it."

• • •

"Some guy named Stettin or Sutton called. Said he met you at the Beta house Monday and was just wondering if you were coming by there tonight?" Toby looks up from his books. "I kind of remember him," he ponders. "Sounds like the Betas are interested in you, Five."

I respond that it's interesting, especially since that the Betas have one of the lower membership dues, along with Aces and someone else. About nineteen dollars a month. "How 'bout you, Tobe? Anyone dangling any hooks?"

"Ahh, I haven't been kicked out of the Phi Delt house yet. Maybe tonight? And a couple of guys at the SAE house have made some comments that are sort of interesting, especially to a guy like me dressed like Henry High School."

"Listen, Tobe? I was wondering… what if I…"

• • •

"Hello, Five. It's good to see you again," Mark Husted says sincerely, arching his eyebrows at my outfit as I climb the steps to the ACE house.

I felt pretty ridiculous at the Beta house when I entered and met Dave Stettin again. But he seemed gracious and genuinely interested in talking with me, despite the fact that I was draped in one of Toby's more conservative one-button roll coats. I figure wearing Toby's coat is as good a test of earnestness in a fraternity as any.

"That's an… ah, interesting jacket you've got on," Husted remarks with a little grin. "I've seen a couple of other guys wearing them during rush. Am I missing out on a trend or something?"

175

"No. I ripped the lining of my other sport coat," I reply sheepishly. "My roomie loaned me one of his. It *is* a little different, I guess."

With the jacket issue settled, Mark takes me around the house, sort of a tour, where I meet more of the ACE brotherhood. Mark hastens to explain the strange, long coat with its peaked shoulder pads and narrow lapels as being my emergency measure for rush. The guy named Curtis gives me a really strange stare.

From one bedroom, I see a building below I hadn't noticed before. "What's that building, Mark? Is it part of Ace house?"

"Oh, that's the Temple Court. Our lodge building. When you're initiated, you'll attend meetings there, all the secret activities that ACE takes part in." *When I'm initiated? What's he telling me?*

• • •

Because it's my night off from rush, Duff has given Darcy Thursday off as well. We're walking home after the OU Theater production of *The Glass Menagerie.*

"God, Five, but that was wonderful! *'Blow out your candles, Laura.'* I could be 'Laura,' Five, couldn't I?" She slides her arm out of mine and imitates Laura's limping walk across stage in the final scene.

"Yeah, Darce. You would be a great Laura." She puts her arm in mine again and snuggles closer. "How 'bout a cup of coffee. Hot chocolate? Here's the Frontier Room."

After coffee, we walk upstairs through the Center gallery and look at Mark Husted's paintings, a special one-man show and rare honor for a student artist. "Pretty strange stuff," she muses. "Dark. Spooky. Look at this one." It's an oil that shows a nude man in a pose reminiscent of the Greek statue *The Discus Thrower.* Except this man is bathed in an eerie orange light and his body glistens with what might be blood. His extended arm holds not a discus, but what look to be strands of hair connected to something in the shadows.

"Strange," I agree, "and Mark doesn't seem that strange

when you talk to him."

"You know him? From where?"

"He's one of the guys I met at ACE. He's really a pretty nice guy and has taken a liking to me."

Walking up Union from the Center, a clap of thunder gives us three seconds of warning before sheets of rain come tearing down. We run for the corner and huddle under the bookstore's portico. Then dash across Court and shelter beneath the door of the College Inn. Giving it up, we make another dash down Union for the green door.

"Man, you could wring me out," Darcy says as she unlocks her door.

"Want me to?"

"No. We'd have to mop the place up. Take off your coat, your shoes. I've got to get into something dry." She grabs something from her chest of drawers and goes into the bathroom. Except for the bottoms of my pants, I'm fairly dry where my soggy topcoat protected me. I mop my soaked hair with her dish towel and flop on the couch/bed.

"Want some wine? A beer?" Darcy reappears in the lighted bathroom doorway. A pair of shiny track shorts and a baggy Ohio State t-shirt her new garb. Her thin figure is outlined through the shirt by the bathroom light.

"No thanks. Come here and I'll dry your hair."

"Not with my dish towel, fool. That's got to last til' next week." She grabs a towel from the bathroom and flicks out the light. Flopping on the couch, she curls into a ball and leans against me as I rub the towel through her short hair. The only light is from the rain-washed windows. I continue to work the towel over her head, then rub her thin shoulders.

"Mmmm, that feels good. Look't the windows, Five. Aren't they gorgeous?" Indeed they are. Great panels of smeary soft light, with streaks of hard color where drops run down the fogged surface. Below us, the flashing red light of a police car or ambulance momentarily adds to the show. "What's that?" Darcy says and leans over on her hands and knees to peer out the window from the end of the couch.

As she does, the t-shirt billows down and I can see her bare stomach and small, neat breasts in outline against the window light. It's the most sensual moment of my life.

"Darce! Don't move." She doesn't, except to slowly peer over her shoulder at me with a soft smile. I stare for several seconds, then close my eyes in concentration, burning that image into my mind forever.

• • •

Friday night's rush sees us going our separate ways. Toby at his most garish heads off for University Terrace to give the Sigma Chi's one last scare before heading for the Phi Delt house. Bear is on his way to Sigma Nu where it seems he'll certainly be a pledge. Wink and Mass are leaning toward the houses on State Street, Theta Chi, SAE. Stolski has several places to visit but announces he's leaning toward Acacia.

I visit the Beta house, dressed this time in my charcoal Ivy League suit. Dave Stettin and his brothers greet me warmly and introduce me to dozens of other rushees, more Beta brothers. Then I leave for ACE.

Horner's Castle is festive. A white spotlight plays on the ice-cream cone cap of its round tower. Other spots cast an orangish glow on the wide front porch, where I'm met by Mark Husted, Dave Gamble and other Aces.

"Hope you got your sport coat mended, Ace," Gamble says with a smile, "you gave us quite a fright last night."

"C'mon in, Five. We've got something new to show you."

Something new is another porch, directly beneath the sun porch, where long tables radiate from a circular bar toward the broad windows. Candles in wax-coated bottles sit on each table and provide the only illumination for the big room.

"The Betas may have their basement," Husted says, spreading his arms to the room before us. "The Aces have their 'Keep.' Welcome to one of the inner sanctums, Five. How 'bout a beer?"

From a frosty pony keg, ACE brothers are dispensing big wax cups of frothy beer. Gamble peers over his and offers a silent toast to me with a serious expression. From somewhere in the room, a voice shouts "Call for Pater Gousha!" And the room responses

Acer, Acer, raise them high!

Aces, Aces, till we die!

Aaaaaaah, Chiiiiiii... Aye!"

And glasses and bottles thump three times in syncopation. As quickly as it stopped, normal conversation resumes. Except for rushees, glasses and cups are empty.

Chet Lee takes my arm and turns me slowly. "Five, I want you to meet John Ehlers. J.E., this is Thomsen Lowrey the Fifth. From Hockingport. I know I've told you about him."

Ehlers is tall. Dark and handsome, Darcy or any of my other female friends would add. His voice is deep. Like a voice from the radio. "Hello, Five. I'm glad to extend my welcome to you."

Ehlers leads me to the large windows and suddenly I realize we're alone, looking at the lighted grounds of the asylum across the river. After a few seconds of silence, he says softly, "Five, a lot of people have told us some very good things about you. You should be gratified to have such friends."

"Uh, well, thanks. I am." *Who in hell's he talking about?* "I *have* made a lot of friends since I came to OU."

"Yes, college is the place to make good friends. Friends that shall last until your death," he continues solemnly. "I would like to think you would find those friends among these halls." He turns and stares at me solemnly. "Please give it a lot of thought." With that, he smiles a bit and turns where Husted and Lee are waiting, smiles on their faces.

"Well, ace, congratulations," Lee says. "I certainly hope we'll see you here tomorrow night."

Husted shakes my hand with warm sincerity. "Let's find a quiet place to sit, Five. I'll bet you have some questions you want answered."

• • •

I'm the first back to Biddle and sit quietly in the darkened 205, my mind awash with thoughts. But soon, Toby returns, followed by Mass and Winkler, then Stolski. Mass and Winkler both want to go SAE but each has his doubts about whether a bid will be coming. Stolski is pretty sure he'll get a bid from Acacia. I keep my counsel. Toby does not.

"You shoulda seen their fuckin' faces when I appear. 'Here I am brothers,' I announce, 'Toby Wolfe, Phi Delta Theta legacy and ready to go!' There's this one guy, Van Sawder, looks kinda like an owl with big ole' horn rims. He looked like he'd swallowed a popsicle whole, sticks 'n all!" Toby chortles and clutches his one-button rolled stomach. "What a scene. I'll bet they're up there right now, shittin' in their hats. Wait'll tomorrow night."

The Bear never does show up at 205.

• • •

On Saturday morning, Toby and I walk over to the cafeteria for coffee and donuts. He's still shaking with laughter at his show at the Phi Delt house last night.

"Tobe, do they *have to* take you? I mean, what if someone blackballs you?"

"Blackball me? Five, do you have any idea how rich my old man is? The Phi Delts blackball me and he'll buy their stinkin' house and flush it down the hill," he hoots again. "Listen, let's go up town and so some shopping. I've got to buy some clothes for tonight."

Figuring that Toby buying new clothes will be a spectacle, I agree to follow along. We hike up the hill toward Court Street. First stop, Kyles. Then Beckley's. Nothing but the best for the ole' Grey Wolfe.

In Kyles, Toby picks out two tweed sport coats, several button-down shirts, two or three rep ties and a pair of bucks. "Christ, look how white these mothers are," he exclaims over the bucks. "I'll have to spend all afternoon dirtying them up."

We enter Beckley's with me carrying Toby's boxes like a

faithful bearer. "C'mon, Five. Try this coat on," he says, displaying a handsome Ivy League gray tweed sport coat. I look at its price tag. Seventy five dollars.

"No thanks, Tobe. Out of my league."

"Bullshit, Five. Mamma Wolfe wants you to have it."

"No way, Toby. I can't let you… or Mamma Wolfe… do that."

"Jesus H. Christ, Five. If it hadn't been for you and your closed mouth, Stacy and I would be out of school right now. Mamma owes you one."

He continues to cajole until I try the tweedy coat on. Fits like a glove. I grin at him. "No. Cannot do it, Toby."

"Done and did. Sold!" he calls to the salesman. "And how 'bout some khakis to go with it?" I try on a pair of polished chino khakis with a strap and buckle on the back while Toby rummages through the spinning ring of rep ties. "Here's a great tie, Five. Bronze and gold. Would look great at the Ace house tonight. Those're their colors."

"What say guys? How're you doing? Hi Toby. Hello Five." It's Dave Stettin, standing there with hands in pockets, smiling at the two of us. "Maybe you'll want a blue and red rep tie also, Five. Beta colors are pink and blue but blue and red would look good on you, as well."

I can feel myself blushing. "Maybe it would, Dave. What're you doing here?"

"Just some Saturday morning shopping. Will I see you at the Beta house tonight? Sure hope so?" He tilts his head quizzically. "And say, Toby, I hear you made quite an impression on the Phi Delts last night. Congratulations." Without another word, he turns and leaves the store.

"Looks like you've got a Beta bird dog, Five. I'll bet you see him again before the afternoon is out."

In less than an hour, Mamma Wolfe has spent over five hundred dollars and Toby resembles the guy I remember from *Esquire.* Come to think of it, I do too. With my new sport coat, khakis, two rep ties, a pair of bronze and gold argyle socks, and a skinny umbrella.

"Gotta have an umbrella, Five. It's the latest. Makes sense in

Athens, too. Don't you read *Esquire,* man? Where's your fashion sense?"

• • •

Toby industriously blows the powdered charcoal from my drawing box onto the new bucks, then pats them with a handkerchief. On my bed, Dense sprawls in his slacks and sport coat, both a mass of wrinkles. Heavy stubble blankets his jaw and his eyes are shot with red.

"So I woke up this morning," he groans, "and I'm on my back behind this couch somewhere. Shit. Somewhere is the Sigma Nu living room. Shit. Fuck. Oh my. I don't have the damnedest idea what I'm doing there. But I think I had a good time last night."

It's mid afternoon and the Bear just staggered into 205. "Can I borrow some toothpaste, Five?" He squirts a worm of toothpaste on his finger and then squishes it across his teeth, around his mouth. "Ahh," he sighs, "I think some Sigma Nu must've taken a dump in there. That's better."

"So? I can take it you're going Sigma Nu?" Toby asks, patting his bucks which are taking on an overall gray hue.

"Going? Fuck Wolfe, I think I've already gone."

• • •

No one at the Beta house pays attention to my bronze and gold rep tie but Dave Stettin. His reaction is just a twitched eyebrow. He leads me into their little library room and we sit on a red leather couch. *I wish I owned a red leather couch factory.*

"Five," Stettin says, "this is Brother Fleming Tewksbury. And you already know Brother Kinslo." I shake hands with Tewksbury and Kinslo.

"Hi, Jake. Good to see you again."

"Five," Tewksbury says in a high, shrill voice. "We have a very important meeting tonight. And I have reason to believe your name will be brought up. We would like to know… if it is brought up… if you look favorably upon Beta Theta Pi if a bid is forthcoming."

"Favorably?" I pause. "Uh yeah, favorably. You guys have really been great to me. I think it's a good fraternity. No doubt. Yes, I do. Uhh, favorably. I guess so. I would have to think about it." *Jesus. Will I never shut up? Stop babbling fool. Quiet!*

"Hmmm, think about it?" Kinslo muses. "Does that mean you're thinking about other houses, Five?"

"Err, well, yes. I guess I am."

Stettin leans in. "Do you have any questions about Beta, Five? Any doubts?"

"Uh, no. You've done a good job of answering my questions. I think I could afford it, f'instance."

"Can you appreciate, Five?" Tewksbury leans in, "what it means to be a member of a Miami Triad fraternity? To enjoy the benefits of brotherhood in one of the oldest fraternities in the world? Certainly the finest?"

I try to remember what the Miami Triad is. I've heard it mentioned one, two other places. The conversation continues. And continues. Earnest. Serious. Am I being hotboxed?

Finally, Stettin sighs and looks at Tewksbury. "I think we had better let Thomsen here give our discussion some thought, don't you Brother Tewksbury?" Tewksbury nods, then solemnly takes my hand.

"Please give it serious thought, Five. It could be the most serious decision you'll ever make in your life."

• • •

"Five! It's an honor... and a pleasure for me... to be the one to ask you to tender your pledge to Alpha Chi Epsilon," Husted says. I've entered the Ace house door and been hustled right to a little room with lots of heavy chairs and a television set. J.E. Ehlers smiles and shakes his head positively in the background.

"We're asking you to become a pledge, Five," Ehlers says. "To join the search for the truth and light of our Order." I can only stare in wonder. After the session at the Beta house, this is a punch to the gut.

"You can give us your answer right now," Husted offers, "or

you can wait and we will repeat it in the morning."

Ehlers takes over. "If your answer is affirmative, Five, you will be one of the first members of your pledge class. And if it is yes, you will have your first Alpha Chi Epsilon secret to keep, for bids cannot officially be offered until tomorrow."

"But we want you with us, Five. We really mean it, man." Husted leans toward me, peers into my eyes. "It's an important thing to us. To you, Five."

Numbly, I blink to keep tears from welling. I look at the floor between my knees. My thoughts are a whirl. Who can I talk to? *Time out while I run up to the Begorra and check with my girl?* The little room reeks with silence and tension. I look up and gulp.

"Yes."

"Good man," Ehlers slaps me on the shoulder. "Good man. Great choice." Husted pumps my hand, his face totally wiped with a big smile.

"Welcome to the club," he says as he continues to waggle my hand. "This one time only. Because you can never call it a club again."

• • •

In a small room off the Keep, I join two other guys I recognize as rushees. Though we've been introduced, their names are blanks to me. They rise as Husted says, "Gentlemen, may I introduce this man as the third member of The Thirteen? Thomsen Lowrey the Fifth. Five. Five's agreed to become one of your number."

"Joe Ransom, Five. Congratulations."

"Clark McClintock, Five. Welcome aboard."

We shake hands and Husted hands me a glass. "Booze and mix on the bar there. Beer in the 'frig, Five. Make yourselves at home but stay in here, if you don't mind." He stops at the door. "And keep sober. We might need your help later on."

McClintock, a stocky guy with brown, well-combed hair, leads me to the bar. I choose a beer and to drink it from the bottle. "So where you from, Five? You a legacy?"

"Uh, place called Hockingport. Down on the river." Pause. "No. I'm not."

They look at me in astonishment. "You're not?" Ransom asks. "No shit?"

"Nope. Didn't even know I was gonna pledge anywhere until about six minutes ago." They continue to stare. I resist the urge to check for my fly being open.

We drink, smoke and talk. Warm in the glow of belonging, in knowing that beyond the door in the Keep, others are being rushed. Others who may join our number.

• • •

When Terry Simpson enters the room with his "keeper," McClintock jumps up with a grin. "All right, Terrence. You're a good man."

Simpson grins back. "Did you ever doubt, Mac?"

The keeper goes through the formalized introduction and we all shake hands. Terry is tall with a blond crew cut that makes him almost bald looking and emphasizes ears that seem designed to detect enemy aircraft.

"Guess what? Terry," McClintock points at me, "Five here isn't a legacy. Ain't that some shit?"

"No stuff, Five? They must've really wanted you bad," Simpson responds. "Congratulations."

"Don't get the bighead, Five," Ransom chuckles. "My dad told me a lot about this pledge stuff. We'll be hot shit for a couple of days and then, bamm!" He punches his fist into his hand.

• • •

By the time our number reaches ten, we're woozy with drink, smoked out and pensive at having been cooped up for hours. Each time a new man is introduced, his keeper goes through the same routine. "The fifth member of The Thirteen. The seventh member of The Thirteen." We're beginning to get the picture.

Our talk is general. Getting to know each other. Prying for what each of us knows about ACE. We're Ransom, McClintock, Lowrey, Simpson, Smith, Able, West, Waller (who turns out to be the son of my friend ROTC Sergeant Waller), Kostic (who seems a bit older and wiser), Salazar and Shivers.

The door opens again. Another keeper appears with a kid who looks slightly familiar. Light hair. Freckles. "Gentlemen, may I introduce this man as the twelfth member of The Thirteen? Chester Steven Husted. Chet has agreed to become one of your number." It has to be Mark's brother. Then, speak of the devil and Mark pops through the door.

"Five, we've got a little problem. Can you help me?" He beckons me out of the room. My heart sinks. I don't want to leave me pledge brothers.

"Relax, Five. It's just ah… well, there's a guy upstairs and… ah, he says he knows you. Could you take a look at him for us?"

"Sure!" I start for the stairs at the far end of the Keep.

"Wait! We'll take the back stairs." Mark leads me to a dark panel set between two huge support beams, pushes on one of the beams and steps back as the panel revolves. *Holy shit! A secret passage!*

I follow his butt up the narrow stairs, lit by tiny orange lamps jutting from the wall. They're designed to look like candles. We go right by the first landing and climb to the second floor, emerging on a horseshoe-shaped landing that overlooks the central hallway.

"Stay back from the railing," Mark whispers. "Over there in that group by the door. The guy in the blue suit and glasses. Has his back to his right now."

I see who he's talking about and the figure does look familiar. One of the others in the group looks up and nods slightly in our direction, then takes the guy's elbow and turns him gently to direct his conversation in another direction. Holy shit!

"Yes. I know him. His name is Chris Cobb." *It's the Martian!*

"Great," Husted says. His expression doesn't say great.

"Come in here. He pushes me into an adjoining room where J.E. Ehlers and the guy I recall as Gamble sit; Ehlers behind a study desk, Gamble on a bunk. "He knows him, brothers. Five, tell us what you know about this guy."

"Well, he's really a pretty neat guy," I start, "although at first glance, well…"

"Yeah, we know," Ehlers says glumly. "Go on."

"Ah, well he's from Blue Ball." They simultaneously cringe. "Ah, it's near Middletown. And he knows this really neat girl who pledged Pi Phi." Again I halt. How much do they expect? From the silence, I can sense Ehlers urging me to continue. "And he rooms with a guy from my hometown." The wince again. "He's Denzel Duerhoff. The Bear. Played freshman football."

"No shit?" Gamble leans forward. "The guy the Sigma Nu's wrapped up last night," he says to the others.

"I think so," I contribute. "Bear, that's Dense… er, that's Denzel," they shake their heads at me impatiently, "he nicknamed him The Martian, Chris I mean. And he seems to take it, Chris I mean, pretty well. He's got a good sense of humor."

"And fanfuckingtastic handwriting, I'll bet," Gamble grouses.

"Well," I continue, "he's a hard worker. Works in the East Green Barfeteria." They smile. "And he's always surprising us with something new. Like he can play the livin' shit out of a clarinet."

"What?" Gamble screams. "He's a musician? Oh holy sainted Acerbus, a musician!" Ehlers is grinning broadly. So's Gamble. I turn to Mark and he also has a big grin.

"Five. I think you've been a big help," Ehlers says. "Thanks a lot. Mark'll take you back to join your pledge brothers."

We pause on the landing overlooking the hallway. The Martian is still down there, talking expansively, waving his skinny arms in their shiny blue suit jacket.

"What was that all about, Mark? He really is a pretty neat guy."

"Well, Five. That ugly fucker marched in here tonight for the first time and announced he is an ACE legacy. We checked the rolls and God help us, he certainly is. Take a good look, Five. He'd better play that mean clarinet because that skinny bastard is about to become number thirteen of The Thirteen."

• • •

It's way past three in the morning before I drift off. Not drunk but not willing to risk waking Darcy up, I walk past the green door with several of the other pledge brothers, Chris Cobb among us, back to East Green. Doug Smith, the tall drum major from West Virginia, halts once to vomit into the bushes by the library.

I feign sleep when Toby rolls in but to no avail. "I'm in Five, I'm in." He capers around the room. "For it's Phi Delta Theta..." he sings, "just one hell of a fraternity..."

"Please Tobe, that's great. Really great. But please lock the door and let me go to sleep. I've got to be up in a few hours."

"You do? Why, for God's sake?"

"Cause I'm in, too, Ace. I'm in too!"

• • •

We're a strange sight. Thirteen young, disheveled men filing across the College Green, led by J.E. Ehlers who is dressed in tuxedo tails, a tall, black top hat with a leopard fur band, and carrying a drum major's baton taller than he is. At the rear is David Gamble, also dressed in a black tuxedo but wearing a strange hat with a flat crown and broad brim. Across the brim dangles a red ribbon. Around his neck he wears a strip of leopard skin which suspends a large, battered gray key.

During our strange parade, the Bataan march comes to mind. I'm wearing an OU sweatshirt grabbed off Toby's dirty clothes pile, a pair of warm-up pants and my penny loafers without socks. Mark Husted allowed me thirty seconds to gather these up and get them on.

Although others of our number are dressed in a similar manner, Waller is in olive drab shorts and matching underwear shirt and barefoot while Salazar sports bright pink pajamas and a pair of flopping mule slippers. Ben Kostic is dressed for battle: fatigue pants bloused into combat boots, an undershirt similar to Waller's and a flat-topped army hat of some sort.

In silence, J.E. turns us in a large semi-circle in the shadow of the main campus gate. Over the tops of Court Street buildings, we can see the stronger light from approaching dawn. Ehlers takes his place before our half circle, both hands grasping the baton placed before him, his feet wide apart. He stares straight ahead sternly. Gamble stands somewhere to our rear with the 'keepers' who followed in our wake. Minutes go by and a small crowd of early-risers assembles on the sidewalk beyond the hedges.

We fidget in the chill morning, looking at each other, at Ehlers, but none daring to speak. Finally... Ehlers pulls the baton toward him and brings his feet together.

"Tiler, how goes the day?" he calls out in a loud, strange voice.

From behind us, Gamble calls, "Acer, comes the dawn and thirteen supplicants."

"Well spoken, Tiler." Ehlers pauses again, then moves to his right to stand about four feet in front of Ransom who led our march across the campus. He raises the baton high above his right shoulder and with ponderous slowness, brings it down to rest upon Ransom's left shoulder.

"Joseph Eric Ransom. You have been chosen to journey in search of the truth and light of the teachings of Acerbus. How say you?"

Ransom gulps, then speaks as we had been coached. "I accept."

"Clark Sims McCormick. You have been chosen to journey in search of the truth and light of the teachings of Acerbus. How say you?"

"I accept, sir."

"Thomsen Lowrey the Fifth. You have been chosen to journey in search of the truth and light of the teachings of Acerbus. How say you?"

"I accept."

The ceremony continues until the tall Ehlers stands before

the scrawny figure of The Martian. Since he's at the far end of the circle, I see the whole spectacle. The graceful swoop of the baton upon the Martian's shoulder. The Martian, standing there in the Bear's warm-ups which droop down his legs and hide his feet, stares into the eyes of the tall ACE man.

"Christopher Watson Cobb. You have been chosen to journey in search of the truth and light of the teachings of Acerbus. How say you?"

"I accept."

Ehlers then moves back to the front of our arc and raises the baton high above his head with both arms. He looks like a successful weight lifter.

"It is my pleasure to present The Thirteen of Alpha Chi Epsilon. Come to this place this day as thirteen individuals. Leave this place this day as one!"

PART 2

Chapter 15

The Thirteen As One

Darcy and I would become lovers. That unspoken pact floats between us, a sweet promise. And it is the most recurring of the jumble of thoughts in my mind on that first day of my pledgeship to Alpha Chi Epsilon.

With the abrupt end of our pledging ceremony, Ehlers turned and marched away toward the Ace house. Gamble moves down our line from the Martian, shaking our hands and depositing a tiny velvet envelope in each of our hands.

"Gentlemen. Welcome to the first plateau of Alpha Chi Epsilon. For those of you who can't remember... or aren't quite awake, I am Dave Gamble. As you heard, I am called the Tiler. Throughout the day, you may hear of my job referred to as "pledge master" or something similar from friends who've pledged other fraternities.

"However, to you I am the Tiler. As your pledgeship progresses, you will learn this first item of ACE lore." He paused. "Each of you has received his pledge badge. All you need to know at this time is that it is worn over your left breast and is never worn with sloppy clothing. Wear it proudly today and tomorrow and we'll discuss it in more detail tomorrow night."

I grip the fuzzy bag more tightly. Gamble continues, "For today and most of tomorrow, you will not come to the Ace house. Your first pledge meeting will be tomorrow evening at seven o'clock — sharp! Wear suits and ties for we'll take photographs." He pauses, looks us over one last time and says, "until then. Walk in the light."

• • •

Emotions are mixed at the cafeteria for Sunday's brunch.

Shaved and decked out in khakis, dress shirt and crew neck sweater to display my ACE pledge badge, I join my friends at a long table.

"Welcome, Five! What did you do?" Bear roars at me. He's dressed in a black sweatshirt with *Sigma Nu* in block letters across his chest. I smile shyly and turn to display the little triangular badge, its three sides bulging out. Upon the bronze field, an abstract shape of white is covered by another smaller shape of black.

"ACE! By God!" Toby exults. "Congratulations, Ace! I guess that's what you were mumbling about this morning? When did you get your pin? We get ours this afternoon."

Winkler rises and shakes my hand. "Theta Chi," he says. "It's great to be a Greek."

Massman has a strange grin as he rises, "Phi Tau. I guess the East Green gang's sort of splitting up, isn't it? And Stolski's gone Acacia." Stolski isn't here.

I pour a cup of coffee and take a seat by Dense. "Where's the Martian?" I ask softly. "I thought he'd be here... or working."

"Still sacked out when I got up. Do you know the little shit went rushing last night? His first night? The last night of rush?"

"Yeah! I heard," I say softly.

• • •

I call the Begorra but no one answers the ring. For some reason, I'm reluctant to walk up town and confront Darcy at home with my Ace badge. Instead, I confront her on paper. Throughout the afternoon I work to transform her image from my mind to the sketchpad. Dozens of sheets are torn out, wadded up. Progress comes in slow, labored steps, each signified by a ball of crumpled paper in my wastebasket.

It's well past three when I finally fold the cover on the sketchpad, wash my face and climb the Bryan steps. The campus is busy with young men in sweaters, swaggering around and flaunting their pledge pins. My badge is on my sweater, hidden beneath my windbreaker.

194

"Hey, Five, how you doin?" Duff greets me from the counter. "Darcy," he yells to the back room, "your guy's here." Darcy emerges through the kitchen doors, leans over the counter and gives me a quick kiss.

"Y'all busy?" I ask, returning her smooch.

"Does it look like it?" Duff responds. "Deader'n hell all afternoon."

"Ah, then, Duff?" He looks up. "Would it be OK if I stole Darcy for about an hour?"

"Sure, kid. Take her away. She's just clutterin' up the kitchen anyway," he grins. Darcy grabs her car coat and we leave the diner.

"What's up, Five? You hung over? Duff said you would be," she grins as she slips her arm through mine and we stroll toward the campus. I don't respond with anything but idle chatter, steering her toward the vacant lot near the Sigma Chi house. We sit on the stone bench overlooking the river. She scrunches closer and shivers.

"I've got something I want you to look at," I say, holding out the sketch pad. "Open it up." She lifts the cover gingerly and stares intently at the sketch for a few seconds.

"Ohh, Five! It's… it's really fine. Ohh, it's me!" She grabs my arm and looks into my face with round, wide eyes. "It is me, isn't it? Oh! Did I look like that? Oh my God!"

"It's you all right," I respond, nuzzling her cheek with a kiss. "I drew it from memory. I'll never forget…" but I stop. "I'm not really happy with it, though. It's not quite right."

"No! It's marvelous." She stares harder at the sketch as if to find something hidden in its penciled line. "Well," she shrugs, "my butt *does* look a little big. And my… breasts? They were showing like that? I didn't realize!" I suddenly grasp that she's serious. *She didn't realize.*

"But it's me," she squeals, "it's really me. Look at that smile. Did I really have that smile. I look… *ornery!* Wicked?"

"Oh, yes. You were beautiful! But it's still not quite what I'm after. I'm going to do another one."

"You are? Can I have this one? Ohh, please?" Again, she pauses and looks hard at the sketch. "Five? Would you… ah, would you like for me to...?"

"Pose for me? Would you? I mean, I wouldn't ask if..."

Darcy throws her arms around my chest inside the windbreaker. "Would I? Of course I would, silly! But... only if I can keep this one." The squeezes me hard and plants another kiss on my lips. "But ohh? What's this?" She pulls her hand back and slowly opens the lapel of my jacket.

"What's that, Five? It stuck my hand."

"Ahh, it's my pledge badge, Darce. I pledged ACE last night."

Darcy looks into my eyes again and blinks. "You did? You really did? Are you happy, Five?"

"Darce, I don't think I've ever been happier in my life." She gives me another rib-crushing hug.

"Then I think it's wonderful. It's a pretty little thing," she exclaims softly. "What's it supposed to be?"

"I'm really not sure. But I'll find out at our pledge meeting tomorrow night, I guess."

Walking back toward Begorra with arms around each other's waist, Darcy chatters away. "Oh Five, I'm so excited. You'll just be the best fraternity man ever. And you're going to do a great drawing. *We're* going to do a great drawing." I nod my agreement and kiss her once more, causing us to stumble on the sidewalk.

"Tell you what," she says. "When you pick up your burgers tonight, I'll drive you down to the Green and then we'll go back to my place and get started. All right?"

"Sounds fine to me, Darce."

• • •

Except for the lack of rain on the windows, Darcy's apartment is the same as it was the previous Thursday night. In her sloppy shorts and baggy t-shirt, she smooches me then flops onto the bed on her hands and knees facing the windows.

"Like this?" The shirt bags down and her breasts are exposed. I experience an instant erection. "Is this about the same pose?"

196

"Not quite," I gasp. "Move your butt a little to the right. A little more. And this leg," I gently grasp her left ankle, "should be a little over here." I realize I'm too close to her on the end of the bed to really get the perspective I want. "Wait a sec'," I say. "Let me get a chair." I drag over one of the kitchen chairs and sit upon it at the end of the bed. "That's perfect."

Taking up the sketch pad, I realize that its surface is in pitch blackness. "Crap," I mutter, "can't see. Perhaps if I turn on the bathroom light." With the light on and the door barely open, I have enough light to see the pad. Darcy hasn't moved, still looking straight ahead. I cross my legs tightly and use the pad to hide my condition. Then start to draw.

"Don't forget now, Five. My butt can't be as big," she says with a giggle.

Amazingly, as my pencil moves across the paper, the erection subsides. Her bottom, not so big this time, and her legs emerge from my mind. Dabny's foreshortening lessons are coming through! Trying to just capture the outlines, I work quickly, limning in her arms, the billow of the t-shirt.

"OK. Relax. Let's take a break for a second." Darcy bounces up from the bed and moves behind me.

"All right. I can see what you mean," she says, throwing her arms around me. I can feel her soft breasts through the thin t-shirt. I stop drawing.

"Five. Do you, ah…" her breasts feel like hot coals against my back. "Would you like to… ah?"

"No, Darce. I want to get this drawing done."

"You sure?" she whispers in my ear. *Christ! Am I sure? Of course I'm not sure.*

"Please, Darce, let's get back at it. Please?"

"Well… all right," she says in a little girl pout. "If you insist!"

Darcy flops right back into the pose as if she'd never moved.

"Now. This time look over your shoulder at me. I have to get your head and your face." Her head turns and that *ornery* smile appears. "Hold still now, hon. This'll take a while."

"Oh I hope so, Five," she whispers. "A really, really long time."

• • •

The Thirteen, minus Kostic who lives in an apartment somewhere off campus, walk as a group across the College Green to our first pledge meeting. I'm beside the Martian who's wearing his blue serge suit again. Each of us has our pledge pin on his lapel.

At the Ace house, the main hall is empty except for Gamble, who greets us warmly and leads us into the living room. Kostic's waiting there, Ivy League in a brown tweed suit.

"All right gentlemen, let's get to work. Tonight begins your next step on the path to the truth and light of Alpha Chi Epsilon." Gamble holds up a thin bronze colored book. "This is *The Shining Path,* your pledge manual. Through the weeks and months to come, *The Path* will be your guide to the lessons you must learn before you can hope to be admitted to our order.

"First of all, as pledges you will never address an active member of this order as 'brother,' either here in the house or in public. Each Ace is to be addressed within the house as 'mister' and his last name. In public and at social functions here, you can call any of the brothers by whatever name he tells you to use. Understood?" We nod in agreement, scribbling into our notebooks.

"I am to be addressed within the house as 'Tiler.' In ancient lore, the Tiler is the gatekeeper and that is my role with you, the Thirteen. I am your guardian, your teacher, and the entity who shall keep you from crossing the bar into our order. Until you are ready.

"As Tiler, I will often seem to be your only friend within this order. *I am your friend.* But more importantly, I am an Acer and any of you whom I judge not fit to cross the bar, I shall serve in my duty and prevent your passage. Is that clear?" Again, solemn nods from the Thirteen.

"Your pledge badge is called the 'roseate.' I know you've looked at them carefully. As you can see, there is neither up nor down to the badge. When you wear the badge, one of the points should point toward your head. The formlessness of the roseate symbolizes the formlessness that each of you has in ACE lore.

"You are called the Thirteen because that is by tradition your number of members. You are brothers within the Thirteen. And as brothers, you shall act as one. ALWAYS!" We jump at this shouted command. "As the Thirteen, you shall become one in your thoughts, your actions, your deeds. And you shall share the responsibility for those thoughts, actions, deeds, as one." We share furtive glances with each other. Ransom gives me a wink.

"Now," the Tiler continues, "every fraternity on this friggin' campus calls itself 'the singing fraternity.' Thirteen. That. Is. A. Bunch. Of. Crap!!! ACE is the singing fraternity!" We start again. "So, turn to page three of *The Path* and we'll start learning…"

• • •

By nine thirty, we've learned two songs and the response to "Call for Pater Gousha" and a bunch of other stuff. I think. Plus we're supposed to have the Greek alphabet memorized by next Monday and know as many of the brothers' names as we can.

"Some last things," Tiler continues. *Does this guy never run down?* "You will be here every Thursday night for study hall. Three hours every Thursday. Got that? And you're getting off easy this week. No Friday night work party. But there will be a work party Saturday morning… nine o'clock sharp. Wear old clothes to work in.

"And finally, Saturday night is your first Ace party. It's the 'Queens To Open' party and if you want to, you can dress up like a riverboat gambler. Dates are mandatory. If you don't have a girlfriend, or someone you are going out with, we'll get you fixed up between now and then. Questions?"

Frank Able, the muscled guy from Cleveland, speaks up. "Can you be someone's big brother, Tiler?"

"No. I cannot. But you are free to ask any other brother in the house with the exception of Acer."

"Acer?" the Martian asks.

"J.E. Ehlers. He's the Acer. He's the president of the order. Anything else?"

West, the guy with the southern accent, raises his hand but his question is cut off…

"PLEDGES! Where'n hell are the fuckin' pledges? Pledges! Get your goddamn worthless asses out here!" A squat guy with short black hair that grows down toward his eyebrows bursts into the room. He's nearly purple in the face with rage. "Goddamn pledges! Are these them, Tiler?" Gamble nods yes with a grin. "Then you dumb shits get your butts down the stairs. Right now. On the double!!!"

We bolt for the door past this madman. The hall is filled with Aces, yelling and hollering, forming a pathway for us to follow toward the stairs to the Keep. The monkey-looking maniac chases behind us screaming at the top of his lungs. "Dumb fuckers. Worthless turds. Move it! Move it!" We move it.

Mac nudges me as we tumble down the stairs. "We're in for it now, Five," he grimaces.

But the Keep is much as it was on Saturday night. Festooned with bottled candles. The actives roar into the room behind us.

"Aces high! Aces high!" someone yells.

Another voice chimes in. "Pledges. Asses to the fore. Attack that pony keg!"

$$\bullet\ \bullet\ \bullet$$

"Way to go, Five. You're a drinker, my man," someone whose name is a blank thumps me on the bicep. I've just been beaten in the semi-finals of the pledge chugging contest and my stomach is churning with beer. I flop on a bench beside Mark Husted and grab for a cigarette.

"God, Mr. Husted. You guys carry on like this all the time?" I gasp.

"All the time, Five. All the time." He laughs and lifts his cup in toast. "But call me Mark when the beer light is on, Five."

"Say Mark, I've been meaning to ask you. Could you be my big brother? I mean, would you?"

"Five, I'd love to. I think you really have a great future. But I can't. I'm a senior and I won't be here next year. I wouldn't be here for initiation… if you make it." My face must show my obvious disappointment. "Not such a big deal," he continues, gripping my arm. "I'll be here to help. When you need it. And I'll help you find a big brother, don't worry about that."

• • •

It's long past midnight when we wobble up President Street past the darkened Begorra. *Oh shit, I've missed my hamburger run.* The black campus rings with shouts and hoots. Fraternity pledges stumble and stagger from many directions toward Mulberry hill or the Bryan steps. Nearly every bit of me has survived my first fraternity meeting. My stomach isn't so sure.

• • •

Andy Logan and I compare chest ornaments in our seats at Fine Arts Appreciation. Her glittering diamond-crusted pin is now replaced with a plain gold Pi Phi arrow. She smiles and whispers, "Gee, I'm so pleased for you, Five. You've got to show dad after class. He'll be tickled."

Indeed, Professor Logan *does* seem pleased. He gives me a hearty handshake and a big smile. "Congratulations, Five. It's a fine order and I'm sure you'll do well… and enjoy the experience."

"Thanks, professor," I return. I've never been on the stage of Mem Aud before. Its empty seats seem to loom to infinity in the darkness.

"If ever you need some brotherly advice, and I mean this sincerely, please call on me," he says warmly.

"I shall sir. Oh, I will."

• • •

No Wednesday MIA movie tonight. Darcy greets me at the door in The Uniform, shorts and tattered Ohio State t-shirt. She throws her arms around me and stands on tip-toe to kiss me firmly. The tips of her breasts are hard against my chest. *Instant tumescence.* "Ohh Five, are you ready to go?" she whispers in my ear. "I am. C'mon in." *Ready to go. Keep this up and I'll have gone. Right in my pants.*

She grabs my hand and leads me through the door. "What do you think?" she says, sweeping an arm grandly. Her room is different. Several posters are gone from the wall above the table and there, matted and in a frame of bronze and gold, is my original drawing. "Isn't it wonderful? I'm so pleased with it, Five. Didn't it turn out beautifully?"

My first work of art hung upon a wall. I gulp back a pain in my throat looking at it. It is wonderful. "God, Darce. It's just… ohh, grand." I hug her to me, careful to avoid my frontal area.

She already has the bathroom door adjusted for backlight. She switches off the overhead light and hops into The Pose. I pick up the big sketch pad and poise my pencil. The swelling slowly eases.

Again I work swiftly, for she can't hold the over-her-shoulder pose too long without getting a cramp. I use my finger to smudge in shading on her breasts. Just touching their image causes that familiar movement in my groin. A kneaded eraser swipes away a highlight on her shoulder. It's foggy out tonight and the windows are steamy. No rivulets running down them but the light effect is right.

We work and work. She poses. I draw. She sweeps her arms around me and squeezes. We kiss. I swell and subside. I sweat. And gradually… the drawing takes shape as I had seen it on that rainy Thursday. Darcy sits on the edge of the bed, arms on her knees, feet flat on the floor. Her head drops. "Enough, Five. My neck is killing me."

"Oh, Darce, I'm sorry. You're right. Enough. My fingers are cramped." I move over beside her and place my hands on her slumped shoulders. I work my fingers up and down her shoulder blades. She drapes one arm over my thigh and droops dramatically.

"Five," she whispers huskily. "Five? Do you think…?"

"Yeah, Darce. I think…"

Chapter 16

Queens To Open

I don't know what we pledges expect from the Saturday morning work party. I arrive right on time. Should have, too, as I only have to walk two blocks. My leaden eyes and aching groin attest to what my life has been since Wednesday night.

On Thursday night, I stopped in Begorra after study hall to pick up my order of burgers. Tobe, who has no Phi Delt study table, took my orders and called them in to Duff. Duff trusts me for the money. Darcy, all smiles and a warm hug, says Duff is letting her off early and she's got the Ford out back to drive me to Biddle.

"Then we can come back and go to work," she whispers in my ear.

On Friday night, we worked some more. Posing. Drawing. Playing and exploring each other. Somewhere around two in the morning, we must've drifted off on her bed.

Because this morning, gray light came through the tall windows and I awoke to find the most amazing girl asleep on my arm. *I've slept all night with a girl! My arm is paralyzed! My bladder's bursting! I've got this awful erection.* Darcy *mmmphs* as I slide my arm from beneath her head and limp to the bathroom. My wristwatch shows five after eight. *God, nine o'clock sharp!*

My bladder convinces my erection of its place in line. I wash my face and run some of Darcy's toothpaste across my gums. She is up on one elbow in bed, the sheet pulled up to her shoulders. A sly smile is on her face. I duck back into the bathroom and flush the commode. I hadn't wanted to wake her.

"Hey love," she says in her 'wicked' voice, "what you doing up so early? And with pants on. C'mon back here. I'm cold."

"Darce!" My pants betray me. "I have a work party in fifty minutes."

"So what? D'ya think it'll take that long to get me warm?"

• • •

"Gee, Five. I was worried about you," the Martian says. "Toby said he didn't know what time you got in. Or left. But your bed was messed up so you must've been there."

"In late. Out early, Chris," I respond with a sheepish grin. "Had things to do."

"God, Five. Looks like you shaved with a lawnmower blade," "Dicky Reb" West says in his West Virginia drawl.

"Or a sharp thigh," Benjo Kostic says with a leer. Darcy's razor hasn't had a new blade in months. *How can her legs feel so smooth?*

Tiler appears on the stairs to the sun porch with Husted at his side. "OK, pledges," he calls, "we've got a lot of stuff to do before tonight's party. The sooner everyone pitches in, the sooner we can get out of here."

Husted points to me. "Five, I've got you for a detail. And you... Cobb? Whatta they call you? Martian?" The Martian nods yes and shows his keyboard teeth. "Any of you other guys know how to draw? Paint?" Kostic holds up his hand.

"I painted a lot in the Army, Mr. Husted," he says, "but I learned to never volunteer. Am I volunteering? Or being drafted?"

"Drafted," Mark laughs. "C'mon you guys, follow me." We hustle down the big stairs to the Keep where a full-fledged workshop is set up in the empty room. "Five, you and Kostic hang on for a second. Martian?" He looks again at Cobb and grins. "Martian, all right. Come over here."

Cobb follows Husted over to the wall nearest the window where an upright piano and drums set are set up. He opens a long, narrow case.

"Know what this is?" he asks the Martian.

"Yes sir. That is one very beat up old clunker of a clarinet."

"The big question is, can you play this old clunker?"

"Probably can. Unless there's a mouse asleep in it. What'ya wanta hear," Martian frowns as he inspects the frayed reed. He reaches into his pocket and produces a thin, silver knife and proceeds to shave on the reed.

"Anything you want," Husted replies. "Jazz? Blues? *Mr. Sandman?*"

Chris smoothes the reed between his fingertips, then slides it back into the mouthpiece which he tightens. He puts the clarinet to his mouth and bends his head forward so the instrument points straight down at his shoes. Then blows gently!

The most incredible tonal wail emanates from that clunker of a horn. Rises, like a scream ripped from a mother bird's chest. Then spirals out and down into a mellow low tone that hippy-hops into the familiar notes of *Mr. Sandman.* Mark Husted's eyes are round with awe. The Martian's face is expressionless. He's somewhere else with the *Mr. Sandman Blues.*

• • •

Kostic spreads broad swaths of white paint on the plywood background while I add the vertical gray stacks. We're each using one of those new paint roller things. "What kind of a nickname's 'Benjo'?" I ask my dark companion. Even smoothly shaved, his black stubble is more noticeable than the chop job on my chin.

"Ah, you heard my name, Five," he replies amiably. "Benjamin Josefus. Big mouthful for Army sergeants. Got to Korea and immediately some old fart sarge starts callin' me 'Benjo.' Means *toilet* in Japanese. As I found out when I got there on my first R.& R." He looks up from his roller. "And whatinhell kind of nickname is Five, anyway?"

I go through the grandpas routine and he gives me a slow nod.

"Then you should know what the fuck we're painting here, then?"

"Yep, and Mr. Husted, Mark, has done a good job on it. Need to put some antlers in front of the pilot house, though, Mark." Husted nods.

"I've seen those in pictures. What'd they mean, Five?" he asks as he details in the frames of the pilot house with a narrow brush.

"I think it has to do with winnin' a steamboat race," I offer, not exactly sure. "Anyway, most river boats have 'em."

Across the room, the Martian is swaying to the beat of drums, bass and piano. A trumpet joins in and the ACE "Riverboat Five" swings into *St. James Infirmary Blues.*

• • •

Covered with sweat and spots of latex paint, I knock gently on the number five green door. "Cmmmin," I hear through the door and try the knob. It opens. Darcy sits on the edge of her bed, nearly covered by a huge pile of black material. Her mouth is filled with pins. "Hey babe," she mumbles and smiles. Pins tumble out. "I'd hoped to have this finished before you got back."

"What is it, Darce?" Then I recognize the material as the stuff that goes under crinoline skirts, except it's black instead of white.

"You'll see," she says with a smile. "Gimme a kiss." I lean down to kiss her upraised mouth. "Ooh," she says, "you're scratchy and you stink. Why don't you go take a shower?"

"All right," I respond, "but I'm gonna shave at home. I damn near committed hairy-kari with that razor of yours." It's a strange sensation, taking a shower in a woman's apartment for the first time. Impossible to do without my friend down there rising to attention. I finish quickly and dry off with Darcy's only bath towel. The smell of her on the towel continues to keep my senses alert. *Really alert!*

When I open the door, she's standing there with her back to me in a spray of stiff, black skirts that reach to the floor. "Looks nice," I observe, "you're gonna be a riverboat lady, all right."

"Maybe it'll look better this way," she says and turns slowly around with her ornery smile turned on. She doesn't have any top on!

• • •

"Want to take another shower?" Darcy asks lazily, tracing her finger up and down my thigh. "Together?"

"Goodness, Miss Darcy," I mimic some movie riverboat hero, "d'yall really think we could?"

"Well… I think you could," she whispers through a kiss, "at least in a few more seconds."

• • •

"Now here's your string tie," Darcy says proudly. "I'll tie it for you when you get here tonight, if you want." She's wearing a t-shirt and shorts because I have pleaded with her to. Otherwise, I may never get shaved at Biddle. "And look what I've done to Toby's old coat. You're sure he said I could have another one. A really awful one?"

Toby's pearl gray coat that once served as Darcy's bathrobe now has some ornate dark gray piping on the sleeves and lapels. She turns the coat and its hem has been split into a pair of long tails. "Damn Darce, but that's gorgeous. You're really a good sewer, er…"

"Seamstress."

"I'll get Toby's longest, lowest button, most vivid pink coat and you can wear it as a bathrobe until you're an old lady," I promise.

"I think he had a purple one," she muses. "Sort of a lavender?"

"Whatever he has, I'll get. See you about seven."

• • •

Queens To Open is the most exciting party I've ever attended. Darcy looks terrific in her lady gambler outfit. It's all black with the huge crinoline skirts. The top is simple, black and form-fitting. Very form-fitting, accentuating all of Darcy's features. An Ace of Spades is tucked into her neckline.

"Toby said this would help your costume," I smile, handing her a long black cigarette holder. "It used to belong to Mamma Wolfe. And… what's that outfit you've got on?"

She flicks an imaginary ash and gives me an eye-shadowed wink. "It's a dance top, you bumpkin. A leotard. Didn't girls dance at Hockingport High?"

"Not in outfits like that, they didn't," I respond. "You can see your…"

"Well, of course you can. I wouldn't look very gambler lady-like with a padded brassiere and big white straps sticking through, would I?"

· · ·

We enter the Keep on what looks like a real riverboat gangplank. In the far corner the Riverboat Five is wailing away on a raised platform. The Martian is dressed in a black coat, string tie and derby, as are the rest of the musicians. At his foot, a small girl in a skirt and sweater sits on the edge of the platform and taps her foot in time with the music.

Darcy's eyes are wide with amazement. Most of my pledge brothers are already here with their dates. After introducing ourselves, we take a seat at a big poker table with Perry Shivers and his date, a familiar face to Darcy and me, O-Annie from the Biddle Christmas dance. I go to the bar to mix a couple of drinks.

"Gonna build a couple of Purple Paralyzers are ya' there?" asks an Ace brother, the monkey-looking guy who yelled so loudly at us at pledge meeting. "That's the way to get in their drawers."

"Uhh, yes sir, ah, Mister…" I can't recall his name to go with the low forehead covered with black hair.

"Aw, don't worry kid. I can't remember your name either 'cept it's some funny nickname. I'm Jim Thoreau." He extends his hand. "Welcome aboard, Pledge…?"

"Lowrey, Mister Thoreau. Thomsen Lowrey V."

"Oh yeah, you're the one they call Five. Better keep an eye on that cute piece you're with. I see Brother Mayhew trying to stare down her dress." I look over and indeed, Darcy has her neck craned to smile and talk with an Ace who's got one hand on her shoulder and standing slightly to her rear.

Thoreau smiles and continues, "G'on. Make those P-Paralyzers in a hurry or he'll have his paw down there where his eyes are trying to get. A couple of those sloe gin numbers and you'll be in her pants before the night is out. Take it from an old pro."

"Gee, thanks. I will, Mister Thoreau." *How much booze does someone have to drink before sarcasm becomes undetectable?*

"Not here, Five. You can call me Kong. But don't ever try to call me Kong when I'm sober."

• • •

After a couple of drinks, the party really picks up. The dance floor is filled with couples gyrating and spinning to Dixieland and ragtime. I'm at the poker table with a hand of cards. Darcy stands behind me, one leg cocked on the edge of my chair to reveal a bright red garter which holds another ace of spades. She flicks real ashes on the fuzzy green top of the table with her long cigarette holder.

"Fold your hand, Five," a familiar voice says over my shoulder. It's Mark Husted. "I've got someone here who says she knows you." I look around to see Trish Spotswood, decked out in a red dress and long red satin gloves.

"Hi, Five. Congratulations on going Ace," she leans down and plants a big kiss on my cheek.

"Hey, Trish. I'm glad to see you." *All of you.* "Is this…?" I nod toward Mark.

"Nope. I've known Mark since I was a sophomore. But he's not *that* one. But, who's this?" she nods to Darcy.

"Aw, I'm sorry. Darcy Robinette. This is Trish Spotswood. Trish was my pre-registration advisor."

"Hi, Darcy," Trish smiles. "I know who you are. Just didn't know your name. We're neighbors."

"We are?" Darcy asks in wonderment.

"Sure, I live behind the green door too. Number one at the other end of the hall. Moved in there about a month ago."

"Gosh, I'm sorry," Darcy says. "I haven't seen you around."

"What do you think of the decorations, Trish?" Husted

chimes in. "Five here was a big help. Riverboats are not my usual thing, but you were right, he is a good artist."

Who's a good artist? How was Trish right?

Husted turns to us and says, "I've had a crush on Trish since I was a freshman. Just followed her around for four years, watching her pick up and drop boyfriends right and left." Trish smiles kind of shyly. "Finally," he says with a grin, "this time I decided to do something when I heard she'd dropped another one."

• • •

We've danced, and drunk, and talked, and drunk some more. The party has settled to a steady pace of boozing, music, dancing and making out. Darcy and I squish into a vacant corner of the big couch in the nearly black TV room. From the sounds, we can detect the presence of other couples.

"I just squished the shit out of my skirts," she whispers in my ear with a giggle. "Will we have to go back to the party?"

"At this stage," I whisper back as I run my hand up her smooth leotarded leg, "I don't think it'll matter much to anyone what we look like." We kiss long and deeply and I feel something snap near my heart. "I think we just broke Mamma Wolfe's cigarette holder," I whisper. Darcy laughs aloud. Several muffled voices out of the darkness chastise. *Either make out or get out.*

• • •

On the darkened sun porch, the kissy face activity is just as frenzied but standing at the north window, we can see the river below and the street lights of the asylum. Darcy has her arms through mine and we look in silence at the beautiful view.

"Look, Five. There's Duff's place and my garage," she points to the right. "See it?" Yes, we can. And as we watch, the light in Duff's bedroom goes off. "If you ever live here," she says softly as she looks up at me in the moonlight, "you can keep an eye on the Ford for me." She runs her tongue along my jaw line. "I really think this is a neat old house, Five. But can we go home now? I feel the urge to… pose!"

• • •

Despite the fact that we don't *pose* long, I'm amazed at the progress I have made on the sketch since Wednesday. I'm proud of the work and feel the urge to show it to one of my instructors. So, when I leave Darcy's apartment early Sunday morning, the big sketch pad is under my arm. I must be a sight as I walk across the campus: pearl gray swallow-tailed coat, broken cigarette holder and the big sketch pad.

What an incredible week it has been!

Chapter 17

The Path Becomes Rocky

"Well, Five. I respond to this as a remarkable achievement upon your part," Blockhart holds my sketch pad at arm's length and looks at me from beneath his bushy gray eyebrows. "Quite remarkable. I take it you were... ah, inspired?"

"Oh yes, professor. Very inspired." I grin back at his leer. We're man to man, artist to artist here.

"Well, I can't blame you. It's an *inspiring* sight. Young woman flesh at that moment... that precise moment! Well," he leers again, "you know that moment?" I nod that I do.

He pauses for a puff from his pipe, looks at the sketch again. "As a sketch, it stands strongly. No doubt Professor Dabny will be taken with it and you may not have to do another figure drawing exercise the entire semester. But? Do you plan to do anything further with it?" He becomes agitated by my blank look, my lack of response.

"A painting, man! Damnit! A painting." He pounds his pipe against the desk, threatening my sketch with glowing embers. "Why are you studying light and color? Why am I trying to teach you the rudiments of brush and pigment? Think, man. Think painting!"

I'm pleased by Professor Blockhart's enthusiasm for my sketch but not prepared for the intensity of his reaction.

"Lowrey. Be a man. This sketch tells me you're no longer a boy. You have talent. I could tell it as soon as I saw the first sketches Jan Dabny showed me. Use that talent. Apply these same highlights and shadows to hues and color. Think painting!"

• • •

Lou Salazar sweats and recites at our second pledge meeting, "...founded at Tusculum College, Greenville,

213

Tennessee... in 1849 as a debating society by Winston Livy Gousha, Kendall Kirkwood and Garret Stowers Thurmond. The Ohio University Chapter was founded in Athens in 1856 and ..."

Tiler has given several of us hell for not having the Greek alphabet memorized. Poor Cobb can't get past *gamma* and looks near tears. Although I've read the first two chapters of *Shining Path* carefully, the lore keeps coming from Tiler's brain like a human tape recorder. Our second pledge meeting definitely is more intense.

We've learned the Acerbus Hymn, although it makes little sense to us.

"In ancient days did Acerbus, strike at the walls of Tyre,

to smite the mighty Saracen, and end his reign of fire.

With book and sword they fought to bring, the word of common good,

and treat their foes with the light of Acer brotherhood."

Once again the meeting breaks up with the screaming entry of Kong Thoreau, herding us down the stairs to the Keep. But this time, the candles are gone and the tables are folded against the walls.

"Line up you fuckin' creep pledge bastards, you!" Kong screeches at us. Deep furrows of rage cut across his reddened brow.

"What's your name, pledge?" someone shouts into my face from three inches. His breath is pretty bad.

"Thomsen Lowrey the Fifth, Mr. Curtis."

"Low-ree? I'll say you're low," Curtis sneers into my face. "You're lower than hemorrhoids on a frog's ass. Lower than..." he pauses for a breath, or a thought? "Lower than worm shit. Let's hear your Greek alphabet!"

I gulp and start, "Alpha. Beta. Gamma. Delta? Iota? Theta? *Oh shit.* Theta?"

"Keep going Low scum from the sewer. Don't stop now our

I'll drop the fuckin' ball on you right here. KEEP GOIN!" All over the room come screams and curses mixed with the tentative chant of faltering Greek alphabets.

Someone else shouts into my ear, "Let's hear the Hymn, Lowrey, you turdhead!"

In a squeaky voice I begin "In ancient days did Acerbus…"

"No! You asshole. Not ass-er-bus. Ace-er-bus!" the voice screams.

"Greek alphabet, Low shit," Curtis screeches. "Don't sing you fucking pansy. Give me…"

"Sing, goddamnit Lowrey! Let's hear the fuckin' hymn"

"…strike at the walls of Tyre, to smite the mighty Saracen, and end his reign…"

• • •

The Thirteen gathers in the Esquire basement, huddled around our beers at the long tables in the rear of the gloomy room.

"Fuck this shit," Smith drawls, "nobody calls me a worthless cocksucker and gets away with it." He takes a slug of Strohs, gulps it and grins. "I am *not* worthless."

"One of those assholes needs a bottle of Lavoris," I comment. "Do you think I'll get blackballed if I leave one in his mailbox anonymously."

"I'm serious," Salazar says in a very serious voice. "That bastard Schmidt called me a 'spic' right to my face. I am not going to take that crap. We may be the Thirteen but you guys had better get ready to be the twelve."

"Ease up, guys. Easy," Ransom says in a calming tone. "Didn't I warn you that we wouldn't be top dogs forever?"

"Yeah, guys," Kostic chimes in. "It's exactly like the fuckin' army. I thought I was back at Fort Leonard Wood in basic. You've got to learn to play their game. Don't you think so, Sarge?"

"Pretty familiar stuff to me," says Waller. "I think Benjo's right. Just take their shit. Learn your lore. Spout it back to them and play the game. What in hell can they do to us besides kick us out of their fuckin' club?"

"Well, I'll stick with it for a while," Salazar says, "but the first guy who calls me a 'greaser' is gonna get my Costa Rican shiv in his ribs.

"Call for Pater Gousha…" someone calls and we raise our glasses.

• • •

It's late Tuesday and Darcy has the helm of the Begorra by herself. I help her wrap my order for 220 burgers as I tell her about the events since Saturday night. I go lightly on details of our pledge 'party.'

"But Lockhart's so enthusiastic, Darce," I go on, "he's really serious and wants me to do a painting from the sketch."

She leans into me. "Does that mean I would *have* to pose some more, Five?"

"You betcha! Lots of posing. I've never done a painting before. You might be posing until next fall."

"We'll have to take lots of breaks. My neck gets awfully sore."

• • •

"Wake up, Andy, f'Chrissakes," I nearly pound Andy Logan with my elbow. Her head's on my shoulder and a thin string of drool hangs from her open mouth. She jerks and starts, eyes wide. In the front of the room, Gessler stares toward our little commotion.

"Did you have something to say, Mr. Lowrey?"

"Ah, nossir. Ah, well… yes. I am a little confused about folkways versus mores…"

Gessler leans forward on the podium. This is the kind of meat he loves to get his teeth into. "All right, once more. Consider a group of tribesmen who come to a stream…"

• • •

Andy French inhales from my Pall Mall, then leans back against the sun-warm bricks of the Ellis courtyard. "Thanks, Five. God, dad would kick my butt if he heard his daughter was *snoring* in a colleague's class. Mores. Folkways. Is that shit boring or what?"

I agree with her. Sociology is about the most sleep-invoking activity I've ever participated in. *With one possible exception.*

"I heard a sociological joke at the house," Andy giggles. "What's the difference between a tribe of pigmies and a women's track team?"

I shrug. "Don't know, Andy. What?"

"Well," she slowly draws a smile, "a tribe of pigmies is a cunning bunch of runts. And a women's track team is... a running bunch of..."

I blush as several people around us share our laughter at Andy's joke. She's learning some new lore at the Pi Phi house.

"Andy... gotta get going to figure drawing. See you tomorrow in Fine Arts."

"Wait, Five. You haven't shown me any sketches in a long time. Y'have anything new?"

"Well? There is this one thing," I say hesitantly.

"C'mon, let's see!" With some reluctance, I hand the pad to Andy. She opens it and looks for long seconds, drawing smoke over her upper lip and into her nose. "Jesus, Five. It's magnificent. She's wonderful. Just wonderful." She looks up with a smile. "How I envy Darcy... to be captured that way."

• • •

"It's a very good work, Five," Dabny says with obvious approval in her voice. "Very fine. The model? She looks familiar somehow. Do I know her?"

"You might, professor. She's a local girl, works in town."

"Not a coed, then? Yes. She does look familiar." She looks again at the sketch, moving the pad around on different axis against the light. "Five, I think this work is good enough to be nominated for the annual student show. Would you mind?"

"No maam. I would be honored."

217

"And well you should be," she says. "Not many freshmen artists get nominated. Very few have their works accepted. May I keep this drawing to show the committee?"

"Well, Jan. Ah, Professor Blockhart is encouraging me to do a painting from it. I'd like to hold onto it for a couple of weeks."

"Aren't you working from life, Five? Is your model no longer available."

"Oh yes, she's still available. I'd just like to have the sketch to help guide my painting. I've never done a painting before."

• • •

We're in the Bear's Den. Dense calls me and says get right over there as quick as I can. There's an urgency in his voice that makes me drop my studies and hustle right over to Perkins.

"Five, this is Sam Hutto." Dense introduces me to a guy who looks more weedy, if it's possible, than the Martian. Hutto nods. The Martian is sitting on his study chair with a strange expression. "Chris is just about to piss himself learning the alphabet. Just can't do it."

"I've got a mental bloc, Five," the Martian whispers. "Those bastards'll ball me right out of Ace if I don't learn it. And I just *can't!*"

Dense leans forward, "We were talkin' about it at lunch and Sam here says he can help us out. He knows hypnotism." *Hypnotism?* I look at Hutto's acne-scarred face, his eyes magnified through the thick lenses of his ugly glasses. He nods seriously.

"So Sam's gonna try to hypnotize Chris here," Bear says, "and then we'll teach him the Greek alphabet. Right, Sam?"

"If Chris is a good subject, and I believe he very well might be, it should work," Hutto says in a surprisingly deep voice.

"But don't fuck around with him," the Bear warns. "Any funny stuff and I'll break your goddamn neck." Hutto's look of fright is a visual contract that he won't try any *funny stuff.*

"You wanna' try it, Chris?" I ask. He nods uncertainly. "OK, Sam. Let's give it a whirl."

Hutto directs a study lamp and pulls a chair up close to the

Martian's, leaning forward against its back. At his nod, Dense turns out the overhead light. He removes a shiny fountain pen and holds it vertically in front of the Martian. The steady pen sparkles in the lamplight.

"Now Chris," he says softly, "I want you to relax and concentrate on the pen. Nothing else. Just the pen and my voice. Relax now," he drones. I find myself relaxing, perhaps too much and snap my eyes away from the pen. "You are very relaxed," Sam continues. "Very relaxed. You're getting very tired. Sleeepy." The Martian's head tilts forward slightly. "Keep your eyes on the pen. Concentrate on the pen. The pen. The pen. The pen. You're now in a deep sleep… but you can see and hear my voice. Can you hear my voice, Chris?"

"Yes. I can hear your voice." The Martian's voice sounds weird.

"Chris. You are sound asleep now. Yet you can hear my voice. And you know I am your friend. No harm will come to you." Again, I jerk my eyes around the darkened room. Dense is leaning far forward, his brows knit in concentration. He blinks a couple of times. I hope he's awake.

"Now Chris," Hutto intones, "you are getting cooler. You feel cold. Don't you feel cold, Chris?"

"Yes. Cold." The Martian shivers. Shivers very realistically. Dense and I stare at each other.

Hutto changes his vocal pace. "But now you're warm. You're getting very warm. You're very hot. It's hot in here!" The Martian's forehead glistens with sweat. A perspiration spot appears at the neck of his t-shirt.

"OK, now Chris," Hutto looks around at us. "You're very comfortable and relaxed. Are you relaxed, Chris?"

"Yes. I am relaxed." The sweat has vanished.

"I think he's there, guys," Hutto says softly, proudly. "What next?"

"How do we teach him the alphabet?" Bear asks softly.

"One of you should do it. Who knows it the best?"

"He does," Dense and I say in unison. "No you, Five. You do it. He's your pledge brother."

"All right," Hutto nods to me. "Chris. Here is your friend,

Five. He's your pledge brother. He's going to help you learn the Greek alphabet."

"Chris," I say gently, "It's Five. Can you hear me, Chris?"

"Yes, Five. I hear you."

I ask Hutto, "Just have him repeat the letters after me? Will that work?"

"Yeah, I'd think so," he says. "Try just one letter at a time. See how that does it."

"All right, Chris. Here we go. These are the letters of the Greek alphabet. You will repeat them after me. And you will remember them." I pause. "Alpha."

"Alpha."

"Beta."

"Beta."

Slowly I work through the letters, all twenty four of them. I'm careful to pronounce each letter slowly and correctly. When we reach *omega,* I turn and give Hutto a questioning look. He shrugs for me to continue.

"Chris? Now you know the Greek alphabet. I want you to repeat the Greek alphabet for me."

The Martian pauses, then in his strange voice begins, "Alpha. Beta. Gamma. Delta. Epsilon. Zeta. Eta. Theta. Iota. Kappa. Lambda. Mu. Nu. Xi. Omicron. Pi. Rho. Sigma. Tau. Upsilon. Phi. Chi. Psi. Omega." We grin at each other with success. Dense makes a champ signal, fists clasped overhead.

"Once more, Chris," I ask gently. "A little faster this time." He whips through the alphabet flawlessly. *Afuckingmazing!* "Faster." Again he does it without a stammer, even faster. "One more time, faster now."

"AlphaBetaGammaDeltaEpsilonZetaEtaThetaIotaKappaLa mbdaMuNuXiOmicronPiRhoSigmaTauUpsilonPhiChiPsiOmega ," he intones without taking a breath.

"How about backwards?" Hutto shrugs. He doesn't know but we'll give it a try.

"Chris, can you hear me?"

"Yes, Five. I can hear you."

"All right. You now know the Greek alphabet... and, even better, you can say it backwards. Can you say it backwards,

Chris?"

The Martian pauses. His brow furrows, then, "Omegapsichiphiupsilontausigmarhopiomicronxinumulamdbaka ppaiotathetaetazetaepsilondeltagammabetaalpha!"

This outburst is followed by small smile.

Hutto moves forward. "Chris, this is Sam again. Now you're very relaxed and when I count backwards to three, you'll be awake. And when you awake, you will not remember anything that has happened here. But you will remember the Greek alphabet. OK?"

The Martian nods. "OK."

Hutto counts slowly. "Three. Two. One."

The Martian's eyes snap wide. He grins at us. Dense turns on the overhead. "Did it work?" Chris asks.

"We'll see," I say with a grin. "Chris? Do you know the Greek alphabet?:

"AlphaBetaGammaDeltaEpsilonZetaEtaThetaIotaKappaLa mbdaMuNuXiOmicronPiRhoSigmaTauUpsilonPhiChiPsiOmega ," he says without taking a breath.

"Ohmygod," the Bear gasps. "Do you think I could learn the table of elements that way, Sam?"

• • •

Darcy and I stand appraising the pile of stuff sitting on her bed. I've just come from the College Book Store where this collection has set my checking account back by at least two Begorra runs. It's a Wednesday afternoon and we're both anxious to get started.

"Just where am I supposed to sleep, mister artist?" she asks with a nudge to my ribs.

"Well, all the paints and brushes go in this tackle box here. And we can push the easel and canvas over against the corner by the window."

"No. I want to be able to see it. All the time."

"Well," I drop my hands in a helpless gesture, "maybe we could put the table and chairs out in the hall?" We shove her big wardrobe closer to the kitchen table and make room for the easel when it's stored. Then I set up the easel and canvas in position at the end of the bed. And place the sketch upright on one of the chairs.

"I'll go get in the shorts and shirt," Darcy says, heading for the bathroom.

"No! I think the first thing to do is redraw the rough outlines from the sketch." She gives me a mock pout but settles in the other chair beside me. With a pencil I draw smooth light lines to delineate the windows, then the bed coming toward me with exaggerated perspective.

"Are you going to redraw the whole thing?" she asks. "This's fun watching you."

"Not all the detail, just the basic outlines, I think. Remember, I've never done a painting before."

I continue with the big lines in the lower right corner where the light falling through the windows creates a pattern across the floor. Darcy hums and runs her hand lightly along my back. Then I begin on her form. As I line her rounded bottom, she increases the pressure of her hand against my back.

"Careful now there," she says. "You're on dangerous ground. Not too big."

I draw the shape of her head. Just bare essential lines to show her eyes. Her smile. Then her arms. And her breasts.

"Maybe a little too enthusiastic there, Five?" she comments. I agree and erase the line with the kneaded eraser. A slightly smaller breast is drawn in. I'm glad she's behind me so she can't see my condition. She massages my shoulders with more enthusiasm.

"Five. Can we *do a little posing?* Just a little bit?" Darcy wheedles.

"Darce! It's the middle of the afternoon!" I respond in mock horror.

"I know," she murmurs, unbuttoning her blouse slowly, "but I'll bet there's nothing in the artist's rulebook that says you can't pose in the afternoon."

• • •

It's Monday night again and the Thirteen is soaking up Strohs in the Esquire basement. Another night of pledge meeting and "pledge party," as the Aces term the periods of harassment in the Keep.

"Man, I thought I'd die, Martian!" Waller laughs so hard that he spits a spray of beer over the table. "The look on Tiler's face when you actually knew the fuckin' alphabet."

Tiler *had* looked amazed when Chris' turn to recite the Greek letters came. The Martian squinched up his face, then slowly, faking great concentration, had begun, "Alpha, Beta, Gamma, Delta…"

Dicky Reb West wipes his brow. "Hah. Hah, hah. Hahahahahah. Jeezus, Martian. Then there's ole' Mayhew, that asshole. Screamin' at you like that and I thought he'd pass out in his crap when you let him have it."

During the "pledge party" Mayhew had been particularly hard on Chris, harassing him and calling him a 'fuckin' fairy.'

"C'mon fairy boy, let me hear your Greek alphabet," he screamed at Chris. Chris again fakes the squinched eye look. "Let's hear it goddamn it!"

And out it comes in a single breath. "AlphaBetaGammaDeltaEpsilonZetaEtaThetaIotaKappaLambda MuNuXiOmicronPiRhoSigmaTauUpsilonPhiChiPsiOmega!"
Then Chris smiles slyly at Mayhew and says, "Wanna hear it backwards, Mister Mayhew?"

Chapter 18

A Turning Point

We're TGIFing in the Esquire, D.D. Smith and his big brother Bob Long, Mark Husted, and my new big brother, Doak Phipps, and me. "Seriously, guys, take this advice but keep it quiet. Keep your women away from Brother Mayhew. The guy just does not know when to stop and 'no' isn't in his vocabulary," Long tells us in a conspiratorial whisper.

"I can protect my woman," D.D. says, "but I don't know about myself. That guy Curtis. He's the one I'm worried about. He's really on my ass."

"Mine too," I contribute. "Wish he'd brush his teeth more, too." *Perhaps that's something I shouldn't have said?* "And Thoreau? Are you guys sure he doesn't come from across the river?"

The Aces laugh to themselves. "Thoreau's OK," Mark says. "He's just making sure the Thirteen doesn't lose its step along the path."

Doak's been silent for a while but he contributes. "Don't piss Curtis off, though. He's the first Korean vet we initiated and he takes his pledge training *very* seriously."

Long adds, "Galen Curtis was a couple of years ahead of me in high school. Good student. Athlete. Class leader. Got drafted and went to Korea. So it was a natural that we'd rush him hard when he came through. Several other vets were rushing and we thought Curtis was a real prize.

"But Korea changed him somehow," Long muses. "He's not quite the same guy I admired in high school."

Doak adds, "Yeah. He's a hard guy to be around sometimes. Funny as hell and really great, then when he starts drinkin…"

"I think Korea changed a lot of guys," Mark adds. "And the vets have sure changed OU. Everyone cusses a lot more. You never used to hear someone say 'fuck' out loud."

Long chuckles. "Yeah. We had a hell of a time with Curtis.

Getting him to quit calling the brothers' dates *mooses*. I thought a moose was a big fuckin..."

"See what we mean?" Husted laughs. "You wouldn't even know Brother Long here is a preacher's kid from the way he talks."

"Do they have to call us all those names?" D.D. wants to know. "I mean, just 'cause I'm a drum major doesn't mean I'm queer. But that's all I hear."

Husted gives both pledges an earnest look. "Yes, D.D. They do. And they will... we will... stay on your ass until the balloon goes up."

"Or the ball drops," Doak says with a chuckle. "Whichever comes first."

• • •

It's a pretty spring afternoon. No party tonight at the ACE house. Just a pledge meeting at midnight. Since nothing big is going on on campus, Darcy and I take her Ford over for a daylight look at The Sharpsburg Hell and just putter around the countryside.

"It's different during the day," I comment, sketching Darcy as she perches on a rock with the smoking vents behind her. "Meaner looking. Nasty place."

"I sure wouldn't want to walk out there barefoot," Darcy says. "Wouldn't want to walk through it at all."

In Washington County, we take a back road and discover the first of four beautiful covered bridges. I do a quick sketch of each. Darcy and I reenact the ages-old custom of snuggling in *our buggy* inside each covered bridge. Outside of Athens, we stop at the Linger Longer for a dinner of minute steaks and their deep fried frozen rolls.

Saturday night, I continue working on the painting letting Darcy *really* pose now as I begin to apply the first light colors with a thin wash. Using the new acrylic paints, I work slowly, testing different densities and mixtures on a scrap of board nearby. Progress is slow and we soon have to take the first of several breaks in the pose.

• • •

Darcy's lying on my chest, circling her fingers through its hairs. "Are you sure you've got to go, Five? Really sure?"

"I'm sure, Darce. Midnight sharp. Or else," they said. "It sounds like a work party as they told us to be sure to wear sweatshirts."

She pecks me a light kiss. "I'm not sure I like this fraternity, Five. It's only fifteen till' twelve."

"Darce!" Mock recrimination. "If you were a coed, you'd have been in the dorm for forty-five minutes!"

"Yeah," she says with a little pelvic bump that rejolts my interest, "and if I were a coed, I would never have posed for the sketch in the first place. And I can *tell* you don't *really* want to go…" as she snuggles tightly against me.

• • •

Tiler has us sitting on the living room floor, a tight circle surrounding him. "Just remember this, guys," he says quietly. "You're the Thirteen. You are One! No matter what happens, keep your heads, remain the One."

"Bring on those fucking worm sucking pledges," Kong's voice howls from the hallway. Tiler nods and we scramble up and break for the door to the Keep.

Chet Husted, who we've elected president of the Thirteen, leads us down the stairs with a chant which we pick up, "The Thirteen. The One. We're The One!" The Keep becomes instant chaos. This isn't an ordinary *pledge party* since more of the Ace brothers are present, all dressed in old, warm clothes.

"Line up. Line up, you swill slurping pig fuckers," Kong screams. Curtis stands beside him, decked out in some kind of green utility uniform, funny little stick in his hand. We line up and instantly are thrown into the cacophony of lore inquisition. *Alpha, Beta, Gamma, Delta* rings throughout the Keep. After about five minutes, a shrill whistle brings sudden silence.

"OK, keep it down," Kong says in a rare normal tone. "Each

of you shitheads give your big brother all your valuables. Everything. Watches, wallets, money, even small change." We scramble through our pockets and empty them into the waiting hands of our big brothers.

"Now you bunch of sniveling assholes," Curtis steps forward. "You're gonna learn a few things. We're not very pleased with your progress. Obviously, Brother Tiler here isn't getting through to you. So we're gonna try another form of communication." Curtis snaps his stick against his thigh like I've seen German generals do in the movies.

"Jumping jacks," he shouts. "Good way to warm up. Ready?" He snaps into an energetic jumping jack and we stand there, slack jawed, watching. "NOOOOO!" he screams. "Not me you pathetic fuckers. *You* do jumping jacks!" We become a hopping, flapping mass of arms and legs as Curtis screeches the cadence... "two, three, four... one, two, three, four." After thousands of jumping jacks, it seems like, he stops us and instantly the other Aces are in our faces, shouting insults, demanding lore.

"Everybody on the floor!" Curtis breaks up the riot with another scream. I can see that he's working up a sweat as well. "Pushups, now! Let's see your pushups... start with fifty. Count 'em out! Loud!" Now the pushup is an alien form of exercise to me and I quickly appreciate that I'm not alone among my pledge brothers. The shouting and harassment begin again.

"F'chrissakes, Waller! You screwin' a mole or something?" one Acer screams into the back of Sarge's bobbing head.

"Not just your ass, Salazar, you spic bastard. Your whole body!"

"Low-ree, you look like you're rapin' a garden hose. Use your arms! Keep that goddamn gut off the floor." Soon my arms are raging in protest, pain rocketing from shoulder blades through elbows to fingertips. Finally... I stay on the floor on gasping surrender.

"Get up you river rat fucker asshole," Curtis screams, whacking me across the butt with his stick. "Give me fifty more, right now! OR GO HOME!" My brain says *fuck this* but my arms respond somehow.

Intervals of shouted lore interrogation are broken by sit-ups, more jumping jacks, and constantly punctuated by pushups. Finally, Thoreau calls a breather.

"All right, you worthless vermin," he says in a quiet, calm manner. "I hope this little sweat party has gained your attention. As you can tell, we brothers of ACE are not entirely pleased with your progress as a pledg…"

"Wait one, Brother Thoreau," Curtis interrupts, stepping in front of Kong. "I for one am not pleased at all with any of these fucks… but this one!" and he points an accusing finger at Ransom, "this nigger-lovin' asshole loser…"

"Now just a minute…" Ransom drawls angrily.

"Shut your fucking mouth you illiterate pussy snuffer," Curtis screams into Ransom's whitened face. Suddenly, he waves his hand before Ransom's round eyes. "See this? See this you pansy asshole? What is it?"

"It's a ball. A black ball, sir?"

"Bet your ass it's a ball, Ransom. And I'm givin' it to you, right now. Understand?" Ransom nods yes. "Cause now you'll have one ball.

"But let me tell you what, Ransom… I do not like you. I do not want you to be my brother. And I have the other ball," he growls, producing a second black marble, "and I'm gonna drop it on your ass right now… if you don't shape up. Understand?" Pause. "Do you understand me?"

"Yessir," Ransom whispers, his nostrils tight and pale.

"Ransom. You'd better believe me when I tell you this…" the room is silent as we watch this bizarre one-on-one. "You will beg to suck my cock before…"

"Easy, Brother Curt, easy," John Ehlers mutters as he firmly pulls Curtis by the bicep. Curtis shakes his head, glances at Ehlers, gives him a sheepish grin.

"Right, J.E.!" An iceberg of tension has crashed into the Keep. Curtis' voice trembles, rises in pitch a little. "I think the best way to let this floating scum of vermin to learn anything is to let them do a little marching." A terrible shout goes around the room. Suddenly, we're each grabbed by our big brothers and hustled up the stairs, into our coats and toward the side doors.

"Get your coat on," Doak whispers. "Don't let on. I left smokes and matches in the pocket. Remember! Unity. Stay as One and you'll be OK."

We shiver in the sudden change from the sweat-steamed Keep to the chilly courtyard.

"Stand right here, in a line," Thoreau says in a quiet voice. We line up facing him as directed. "Don't be alarmed now. Nothing's gonna happen to you… yet. And your big brother will help you."

Something drops over my head and even the blackness of the night becomes blacker.

• • •

Riding in a car with no visible reference is a new and strange experience. Soft conversation between the Aces in the front seat doesn't give us any clue as to what's happening. I guess *us* is accurate because I can feel a very warm body on each side of me in the back seat.

The car seems to take many turns. We alternate over smooth and bumpy surfaces. We stop a couple of times.

"Keep your hands down. Don't touch your hood," comes a soft warning from the front seat. Evidently one of us has tried to sneak a look.

The aimless driving seems to go on forever. Again we stop but this time the sound is of both doors opening in our car. "We're alone," Terry Simpson whispers from beside me. I tug at the drawstring of the hood around my neck and timidly lift its hem above me eyes. In the road ahead, flashlights bob around another car.

"Watch it," the voice beside me hisses. "Here they come." I recognize Waller's voice, even in a whisper.

"Out of the car, pledges," a strange voice orders. We shove the front seats forward and crawl out of the back of the two-door. The gravel surface of the road seems unsteady and treacherous. "You can remove your hoods," the voice instructs.

"Up here, vermin," Thoreau's call brings us together. We huddle in a group around Kong whose face has an eerie

230

Halloweenish look as he holds a flashlight beneath his chin. "Listen carefully. This is your first major test as the Thirteen. It's important for you to remember what you've been taught. And..." he pauses dramatically, "do not miss pledge meeting Monday night. Under no circumstances... will you miss pledge meeting!"

Kong flicks off the light and turns to get into his car.

"But I've got a geometry quiz in the morning!" Salazar cries out.

Once more Kong says ominously, "Do not miss pledge meeting Monday night." Car doors slam. Engines start. We jump out of the way as the four vehicles with Ace decals in their back windows roar off down the dusty road.

• • •

Our general grousing and bitching has diminished after about five minutes' worth of stumbling down the dirt road in the direction the Aces had driven. "What makes you think this is the way to go?" A.A. asks. Because of this last two initials and his reluctance for booze, Frank Alfred Able has been awarded the first of new pledge class nicknames.

"You're right," Sarge Waller responds. "All that driving around, stopping, that could just be bullshit. Doesn't mean a thing... they went that way."

"Let's stop a minute," Kostic contributes, "and think about this. Anyone got a smoke?"

"Bastards took mine."

"Mine too!" General agreement within the group.

The Thirteen is the One. I hesitate for a second. "I do," I say softly. "Doak slipped a pack and matches into my coat." No one says a word.

"My big brother left me a candy bar," Ransom volunteers softly.

"I've got a packet of Cheezits," another voice chimes in. D.D. Smith's.

More quiet as we think. "Anyone get a flashlight? A map?" It's a few seconds before we realize we're afoot somewhere in

231

the dark with emergency rations only.

• • •

After half an hour, it becomes frighteningly apparent that we don't know where we are. The darkness isn't as bad because our 'night vision,' as Kostic terms it, has kicked in and we enjoy pretty bright illumination from a heaven full of stars. We can even see Kostic's silhouette against the skyline as he turns slowly scanning for some sign of life. "There's a glow on the horizon over this way," he calls, "really faint though. Nothin' else... so it's probably Athens."

"But the road doesn't go that way!" McClintock says with a whine. "We're not going cross country, are we, Benjo?"

"No fuckin' way," Kostic grunts as he scrambles down from the knoll above the dirt road. "Let's have a smoke break and try to figure out what to do. Five, break out those cigarettes."

Pulling the pack out of my coat, I realize in the darkness that it's mashed and obviously not the Pall Malls I had taken to the pledge party. Feeling over the matchbook, I make a scary discovery. "We've only got three matches!" I count them with my fingertips. "Those bastards only left me three matches."

"Well, we'll just suck off one smoke after another," Terry Simpson says in a practical, smug voice.

"Not for long," I answer. "Close your eyes everyone and I'll light up.' I extract a cigarette from the mashed pack and carefully scratch the match against the frayed striker pad on the folder. It sputters, then lights, revealing the pack of cigarettes while I light my smoke. "Ooh, shit, Phillip Morris," I grunt as I inhale the peculiar flavor of this charcoal filtered non-favorite."

"And the assholes only left us a half a pack," the Martian observes. "Hold the match, Five, while I light one up." Cobb grabs a cigarette and puffs it against the match now burning my fingers. In the dark, I finger the remaining cigarettes in the pack.

"Seven left, guys," I caution. "Pass these lighted ones around and enjoy 'em."

"Aw shit, Martian. You nigger-lipped this one, you fart!" Chet Husted grumbles.

Three smoke breaks later, we're down to four cigarettes and half a candy bar. The cheese crackers were easy to break in two, making the portions relatively fair. We all rag on Ransom when he sheepishly reveals he's eaten half his candy bar.

The glow on the horizon *seems* a little brighter. Maybe an hour before, we chose a left turning at a fork and this road seems to meander a little toward the glow.

"C'mon you guys, keep up!" Benjo calls to Salazar, D.D. Smith and Simpson who trail behind, muttering curses and complaints.

"You're goin' too fast, Benjo," Smith whines. "What're we in a hurry for? Someone will pick us up. I know it."

"I'm glad *you* know it, 'cause I fuckin' sure don't," Kostic grumbles his response. Step after step, yard after yard, we trudge on.

• • •

Huddling in the road, we listen to dogs barking at us from the darkened farmhouse. "Shit, they've got to wake up sometime with all that racket," Mac says. The dogs have been raising hell since our arrival five or so minutes before. But no light shows in the farmstead.

"Go on, Husted. Walk up there and knock on the door," Waller urges. "That's why we elected you president."

"Bullshit," the freckled towhead snaps. "Get my balls bit off or my ass shot off? No way. It must be two, three in the morning."

Lights never do appear and we trudge on, fearful of trespassing upon the dark farm in the middle of the night. To keep up morale, we try talking about different subjects. Food doesn't work.

"A big plate of spaghetti and meatballs, swimming in sauce and covered with that shaky kind of cheese," D.D. dreams aloud. "And three-stripe Jell-O with whipped cream for dessert."

"I'm so friggin' hungry," Terry "the Pirate" Simpson moans, "I'd even eat the East Green meat loaf, baby shit gravy and all."

• • •

"So where's fuckin' New Marshfield, Sarge?" Shivers wants to know. Waller and Kostic, our military leaders, chose another fork a ways back because a tiny sign pointed to what is obviously a tinier, or maybe non-existent, New Marshfield.

"Shuttup and march," Benjo Kostic growls. "I'm gettin' sick and tired of this grumbling in the ranks. You bastards woulda been dead in Korea by now." He huffs on down the road. "C'mon D.D. It's your turn."

"Well, as you know, I'm from Weston, West Virginia. My ole' man owns the movie theater there. Got an Italian guy out on the sidewalk with an old-timey popcorn wagon and he has real melted butter in a coffee pot…"

"No food, damnit," I cut him off. We've been reciting autobiographies after our stomachs rebelled at food fantasies.

"Yeah, sorry. Well… I was good in math, and played drums in the band. Had a girlfriend but she went off to Marshall so I guess we've broke up. Came to OU and went out for the band. But that little Minelli guy tells me he's got enough good drummers already… but he's got a drum major's uniform that'll about fit me and would I like to be an assistant drum major."

"All drum majors are queers!" Mac mimics the psychopathic Curtis.

"Your turn, Five," Waller says. "I've had enough about queers and drum majors."

"Well, you guys all know about my dad, the river boat captain, and my four grandfathers who were river boat captains," I start.

"Yeah, and we've heard about the dildo, too," Frank Able sneers. "Tell us something new."

"OK, my great-great-great-great-great grandfather… that's five of 'em isn't it? He didn't have my name. But he was a river man too. His name was Mean Mike Lowrey and he was a river pirate who drowned in the Ohio rather than get hanged. But he

234

was the meanest, nastiest fucker on the river while he was alive. Wrestle with an alligator and make him eat his tail 'til his nose was stickin' out his asshole." The all laugh at this parody of what I've heard Captain do at the barber shop.

"Only problem was… Mean Mike couldn't swim."

• • •

"Lewis Alfredo Salazar. That's the three names I got here in Athens," Salazar intones. "But I got a fourth, secret name that I only tell my pledge brothers." I can almost see his grin as he apes the Costa Rican accent we expect and he does not have. "Ees Jesus."

"Jesus?" we shout. "Then get us out of this mess," the Martian says. "I'll pray. Yes Jesus, I'll pray."

"Noo, my frien', not Je-zuss, like you say in Norte Americana, but as we say in Costa Rica. Hey-soos."

We bicker for at least a half a mile about Salazar's new nickname but finally prevail upon "Soos."

• • •

"C'mon Joe, you gotta get up," Benjo urges the whimpering Ransom. "You'll freeze to death sittin' there."

We're slogging along when suddenly a far-off moan turns us around on the darkened road. Kostic, the *point man,* counts dark forms in a whisper. "Twelve. Someone's down back there. C'mon."

We head back the way we'd come cautiously and in just a few yards find the sobbing Ransom sitting on the ground near the ditch of the road.

"Can't go any further," he whimpers. "Feet hurt, head hurts. Fuck it. Just can't do it."

Waller leans over the downed pledge brother and in a surprising tone blasts ole' Ransom. "Off your ass, Ransom. Right now. We're in this together and if, by God, you don't stay with us, we're not One any more. So quit doggin' it and get on your feet." To our amazement, Ransom slowly crawls off his

235

butt. "Seen my old man enough times on the parade ground to know what to do," he chuckles in a whisper into my ear.

• • •

McClintock sways from the skinny top of a roadside tree, his figure barely visible against the night sky. "I'm not shittin' you guys," he cries in triumph, "it's a red blinking light, right over there." We can see his arm point. "And there's a brighter glow on the horizon."

"OK, Mac, c'mon down," Kostic calls. We've each taken turns — except for the limping Ransom — climbing trees, tall rocks or knolls to look for some sign of life. Benjo says to us in general, "I hate to mention this but you can see a glow on the horizon from here. I think it's gettin' near daybreak." He shuffles off. We follow. "C'mon Dicky Reb, let's hear more of your life story."

"Wellllll," the rebel drawls in about four syllables, "down home we got these things we call drive-in movies."

"Yeah, we call 'em that here too."

"Yeah, but down home, you get an ole' girl to go to a drive-in, it's just as good as sayin' she puts out. So there I was…"

"Reb? Is this gonna be another Georgia pussy story?" Simpson asks. Plain to see our tempers are fraying short. "We done heard fifteen of those. If everyone in Georgia puts out like you say, why aren't there more white people?"

• • •

Even with the last cigarette long smoked, our breaks become more frequent and longer. Ransom cries openly from time to time. Chris Cobb sits in the middle of the road, wrapped in three coats and still shivering uncontrollably. Although the sun hasn't come up, it's that watery time of morning when dark is gone but light hasn't quite gotten here. The Thirteen sits in the middle of a summit in the road, back to back, so we can see in both directions.

"That fuckin' blinker has got to be Athens," Kostic says to

236

himself. "Can't be more than a couple more miles." He looks at us. He's dubbed us the "lost patrol" and the pity he feels for us is apparent. "Y'all want to wait here and I'll try gettin' on in to town."

"I think you could do it, Benjo," Husted says, "but it'll be twelve and one. Not Thirteen. Not One. I say we stick together." Several of us grunt affirmative votes. Ransom just blubbers. Our joints and muscles creak as we rise slowly to continue the march.

"What's that?" Waller shouts, pointing down the road. "Lights? Lights! Man, somethin's coming!" Indeed, behind the next rise in the undulating road, a bright glow gets brighter. Then a pair of headlights pops over the top and heads down the road toward us, a rooster tail of dust boiling behind.

"Get out of the road," Benjo orders. We scurry for the dusty ditch. Kostic stands in the road's center, his arms upraised. "Stop! Stop you sonofabtich. Stop 'cause I'm too goddamn tired to jump out of your way."

On come the lights and through the dusty gloom, the form of a vehicle takes shape. A familiar shape!

"Oh holy shit!" I scream to the skies. "It's Dense. It's the Bear come to save us."

• • •

We stand around the Bearmobile, puffing the Camels Dense has brought along. The battered yellow pick up truck has never looked so handsome, even on the day it rolled off the I-H showroom floor in Parkersburg.

"I checked over at Biddle," Dense says with a grin, "and Toby said he hadn't seen you since early evening. The Nu's took us for a ride too, but someone had a dime and we called from some service station. Home almost as fast as the actives were."

"So I just hopped in the ole' Bearmobile and started drivin' around the back roads, hopin' I'd run into you. Just about to give up when I topped that last hill and saw you sorry bastards sittin' there in the road. Can't believe you poor suckers have been walkin' all night."

"Bear, dammit, you're a good man," Benjo says punching Dense on the shoulder, "but even if you weren't, you're the first sign of human life we've seen since those assholes let us out back there wherever."

• • •

We manage to stuff the wet-eyed Ransom, shivering Martian, and the two littlest guys — A.A. and Terry the Pirate — into the cab with Bear. That leaves ten of us to stack ourselves onto the flat plywood bed in back.

"Drive slow, Dense," I call down, "Sarge and I are gonna sit on the roof."

"OK, here we go," Bear says, "I'll go really slow and you guys hang onto whatever you can." Bear has turned the truck around and we start toward the blinking beacon which he tells us *is* WOUB's tower in Athens. "There's a filling station, store, whatever, down here about six miles," he yells out the window. "We'll ease down there, let some of you guys off and I'll drive half into town, then come back and get the rest of you."

• • •

My entrance into 205 doesn't even break the cadence of Toby's snoring, even though one leg gives out and I crash against my study chair before collapsing on the bed. Before my eyes shut, my brain registers the clock on Toby's desk reading eight fifteen.

• • •

"Five! Five, c'mon man. Wake up!" *Why won't some fool quit shaking my shoulder and yelling?* "You wanna talk to Darcy? She's on the phone."

My eyes can't open. Then, with supreme effort, the glue that holds them shut is cracked and I realize where I am. But it's still eight fifteen. Dark out! Was the whole thing a bad dream? I stumble down the hall in the same clothes I'd worn to the Ace house Saturday night. "H'lo?"

"Hi, Five. It's me! Are you OK? I thought I would've heard

from you by now."

"M'fine, Darce. Js'fine." My eyes are open. Why won't my mouth work?

"You don't sound fine. You sure you're OK. Are you gonna call a burger order?" *Jesus. Is that all she cares about? Selling hamburgers?*

"Not tonight, Darce. Let 'em eat tuna salad. Bye. Talk to you later." I turn and stagger toward the john. Behind me, Toby talks into the receiver then softly hangs it up.

• • •

For the third time I see eight fifteen on Toby's clock but now it's daylight again. Something stinks in here. *Oh! It's me.* After a long, scalding shower and an equally hot shave, I feel as if I could go back to bed and get a decent night's sleep. So I do. Sleeping through English comp, western civ and almost through lunch, except Bear and the Martian are shaking my shoulder to prevent that.

I cut seasonal sports in the afternoon and grab a few extra winks. Finally, at five, I shower again and dress to walk up town. Darcy comes around the counter and swings her arms around my neck, giving me a huge kiss and hug. Two or three other customers whistle and cheer.

"I was worried about you, hon," she whispers. "You OK? Sure?"

"OK Darce, really OK. Just a little tired."

"Bear came by this afternoon and told us what happened. That was terrible. Did you quit?"

"Quit? Quit what?"

"ACE of course! You're not gonna put up with that kind of stuff are you?"

"Darcy, that's part of it. Part of being a pledge! We stuck together. Course I'm not gonna quit." She gives me a look that indicates I might need a rest in the asylum across the river. I linger over coffee and Begorras until it's time to walk over to the house.

"Darce," I'll see you a little later. "I'm promise." Sarge

Waller, Chet Husted and McClintock come in just as I'm ready to leave and the three of us limp to the pledge meeting.

•••

"I just cannot believe you guys walked the whole way... stayed out the whole night?" The Tiler paces back in forth in front of the Thirteen, seated in the ACE living room. "That's just... magnificent!" he says with a broad smile. "Unity. That's what you showed them. I'm proud of you. Really proud." He goes slowly around the circle, stopping to gaze into the face of each of us. Ransom gives him a blank, bleak look but says nothing. The Martian continues to shiver.

The pledge meeting is more of the same. *When was Garrett Stowers Thurmond born? Where? (Who gives a shit?)* We may have solidarity but our collective spirits are worn thin. We weakly repeat the verses of another new song.

"Aces high, aces high, that's the song this week.

If you're from another house, then you're just a Greek.

Bet your hole card on the pot! Put him in with all you got.

For when the dealer calls his cry, Your bet is aces highhhhh!"

It's nearly ten o'clock when Kong's hated growl echoes up the hall. "Pledgessss... where are the fuckin' pledges?" We collectively groan but Tiler gives us a sympathetic, strange smile.

"Outside you asshole pledges. Hurry it up. Get your stuff. Outside!" Thoreau and Tiler herd us toward the front door. We burst through it onto the porch and are met by a great cheer.

There, below the steps, are thirteen big brothers, clapping their hands and yelling. Kong herds us down the steps and I trot into the grip of Doak. "Come on you fucking pledges! Come on little brother! We're gonna go drink some beer!"

• • •

"Aces high, aces high,   that's the song this week.   If you're from another house, then you're just a Greek..."

The singing Aces are living it up in the Esquire basement. Free beer just keeps coming our way as the brothers, even assholes like Mayhew and Curtis, slap our backs and shake our hands.

Ransom seems to have broken out of his long march shell. Standing on his chair, he chugs another National Bo right from the bottle. "I'm so fuckin' happy I could just..." he looks around with a silly ass grin, "just... crrrrryyyy!" Bursting into tears, he spins on the share and crashes to the floor.

"What's the matter with the Martian, Tiler?" someone asks. Chris is sitting in a booth with both hands gripping a beer bottle. Staring straight ahead, he shakes constantly. "C'mon Chris, drink up!"

"I think am sick," he responds in a monotone. I look at the Tiler. He blinks.

"I think we'd best get his ass over to the infirmary," he says to a couple of actives.

"For when the dealer calls his cry, Your bet is aces high!"

Chapter 19

Some Interesting Revelations

My high rank on Darcy's shit list is confirmed early Tuesday. As Andy and I leave Ellis from sociology, she mutters "uh oh, looky there" and gives me a nudge. Darcy sits on the courtyard wall, her determined frown unchanged when she obviously spots us.

"I think I'll just keep on motorin'" Andy tells me, "see you tomorrow, Five." as she blends into the crowd of milling students.

"Hey Darce, what're you doin' here?"

"I had a meeting here. And I *keep* my appointments. My promises." No peck on the cheek this morning.

"Aw Darcy, I'm sorry. Things just got carried away... we just got carried away. I came by Begorra later and it was closed. And your light was out so..."

"I'll say you got carried away, Five. I kept Begorra open an extra fifteen minutes. And I didn't go to bed until nearly 1 a.m. Besides, I saw Trish and Mark on the stairs and he told me you pledges had gone drinking with your big brothers." She gives me a stern look. "I hope you had a good time... with your *pledge brothers.*"

I light up a pair of Pall Malls and hand her one. At least she takes it. I'm not out of the woods but I *can* see the meadow. We sit there in silence for a few seconds, watching the student throng thin out just before the bells ring for the next class.

"Darce. I do apologize. You just have to be there, I guess, to understand how this pledge thing works. I couldn't take off. Believe me."

"Oh Five, I do believe you. That's the problem I have with the entire pledge business. You tell me you'll do something and then you can't because the *pledge class* does something else." She takes a deep breath. "Five... I didn't go out with a pledge class, that first date. I don't feel what I feel for you for a goddamn pledge class." She lowers her head and turns slightly away from me. The first class bell rings.

"C'mon Darcy. It's just for a little while longer. Then I'll be an Ace and everything'll be OK."

"Will it, Five? Will everything be OK?" She looks up at me with filmy eyes. "Don't you have a class to go to?"

"It's just figure drawing. I can be a little late."

"What about us, Five? What about the painting? You haven't worked on it since Saturday night. Do you want to work on it tomorrow night?"

"Jesus, Darce. I can't. At least not early." She snaps her eyes up to meet mine. "We've got a pledge dinner set with the Pi Phi pledge class tomorrow night. But I'll be up as soon as I can afterwards." The second class bell rings and Darcy rises.

"Better get to class, Five. I'll see you."

"Tomorrow night?" I ask.

"Maybe."

• • •

The Pi Phi pledge dinner is our first big social test as a group and it's not a home game. Tiler has drilled us on quick drawing our Zippos. "No woman or active ever gets a cigarette to lips before you are there with a light." We practice on each other, incinerating our nose hairs. Mom Holmquist — I privately think of her as 'Katherine,' her real name since Mom somehow doesn't seem appropriate — has taught us the niceties of etiquette, table settings and which fork to use when. *We hope.*

Soft drinks and smoking on the Pi Phi patio, sort of a mock cocktail party, are followed by the sit down dinner. The Pi Phi pledges look pretty great in heels and nice dresses. The Thirteen doesn't look very shabby, with the exception of Ransom whose personal habits have slipped a lot since the long march. Even the Martian, recovered after a night in the infirmary, looks pretty spiffy in a blue blazer and rep tie.

Although I've hung on the comfortable fringes of Andy Logan's circles of conversation, I find myself seated between Jackie Adamson and a blonde girl named Norma. Andy shoots me a wink from the far end of the table where she sits, surrounded by my pledge brothers.

"I was so thrilled when I heard you'd gone ACE," Jackie coos as the soup is removed. "But I had hoped you would go Sigma Chi," she adds. "You would make the perfect Sigma Chi, Five. They're just groovy."

"Jackie's *very big* on the Sigma Chi's," Norma contributes from my left. "She's going out with Dan Nofzinger." Dan Nofzinger doesn't ring any bells for me but obviously counts for something in the Pi Phi house. Jackie reaches for her red leather case and produces a king sized Kent. My lighter flames beneath her delicate nostrils in an instant.

"Jacqueline," the soft voice of the Pi Phi house mother drifts down the table like a layer of freezing fog. "Not between soup and salad, my dear." Jackie doesn't blush but is obviously flustered when she realizes there is no ashtray on the sparkling table.

"Mother Exner, may I be excused from the table for a moment?"

"Why certainly, my dear," the housemother replies sweetly. All of the Ace pledges rise as the lovely Jackie leaves the room in search of an ashtray, a thin trail of smoke behind her. Simpson causes a mild stir when he nearly knocks over a candlestick as we rise again for Jackie's return.

Norma leans over and whispers in my ear, "That's how they do it at the Sig house. Smoke between soup and salad. Hell, smoke between bites."

After dinner, we gather in the living room. Some of the Pi Phi pledges are like me, ready to bolt for other matters. Others mingle happily with my pledge brothers, playing the game, hustling for dates. Since we're considerably outnumbered, the pickings should be good.

"A couple of us are going up to the Frontier Room, Five," Andy Logan asks me, "want to come along?"

"Gee thanks, Andy, but I've got somewhere I've got to be. Really like to but I've got to run."

"Oh yes, of course you do," she smiles with a knowing nod. I make my good-byes to Mrs. Exner and the pledge mistress and am out the door.

• • •

The note on Darcy's door reads
"Gone to MIA movie with Trish."
I decide to hang around and go downstairs to duck into the
Wonder Bar. It's a dark and noisy place. I buy a Strohs and settle
into a spot at the stand-up bar by the window where I can see
them when they return. I take a couple of sips, then my beer
suddenly sloshes out of its glass as someone gives me a shove.

"Well look here, if it isn't the burger boy?" The slab
cheekbones and short crew cut of the Sandwich Man appear at
my side. "What're you doin' in a man's bar, burger boy?"

Another voice behind me, "Back off, Bodine. This one's
mine. All mine."

"Whatta you mean, Curtis? I owe this asshole big time." I
recognize the source of most of my recent nightmares, Brother
Galen Curtis.

"You must be shell-shocked, Bodine. You don't hear too
good. I *said* he's mine. Understand?" Bodine the Sandwich Man
gives me a black look and moves off into the dark rear of the
bar.

"What *are* you doin' in here, Low-ree?" Curtis asks,
elbowing his place into the stand-up bar?

"Hello, Mister Curtis. Just thought I'd have a beer while I
wait for my girl."

"Wonder Bar's a pretty strange place for a pledge, even an
Ace pledge, to wait for his girl. Nothing much in here but
drunken jocks and Korean vets waiting for the eagle to scream,
reliving the glory days at Long Dong Po." He gives me a look.
Just a look. "You look more like a Towne House type, all
dressed up like that."

"Been to a pledge dinner with the Pi Phi's Mister Curtis."

"Ah yes, the pledge dinner. And how'd the Thirteen do at
the Pi Phi house, Low-ree?" I tell him we did fine.

"Even Ransom? He didn't barf? Or burst into tears? What a
shitheel," Curtis snarls. "I'm gonna ding his ass. He'll never
make it to the balloon going up. You tell him that."

246

"Yessir, Mister Curtis." Down the sidewalk come Darcy and Trish. "Good talkin' to you, Mister Curtis. Gotta go. I'll see ya." I leave my beer and head for the door. Out of the corner of my eye, I see Curtis slide my bottle toward him and pour my half full glass into his.

• • •

Trish and Darcy *seem* friendly enough. Darcy asks me if I want to come up but there's a definite lack of enthusiasm. "Did you have a nice time with your little Pi Phi pledges, Five? Is that Chanel Number Five, I smell?" We say goodnight to Trish as Darcy rips off the note and unlocks the door to number five.

"No posing tonight, Five," she says, kicking off her loafers and sitting on the bed against the wall. "I'm exhausted."

"I just want to apologize, Darce. I mean it. I'm really sorry about Monday night. I just didn't have any control over what happened." I try on a truly sad expression. "Forgive me?"

"Aw Five, I forgive you. It's just that I worry about you. And us." Darcy leans over and gives me a soft kiss. "And that damned fraternity."

I return the kiss and she leans back against my arm, pulls her legs up onto the bed. "God," she murmurs, "my feet are frozen. And killing me. Too many hours at the Begorra." I rub her foot tentatively. She scoots away a little and reclines on the pillow. "Foot rub, Five? That'd be nice."

Darcy hums and purrs as I sit there with her icy feet in my lap, rubbing warmth into them. She squirms in happiness.

"Ahh, that's wonderful. Don't stop, Five. Keep it up." She twists her feet in my lap, exploring what lies beneath my trousers. "Five? You know what would really be nice? Really delicious?"

"Ah, no, Darce? What?"

"If you were to lick my feet all over. Like a cat. Would you do that for me, Five?"

• • •

It snows hard on Saturday, unusual for Athens even in mid-March. The drifts around the porch of the ACE house force the brothers to alter their plans for tonight's *Nights of Olde* party, much of which would take place in the courtyard. In the Keep, we place streamers of many colors radiating from a throne on the bandstand by the windows.

"I've been talking with Jan Dabny, Five," Mark Husted tells me as we take a smoke break from touching up coat of arms placards that will decorate the *great hall.* "She says you've got a sketch accepted for the student show. Congratulations."

"You mean really accepted? No shit?"

"That's what she said." Husted grins at me. "You know… next year you'll probably be the resident artist at the ACE house."

"If I make it." We've learned this doubtful sentence is the proper response for almost any reference to initiation, going active.

"Aw, you'll make it. Even if I have to come back and ride herd on your ass through hell week." *Hell week! The first time it's been said out loud to me… or any of my pledge brothers that I know of.*

"Come back? You mean we won't be initiated until next year?"

"Looks that way. A few of the brothers are pretty upset with your class. Some of your guys just have to shape up before the balloon'll go up." He gives me a sly smile. "But back to your artwork. Are you doing anything for the show in painting class?"

"Yeah… I've got something started. Professor Blockhart is really encouraging. He's seen my sketch. So I'm working on it. Hope to show him next week."

"Would you like for me to look at it? Give you a, say, peer's opinion?"

"That would be neat, Mister Husted, but…"

"Mark! Mark, Five. Here between us."

"Right, Mark. But I'd have to check with Darcy about showing it to you. She's my model."

"She's the girl in the sketch, too?" I nod yes. "She must really be something. Dabny really carried on about the sketch.

Damn Five. If you get two works in the student show… that'd really be something for a freshman."

• • •

Nights of Olde isn't such a terrific party. Maybe the snow, which keeps coming down, has taken a lot away from the medieval theme but right now, the theme seems to be let's get *really* drunk and raise hell. Ransom gets in a heated discussion with Waller about the army and their dates look on in disgust, drinking more than they should from their cups of Seven and Seven.

Darcy giggles when she first hears the words to the Kangaroo song, then flirts with Mayhew to make him repeat them until she's learned the song.

"My father killed a kangaroooo! Now wasn't that a grisly thing to do? To give me to chew the grisly piece of a dead Kangaroo.?"

Ransom's date, a muscular girl from back home in Dayton, curls up on the bench with her head in his lap and goes to sleep. Waller's date excuses herself and wobbles off in search of the little girls' room. Mayhew leaves shortly after she does.

Curtis and Gunner Schmidt, the other Korean veteran, sit nearby chugging vodkas and yammering about the Reservoir, whatever that is. Their dates, a couple of ugly Wonder Bar mooses, slop down their drinks in bored but steady fashion. I expect the four of them to hop up and start wiping out gooks any minute.

Someone starts a game where a girl sits on a bedspread in the middle of the Keep's floor, then four brothers each grab a corner of the cloth and run in a tight circle, spinning the girl like a top and themselves into falling-down dizziness. I persuade Darcy it's time to leave before she gets recruited for the game.

Upstairs in the coatroom, we hear loud voices from the library. "I don't give a shit if you're god. You don't try that stuff on a date of mine." Waller has Mayhew backed up against the bookshelves, a fist cocked ready to smash the active's face. On the couch, Waller's date is busy trying to stuff her breasts back into her brassiere and straighten her blouse.

I grab Waller's arm and Darcy runs over to help Waller's date. "Easy, Sarge. Go easy here. It's just a… misunderstanding. Right Mister Mayhew?"

"Fuck you, Lowrey. And forget this brotherhood, you dickhead," Mayhew spits at Waller. "I'm going to drop the ball on your ass Monday night," he snarls.

"No way, Mayhew, you horny asshole. You'll never have the chance 'cause I'm gone. You can tell this bunch of clowns to forget their goddamn Thirteen." He turns to his date who's now in a coat. "Come on, Jeannie. Let's get the hell out of here!"

"Wait up, Sarge. We'll go with you," I call as Darcy shrugs on her coat. I turn to Mayhew. "Listen Mayhew. No! Don't give me that shit. Not Mister Mayhew. MAYHEW! You may have just fucked up big-time. If we lose Sarge, ACE'll be the loser. You think about it and I'm gonna have a talk with my big brother." The four of us leave the brightly lighted house and shuffle into the snow-packed courtyard.

• • •

Standing outside the green door with Waller and Jeannie Cavellero, his disheveled date, we quietly talk about Mayhew and I try to dissuade Waller from doing anything rash.

"Would you guys like to come up?" Darcy asks the couple. They look up, questioningly. "Upstairs! To my place?" She grins at them. "I live up there, right over the sign. We can make some coffee. Coffee'd feel good right now."

Four people inside number three makes for coziness. "Gosh, Darcy, it's a neat place," Jeannie exclaims.

"Well, small for sure. Neat, I'm not so sure about? But it's home. And it's cheap. And it's warm. How 'bout coffee?" She puts the pot on to boil on her hot plate, pouring grounds right into the pot. When it's finished, she'll crack an egg into the whole mess, something that made me want to gag when I first saw her do it. But it tastes so good.

"Lord, Darce. This is you, isn't it?" Waller's examining the framed sketch over the table. "Who did this drawing?"

"Why your brother Five, Sarge. You know he's a great artist, don't you?"

"Well, yeah, but not anything like this. Ah... it's very... "

"Moving," Jeannie contributes. "Darcy, I don't know that I'd have the courage to pose like that."

"Oh, it didn't take courage. I didn't even know what Five was seeing when it first happened. You think that's something, look over in the corner. Show them, Five."

I turn on the overhead light which reveals the painting on its easel.

"Oh my!" Jeannie exclaims. "Ohhh my!" Waller just stares at the painting, then at me. Then he smiles, slowly. Very slowly.

• • •

"That was fun, Five," Darcy snuggles closer to me. Sarge and Jeannie have been gone five minutes or so. It's very close to midnight and the snow keeps falling. The Wonder Bar's light show is different tonight, but really something with the snowflakes making flickering reflections. "They're nice people. And I felt so sorry for Jeannie. That Mayhew is a real jerk. He can *seem* so nice, then once you're alone with him... bam!"

"He try that stuff on you, Darce? Doak warned me about him."

"Aw, just a quick grope at the first party. I just slapped his hand and joked him away. No big deal."

"They really seemed to like the painting, didn't they?" I ask softly.

"Yeah, they did," she responds, "I think it's going to be a pretty great painting myself. But what do I know about art?"

"You didn't mind that Waller saw it?" I ask. She shakes her head no. "Would you mind... ah, if I brought Mark Husted up to see it sometime? I need to take it to Blockhart next week for him to look at it and... I'd like someone else's opinion before I do."

"Sure, that'd be fine." She stretches and yawns. "God, but I'm done for. Can we start drinkin' something beside that sloe gin? It really makes me sleepy." She curls against my shoulder and snuggles. "You're not gonna go out in that stuff again tonight, are you?"

• • •

Sunday morning is blindingly bright. About five inches of new snow have fallen during the night and Athens is blanketed in at least a foot of pristine white stuff. Nothing moves outside.

"How about Cream of Wheat?" Darcy calls from the *other room* as we've come to call the kitchen-bathroom-alcove. I'm still under the covers, soaking up the warmth and coziness that only a morning of being snowed in can produce. "I'll go check with Trish and see if she's got any milk."

"You think she's up?"

"Five! It's nearly eleven. She and Mark didn't even go to the party. Sure she's up." She disappears out the door. Reluctantly, I get up and make my way to the bathroom. I'm just about to open the door when I hear voices. *Voices?*

"You decent, Five?" Darcy calls. "Oops, no you're not." Her arm with my pants and shirt pops through a slight opening in the doorway. "We've got company for breakfast." I quickly jump into my khakis and pull the shirt over my head. Trish Spotswood is standing at the window, looking out.

"Hey, Trish, how're you?" I can feel blood flowing to the edges of all my skin.

"Mornin' Five. You're up here pretty early today." She turns and smiles. "Funny, though. I don't see any tracks out there in the snow." Trish grins broadly. "Look at that, Darcy. Five's blushing. Aww, Five!"

"Well, I ah, er" I look at my bare feet as I stammer.

"Joke's on you, Five," Trish laughs. "Guess I don't have to ask you how your love life is any more, do I?" Darcy giggles. I grin. "Don't shake that milk, Darcy. I don't want the yellow part. Gotta keep my waistline."

Darcy holds the bottle of Broughton's Dairy milk, its paper cap pried off. "You mean we can have the cream? Oh, Trish. I just love real cream on Cream of Wheat." She carefully spoons out the thick yellow cream from the neck of the bottle and plops big dollops on two bowls of steaming cereal.

What can be better than to be snowed in with *two* beautiful women?

• • •

We leave Trish at the corner of Congress and Union. She's going to walk down to the depot to hopefully meet Mark's train from Cincinnati, where he's been on a job interview. I'm walking Darcy over to Begorra, then on to Biddle and a clean up. But Begorra is locked tight with a note on its door:

"Closed til' snow is gone."

"Terrific!" Darcy chortles. "I know Duff'll pay me for today. Act of God and all that." She falls backward into the thick snow on the street and flaps her arms and legs into a snow angel. "We can play, Five. All day! We can play in the snow."

"OK, I'll go along with that. And I've got an idea. Let me go home and get shaved and cleaned up. I'll be back to pick you up. An hour. Couple hours? However long it takes. OK?"

• • •

Showered and shaved, I follow the deep tracks from Biddle over to the East Green Cafeteria. Surprisingly, it's doing a good business for the early Sunday hour, considering the snow. With a cup of coffee in hand, I go in search of the Martian, finding him in the kitchen ordering second-semester new guys around.

"Hey, Chris. How'd you do at the party last night? Looked like you were having a good time." He grins in response. His steady date, Dawn Morgan, doesn't live up to her exotic name with thick glasses and straight lanky hair, but she and the Martian have a great time together.

"Terrific, Five. You guys left pretty early. Missed all the excitement!" I give him a questioning look. "Curtis and Ransom got into a real argument and Ransom's date barfed all over his feet."

"Ransom's feet?"

"No! Hah, hah, Curtis. He just about went apeshit. Said he's gonna blackball Ransom Monday night." We talk some more about the party and Chris gives me the word that the Thirteen is going to meet in the Esquire basement an hour before pledge meeting.

"Listen, Chris. Can I ask a favor?"

"For a member of the Thirteen," he grins. "Anything!"

"Well, I need to borrow a couple of the biggest serving trays…"

• • •

As we start across the President Street bridge, a B&O Pacific whistles its eastbound departure from Athens. We watch the black engine move toward us, then run from the plume of black smoke that blossoms up.

"C'mon Five. Let's go back to the Ace house and meet Trish and Mark," Darcy urges. I'm reluctant to go there uninstructed but, what the hell, it's a snowy Sunday.

We discover Katherine Holmquist in the living room in jeans, a sweatshirt and with a scarf tied around her pretty golden hair. She surveys the shambles of overturned furniture, half full and empty glasses, and looks up with a smile. Beside her, the Ace vacuum sweeper is poised.

"Gosh, Mom Holmquist," I say, "you shouldn't be doing this. Let me help." I immediately pitch in to right heavy chairs. Darcy starts gathering up plastic cups and empty bottles.

"That's all right, Five. It's nice of you to help. But I've got all day and the brothers certainly won't get the pledge class up here today. You'd better scoot before someone discovers you're here."

Just then Mark and Trish come through the front door. Mark rushes over to Katherine and gives her a big hug. "I got it, Mom. You're looking at an employed Ace!" Trish smiles broadly behind him.

"Terrific, Mark," Katherine responds. "Congratulations."

He turns to us. "Associate art director! Bowles and Cochran. Biggest ad agency in Cincinnati," he beams. I shake his hand

and Darcy gives him a kiss. "What're you guys doin' here, anyway?"

"We're going to the asylum grounds, sledding on these trays," Darcy says. "It's Five's idea. Isn't it great. Come on and go with us."

• • •

The sight that greets us at the asylum grounds tells me that my idea isn't all *that* original. The slopes are covered with figures of students, sliding on trays, riding sleds, big sheets of cardboard, even a six-person toboggan. It's a blast.

As the afternoon wears on, heavy clouds move in to cover the sun and the first of more snowflakes begin to fall. At the bottom of the hill, a bunch of Ace brothers have started building a bonfire. Other groups nearby are at work on theirs.

Darcy and I wrestle in the snow. Hug and kiss. Generally act like little kids. So does everyone else. It's nearly dark when we join the group at the Ace bonfire. "Hot buttered rum!" shouts Doak Phipps, gesturing to a huge pot from the Ace kitchen bubbling over the fire. Someone else produces mugs. Gunner Schmidt brandishes a bayonet. I secretly hope he's not planning to run a pledge through with the evil looking weapon.

We sit on our trays around the fire and join the singing…

"Oh college boys from sea to sea… don't ever go on cruise.

They stay at home and date our girls, and drink up all our booze.

They wear white bucks, bermuda shorts…

Doak drops a stick of butter into a pitcher of steaming rum, then Gunner plunges the glowing bayonet in, producing a huge cloud of hissing steam. Doak quickly begins pouring the mixture into mugs and others pass them around.

"Holy shit!" someone screams. "I can't even get this stuff to my mouth! What's in it?"

Gunner and Doak shrug. "Let's see? Five fifths of 200 proof rum. Lots of cloves and cinnamon and stuff. A stick of butter?"

Bob Long grimaces as he takes a sip. So does Darcy at my side. The stuff is hot, warm, glowing… fiercely strong and good! Long muses, "I'm not sure but it seems to me there should be some water involved…"

• • •

Each armed with a symbolic bottle of beer, the Thirteen gathers in the Esquire basement. The bitterness from Saturday night's party has been eased somewhat as we recall the scenes from the now legendary asylum snow party.

Mayhew being led off by a couple of the brothers to get his bleeding hand repaired at the infirmary. O-Annie protesting in girlish giggles… "I didn't realize a zipper is *that* sharp. *Giggle.* I just said 'oooh, your hand is icy' and yanked on that ole' zipper ring and…" she rolls back into the snow shaking with laughter.

Mark Husted and I directing the others as they march up and down a pristine slope to stomp giant Alpha, Chi, Epsilon symbols in the deep snow.

Curtis, passed out face down in the deep white stuff. After carefully swinging his arms and legs to create a snow angel, the Thirteen poses in a semi-circle behind him. O-Annie kneels in the foreground, holding his head up for the flash camera. A hand cocked on her hip, Darcy has one foot on his big upright ass like Osa Johnson with a prized cape buffalo.

Chet Husted taps his bottle on the table and brings us back to reality. "Drink up, Brother Ransom," he chides. Ransom makes a face and shakes his head no. "Ohhh, yes," Husted says. "We're the Thirteen and we're the One. If we go to pledge meeting with beer on our breath, we *all* go with beer on our breath." Ransom looks unhappy but takes a modest sip from his bottle. We wait, expecting him to barf or cry.

"Brothers Kostic and Waller have some things to tell us and we're runnin' out of time. So listen up," Chet says with surprising authority.

Waller and Benjo stand, each holding their jackets. "No way they'll take us for another ride tonight," Kostic says with a grin. "Can't even drive out there."

"But by next week, each of us needs to be ready," Waller says. He opens his jacket and carefully unfolds its lining revealing a small slit from which he extracts a square plastic flask. Kostic does the same. "I got a couple of these survival bottles from my dad's stuff. We're going to use them to make our own pledge class survival kits."

"They're no good for drinking," Kostic adds, "tastes like iodine and they do leak, too. But new, they come with all sorts of rescue shit. A silk map of Okinawa. Compass. Signal mirror. But we'll show you what we've done with ours." He unsnaps the metal bar that holds the removable top and spills out the contents on the table.

"Matches. The old fashioned kitchen kind. I've wrapped mine in wax paper. A couple bucks in quarters, dimes and nickels, wrapped in a handkerchief so they won't jingle. Some first aid stuff. Band-Aids in several sizes. Iodine. Needle and thread."

Waller picks up a pack of Pall Malls. "Cigarettes. And I picked up a map of Ohio from the Sohio station on Court Street. Also a little pen flashlight."

Holding up a white block, Kostic adds "This is D-ration. Don't make faces. It's rich chocolate and it tastes good. Sarge will get some from his dad. It's nourishing and won't melt." Around the tables our faces light with comprehension. "Each of us should have at least matches, change for phone calls, cigarettes and chocolate hidden in a coat. Don't try to pack too much stuff in, it'll bulge and the asshole actives will notice it."

"And memorize some telephone numbers," Waller adds. "People who can get some cars to come and get us."

We move on to other subjects. After Saturday's urging from Darcy, me and Jeannie Cavallero, Waller decides he's not planning to depledge.

"But if those assholes try to blackball Ransom, or me, or anyone else in the Thirteen. I am gone. And I hope that each of you is with me," Waller thumps his bottle on the table. "Call for

Pater Gousha!"

• • •

Pledge meeting is surprisingly subdued. Almost routine except for the extraordinary appearance of Mayhew, who apologizes to Waller and all of us for his actions at the Saturday party, and Curtis, who smiles a lot but mumbles through a half-assed speech about being sorry for some of the things he's said...

Even the interrogation party afterwards is pretty calm. Kong Logan seems in better spirits as he herds us to the Keep. But no calisthenics. Just shouted questions and quicker answers. The Thirteen seems to be growing up.

After the meeting, I stop by Darcy's apartment to say goodnight. With classes canceled and the Begorra still closed, we spent the entire Monday painting, messing around, and even me getting a little studying done.

"Just wanted to see how the paint is drying," I tell her. She's dressed in a long flannel nightgown, a garment I've not seen before. She gives me a hug and kiss and we examine the surface of the painting. "Professor Long says oil paintings sometimes take years to dry but this gouache stuff feels pretty good," I say, running my fingers across the image of the subject's pendulous breasts.

"I thought Mark was genuinely pleased with it," Darcy says, her arms around my waist and leaning into my back. At our invitation, Mark and Trish had stopped by in the afternoon to look at the painting and drink coffee. Husted's enthusiasm was heart-warming.

"Wanna stay a little while, Five?" she asks as I shrug back into my coat.

"Aw Darce, I've got to study sosh and finish my comp paper just in case they start classes again tomorrow."

"Oh they are," she answers, snuggling again in the doorway. "I heard it on WOUB a little while ago." We share a long kiss and she runs her tongue along my jawline. "Five? Remember my big surprise?"

"The new job?"

"Uh huh. Well, I start tomorrow."

"Gonna tell me what it is?"

"Nope," she breathes into my ear. "You'll find out soon enough. And you'll be… really surprised. Nite now."

Chapter 20

More Truths Unveiled

If OU started classes at eight o'clock on Tuesday morning, they did it without me. I woke with Toby's clock staring accusingly at me. 8:15 again. Doesn't the damned thing ever move? Fortunately I shaved and showered when I got in last night. So I grab my sketch pad and start up the Bryan stairs. They're like the south face of Everest, glazed and icy in sloping, uneven footprints that have thawed and frozen again.

Crossing University Terrace, I can hear the second class bells rattle across the snowy campus. Stomping snow off my boots, I hurry down the hall and enter the figure drawing studio. A few empty easels but not many. Jan Dabny looks up and nods, butts her cigarette.

"Well, I guess everyone's here that will be here," she says. I hurriedly set up my pad against the bench back and dig in the box for my pencils.

Dabny continues, "Today, we have a new model. I'm quite pleased with her and I believe she'll give you a different physique to challenge your skills. Monique? Are you ready?"

I look up as the model, her back to us, demurely removes the class kimono. With a graceful wave, she drops it to the edge of the podium and turns slowly to face the class.

Great galloping Christ! It's Darcy!

I feel blood racing everywhere throughout my body in a hell of a hurry. Darcy has a shy smile as she stands there, hands folded down over her groin. She doesn't move. Except her eyes which slowly rove over the class until they rest upon me. Her smile increases a degree.

"All right everyone," Dabny gives us the familiar chant. "Monique? Ready? Pose!"

While my classmates sketch furiously. I run the pencil around the surface of the pad, try to draw from the soul but not drawing anything at all. I'm not sure what my soul feels. After our weeks and months together, I've never drawn Darcy except from her pose on the bed or clothed at various places we've visited.

Her body looks exquisite. She trembles slightly from time to time, sways ever so little. But she holds the pose perfectly. I sense Dabny's presence at my shoulder.

"Trying something different, Five?" she asks in a low tone. "Our new model have you at a loss for... ?"

"Words, Jan. Yep, I'm at a loss for words." I turn to look at her and her expression tells me that she has been in on Darcy's surprise all along.

"OK, folks. One minute," Dabny calls. Pencils scratch and scrape. I line in a few more features but the sketch on my pad is the roughest, lightest of studies. "Time everyone. Relax, Monique."

Darcy slumps for a second, then bends gracefully to scoop up the kimono and slip into its billowing form. Thank God she didn't learn Anique's graceless beaver shot technique of picking up the robe. But she has learned that the model is free to roam the room during the break and inspect the work of the students. She moves slowly from easel to easel, nodding, smiling, making low comments.

Then she's beside me, bending over, arms holding the kimono wrapped tightly, her chin nearly on my shoulder.

"Like my surprise, Five? You should've seen the look on your face!"

I still feel in shock. All I can do is look up at her. Finally, "God, Darce. It's a surprise all right." I puff furiously upon my Pall Mall. She removes the cigarette from my fingers and takes a drag. I can feel the eyes of my classmates upon us.

"Are you angry with me, Five? Did I do the wrong thing?"

"Angry? Jesus, Darcy... I don't think so. I don't know what I am. Stunned, I guess. And... what's this 'Monique' crap?"

"Aw," she whispers, "Professor Dabny's idea. Thought I might want to protect my privacy. She has another model named Anique..."

"Yeah, Anique Dottreau. She's a research librarian and built like a research desk," I snort.

"Is that how you talk about *all* your models, Five?" Darcy giggles a whisper.

"No Darce. As you know, I don't talk about *my* models at all. I've only had three and I sure don't talk about my favorite one."

"Will you buy me a cup of coffee after class, Five?"

"Yeah. That'd be a good idea. Looks like Dabny's ready for you. I'll *try* to concentrate on this pose."

She starts back toward the podium, pauses, and takes a step back. "I don't care about my privacy," she whispers. "Do you?"

Do I? I shrug no and watch her bounce back to the posing platform. She again gracefully swings the robe away and turns to face us, legs slightly spread. She shakes her head as Dabny begins to speak.

"Excuse me a second, Professor Dabny. There's something I want you all to know. My name's not Monique. It's Darcy. And I work over at Begorra." She pauses and smiles shyly. "I've never done this before… posed for a bunch of people like this… and I hope I can do a good job for you. When I get rid of the goose bumps, it may even be fun."

"And… in case you think I'm showing favorites in this class… well, maybe I am a little." She pauses, glances my way and smiles. "Five and I have been friends for a long time."

• • •

Darcy's never been in the Frontier Room in the morning before and expresses amazement at the dancers.

"God, *Rockin' Robin* at 10 a.m.," she shudders. "It's not natural."

"Neither is standing naked in front of a bunch of strangers," I blurt, instantly wishing I could take the words back as I see the hurt in her face.

"Aw, c'mon Five. They're not strangers. They're *artists*. Just like you. Besides," she pauses, "I'm getting paid fifteen bucks an hour. Two beginner and two advance classes a week, that's more money than I make at Begorra.

"It really bothers you, doesn't it?" she bites her lower lip.

"Five… if you're ashamed…?"

"I'm not ashamed, Darce!" I protest. "I love your body. It's just…"

"Yeah," she interrupts, "you love my body all right. My body and that dumb fraternity. Sometimes I think that's all you love."

"Aw, Darce," I whine. "You know that's not true! It's just… well, I guess I just don't like sharing you with everyone else."

"Sharing me? You're not sharing me! They're looking at me. Drawing me. I'm posing. You sound like you think I'm a whore!"

"No, no, Darcy. No way. I'm proud of you, hon." I pause. Surely there's something else I can say? Something that gets us back on an even plane. "I guess it'll just take some getting used to."

"Well, I hope you do, Five. I need the money and, frankly, it *was* kind of fun." She glances at her watch. "Jeez, fifteen til. I've got to get changed and over to work." She rises. "Will I see you tonight?"

"Sure," I say. "I'll be up for my Begorra order."

Darcy leans up and kisses me gently on the cheek. "It'll be all right, Five. It will. If it isn't, I'll quit. Promise." And she picks her way through the gyrating dancers and out the door.

• • •

Professor Blockhart leans forward at his desk, puffing his pipe furiously as I carefully unwrap the canvas. Darcy and I haven't worked on it for three nights to ensure the acrylic is dry before wrapping it in the big muslin bag she sewed.

I timidly proffer the canvas toward him. He takes it in both hands and leans back in his chair to study it in the light from his window. Clouds of smoke erupt from behind the expanse of canvas. I sit quietly, examining his office for the first time. A painting of a giant nude, her legs sprawled apart, dominates one wall. Marching into her huge vagina are tiny figures. Students obviously since some carry little tightly rolled umbrellas.

Lord! This guy's weirder than Husted. And I really have him

264

as a faculty advisor? I hope I can graduate without getting arrested.

"Interesting, young Lowrey. Very interesting." These words float up from the smoke that I now identify as *Mixture 79.* "I do believe you have captured something very special. How do you feel about it?" He tilts the painting and peers at me over its top. An owl wreathed in pipe smoke.

"Gosh Professor, I think I'm pleased with it so far. But somehow... I don't feel it's quite finished, quite there."

"Nonsense," he snorts. "And yet true. It could hang this minute. I would be proud to hang it here upon my walls. Yet..." he pauses, "I know the feeling. I get it with every canvas I touch. But there's a time when you have to say halt! Fini! Done!"

He puffs and studies some more. I sneak glances at some of the other paintings, then find courage to rise and look more closely at one of a woman standing in what appears to be a swamp. She also is nude and her body shines with a coat of green slime. Still, she looks familiar. *Well, she should. It's Jan Dabny. Perhaps a few years younger but just the same.*

"I think, Lowrey, you're very nearly there. Am I to take it that this is a painting from life? This spot exists? Not just in your mind?"

"Yes sir. It exists all right. In my mind." I pause for a second, then blurt, "and in my soul."

"Excellent, Lowrey. I'll give you a week. A week from today. That's the deadline for entries in the student show. Have it finished by then and it shall have my nomination to hang. You'll need to sign it... and give it a name. Good enough?"

"Good enough, Professor Blockhart. Thank you very much sir. Thank you." I accept the canvas back and gingerly slip it back into its bag.

"Oh no, Lowrey. Thank you. You're confirming my belief in you. And I find it very gratifying." He smiles and explodes a giant cloud of aromatic smoke at me. "If I were you, I would proudly march across that campus with the painting unsheathed for all to see." Pause. "But then, perhaps it will make a far greater impact upon the public when first seen at the student show."

• • •

Darcy hunkers on a backward kitchen chair beside me as I put finishing touches on the painting. What finishing touches? What does it need? A light wash of yellow in the lights shining on the floor. Tiny strokes of magenta in the highlights in her hair. I drop the brush and droop in my chair.

"Darce. It's got to be finished. I can just paint and paint and it'll never be done if I keep this up."

"I think it's finished, Five. I think it's perfect. Sign the damned thing and let's call it done."

I pause for several seconds. How to sign it? "I think my full name is kind of, what, pretentious?"

"Didn't you say Rembrandt signed his full name?"

"Yeah, but I'm no Rembrandt." I pick up a fine brush, dip its point in black acrylic, then quickly scrawl *Five* in the lower right hand corner. "There!"

"Perfect," she says with finality. "Now, what are you going to call it?"

"God, I don't know. We called the sketch *The Window.* How 'bout *Window Number Two?"*

"Nah, that's pretentious too." She bites her lip in thought. Silence.

"What do you think of…" I give her a glance, *"Light Show?"*

Darcy looks at the painting. Then at me. She smiles. "That's kind of what? Dirty? It has a double meaning, my boobs and all." Another pause. "I like it. *Light Show."*

• • •

The days and weeks that follow are frenzied. Pledge meetings and sweat parties. With two assignment paintings still to do, I begin work on a second nude of Darcy, using sketches from her figure drawing poses. I've become accustomed to the idea of *my girl* posing before the class and find the objective study of her body beneath the classroom skylight fascinating.

A second painting, this one a fantasy landscape of a covered bridge wreathed in fog, alternates on the easel in her apartment. *My studio.*

The Thirteen continues to survive the harassment from the Ace house. Harassment which intensifies with every week. Our weak link seems to be Ransom, whose fragile personality unravels a bit more with every screamed order for pushups. Benjo and Sarge have assumed roles as our military leaders. Chet Husted guides us gently, playing politics with the Tiler and the other active brothers.

Somehow I continue to juggle four Begorra runs a week, pledge dinners and teas, work parties and sweat parties, painting, and above all, loving Darcy. Attending classes is no problem but sitting in them without proper preparation becomes nerve-wracking. I ease by mid-terms with B-minuses and C's. A couple of times I catch myself day-dreaming about the good old, easy days of high school.

● ● ●

The Ace house is silent. It's nearly ten o'clock and most of the brothers are out on campus somewhere, smooching their dates goodnight, shooting the shit in a smoky bar. I stare glazedly at the Western Civ text on the dining room table before me. It's the second time I've had pledge duty and I know that soon, the quiet will be altered by the return of rowdy Aces.

"Pledgge!" The cry echoes down the stairs and I leap up to find its owner. Someone needs some shoes shined? As I reach the top of the stairs, the call rings out again. I find Galen Curtis, clad only in boxer shorts, standing in the doorway to his room.

"Aw shit, not you Low-ree, you fuckup," he grins. "I'm starving. Here's two bucks. Run up to Begorra and get me 15 burgers and a Coke." I take the money and whirl to run his errand, hoping to escape the house before others arrive to add to the order.

Darcy wipes the hair from her forehead and gives me a smile as she serves the throng of customers at the counter. Duff looks up from the kitchen, calls to me, "You didn't call in an order,

Five. What's up?"

"Rush order for the house, Duff. Fifteen and a Coke, fast as you can."

"What're you doing here so early, Five?" Darcy asks as she draws the Coke.

"Got pledge duty tonight, Darce. These are for Curtis. I'll probably be back again unless they want pizza." I pay for my order, wink at Darcy and whirl to get back to the Ace house.

I knock on Curtis' closed door and enter when he responds. I pass through a dark short hallway that leads to the two-man room he shares with Gunner Schmidt. Curtis is seated at his desk, the only illumination from his study lamp.

"Here's your burgers, Mister Curtis," I say.

"Bring 'em over here, Low-ree," he says softly. He turns slightly in his chair and I can see his erect penis poking from the open fly of the boxer shorts. He smiles and asks gently, "Is there anything you'd like to talk about, Five? Anything bothering you?"

I try to look over his head, anywhere but at his swollen member. "Uh, no sir. Nope, Mister Curtis. I've got to get going." I turn and flee from the room.

As I leave, I hear him say, "Any time you want to talk, Five, come and see me."

• • •

"Darcy! Darce! It got accepted!" I burst into Begorra and grab her around the waist, picking her up and swinging her around. Duff looks on from the cash register in mild surprise. So does the pair of customers.

"It did?" she squeals. "It really did? Oh my God!" Throwing her arms around me, she gives me a big kiss.

"Yeah. It really did. I just left Blockhart's office. Scared the crap out of me when he left a note for me to come see him. But he seemed really pleased and said that both *The Window* and *Light Show* will hang in the student show! You're gonna be famous!"

Darcy blushes and grins at Duff and me. "Nope, Five. I'll be notorious. You're the one who'll be famous."

• • •

Mark Husted knocks at the doorway and waits while Tiler finishes his instruction at another pledge meeting. "…so the leopard plays a great role in the symbolism of our brotherhood. As you learn about the leopard, you will discover that he is not only a symbol, but he is your guide on the pathway to light and truth." He pauses while we scribble our notes. "You have something for us, Brother Husted?"

Mark comes in and sits on the arm of one of the overstuffed couches. "Well, guys. We just voted on our theme for J-Prom and candidate. Brother J.L. Simmons will be our J-Prom king candidate. And the theme is *Aces On The Half Shell*. We're going to use the musical *Carousel*."

We Thirteen stare at each other in wonderment. *What in hell is this J-Prom stuff, anyway?* Husted grins at our obvious ignorance.

"Don't worry," he says, "Brother Phipps is the chairman and he'll be out in a little while to fill you in. I'm in charge of building the float and the sets for the skit, so I'll need some help. Five, you're drafted. Anyone else interested? Kostic, you and Waller did a good job on the party stuff. You want to help?"

Kostic, who doesn't like to volunteer, shrugs. Waller follows his example.

"Well, the rest of you guys are going to have to help build stuff as well rehearse the skit songs and dances, and help sew costumes…" Kostic and Waller shoot their arms up in a burst of volunteerism.

• • •

Working furiously, Darcy and I have fashioned our costumes for tonight's *Up or Down* party at the Ace house. A clothes hanger and gold glitter have created a halo for her angel outfit — a white robe made from an old sheet with a pair of cardboard wings I've painted and covered with feathers from her pillow.

Another bent coat hanger supports a long, swaying tail for my devil outfit.

"Hold still, Five," she says with pins in her mouth. "I'm going to cut out this seam in your pants..."

"Darce, these are my good flannels," I protest.

"Just a little hole," she says, "and I'll put some stitches around it to keep it from ripping the rest of the seam. All we've got to do is stick the tail through and hook it onto your belt."

The tail is a long tube of red material which she's stitched, then turned inside out. Its point is stuffed with a piece of rag and the whole thing then slides onto the coat hanger armature. I admire the way it sways to and fro in the mirror on her bathroom door.

A battered porkpie hat from Trish's closet is now festooned with a pair of stuffed red horns. Darcy applies mascara liberally to my eyebrows, then paints on a fiendish looking mustache.

"Now me," she orders. "The wings'll go through the slits in the robe like this." Her fuzzy wings are taped to her brassiere strap. Carefully, I lower the robe over her head and urge the wings to appear through their openings. Darcy cinches the robe with a piece of tasseled gold cord we've stolen from a beer display in the Esquire.

"Ah," I stammer, "aren't you going to wear any... ah, panties?"

"Oh gosh," she blusters. "How am I gonna get them on without crushing my wings? I guess you'll just have to do it for me, mister devil."

• • •

For *Up and Down* the Keep is decorated with stalactites of red and orange crepe paper and rotating red lights keep the hellish atmosphere alive. Upstairs, "heaven" is the dining room with a few blue bulbs, the floor covered with mattresses, and soft romantic music wafting from the speakers.

As parties go, it's pretty much the usual... lots of drinking, dancing, singing and looking for sexual opportunities as brothers and their dates get drunker. Darcy and I avoid the mattressed confines of Heaven as we've mutually decided we don't like making out in public... even in a dark room with blue lights.

We're sitting at a long table with Waller and Jeannie when Ransom's date, the Pi Phi pledge named Norma, slides onto the bench beside us.

"Have you guys seen Joe?" she asks. "I thought he went to the john but that was a long time ago." She reaches over and picks up my cup, taking a big slug without asking. "He was pretty smashed already," she grins. "Now I've got to catch up." She lurches away toward another table, calling back "tell him to come and get me if he shows up."

The four of us leave right after the climax of the party — screaming, squealing O-Annie being rolled in strings of orange and red crepe paper, clad only in a black bra and red panties.

• • •

My eyes are barely shut when there's a sharp knock on the door of 205. Toby's still out so I lurch up to get the door for him. Obviously, he has once again lost or forgotten his key.

Instead, I find a pale Terry Simpson. He bursts through the door, "Get your clothes on quick, Five. We've got a problem." He sits on Toby's bed as I scrunch into khakis and a t-shirt, slide into my loafers. "The Thirteen's meeting over in Gamersfelder as soon as we can round everybody up."

Kostic and Dicky Reb arrive at Gamersfelder Hall just as we do and Simpson leads us up the stairs and down a hallway. He knocks softly on a door and Chet Husted answers it, his face pale and grim.

"OK, guys, pull up a floor and listen," he says. A single study lamp lights the room, revealing all of us and especially Ransom, curled on a bed and reeking of booze and vomit.

"What happened to Ransom?" Shivers asks, "he barf on someone's date again? We gonna have a sweat party for it?"

"No... worse than that," Chet responds in a low tone. "A lot worse than that. I want him to tell it himself if we can get him awake." Soos Salazar comes in from the hallway with a soaking towel. Chet and Waller lean over Ransom, wiping his face with

271

the cold cloth and urging him awake.

He blinks, groans and shuts his eyes again. "C'mon dammit, Joe. Wake up. It's OK. We're all here with you. It's OK." Ransom's eyes pop open and he rolls them at us. Husted helps him to sit up against the head of the bed.

"C'mon Joe. Try to tell us all what you told me, OK?" Husted urges softly. "Everything, OK? Everything you can remember."

Ransom sobs loudly, then retches. Husted quickly puts the towel beneath his mouth. But nothing happens. "I guess I got pretty smashed at the party," he stammers out between sobs. "I was in the john, sort of trying to wash my face... and Curtis comes in... says 'whatsa matter? Can I help?'" I look around the room. The intent, serious stares of my pledge brothers meet mine.

"Then... he sort of helps me into his room, tells me to lie down, I'll feel better..." more sniffs and gasps. "I guess I did... and passed out. Thought I was havin' a dream..." Sob, sniff. Ransom looks around the room again, his eyes narrow slits in his puffy face. "You know... a dream... like...a wet dream but it wasn't. I woke up and there was Curtis... it wasn't a dream!" He shudders and curls into a ball.

"What was Curtis doing?" Chet asks gently. "Come on, Joe. You've *got* to tell us everything."

"Uh! He had... he had my penis... in his mouth... I was hard... and he was... I guess I passed out again." He grasps his arms tightly around his chest and tears roll down his cheeks.

"Then... I'm awake sort of... again... and he's kind of holding me up, sitting on the edge of the bed. And he... he's trying to get me to open my mouth... and there's his cock, right there in my face!"

Ransom's look is sheer terror, desperation. "I pull my head away and he grabs me by the hair and... before I can do anything... he... he *shoots* all over me!"

"Sonofabitch!" someone mutters but Ransom is talking now, fast, almost without a breath.

"I jump up and try to get to the door, but my pants are down around my legs. I fall... hit my head... guess I passed out." He

272

stops dramatically, then slumps back against the headboard with his eyes closed tight.

Frank Able picks up the story. "His date, Norma, was pretty well bombed and my date and I walked her back to her dorm. Then when I came home here, I decided to check on Joe.

Able pauses, sighs, "found his door wasn't locked. But it wouldn't open. So I shoved hard and budged it open. He was lyin' there on the floor, against the door and that's when I went to get Chet."

"I'll be a sonofabtich, the rotten bastard," Waller snarls. "Curtis *really is* a cocksucker!"

"Listen up," I say urgently, "let me tell you what happened to me last week." And I relate the story of the hamburger delivery to Curtis' room.

"That motherfucker," Waller says through clenched teeth. "He pulled the same shitty stunt on me. I didn't say anything… just thought it was best I kept it quiet."

McClintock, Ransom's fellow legacy and rush buddy, has been silent until now. He asks, "do you suppose he did anything else to Joe?"

We're all standing and we stare silently at each other. We look down at the form of Ransom. "We've got to check," Husted says. He and Mac pull the cover down from Ransom's bed. His pants are down around his ankles, his underwear missing. Gently they roll him over.

Chapter 21

Did We Miss A Turn In The Path?

Coffee, cigarettes and endless words help take the edge from our rage. After Benjo, who admits he has seen lots of carnage in Korea, examines Ransom and cleans him, we leave him sleeping with a double dose of cough medicine in him. The Martian guides us to the East Green Cafeteria where he uses his key to gain entrance to the kitchen and brew a huge pot of coffee.

Ransom's condition is the biggest subject of concern. "I don't think he's got any internal injuries," Kostic said, "but then, I'm no medic. But... he's probably gonna be pretty fucked up in the head."

"Even more so," McClintock mutters. "So... should we get him up to the infirmary?"

"Same answer as to the question of calling the cops," Husted says firmly. "We'll do what Ransom wants to do... when he can tell us."

"If he wants to go to the police, that'll probably be the end of us as a pledge class... and the end of ACE as a fraternity at OU," D.D. Smith observes.

"So fuckin' what? I'm not sure I want to belong to any chickenshit outfit that would take a pervert like CC," Soos Salazar spits out. 'CC' is the code nickname we've made up for Curtis to prevent the secret from accidentally spilling into the wrong conversations. It stands for *Cocksucker Curtis.*

"Aw, ease up guys. They've got predatory homos like CC in the army, all of the services. It's pretty hard to weed 'em out," Kostic says. Twelve sets of eyes roam the table, each peering for someone to weed out.

"Yeah," Waller chimes in, "in my dad's basic training companies at Fort Benning, they'd get one of these guys, throw a blanket over his head, and toss his buttfucking ass down a set of stairs."

"Now there's a pleasant thought," McClintock says. "Maybe we can set him on fire first?"

This sort of banter goes on for hours. Somewhere around four, Mac goes back to Gamersfelder to check on Ransom. Chris Cobb starts another urn of coffee so one will be ready when the Sunday cooks come in.

And in our daze, we realize we haven't agreed upon much. Except to abide by Ransom's wishes in the matter, if he has any.

"He's still out like a light," Mac reports back. "Anyone needs a smoke? I got two packs of Pall Malls from the machine."

Kostic says tiredly, in a slow drawl. "I'll tell you what. I see this as the kind of challenge to the Thirteen that Tiler's been talking about. None of that chickenshit 'what was Kendall Kirkwood's collar size?' stuff."

"Agreed," I chip in. "If Ransom wants to handle it as a revenge thing, then by God the Thirteen is One and we get revenge." I find it difficult to think of Curtis without envisioning his erect penis popping through those shorts. *It could've been me.*

"In Costa Rica, my father's friends say the flavor of revenge improves with age, like fine wine and cheese." We all chuckle at Soos' father's adage, even though most of us have never tasted fine wine.

"I'm in favor of keeping it within the Thirteen," Husted says. "We don't let the sonofabtich get away with anything else, and, unless Ransom wants to, we don't say anything to the actives. Once we've been initiated…"

"If we make it," the Martian intones by custom.

"Once we're initiated," Husted continues, "we have two years to figure out how to take revenge on CC." He pauses to stretch and yawn. "In the meantime, let's get some sleep. Mac, you keep an eye on Ransom and let me know if there's anything new. Everyone… keep your eyes and ears open… don't let Curtis get you alone… keep your peckers in your pants… and your pants on."

• • •

It's early afternoon Sunday when Dense shakes me awake in 205. I blink at him and wonder how he got in the room.

"C'mon man, it's too nice a day to spend in the rack. Even Toby's out… left the door unlocked again too."

Strangely, I feel alert and awake after several hours of sleep without dreams… without nightmares.

"Page and I are gonna take the Bearmobile on a ride out to a place called Ash Cave. Come on and go with us." I nod agreement and he says he and Page will wait in the truck while I clean up. Ready to leave, he turns as says, "by the way, the Martian said for me to tell you he'd heard from Ransom. Everything's gonna be OK."

To my surprise, the Bearmobile has a new paint job. Big black Sigma Nu initials on the door panels. Plus an old car seat and pipe handrails bolted onto the flat plywood bed. "The brothers thought it needed a little dressing up," Dense says proudly.

In the cab with Page and Dense, my stomach growls loudly enough for them to hear. "Can we swing by Begorra and pick up some burgers?" I ask. "We had an all-nighter and I haven't had anything to eat since… God, since I don't know when."

Darcy gives me a big smile as I enter, then squeals, "Oh, am I invited?" when I tell her what we're doing. "I'm sure Duff would let me off *if* I ask him nicely," she says in a stage voice that can be heard in Nelsonville, much less the kitchen.

"Sure kid, take off," Duff says. He leers at me. "I understand she's about to come into some *additional* wealth, Five." I grin back sheepishly but don't acknowledge Darcy's *other* job.

While Page and Dense wait in the truck, Darcy and I clomp up the stairs so she can change. "I don't want to smell like hamburger grease and onions," she says. "Do you think I smell greasy and onion-y, Five?"

"Darce, you always smell good to me. The way you smell always does something to my appetite." She returns this grease-spotted compliment with a silly leer.

As she's unlocking her door, Trish Spotswood opens her door and yells down the hall. "Hey guys, what're you doing? Want to come down and listen to records with Mark and me?"

"We're going to Ash Cave in a pickup truck," Darcy calls. "Why don't you come with us?" She looks at me. "That's all right isn't it?"

"Sure," I reply. "We may have to stop and get some more burgers."

Darcy strips off her tan Begorra shirt and wriggles out of her brassiere. I have a momentary wish to spend the afternoon but before I can express it, she's thrown on a sweatshirt and runs into the alcove to wash her face.

Back downstairs, we introduce Mark and Trish to Dense and Page. The newcomers are happy to ride on the back seat and Trish runs back up to her place for a blanket.

I pile into the cab with Dense and Page, Darcy snuggling on my lap. Her breasts are warm and soft against my arm and I involuntarily signal to her my enthusiasm. She giggles and bites my ear.

• • •

Ash Cave is a giant arch hollowed out of a steep hillside. From its cliff-like top, a thin waterfall splashes down several hundred feet. Mark and I sit on a rock and sketch the scene before us. Near the pool, the Bear cavorts with the girls, throwing big rocks into the pool to try and splash them.

"Mark," I say tentatively, "you said once when I asked you to be my big brother that you'd always be happy to give me any help… any advice you could."

"You need some advice, Five? Got a problem?"

"Not just me. It's the pledge class."

"And you don't want to ask Tiler?" he observes.

"Not just that. We don't want to ask anyone. This's just me, asking you."

"And?" I ponder for a few seconds, continuing to sketch details on the pad.

"Well, say we have an active who's really giving us a bad time. A really bad time."

"You mean something beyond the pledge party horseshit? The harassment?" He pauses. "I'm sure you realize by now that a lot of that is part of the game… kind of an act. Necessary though."

"No, this is not that chickenshit stuff." He smiles at my term. "This is important. Could be *really* important."

"And you don't want to tell me any details."

"I can't. You understand, don't you?" He nods yes. "Is there some way that we can get a message across to him? A message that he'll understand. Loud and clear?"

He stares at me steadily. "I would guess you're talking about Brother Curtis?" I nod slowly. Mark sights and looks at the sky. "He's a hard guy to figure, almost like one of those split personality things. He can be funny and great, then in a second he's madder than hell."

"Yeah, that's what we've been told. Mostly, he's been madder than hell at the pledge class and I don't think it's just part of the game."

"Well, this is just friend to friend. Outside ACE. But I *have heard* of pledge classes taking certain active members on a ride."

"On a ride? Like you guys did us?"

"Yeah. It could be done, you know. But you'd have to be very careful…"

• • •

Dense idles the truck for ten minutes, then pops one of its hoods. The bags of Begorra burgers are placed on the engine's flat block. In a few minutes, we can smell the familiar aroma of grilled onions. "Guess we'd better turn 'em once, don't want 'em to get burned," he observes.

"Chef Bear!" Trish looks at my big friend with admiration. "Who would've ever thought someone out of the Sigma Nu house could cook anything other than home brew or Spam?"

The burgers *are* delicious, warm and still juicy. Darcy has a smear of mustard on the tip of her nose. "Can you guys believe that *even I* like the way these taste? Wait'll I tell Duff he can sell his griddle and just install an old Harvester pickup out back."

On the way home, we trade places with Mark and Trish and

snuggle on the car seat beneath Trish's blanket. I have a hard time keeping my eyes open and finally, realize with a jolt that I've been asleep with my head on Darcy's lap.

"I was afraid you would fall off this thing, love," she murmurs to me. "Did the nasty old Aces keep you up all night?"

"You might say that, Darce. Thanks for giving me a soft pillow." We kiss and watch the sunset through the trees. It's still winter but the days are getting longer.

• • •

We're beginning to call ourselves the 'Esquire Thirteen' with another Monday night session before pledge meeting and we're at the big round table in the Esky basement. All thirteen of us with Ransom looking more alert, more chipper than he has in weeks.

"Believe me, brothers. I'm all right. I mean, what happened, that's a bitch. But I'm OK. I don't hurt. At least not inside. You know…" his explanation has a sincere ring but each of us knows it cannot be true.

Without giving credit to my source, I outline *my* idea for revenge. Ransom has said no to either telling the actives or calling the police. "We're the Thirteen goddamnit, and we'll settle it our way," he says with determination.

Smiles light up around the table as each pledge brother comprehends my scheme and begins embellishing it in his own mind.

At the Ace house, the pledge meeting itself is certainly different from previous ones. Tiler spends much of the meeting out of the room, leaving Chet Husted to drill us in lore and songs. Tiler looks grim when he returns.

"Pledges. We're going to have an interrogation party after the meeting. No sweat party. And this'll be your last interrogation party… for a while." We exchange glances around the room, seeking some meaning of this announcement. The Tiler continues, "The first J-Prom practice is tomorrow night, six thirty here at the house. And the same every night for the rest of the week." We groan in unison.

"J-Prom practice here Saturday morning and the rest of that day. If you've got dates, cancel them. J-Prom practice on Sunday, from noon through night. Cook'll serve you all sandwiches both days this weekend." He pauses, takes a breath, then continues.

"Things are happening guys... things that are going to make this J-Prom and the rest of the spring's schedule a little more hectic. Get as much sleep as you can and by all means, try to study every spare moment you get." *Call for Pater Gousha?*

• • •

The "pledge party" *is* strangely different as well. An air of intensity pervades the Keep and many of the actives looks as stressed as we pledges feel. After about thirty minutes of relatively quiet interrogation, we're dismissed and told to go home. We head for the Esquire basement.

"What was *that* all about?" Ransom's general question echoes the puzzlement we all feel. It's just not like the active chapter to undergo such a sudden change. After two beers, I head upstairs for the john, where I encounter Dense standing at a urinal.

"Five! Great news, man. It's supposed to be a secret but we're going active this week. Start Hell Week tonight."

"Tonight? Good luck! That's great, I guess. But isn't it pretty early?"

"The poop we got is that IFC is changing its rule on deferred rush. So we're gonna be initiated early so we can help prepare for a big rush next fall, first semester."

I deliver this news to the Thirteen at the round table in the gloom. "Holy shit," Chet Husted exclaims. "D'ya suppose they're down there prowling the East Green right now for us? That we're starting tonight too?" We chug our beers and hustle for the East Green hill, thoughts full of not being in the right place when the balloon goes up.

But in 205, all seems normal. Toby is asleep on his bed with a textbook on his chest. Obviously, the Phi Delt's are not harassing their pledge class as hard as the Aces do. "Wake up,

Tobe. Did you go to pledge meeting?"

He blinks and shakes his head. "Yeah. But we got sent home early. Something's going on, but what? Do you know anything?"

• • •

By the next afternoon, the news is all over campus. *The Post* has the official version that deferred rush is dead, attributing IFC's sudden decision to "make an effort to improve the social and study opportunities for freshmen men by returning to a first semester rush." The general consensus is that this is a line of bullshit; the fraternities just want to get pledge money in their coffers earlier. Whatever, the decision is made and the spring of '55 suddenly becomes different.

The Sigma Nu's are the first to have their "initiation week" but the few times I glimpse the Bear, whatever hell they're passing out up on Congress Street doesn't seem to faze him.

I'm busy working with Husted designing the guts of our float — a rolling carousel with lobsters instead of horses. In the parking lot, McClintock and Simpson learn their steps as dancing lobsters while Soos Salazar practices his lines as a talkative clam with a Spanish accent. The other members of the Thirteen join the actives in a chorus line of the damned, shuffling through the ragged steps and counting cadence aloud. The sight of dancing seafood makes me wonder what *Carousel* is about.

Husted drives Kostic, Waller and me out to the airport where an abandoned World War II hanger shelters the Ace "secret weapon" which turns out to be a stripped down '39 Reo truck. "We got this baby last fall but couldn't get it running in time for the homecoming parade," he says proudly. The truck and its frame are festooned with angle-iron bars running its length and width.

We follow in Husted's car as Kostic drives the skeleton truck through the darkened streets to Beasley & Matthew's' Ford garage, where one of the owners has offered to let us build the float in an empty building.

• • •

"Five, are we going to J-Prom?" Darcy asks in a matter-of-fact tone as she wipes the Begorra counter.

"Well sure, we're going…" I hesitate. "I mean, aren't we?"

"You haven't *exactly* asked me," she returns. "I mean, a girl's gotta make plans."

"Oh God, Darce. I'm sorry. I've just be so damned busy with the stupid float and all…" I get down to one knee on the Begorra floor, clasp my hands and plead, "Darcy honey, will you go to J-Prom with me?"

Shrugging, she grins. "I'll think about it." Customers applaud.

• • •

"It's a perfect plan. I love it!" Waller exclaims. He, Kostic and I are working in the Beasley garage. Husted's somewhere scouting up some more lumber and bolts while we assemble the two-by-four frame that will support the carousel.

Kostic grins his approval. "You've really got an weird mind, Five. I mean… just dumping his ass out in the cold is one thing but this!"

"It's genius!" Waller shouts. "Sheer fucking genius. When do we do it?"

"Any time after J-Prom," I guess. "Don't forget we've got to get the rest of the Thirteen to agree. I've just mentioned it to you guys."

"And it's the sort of thing we have to really work out. Even rehearse," Kostic adds. "Lots to go wrong if we don't carry it off to perfection."

• • •

J-Prom Thursday arrives… the night when fraternities and men's dorms traditionally troop around to women's residence halls with their skits, campaigning for their candidates. Our skit gets off to a rough start at Boyd Hall and improves only slightly

283

when we put it on in front of the ADPi house on South Court. In our spare time from float building, the art team has created a two-sided set of background flats that represent a fishing wharf and when twirled around, a carnival midway.

The skit's problem seems to lie in the fact that our candidate, J.L. "Curly" Simmons, owns one of the flattest singing voices to ever make an ear cringe. Even with the "Fishing Boat Five" in the background, J.L. flats his way through one embarrassing performance after another.

He saves the show, however, by providing a very romantic embrace and a long kiss to the queen candidate at each finale. Jesus Salazar, the funniest bivalve on the Hocking, also leaves a trail of laughs as we slog through Athens. *Thank God I don't have to wear a lobster suit.*

At Lindley Hall, Darcy pokes me and grins. "Duff said I could come up and watch 'em go by here as long as I'm back when the rush starts. J.L.'s pretty awful, isn't he?" I grimace. "Don't worry, I've seen Gamersfelder and Phi Tau so far, and they were just about the bad," she says encouragingly. "You're gonna pick me up after work?"

Our twelve minutes is up and I jump to grab the set and roll the Ace show toward the far end of sorority row on College Avenue. The show must go on. I give Darcy a quick wave as we march off in the wake of the band playing *It's Been A Real Nice Clambake.* The long trek up Court Street is punctuated by actives ducking into the Esquire and Tavern, a definite breach of skit rules and Ace discipline.

The star of our show fortifies himself frequently from a flask carried for him by McClintock in his lobster suit. Mac and Simpson seem to be growing more graceful in their crustacean dance so I suspect that Mac may be hitting on the flask himself. By the time we're ready to start at Sigma Kappa, J.L. seems more confident in his role as Curly. His off-key rendition of *If I Loved You* earns more than the usual embarrassed applause from the Sigma Kappas. At Phi Mu, J.L. hits the peak of his singing career, notewise, but has his first encounter with lyrics that vanish on a cloud of booze.

As we march away from Phi Mu, Doak Phipps rushes over

to J.L. and has quiet but serious words with him. Simmons answers with nods and a silly-assed grin. I sidle up to Lobster McClintock, "I think you'd better stash that booze. Doak's on J.L.'s ass and the whole thing goes to hell if Simmons forgets any more words."

"Don't worry, Five, ole' buddy," the lobster replies, "the booze, she is gone." From the wiggle of his feelers, or antennae, or whatever they, I sense that he is nearly gone as well.

Pi Phi, Chi O and Alpha Xi — the heart of sorority row. The lobsters shuffle and dance, serve as straight men for the cornball jokes from Soos the talking clam. The Fuzzies go wild when J.L. hits something that resembles the high note at the end of *If I Loved You.* We're on a roll.

Somewhere between the stop for Howard and Center Halls and Zeta Tau Alpha, McClintock suffers lobster blindness, walks into a tree and knocks himself cold. A neat trick since there are only one or two trees on this part of the route. "Lowrey, get your ass into the lobster suit," Doak shouts. "Someone else can carry the damn sets."

"But I don't know the steps, the lines, Doak!" I protest. But already I'm being dragged into the alley between Howard and the Zeta house. Thank heavens we only have about seven more stops.

"Fake it," Doak grins. "That's what Mac was doing. What'n hell got into him anyway?" he asks as I wriggle my arms into the paper mâche claws. I shrug ignorance. Then comes the lobster's head, reeking of whiskey. Gamely, I peer through the slit and gambol into the street before the Zeta house. *It's gonna be a hell of a clambake.*

From a lobster's vantage, I guess I don't harm the quality of the skit. We make it past Alpha Gamma Delta, Bryan and Lindley Halls and now the band strikes up *Carousel Overture* as we start our last show at Scott Quadrangle.

After I shuffle off from our comic bit, I stand on the sidelines waving my claws in time to *Clambake* while the chorus line sings and bobs. Someone pokes me in my back, er, carapace.

"Five? That's you isn't it?" I turn and squint through the

limited vision slit in the costume. There stands Judy Graham, a big smile on her face. "It is you! I thought so. I loved your little dance. You must've practiced for a long time."

"Hey Judy, how are you anyway?" Lobsters aren't known for their witty cocktail conversation.

"I'm just great. Just wanted to say hi. And tell you, the Alpha Gam's have asked me to pledge."

"That's terrific," I reply. "I see Page every once in a while but she didn't say anything about it."

"No. I just got the bid a couple of days ago. I told them I'd think about it." Just then, the band hits the first chords of *If I Loved You,* and I say a quick good-bye and bob onto the scene to wave my claws in time with J.L.'s boozy solo.

• • •

Friday night is unseasonably cold and the scantily-clad coeds who present their skits shiver through routines, their voices thin and reedy and producing puffs of vapor as they sing. Darcy and I huddle under a blanket on the porch roof of the Ace house, sharing our critiques with other members of the Thirteen and their dates.

"Ooh, look at her," Darcy exclaims as Susan Mackey, the Chi O's queen candidate, emerges at the finale of their skit. "Isn't she gorgeous? She'd be a real knockout if her skin weren't so blue." Susan and J.L. go into the traditional clinch that ends every skit. Out of the corner of my eye, I can see Lisa Nelson glowering as her boyfriend accepts another layer of lipstick.

After the last skit, we warm up in the Keep, then everyone troops down to the Beasley-Matthews garage for our parade all-nighter. Earlier in the day, Husted, Waller, Kostic and I installed the giant clam shell that opens in time with the music to expose large block letters spelling ACE. If all goes well, Waller will keep steam erupting from the clam with a big bucket and 200 pounds of dry ice.

After a few hours, our wood, wire and cable contraption begins to assume the form that was born on Husted's drawing pad. From an overhead painter's scaffold, O-Annie and Darcy hang over to stuff the brightly colored panels of the chicken wire roof.

"Look at those asses," Mayhew comments to his buddy Curtis. "Like to get my hands on those cheeks for an hour or two." Curtis grins and winks, then nudges Mayhew when he realizes I'm standing right beside them.

At half past twelve, many of the brothers leave to take their one o'clock dates home. By two, we're furiously working to fill the last holes in the chicken wire. "Don't bleed on the white paper," I caution O-Annie. Her fingers are covered with pricks from the chicken wire. At three, Husted declares the project done. Walking back to Darcy's, I reflect upon the work involved and compare it with my simple Biddle Hall display.

• • •

"Aw, Doak. C'mon, man. You've gotta be kidding." I am pleading for my J-Prom sanity with the Ace chairman who has decreed that I will wear the lobster suit to guide the float down the street.

"Five, dammit. You can't just walk down the street in a sweatshirt. It'll ruin the theme. Besides, Mac is still dizzy and I don't think he'll make it through the parade." And so, I don the lobster outfit again. Just before the head goes on, D.D. Smith hands me a flask.

"Better take a big slug, Five," he advises. "We got nearly three miles of downhill to walk on brick streets." D.D. is resplendent in his assistant drum major suit... tall white shako, white tails with green lining, shining black boots that come nearly to his knee. I accept his offer and swallow a huge portion of straight vodka. It burns good as it goes down and I enter the life of the lobster.

• • •

The claw signals that Benjo and I have worked out get us all the way to the reviewing stand at Court and Union where we'll have five minutes for the chorus line to do a part of the skit. And where I'll have to steer the float around the sharpest corner on the route.

Aces On The Half Shell has been received with lots of laughs, applause and catcalls all along the route. The clam opens and closes its mouth beautifully, expelling a cloud of steam blown by the never-flagging Waller.

J.L. sits atop the Carousel in his gold and bronze 'Curly' suit, waving to the admiring crowds. No one sees the pledges toiling inside, a pair of sweating guinea pigs on an endless merry-go-round and their whirling rope puller companions. The only evidence of their toils is the occasional puddle of barf left in the wake of our float.

Finally we start the turn from Court to Union, me clawing frantically as the gasping clam threatens to chomp down a stop sign. Spectators draw back in apprehension. Despite our band playing beside me, I can hear Benjo cursing inside the float, "I rode in a fuckin' tank once but this is terrible... ten times worse."

The tail of the float barely clears the other corner and we're on the home stretch on Union Street. Most of the parade will turn left on Congress and disperse to the athletic fields across the river. We'll continue on down to High and then park the float in the Ace parking lot overlooking the bridge.

As we near the Wonder Bar, a huge cheer goes up. There's our crowd, sitting on top of the Wonder Bar sign... Darcy's *front porch.* I wave my claw in joy at nearly being done and do a little lobster heel-click, landing flat on my ass! With a ton of clam-chomping carousel bearing down. I scuttle out of the way on all fours and barely escape with my tail intact. A roar of approval swells from the crowd.

Taking deep bows in every direction, I can spot O-Annie waving a bottle of Strohs and making *come on up* gestures. I blow them a kiss and we head home.

• • •

The party behind the green door is one to remember. Trish and Darcy have thrown open their apartments and a tub of iced beer dominates the hallway. The girls have already refilled the tub once by the time the Thirteen arrives.

I arrive with Benjo and Waller. I'm plastered with bits of the *Athens Messenger* and *OU Post,* artifacts of the rapidly deteriorating lobster head. Except for Waller, none of my pledge brothers has been in Darcy's place before. I watch with contentment as they examine the framed sketch over the kitchen table.

"This is the last one, lobster boy," Darcy says as she hands me another sweating Strohs. I wondered why the crowd was thinning. "Trish and I are gonna ride up to Nelsonville in the Ford. You want to come, get some sun in the rumble seat?"

"No way," I respond. "Gotta get a shower, shave, be ready for you tonight!"

"Hah! You'll probably fall out before the first dance," she laughs. "OK, get outta here, then. We're going to Nelsonville for a surprise!"

• • •

The J-Prom dance is one of the wonderful nights of our lives. We start at the Ace house, where Darcy's dress is a sensation. "Aunt Ida dug it out of a trunk last week," she says with a grin and wiggle, making the tassels shimmer all over the bright red dress. "She wore it when she was seventeen... back in the Roarin' Twenties!"

Once again, committee fairies have transformed musty Men's Gym into a romantic cavern. Couples swirl beneath sparkle balls that shoot tiny beams of colored light upon the floor. But the best part is on the band stand! None other than Benny Goodman and his Orchestra!

After several dances, we join Dawn and the Martian to stand and sway at the edge of the stage. Benny Goodman, who looks like anyone's bespectacled uncle, is playing just feet away. The Martian's face is rapt as Goodman leads his band into *Sing, Sing, Sing.* We get back on the floor and jitterbug until the sweat flies to *Stompin' At The Savoy.* A hole in the dancers opens for us as we shag to *One O'Clock Jump* but I'm sure it was due to

Darcy's flailing tassels.

No one seems to care at intermission when J.L. Simmons isn't elected J-Prom king. I watch carefully to see who Dan Nofzinger's date is when the tall Sigma Chi is announced as king. It isn't Jackie Adamson. Nor is anyone surprised when the stunning Chi O Susan Mackey is presented as queen.

Tension settles in for skit awards but again, Ace is shut out, despite the best efforts of the seafood players. Now it mounts as Phi Tau is announced as the third place winner in the float competition. Then the J-Prom chairman intones, "Second Place, Tau Kappa Epsilon." The TKE's cheer and shout in a knot across the gym.

"And now... first place in the float competition... and not a half-shelled job either... Alpha... Chi... Epsilonnnnn!!!" We dance around, hop up and down, hug each other and our dates. Husted waves the float trophy and we cheer as if he'd just won world peace.

• • •

Darcy leans back against me. With my arms around her waist, I run my fingers along her tassels. We're standing on the sun porch of the Ace house, its windows open for the first time this spring. The lights of Athens sparkle in reflection on the river. From the Keep below, singing and yelling keep track of the Ace celebration.

"Ahh, Five... thank you for this wonderful evening. It's the best night of my life. Can things ever be this good again?"

Chapter 22

Time To Take A Break From All This Hiking

Hell Week doesn't start on the Monday following J-Prom so it's time for the Thirteen to take action against Curtis. After a night of rehearsal, we are in our places on Tuesday night — along shadowy Lash Alley that leads from College to Congress.

"Remember, no one says a word," Benjo Kostic instructs in our final meeting in the Esquire basement. "If he sees us, or hears anything he can recognize, we just go on with Plan B. Take his ass out in the country and let him walk home."

I'm at the Court Street end of the alley where I have a clear view of Trish Spotswood's lighted window above the Wonder Bar rear door. The Martian is in Trish's apartment, ready to turn out the light when Curtis makes his usual departure from the Wonder Bar by way of the alley.

We've trailed Curtis for several weeks now and know his habit to drink in the Wonder Bar Tuesdays until nearly midnight, then walk up to Congress Street to play cards with some of his Korean vet cronies back from their Sandwich Man runs. Tonight, he holds true to form.

Trish's light goes out and I can see Curtis' figure in the alley, turning away from me toward Congress. If he turns toward me, I leave and we abandon the plan for another night. But as he turns away, I click Kostic's little flashlight.

A few seconds later, figures emerge from behind the silhouetted Curtis. I immediately start up the alley as quietly as I can. Ahead, there's a brief, silent scuffle. I see the figure of Curtis slowly lowered to the ground. By the time Cobb and I arrive, he is bagged and taped, ready for transport. Kostic gives me a grin and a thumbs up sign. I flick the light back down the alley toward College Avenue. Headlights blink in response.

Waller works quickly to wind black electrical tape around Curtis' hooded head to hold cotton-padded falsies over his eyes.

We hope this will keep him from being able to see anything. As the car approaches up the alley, Waller puts a falsie over each ear and gives these a couple of winds of tape. Tape fastens the hood tightly to his chest and this hands are taped behind him.

Ransom pulls the borrowed car up and dims the lights. Waller enters the back seat and then Kostic guides Curtis in. For the first time, Curtis struggles a bit but Kostic firmly shoves him into the car, then gets in beside him. Another thumbs up from Shivers in the front passenger seat and they pull on up the alley. Not a word has been said.

• • •

Thankfully, small groups of young men are not unusual in the streets of Athens after midnight. We walk in twos and threes down Lash Alley, scattering near the Center and the Speech Building. Shivers and Able, who work in the Center as busboys, use a "borrowed" key to check the alley delivery door. They signal all clear and enter the silent building.

Roughly forty minutes later, the car returns and pulls into the alley. Quickly, Kostic and Waller pull the hooded Curtis out of the car and through the unlocked delivery door. Ransom drives the car away and the rest of us follow into the building.

Softly we climb the darkened service stairs to the third floor and turn into a hallway by the Ohio Room. In the distance, we can hear the sound of women's voices; the seniors who live in the exclusive Center Dorm one floor above. Shivers guides us into a small room off the main banquet hall, empty except for a single straight chair in its center.

Several of us hold Curtis firmly by the arms while Kostic and Waller move into the final phase of the plan. Waller uses a pocket knife to cut away Curtis' shirt and applies new tape to hold the hood down. Kostic removes his shoes, pants and underwear. I am gratified to notice Curtis' penis, a tiny shriveled thing which looks as if it would happily crawl up into his groin.

They firmly place Curtis in the chair and Kostic winds many bands of black tape around his chest and the chair. His arms are cut free and then each taped to the side of the chair. Finally, his feet are spread apart and his ankles each taped to a chair leg.

We softly move to the doorway at Waller's signal. We wait as he cuts away the tape that bind the falsies over Curtis' ears. In his best imitation of Ray Milland, Waller whispers, "Can you hear me, fuckhead?"

Curtis nods yes.

"Do you know where you are, fuckhead?"

Curtis nods no.

"Well," Waller whispers, "I'll tell you. You're in a women's dorm. A small room just off the lobby." As if on cue, a girl's shriek is followed by a chorus of female laughter from the dorm floor above. "If you want to yell for help, you can. But just remember, they're gonna come in here and find you with your cute little dick hanging out."

We leave the room with Curtis in the gloom, illuminated only by the light of an exit sign. Safely in the alley, we shake hands in silence and walk toward East Green. Kostic throws Curtis' shoes and clothes in a garbage can. At the top of the hill, Ransom and Shivers meet us from having returned the borrowed car. We march down the hill in silent jubilation. The Thirteen. The One.

• • •

Wednesday seems like a nearly normal college day. Sarge Waller and I take Darcy and Jeannie to see the MIA movie — *Picnic* with William Holden and Kim Novak. After the movie, we repair to the Towne House where the girls are now in the john. Sarge takes the opportunity to fill me in on the events of the day.

"I go up for pledge duty this afternoon. I guess they found the note pretty early, went down and found Curtis, still there in the chair and a puddle of piss." He grins at the vision. "No one really said anything to me but you could tell the actives think it's pretty damned funny, except when Curtis is around.

"Then about four, who shows up but Kostic? Couldn't stand not knowing anything. Pretty soon , Curtis has the two of us up in his room, doing push-ups. Gunner was there, watching the whole thing.

"Curtis keeps asking about last night. I say as little as I can... afraid he'll recognize my voice. But we just keep denying we know anything." Waller takes a long sip of his beer and continues, "Then they start giving ole' Benjo a line of shit about how the vets have to stick together, that kind of stuff. He just grins and keeps on doin' push-ups."

"What are you two giggling about?" Darcy asks as she and Jeannie return to the booth.

"Oh? Just fraternity secrets," Waller says slyly.

• • •

On Thursday morning, I wait for Darcy to get into her clothes after figure drawing class. Jan Dabny is obviously pleased with Darcy's work as a model and the class has a light-hearted air that makes it fun for everyone. As Darcy emerges from the dressing closet, Dabny beckons to me.

"Five, Professor Blockhart wonders if you could stop by his office for a second?"

"Sure," I say. "Want to come, Darce?" She nods enthusiastically.

As usual, Blockhart's office is a spooky mix of pipe smoke and window light. "Ah, young Lowrey! Come in. Come right in."

"Professor Blockhart, this is my friend Darcy Robinette." Blockhart rises and reaches out to grasp Darcy's hand with both of his.

"Miss Robinette! I'm very pleased to meet you. See quite a lot of you around the fine arts building but never... er, in person," he stammers. A short *bloop* of smoke erupts from his pipe. He turns to me.

"Mister Lowrey, as is customary, there will be a silent auction at the opening of the student show Saturday night." He looks at me, then a long glance at Darcy who's studying the paintings on the side wall. "I believe it's very likely, highly likely, that your painting might be sold."

"You do, professor? Do I have to sell it?" I look at Darcy

who has a broad smile on her face.

"Not at all, but I just wanted to mention it to you. If you do wish to have it for sale, I would suggest a refusal bid of, say, two hundred dollars."

"Two hundred?" I'm amazed. "What you say, Darce? It's as much yours as mine?"

"Oh, Five, that's sweet but… two hundred! That's a lot of money. Let it go if it'll sell for that kind of money."

"All right, professor. I guess it's for sale."

• • •

Darcy looks sensational in the black velveteen cocktail dress she made for the Biddle Christmas party. A choker of pearls is her only jewelry, on loan from Trish Spotswood. Mom looks pretty snappy also. She drove up from Hockingport for the private cocktail party before the opening of the show. She and Darcy chatter away like they'd known each other for years. Captain is somewhere on the river, down near Cairo.

Duff Noonan, my third invited guest, chats amiably with Mark Husted, Trish and me. For the first time since I've known him, he wears something other than his Begorra t-shirt and greasy apron. He looks downright natty in a tweed suit.

"Listen Duff," I whisper, "do me a favor and stand near my mom when we go in to see the show. I'm afraid she'll faint when she sees my painting."

Husted chuckles. "I invited my parents up to see my first student show, my sophomore year. Thought my mother would die when she found out I was painting naked people."

I introduce everyone to Professor and Mrs. Logan. Mrs. Logan gravitates to my mom like iron filings to a dime store magnet. *Perhaps she'll catch her when mom faints.*

"Five, these manhattan things are yummy," Darcy says. "They sure taste better than that ghastly sloe gin." She stops and nods for me to glance over my shoulder. "Jan Dabny. Isn't she pretty tonight? But after visiting Blockhart's office, I'll never think of Jan again except covered in shiny green slime." She giggles and takes another sip of her manhattan.

Then Professor Logan chimes his glass and announces that the show is open. We quietly walk into the large Ohio Room, its overhead lights dimmed with baby spots highlighting the individual paintings. Several sculptures break the vast expanse of the room. I suddenly realize that the room where we've been enjoying cocktails is the one we left Curtis in. I chuckle softly to myself. Darcy gives me a puzzled look.

A glance around three of the walls reveals perhaps twenty five paintings and drawings but none of them mine. Just then, a voice gushes in my ear, "Ohhh, Five. It's just so neat." It's none other than O-Annie whose bright red dress makes me want to look for her dog Sandy. She takes my arm and turns me gently.

Light Show is *so neat*. Surrounded by an inexpensive gray mat and framed by a plain black border, it glimmers beneath its baby spot. Darcy takes her arm and gently turns mom toward the painting. "Look Mrs. Lowrey, there's Five's painting."

Mom stuns me by taking a step or two closer and examining the surface as if looking for dust. "Why, Darcy," she exclaims softly, "it's you. Five! I am surprised. It's a beautiful painting." And then she hugs each of us and gives me a huge kiss.

Duff Noonan stands before the painting, hands behind his back. "Gee kid, all these months I've been tryin' to sneak a peek and now I have to see 'em on canvas." He grins broadly and gathers each of us into his arms. "I think it's grand. Congratulations, Five. I really like it."

We stroll the room, examining each of the exhibited works. Mark Husted's painting is a huge affair, graduating from black at the bottom to a deep blue at its top. A ragged horizontal bar of orange blends into a vivid blue near the top and two tiny figures sit upon it, their naked legs dangling.

Trish jokes with us, "I think one of them's me, but you can bet that Mark painted it from his imagination."

The other works include several done in the Jackson Pollock school of paint dripped from a height. Although I've been taken by Pollock's work, I'm glad I didn't succumb to his techniques. One sculpture is smooth and sinuous, influenced by either Henry Moore or Brancusi. Perhaps both.

The Window hangs near a corner, dwarfed by larger

drawings to each side. Mom exclaims, "Oh Darcy, there you are again!" I cringe until I realize she's genuinely pleased and impressed by the drawing. "Five! It's so nice. Could I... could I possibly have it?" *And watch the Captain leap out the window when he sees it?* Her expression is the same one I saw the night I told her I would go to college.

"Certainly you can, Mrs. Lowrey," Darcy says. "Right, Five?"

• • •

On our last tour of the room, *Light Show* has a new adornment on its frame. A small orange sticker declaring *Sold!* I don't know *how* a silent auction works but someone now owns our painting. Darcy and I squeeze each other's hands in pleasure. Then Professor Logan signals for quiet and moves behind a small podium with a microphone.

The mike shrieks as his lips move and he jumps back in alarm. A student rushes to adjust the sound system. "On behalf of the Department of Fine Arts and the Ohio University Art League, I welcome you to our 1955 Student Show." Polite applause.

"I don't think I need to tell you that this year's show is testimony to the outstanding talents of our student artists." Scattered hand claps. "We of the faculty are so proud of this group of students, especially many of the younger ones. So, with no further ado, let me announce the awards. If your name is announced, please come forward and stand to my right."

Name after name is called, including mine for an *Award of Merit* and a twenty-five dollar prize for *The Window.* I join my fellow students and grin madly out into the crowd. Sculpture awards are presented, then Professor Logan moves to the painting category.

Awards of merit. Then third and second prizes. "Finally, the award for first prize. The artist is familiar to us all and one of our most talented students. Employed as well, I might add," Logan chuckles into the mike. "For his painting entitled *Dawning Of Realization,* the first prize and an award of two hundred dollars goes to Mark Husted."

A great cheer goes up as Mark comes to the front of the room. He shakes our hands and then moves forward to accept the congratulations of Professor Logan and a long white envelope. Then Logan raises his hands for silence.

"At last," he sighs. "As one of the panel of judges, I can tell you that it's unusual for a freshman to have a work accepted for the student show. For a freshman to have two accepted is exceedingly rare." My guts churn as if an icy hand has gripped my colon.

"But tonight we have among us an artist whose talent I feel is filled with promise." A small *yeah!* squeaks from the crowd and I know who its owner is. "This young man made his mark upon the Ohio University art world very early last fall." Logan grins and several of the faculty members laugh aloud.

"But thank God, he has channeled his talents from billboards to the canvas. For his excellent painting *Light Show,* I am pleased to announce the Best In Show award goes to Mister Thomsen Lowrey the Fifth!"

I'm pummeled from all sides. Darcy is around my neck, kissing me. Mom beams on. Husted reaches across to shake my hand. Professor Logan steps over and takes my arm, leading me to the podium. "I might add, that not only does Five's fine painting have a Best In Show ribbon, but that ribbon is accompanied by an award of two hundred fifty dollars!" Darcy's shriek rivals the feedback from the microphone.

"Want to say anything, Five?" Professor Logan asks gently. I nod no but he hands me the microphone anyway.

Staring into the crowd, I'm tongue-tied. Finally I stammer. "Thank you. Thank you very much. Thank you Darcy. And thank you mom, for encouraging me to come here."

Again I'm surrounded by congratulating people but once more, Professor Logan taps the mike. "I want to add my congratulations. And I want to thank each of you who has so generously supported this event by your donations of prize money and your purchases in the silent auction." He pauses for a second, then looks directly at me.

"One of those purchases, Five, was of your painting *Light*

Show. An anonymous patron has bought your painting for what my faculty colleagues and I believe is a record sum!"

•••

Our jubilant party closes up the Towne House. We see mom off to the Chevy where she assures us once again that she can drive back to Hockingport just fine. Now we're sitting on Darcy's "front porch," the Wonder Bar sign, Mark, Trish, Darcy and me, watching the reflection of the Towne House neons die as Manuel locks the place for the weekend.

"Eleven hundred fifty dollars, Five!" Darcy exclaims. "I just can't believe it. Someone paid nine hundred dollars for your painting!"

"Eleven seventy five, Darcy," Trish reminds us. "Don't forget the award of merit."

"Ohmygod," she rasps again. Her voice is nearly gone from the squealing and screaming she's done. "I just can't believe it. Your painting for nine hundred bucks. And Professor Logan won't tell you who bought it?"

"Our painting, hon," I say. "And Logan said I might find out someday. But certainly not until the show is over."

"Ohmygod, ohh my God! This has been the best night of my life," she croaks.

"No Darce! That was J-Prom night, remember?"

•••

The Thirteen attends Monday's pledge meeting pretty sure that Hell Week isn't here yet. Not with the Ace *Queen of Sweethearts* ball scheduled for Saturday night. And the getaway for spring break in the middle of the next week.

The post-meeting pledge party is the most intensive yet. The brothers scream and shriek their questions and we chant our answers at the top of our lungs to be heard. Curtis accosts each of us with a barrage of questions, sometimes nearly incoherent. He also passes out push-up orders as if they were cookies.

"You fucking spic pansy," he screeches at Soos Salazar who

has sinned by not remembering Kendall Kirkwood's middle name. We all register the fact that the Ace founder had *no* middle name as Soos counts off his push-ups.

On Wednesday night, we're summoned again to the Ace house and each of us fears the worst. The balloon goes up! But no balloon. Just another vigorous sweat party, followed by the schizophrenic change in the brotherhood that we're growing used to; a pony keg on the sun porch with much boozy fellowship and singing.

● ● ●

Although I want to use some of my prize money to buy her a new dress, Darcy insists she'll wear the red flapper dress. "I just feel so great in it when I dance," she chortles. Trish too has a Roaring Twenties dress on, white with tassels and beads in the same style as Darcy's.

"I know what she's saying," Trish agrees. "The dress kind of moves in a life of its own and you can feel your body moving inside it."

"Especially since you don't wear a bra with it," Husted comments wryly.

"Aw Mark, wouldn't a big old pink bra strap look nice with this dress?" Darcy says in her "Aunt Ida taught me" pout.

With Darcy on one arm and O-Annie on the other, I'm having the time of my life. "Don't forget, Five, you promised me you'd autograph your drawing of us in the Frontier Room," O-Annie says loudly. D.D. Smith, O-Annie's date for the *Queen Of Sweethearts* ball, returns from the bar with two more Orange Blossoms. Deceptive drinks with lots of orange juice and some ingredient that's going directly to the redhead's brain.

"Fiver. My glass is nearly empty too!" *Fiver?* Darcy's never called me Fiver before. But then, these manhattans do taste good. I take her glass, finish the dregs of mine and head for the bar.

The Ace Sweetheart dance is pretty elegant. Real bartenders, not pledges. And a real band, not the Martian and his cohorts. Right now, the trick is to make it through an hour of cocktail party before the music starts.

The Athens Country Club is festooned in gold, bronze and white streamers. Most of the active brothers are wearing tuxes. We pledges are in our most formal suits. Most of the girls wear pastel formal gowns or exceedingly snazzy cocktail dresses. Our two flappers look great.

• • •

The dance goes on. Lisa Nelson, our newly crowned sweetheart, Trish and Darcy do a crazily drunken shag in the middle of the dance floor. Beads flying, tassels swirling, the girls are a wonderful sight, especially Lisa's tiara which keeps creeping down over her *glowing* forehead.

The band members, who've been doing their own celebrating on breaks, keep the rhythm pumping and the crowd forms a big circle around the prancing girls.

"Buncha goddamn lesbians, looks like!" a familiar voice mutters near me. It's Curtis muttering to Mayhew and Gunner. Their mooses from the Wonder Bar are at the bar, guzzling free booze as long as it lasts.

"Watch your mouth, Brother Curtis," Husted warns from nearby. "And you watch your mind, Brother Mayhew. What's going on in there is written right on your forehead."

Later, I return from the john but can't find Darcy in my crowd of friends. I don't think much about it, reckoning that she too has answered nature's call. But in a few minutes, she appears from behind us. The bodice of her flapper dress is pulled slightly down and her hair is messed up. Her eyes are filmed with tears.

"What's the matter Darce?" I lean over her. She just jerks her head toward the outside. Waller, Mark Husted and I rush for the door.

"Jus'a fuckin' cock teaser, tha's all y'are," Curtis yells toward the door. I turn and Darcy's standing there, staring coldly at the drunken Aces. "Need a good dick in ya, s'whas ya need. Stop fuckin' aroun' with goddamn sissy civilian pledges," he slurs. Mayhew drunkenly nods his agreement. I lunge for him but Husted has me by the arm.

"Don't hit him, Five," he cautions. "Take Darcy home. I'll take care of *Brother* Curtis.

• • •

At the foot of the country club drive, I stop the Ford while Darcy leans out the door and heaves. Trish is in the rumble seat and eases forward to whisper, "Let her get it up, Five. She's had a lot to drink and she's upset." I walk around the car and gently help her out to walk along the roadside.

"That Curtis bastard grabbed me, Five," she sobs between heaves. "And held my arms back..." *Sob!* "And Mayhew pulled my dress down and tried to kiss my..." and she burst into tears again. We walk back toward the car.

She curls up in the front seat and whimpers, "Then Curtis called me a whore. Said I should put out for them 'cause I put out for everyone. Show my tits to everyone..." she breaks into heaving sobs again. Trish pats me on the shoulder from the rumble seat.

As we near the garage, Darcy wails, "Oh Five, this was certainly the very best night of my life... and now it's the very worst night of my life!"

• • •

The last pledge meeting before spring break again reflects the overall mood of the Ace chapter. Tiler drills us on our lore and calls our attention to new snippets we must memorize. But his heart doesn't seem in his job.

First Mayhew, then Curtis, come into the meeting to offer their apologies. But they too, don't seem to be honest in their sentiments. From the back of the room, someone mutters, "Why don't you make a record of it, asshole?" Curtis gives the room a ferocious look and spins on his heel.

Tiler brings the meeting to an end with cautionary tales for those of us planning to go to Fort Lauderdale. And then he quietly sends us home.

At the Begorra, I load my crates with hamburgers. Darcy is

302

somber. She walks me to the door, then hands me her keys. "The Ford's out back, Five. Use it for your delivery. Then come back and see me, please?" The look in her eyes makes me want to cry.

• • •

After locking the garage, we walk hand-in-hand up high street. Darcy shudders and gives the almost dark Ace house an evil look.

"Darce? Please don't judge all those guys by two... two animals. Please?"

"Aw, Five, I know your pledge brothers are all nice guys. And Mark. And some of the actives. But I can't help thinking about what they called me. I can't help thinking that's how they all think about me."

"Not true, Darcy. Everyone I know loves you. They think you're great. Everyone I know thinks Mayhew is an oversexed asshole. And... well I won't tell you about Curtis."

"Are you going to make it, Five?" she asks in a quiet voice, her upturned face looking into mine. "Do you want to be initiated?"

"Makes you wonder, sometimes," I reply. "If you only knew. But still, we're so close." I put my arm around her waist. "So close. And we can make a change."

• • •

With frosty glasses of iced tea, we sit on the windowsill of the apartment. Below us, Union Street looks quiet and peaceful. Just the security light glows from Quick's Drug. Even the Wonder Bar is locked and silent.

"Darce? Would you come down to Hockingport and spend spring break? I know mom would love to have you there. And so would I."

Her smile is faint and she shakes her head the tiniest bit. "Five, that's really nice. But Trish has asked me to spend the week with her at her folks' house in Cincinnati. She thinks I need a change of scene."

There's a lump in my throat. "She's probably right. But I wish you'd reconsider."

"No, I can't. I've promised her. We're driving down Wednesday morning, right after her last class."

"You're driving the Ford?"

"And why not? It got me this far, didn't it?"

• • •

On Wednesday morning, I stand in front of the green door, helping Trish and Darcy pack the Ford. They're going to run me down to the B&O station where I'll catch the eastbound for Coolville.

"Take care of yourselves, gals," I say softly, "giving Trish a hug. Then Darcy a long hug and lingering kiss."

"Don't fall in the river, Five." Darcy whispers. "I'll see you in a week. OK?"

"You bet." I've called mom and asked her to check with Captain Scullen about working on the *Ernie M.* for the week. It looks like I'll pick up a few bucks.

But as the Ford chuffs off up Union Street, why do I stand on the station platform feeling as if I'm losing something instead? Something important?

Chapter 23

The Balloon Goes Up — Or Bursts

Everyone returns from spring break with a tale to tell. Mine is simple; a quiet week on the *Ernie M.* which puts another hundred dollars in my Bank of Athens account. This first day back is grim and dirty. Rain which threatens to turn to sleet glazes the brick walks where hundreds of students brave the elements in short sleeves. Florida tans *must* be shown even though the result may be another flu epidemic.

In fine arts, I comment on Andy Logan's peeling nose. "Florida?" She shakes her head negatively.

"Myrtle Beach," she whispers. "Dad's been taking us there for years so I took the family car and showed some of the sisters the sights."

"Have a big time?"

"Well… you should see the backs of my knees," she says. "Worse than my nose. I spent most of the week rubbing on cold cream and groaning. Congratulations, by the way. I went to see the student show and your painting is great. And Dad says it sold for some big money?"

"Pretty big money, all right, " I respond. "Enough to get me through a year of school." Andy squeezes my hand and grins. "I'm just afraid the painting will vanish somewhere and I'll never see it again." Her smile grows bigger but she doesn't respond. Her father clears his throat into the lecture mike and we turn to our note taking.

• • •

Easing back into social life, I take Darcy for a pizza at the Tavern. Then Sarge and Jeannie come in after the MIA movie — *Picnic* again which Darcy and I declined to repeat. Darcy is taken with Cincinnati, her *second* big city.

"Oh guys, Columbus is flat, and ugly. I swear, you look west at Broad and High and you can see cornfields and Dayton! But Cincinnati!" She lights up when the describes the Queen City. "The river curves and these big hills come right up to the bank. It's beautiful. Just gorgeous at night when the lights are all on."

She's just beginning to tell us about Trish's search for a teaching job at Xavier or U.C. when Trish herself comes in with Mark Husted. "I was just telling them about the apartments we looked at for you," Darcy bubbles to Trish. "The one you liked best. Where was it? Mount Adams?"

"Yeah. This really neat neighborhood," she says. Husted nods in agreement. "Pretty run down but lots of great old apartments on the hill. Look down on the river."

"And we saw some *beatniks* too," Darcy bursts out. "Y'know, real people reading poetry and smoking dope!"

"And smelling bad," Husted adds. "Those are the prime rules for becoming a beatnik. Don't bathe. Smell bad."

The conversation turns to Fort Lauderdale. None of us went but we've all heard bits of gossip. "Ransom came home with a big bruise on his cheek and totally clammed up, worse than ever," Waller relates.

"The poop at the house is that he got in a pretty bad scuffle with Curtis at the Elbo Room," Husted says.

"And I talked with O-Annie this afternoon," Trish says. "She had an awful experience with Curtis and Mayhew." She hesitates, then gives Darcy a pained glance. "I guess they were mauling her around somewhere but Ransom and some guys from Notre Dame stepped in and stopped it."

"Yeah," Waller adds, "that's what I heard started Ransom and Curtis. Curtis blamed Ransom for the Notre Dame guys."

"Not to change the subject but is everyone going to the *Rites of Spring* party Saturday?" Husted asks. "It's usually a pretty good blast. Free beer and everything."

"I'd go to the lion house of the Cincinnati Zoo if they served free beer," Waller comments.

• • •

Even though she seems over the country club episode, Darcy's mood at the *Rites of Spring* party can't be called effervescent. Free beer there is. A full keg of Hudepohl and a pony keg of Stroh's *bock,* black viscous stuff that tastes good going down then sloshes around threateningly.

Rites of Spring is sort of a beer-drinking olympic games. The sounds of chugging contests echo around the Keep. At our table, rhythmic tapping and clapping signifies a round of "Cardinal Puff."

Here's to Darcy, she's true blue… she's a drunkard, through and through…

Darcy bravely tips up her cup and lets the evil bok beer slide down her throat, but for a few trickles that make their way down her chin.

Even later, a group of brothers sets up "Fort Zindernuef" with overturned benches and challenges the "saracens" to breach its walls. Many gallons of beer are thrown in the process, which quickly turns into a laughter-filled brawl. Ransom crawls out of the bottom of the pile with a silly grin and blood streaming from his nose. "Got the bastard," he whispers to Waller and me.

As we steer the beer-soaked girls up the stairs for home, Tiler stops us and whispers "Back at the house by one o'clock. Sharp!"

• • •

When we walk in a mob up Union Street, the temperature begins to drop and the awful rains fall once more. All of us, pledges and dates, shiver in our beer-soaked t-shirts and shorts. Darcy and I bid everyone good night at the green door and I climb the stairs with her.

"Can't come in, Darce. I've gotta get going," I say as she shakes in the doorway. "You gonna be all right?"

"Sure I will, Five," she says as she gives me a beery kiss. "I'll just go in now and barf. And maybe, if I'm lucky, I'll die."

On the stairs, I meet Husted and Trish. Trish gives my arm a

307

squeeze and winks. Husted looks grim. "This just *could* be it, Five. Be like a Boy Scout." I nod and start to move by them. "Oh yeah, Ransom's still at the house. But I've got someone looking out for him."

• • •

In 205 I discover Toby packing his gym bag. "Man, am I wasted!" he groans. "And we're starting Hell Week tonight."

"We may be also," I say, checking my windbreaker to make sure the D-rations, smokes and matches are still there. From my desk drawer, I retrieve my list of phone numbers and slip it into my tennis shoe.

The Thirteen meets at the foot of the Bryan steps. "Where's Ransom?" Chet Husted asks.

"I saw Mark at the green door and he said he's still at the house."

"Oh, shit," someone exclaims.

"No, he said he had someone looking after him," I reply. We climb the steps through the rain.

• • •

At the Ace house, Tiler has us throw our jackets in the library and go down to the Keep. But once again, the Aces surprise us. Ransom is all right, head down and asleep on a table. But the brothers are all there and apparently having a good time finishing the kegs.

"C'mon in pledges," Gunner Schmidt calls out jovially, "got some beer to finish." There's a call for Pater Gousha. The *Rites of Spring* roll on.

"Aces high, aces high, that's the song this week

If you're from another house, then you're just a Greek.

Bet your hole card on the pot! Back it up with all you got.

For when the dealer calls his cry, Your bet is aces highhhhh!"

Songs and jokes fly around the room. Beer gushes from the kegs. We pledges share questioning looks among ourselves. But slowly, the mood changes from party to something else. Curtis and Mayhew have Ransom against a wall where he weaves and blinks. Curtis and Ransom share similar streaks of dried blood running from their nostrils.

"No you fuckhead," Curtis shouts in Ransom's face, "it's Garret Stowers Thurmond. Not Starrit Gower Thurmond." Ransom winces, looks as if he'll cry.

"Give me fifty, Ransom you shit eater," Mayhew screams. Obediently, Ransom flops to the floor to begin chanting his push-ups.

"Thirteen!" Kong Logan screams, "where is your unity? Are you going to let your brother do push-ups by himself?" We instantly hit the floor. I can see my reflection bob up and down in a puddle of spilled beer beneath me.

It turns into the loudest, meanest sweat party yet. Soos Salazar flops on his belly from exhaustion and we rush to hold him up for a stint of running in place. Finally, someone calls a halt.

"Take five," Curtis growls. "Sit on the floor and shut up." We sit.

"You guys are a bunch of pussies," he continues. "I would not have lived five minutes with a bunch of assholes like you in the trenches with me on Hill Two Oh Five."

"You got that right," one of the Thirteen whispers.

"See this ball?" Curtis says, producing his familiar black marble. "See this, you worthless turds? When the balloon goes up, this ball will have dropped on one of you. Mark my fuckin' words, one of you dickheads is not gonna make it."

Then we're being hustled back up the stairs and into the living room. "Don't sit down," Logan yells. "Give your big brothers all your belongings. Everything. Brother Curtis, pat 'em down to make sure none of these gook loving bastards is hiding anything." I feel Curtis' hands run across my butt, pause at my crotch, then move on.

"Grab your coats and into the courtyard," Logan orders. We hustle into our coats and then out into the rainy courtyard. Cars are waiting. So are the hoods.

· · ·

This ride is not quite a repeat of the first. I'm sitting on the outside in back and no one yells at me when I slip the hood up from time to time to peek out the window. In the front seat, Tiler drives and Mark Husted is riding shotgun.

"Why's he driving so fast?" Tiler mutters. "We're supposed to stick together."

After many turns, Husted stage-whispers to Tiler, "Have we lost them? We still have two cars behind us? That was Chauncey we just went through." Whoever's riding beside me nudges my knee. We've all spent hours studying the map to memorize towns around Athens. *Are they playing more games with us?*

We stop once and the front doors open. Husted says to us, "Stay here. No one gets out." I lift my hood and can see the brothers gathered in the headlights behind us. There's a lot of pointing in different directions and excited discussion. The surrounding countryside is devoid of anything but the lights of our caravan. The rain continues to whisper down.

We're rolling once again. Husted says to Tiler, "There's the sign for Jacksonville. So we turn left here. Toward Buchtel." *Jacksonville. Near where Darcy grew up.* We lean as the car swerves through a sharp turn. A few minutes later, we stop again and the actives leave the car.

"All right, get out now," Tiler orders. "Give me your hoods. Your brothers are down the road a couple hundred yards. Start walking. Good luck!" As we remove our hoods, we can see the glow of headlights in both directions. Tiler and Husted roar off through the rain, leaving Frank Able and Soos Salazar standing there with me in the darkness.

"Where are we?" A.A. asks. "You guys have any idea?"

"Northwest of Athens about thirteen miles, if what Husted

was saying is true," I respond. "If it wasn't, we're fucked."

Shouts direct us down the road and into the gloom. After a couple of minutes, we see the lights from smoldering cigarettes. We rejoin the pledge brothers.

"C'mon guys, line up and count off," Kostic orders quietly. We form a line and slap the next guy's shoulder as we count our numbers. *One. Two. Three... Eleven! Twelve!* Silence. Kostic's flashlight clicks on. "Twelve! Who's missing?" He shines the light around the circle of faces. Ransom is missing!

"Now what the fuck?" Chet Husted says. Chet, who rarely curses, is obviously upset.

"Maybe they took him back," Dicky Reb West ventures. "He was really shitfaced and sick, too."

"No! Someone would've said something if they took him back," Chet Husted says.

"Well, we can't leave here 'til we find out," Waller says flatly. "So what do we do?"

"Look!" Soos shouts. "Over there!" Against the rainy horizon, a moving glow shows for a few seconds, then disappears. "Car lights?"

"Maybe?" Kostic ventures. "OK, I suggest we head that way. Does anyone know for sure where we are?"

"Mark Husted was dropping hints in the car," I contribute. "If he wasn't lying, I think we're between Jacksonville and Buchtel. Buchtel's near Route 33. But which way's Buchtel?"

"I don't think Mark would pull that shit," his brother says. "He likes you, Five. I think he'd try to help. Besides, mom would kill him if she found out he screwed us up"

So we set off through the rain toward where we saw the last car lights. Kostic and Waller intermittently flash their lights along the roadside. Every couple of minutes, we stop and shout for Ransom. The rain lets up a little as we trudge on.

After forty minutes or so, Kostic's light reveals the roadside where a car has mashed ruts in the weeds. We huddle as he and Waller explore each side of the road.

"Jesus Christ!" Waller hisses. "What's this?" We all shuffle up to where he stands on a slight rise above the roadway. Beneath us his light reveals a strange landscape of mud and rock. The rain comes down again.

"Old strip mine," Dicky Reb says. "They're all over West Virginia."

"Here are footprints," Benjo Kostic shouts. "Spread out and let's walk down this hill. Be careful. It's slippery."

The Martian's scream startles all of us a few minutes later. "Here he is," he screeches. "He's here. Hurry!"

Ransom is lying at the edge of a huge puddle, his face nearly under water. He's covered with mud. Kostic leaps down and puts his hand to Ransom's neck just beneath his ear. "He's alive. He's got a pulse. Ransom! Ransom! Can you hear me."

Ransom responds with a weak groan. "He's alive," Mark Husted whispers, "but are we in some deep shit?"

Kostic and Waller examine Ransom carefully. He appears to have no broken bones. Gently we make a human stretcher and carry him to the top of slope and down to the roadside.

"Everyone shuck outta those jackets," Kostic orders. "We've got to keep him warm." Kostic is in charge, just as he's been in every test we've faced as a group. "Waller, you and a couple guys see if you can find some dry wood. We walked past some pine trees a way back and they ought to have some dry tinder underneath them.

"The rest of you dig out any paper you might have, cigarette packs... not the foil part... keep it dry but ready. We've got to get a fire started." By the light of a Chesterfield, I study my sheet of numbers intently. I've memorized Dense's and Trish's numbers but want to make sure.

Several guys run back with armloads of pine branches, needles and cones. "I'll build the fire," Terry Simspon volunteers, "I was a hell of a Boy Scout." True to his word, the Pirate soon has a flame flickering beneath a small pile of pine twigs and needles. Gently he feeds it, twig by twig. In the flickering light, Ransom's face is pale as chalk. A mud-spattered, chalky mask.

• • •

Waller and I run along the muddy road. After getting the fire

312

burning vigorously, we follow Kostic's orders. A group of four starts off running in each direction down the road. The other four stay to watch over Ransom and tend the fire.

As Benjo directed, Waller and I split from Shivers and Able at the first fork of the road.

"Run five minutes, walk one. Then run five more," Benjo told us as if he were planning an attack on some Korean mountainside. "Stop at the first place you see. Lights or no lights."

As we top a rise in the road, the geometric shapes of buildings loom up from the rain. "A farm," I gasp as we jog toward the buildings. Indeed, the barking of a dog soon greets us from the darkened farmstead. We clomp up onto the porch and knock loudly at the door. In the back of the house, a flickering light comes on. A kerosene lamp?

"Who is it? Who's out there?" The querulous voice is indistinct behind the solid door.

"Please. Open the door," Waller says urgently. "We need to use a phone. It's an emergency."

"Who's out there, Asa?" a woman's voice calls.

"Just some more of those damned college kids." There's a pause. "You kids go away. Leave us alone."

"Sir!" I cry. "Please open the door. It's an emergency. Someone is hurt. We need to get help."

"I've heard that line of crap before, kid," the farmer's voice comes through the door. "You better be telling the truth. Because I'm calling the sheriff and if you're not, you'll spend the night in jail."

• • •

In the lamplight of a kitchen from the last century, we stand dripping as Asa Benquist calls the sheriff's office. Mrs. Benquist scurries to produce a couple of towels for us to dry with. Then, I use the phone to call Dense at Perkins Hall. He says he'll have the Bearmobile on the road in five minutes. I call Trish Spotswood's apartment and after a couple of rings, she answers the phone with a sleepy voice.

"I'm not sure Darcy's in any shape to drive, Five," Trish responds. I tell her our problem in more detail. "But I'll get her up and I'll drive if I have to. Now tell me how to get there."

• • •

By the time Mister Benquist drives us back through the rain, the flashing red lights of a sheriff's '54 Ford add illumination to the roadside scene. The farmer silently gets out of his old truck and walks with us over to the crowd along the road.

"You made good time, deputy," he comments to the cop who is digging a blanket from the Ford's trunk. "You know I hate to call you boys out just for another one of these damn college kid pranks but these fellas seemed pretty upset."

"You did right, Mister Benquist," the deputy responds. "I think we've got a pretty sick boy here. I'm going to run him in to Nelsonville Hospital right now. We'll have another car out here to talk to these boys in just a few minutes."

We help the deputy load Ransom's blanket-wrapped form into the back seat of the squad car. Chet Husted climbs into the front to accompany them to the hospital. They move off into the rainy night, red lights flashing.

Soon, a second sheriff's car pulls up and another deputy gets out. His arrival is followed by that of the Bearmobile, Darcy's Ford and McClintock's roommate in a battered Pontiac. I walk over to the Ford where Trish rolls the driver's window down.

"What happened, Five?" they both ask at once. Darcy is dressed in a sweat suit but her hair is still wet and plastered to her head.

"They took us for a ride," I say grimly, "but Ransom got lost somehow. We found him lying down there in the mud."

"Are you ready to go home, Five?" Darcy asks grimly.

"I'd better find out what this cop wants first. Do you guys mind waiting? Please?" I turn to rejoin the group around the hood of the squad car.

"No officer, I just don't know. It was fraternity stuff, y'know," Benjo Kostic is telling a deputy of about his own age. "I guess he just got lost and went the wrong way. Fell into that pit over there, we think. That's where we found him."

"You fraternity guys get in more trouble wandering around out here," the deputy says. Clearly, he's not very sympathetic. "Last year, a bunch burned down Mister Benquist's shed just to get warm. You're lucky he didn't shoot your ass off."

He pauses and stares at the circle of soot-covered, anxious faces. "But if he just wandered off, I guess we just call it another stupid fraternity prank accident. That OK with you guys?" We nod uncertainly. The deputy folds his notebook with a snap. "I'm going back to Athens. Any of you need a ride?" Kostic instantly says no, we should be able to make it with the cars that are here. I hope the cop doesn't inspect the Bearmobile too carefully.

• • •

With its top up, the Ford reeks of beer and the remnants of perfume. Trish drives with Darcy snuggled up in my shoulder. "Mmm, Five, you really smell," she murmurs. I probably do... of sweat, wood smoke, beer, cigarettes and the fear of death. At a stop sign in Nelsonville, I pull down the rear window and check on Soos and Waller, huddled in the rumble seat beneath a soggy blanket.

We stop at the emergency room of Nelsonville Hospital where a kindly nurse informs us that Mister Ransom has been moved to Athens General. And she'll tell us no more. So we pile back into our assortment of cars and head for Athens.

Chet Husted is standing in the portico of the emergency entrance, puffing on a cigarette. "They won't tell me much," he reports. "The doc in Nelsonville said he was suffering from something called hyper... hypotherma..."

"Hypothermia," Kostic says, "can get your ass good if it's not treated promptly. Can we see him?"

"Nope," Husted says flatly. "They say he's resting comfortably and they'll call the house if there's any change. They told me to go home but I knew you guys would come here."

Chet climbs onto the bed of the Bearmobile and our caravan

heads for East Green Cafeteria. I kiss a nearly-sleeping Darcy on the cheek, then walk around and do the same for Trish. "Thanks a million guys," I say. "I really hate this but you sure did help save our butts."

Darcy's whisper comes from the darkened car. "What do you hate, Five? Do you hate the Aces? I think I would."

• • •

"So I called Mark at the house from Nelsonville," Chet tells us through the steam rising from his cup, "and then talked to J.E. Ehlers. They were both at Athens General when we got there."

"What did Ehlers say?" Soos asks impatiently. "What're they gonna do?"

"What's there to do?" Waller asks.

"It's just another stupid fraternity stunt accident, boys," I mimic the deputy. "So let's all go home and be more careful next time."

"Ehlers was pretty upset. So was my brother," Chet says. "They're going to look into what happened. Try to find out."

"I'm sure they'll find that Ransom rode with Curtis if they check hard enough," Waller comments.

"In the meantime," Kostic speaks up, "I want to go out there in the morning and take a good look at that place. Five? Do you think we can borrow Darcy's car?"

"I'm sure. Or the Bearmobile," I answer. "I'll be ready whenever you say."

"One more thing," Husted says. "I'll call the hospital in the morning and if it's OK, I think one of the Thirteen ought to be up there around the clock. That sound OK with you guys?" We rumble our assent. "OK, I'll use the pledge duty schedule to set us up. We'll do four-hour shifts if we can. That way no one should have to do two late nights or mornings in a row."

• • •

Kostic, Waller and I jump out of Darcy's Ford as soon as I pull up to the soggy ashes of our fire beside the road.

316

"Careful," Kostic warns. "I don't know what we're looking for but keep your eyes open. Don't step on anything." Half asleep, Darcy had handed me the keys without a word from either of us. Retracing our route was fairly easy, a snap once we passed the buildings of the Benquist farm.

"Someone definitely went up that bank," Waller says, pointing to the steep three-foot slope where yellowish-red clay reveals a fresh scar.

"But could a falling-down drunk? All by himself?" Kostic asks aloud. The scar in the clay is nearly smooth, washed by the rain. Even our trampled footprints around the roadside are just little water-filled depressions. At the top of the slope, we look down to the ugly terrain of an abandoned strip-mine. The earth ripped away for its coal, then left there like a rumpled bed.

Carefully, we slide down the bank. Again, our tracks from earlier this day have been scoured by the rain. The place where we found Ransom is totally under water now. We shudder at the thought of not having found him.

"Here's a cigarette butt," Waller says. Indeed, near where Ransom had lain is the soggy butt of a cigarette. No filter. Just a flattened inch of grayish paper and shreds of unsmoked tobacco. "But whose is it?"

"Wait a second," I say. "Ransom didn't go to East Green and get his other clothes on. He didn't have any smokes or matches. Would he have? When they searched us at the house?"

"Five? I think you've just made an important point," Kostic says grimly. "Someone else was here." He pauses as we scan the ground at our feet. "But who?"

• • •

"I hate to be a bitch, Five, " Darcy scowls up at me from her table. When I return her keys, she's smoking and drinking coffee and generally looks like hell. A bath and a comb through her tangled hair would help. "But that shit last night is just plain stupid."

My response is silence. My arms on my knees. My tired head is bowed.

317

"I think you ought to walk over there and tell those Ace bastards to just shove their dumb pledge pins. All of you! See where they'd be without any pledge class."

I continue to stare at the floor. I cannot answer the logic of her argument with any words.

• • •

Monday's pledge meeting is solemn to the lowest degree. Brother Ehlers talks to us for a long time, asking questions, answering ours. But we get no satisfying answers. And we realize we've asked no really pertinent questions.

It's nearly midnight when I walk up to Athens General to relieve Soos who was excused from the meeting to sit outside Ransom's room.

"Anything going on, Soos?"

"Pretty quiet, Five. Nurse says he's resting. Not out of danger but comfortable. What'd I miss at the meeting?"

"Not much. Just some soothing bullshit from Ehlers. Some new lore from Tiler... nothing important. Fuck! What's important?" I say in disgust.

"Ransom's important," Soos responds vehemently. "But you're right. Who gives a shit if the balloon ever goes up?"

• • •

"Are you Mister Ransom's friend?" A young nurse has her hand on my shoulder, waking me gently. I nod yes.

"Well, he's awake and wants to see one of his friends." I rise from the chair and my knees and ankles protest with stiff pains. "But just for a minute and be quiet. It's nearly two and most of my floor's asleep." She gives me another warm smile and opens Ransom's door.

A bedside lamp is on, its shade turned against the wall to throw an indistinct light over Ransom's form.

"Joe? Are you awake?" I whisper. Where a streak of blood once marked his upper lip, a plastic tube now snakes into his nostril. His eyes flutter.

"Who's it?" he whispers hoarsely.

"It's Five, Joe. Five Lowrey." Ransom slowly moves his hand from beneath the sheet. An IV tube is connected to the wrist. He frowns and moves the other arm. A free hand appears and he extends it to me.

"Five? S'you, isn't it? M'in the hospital aren't I?"

"Yeah, Joe. You're gonna be fine, Joe. They're takin' good care of you."

"Five?" He pauses, his eyes fluttering rapidly. I wait for his voice again. He breathes deeply.

"Five. He got me again…" his voice drops into a shallow whisper. "He did it again, Five." A tear forms at the edge of his tightly closed eye.

"Who did it, Joe? Who got you?" I lean close.

"Curtis," he whispers. "You gotta get him, Five. You gotta…" and his head lolls to his chest. I move to the door and look out for the nurse. Beckon her.

"He's asleep," she whispers. "Why don't you go home now, and get some sleep yourself?" she asks nicely. I shake my head and plop my aching body onto the straight chair by the door.

• • •

I'm lucky to catch Chet Husted as he's about to enter Wilson Hall for his eight o'clock. When I tell him my news, he slams his books to the wall and mutters "sonofabtich." Then he looks squarely at me. "What do I do, Five? What do we do?"

Using the hospital watch schedule, we manage to round up Waller, Dicky Reb, McClintock, Pirate Simpson, and the Martian. The seven of us crowd into the corner back booth at Quick's Drug.

"I've got to tell Ehlers," Chet says after I repeat my conversation with Ransom. "I mean… the bastards have got to do something about that sadist!"

"What exactly," Waller looks at me, "did he say again, Five? At the end?"

"Curtis,' he whispered to me. 'Curtis.' Then he kind of rasps out 'You gotta get him, Five. You gotta…' and he fell asleep again."

"Then we've got to get him," Waller says with grim determination. "That's what Ransom wants. When he's healthy, we're going to get that bastard. Whatever way Ransom wants to do it."

• • •

I sleep in and miss my sociology class on Tuesday morning. Then Darcy doesn't show up for figure drawing and Dabny dismisses the class. Sitting on the steps in front of Cutler Hall, I contemplate the quiet morning campus. The first buds of green are showing on the elms and maples.

Coming up the walk toward me is a familiar hunched figure. As he gets closer, I recognize Jesus Salazar. I flip my cigarette away and stand as he strides up to me. His face is set and streaked with tears.

"He's gone, Five."

"He's gone? Ransom?" He shakes his head. "What'ya mean he's gone?"

"Dead, Five. Joe Ransom died about an hour ago."

• • •

The days that follow are a whirlwind of gray impressions for each of us. J.E. Ehlers calls a special pledge meeting and once again counsels us quietly. Each of us leans forward, expecting another member of our class to ask the fateful question. None does. Before the meeting breaks up, an assistant from the Dean's office joins us.

He is a young, kindly man who questions us as a group as to exactly what happened on Sunday morning. Our answers are vague as we adhere to the story that Ransom somehow got separated from the group and wandered off. None of us knows who Ransom rode with and none of the actives volunteer the information.

On Wednesday evening, I work furiously on my paintings in Darcy's apartment. She watches in silence, filling cups of coffee

320

from her hot plate, rubbing my shoulders. I declare the moody portrait of her finished.

"It's so dark, Five. So sad. Why do I look so sad?"

"It's not meant to be that way, Darce," I reply softly. "I mean, I haven't really done anything to make it different since…" a sob builds in my throat.

"I know, hon," she hugs me gently. "But still. I look at it and feel so terribly sad."

• • •

On Friday afternoon, we load into four of the actives' best cars for the drive to Dayton and Ransom's funeral. I ride in the back of J.E. Ehlers' Oldsmobile with Salazar and Waller on each side. The Tiler sits in the front seat.

"We've appropriated money to pay for your motel rooms," Ehlers says during the drive. "We've got to be at the funeral home tonight, then tomorrow… tomorrow, the funeral's at its chapel at ten o'clock."

• • •

At fifteen until seven, we arrive at the funeral home from the motel. All of us, brothers and pledges, are dressed in our best dark suits. In the lobby, we meet Ransom's mother and father. Mrs. Ransom hugs each of us tightly, crying soft tears. With us are Ehlers, the Tiler, Mark Husted, J.L. Simmons, Doak Phipps and Kong Thoreau.

Mr. Ransom shakes each hand firmly, his eyes glistening with tears, his lips quivering. Then the twelve pledges, followed by the brothers, file into the chapel where Ransom's casket lies surrounded by flowers.

He looks as pale as that last morning I saw him in the hospital. The ACE roseate glistens from the lapel of his black suit. His hands are folded across his lap. Below his hands lies a small, flat bronze pillow and pinned to it is the Alpha Chi Epsilon badge; its rampant leopard, sitting on the shield, one paw raised to hold a sword, the broken chain in its mouth. The bronze, gold and white badge gleams beneath the lights of the chapel.

Mr. Ransom's voice, soft and gentle, comes from behind us. "He would have worn that badge… my badge… at his initiation."

Six of us return to the lobby to meet visitors who are coming into the funeral home. The other six take their places, three to each side of the casket, hands folded in front, backs to the room. We'll spell each other in this guard of honor every fifteen minutes.

• • •

Saturday morning is bright and clear. The chapel is filled. Many familiar faces from people we met the night before. Ransom's classmates at Stivers. Pretty girls whose beauty we recognize but whose names we cannot recall.

The pastor, a young man not much older than ourselves, conducts the service. His words are sincere but to our ears, may as well have been in a foreign tongue. Then J.E. Ehlers rises and walks slowly to the pulpit.

"We are here in sadness…" his adam's apple bobs in a negated sob, "to bid farewell to our Brother, Joseph Eric Ransom." He turns his head slowly toward the casket. "Brother Ransom! You have seen the light. You have found the truth. May they be of comfort to you in your rest."

Ehlers solemnly moves back to his seat beside the Ransom's and the music from the chapels organ begins the chords of what we recognize as *The Acer Hymn*. The six who are pallbearers rise to stand beside the casket. The chapel empties.

• • •

At the cemetery, I am among the second six to bear Ransom to the graveside. The Ace brothers and our pledge brothers follow us in a simple procession. The casket is surprisingly light, as if the weight of Joe Ransom's tortured soul has already left us.

Then it's finished. We stand beside the open grave and following the lead of Mr. and Mrs. Ransom, the brothers, each takes a handful of earth and drops it gently onto our brother's resting place.

The Thirteen is now twelve strong.

Chapter 24

Can You Hear The Leopard's Roar?

The mood of the funeral continues into the next week. Monday's pledge meeting is serious, more intense than ever. The Tiler drills us on new lore regarding the Order. We practice our songs. I find a lump coming to my throat as we stand and sing...

"In ancient days did Acerbus strike at the walls of Tyre,

to smite the mighty Saracen and end his reign of fire.

With book and sword they fought to bring..."

We depart the Ace house in a somber group, puzzled as to why the pledge meeting was not followed by a sweat party. Waller and I leave them to stop by the Begorra. No Biddle order tonight because Toby Wolfe is a newly-minted Phi Delt is celebrating with his brothers.

Darcy greets us with a wild, strange look on her face. "Oh Five, please, please don't be angry."

"Angry, Darce? What about?"

"Just a minute, you'll see." She turns and yells to the kitchen. "Duff! Duff, Five's here." She turns back to me; a strange smile, big round eyes. Duff emerges from the kitchen, wiping his hands on his apron. He walks to the far wall and stands beneath a shrouded shape. He too has this weird smile. He grasps the corner of the drape and slowly pulls it away, revealing *Light Show*.

"Surprised, Five?" Darcy asks anxiously. Duff just stands there, grinning like a madman, the rumpled drape in his hand.

"Duff? You bought it?" He nods his head up and down.

"You're the anonymous patron?" I don't know whether to laugh or cry. In my present mood, crying seems closer.

"And it's going to hang in the Begorra?" I continue. "For everyone to see?"

"That's what I asked, Five," Darcy says, squeezing my arm as she stands beside me looking up at the painting.

"Naw," Duff responds, "just for tonight. Just wanted to give you a little jolt," he grins. "Sure would help business, though. Don't you think, Darcy?"

Her jaw drops in amazement. "Duff! Really!"

"Well, I was thinkin' of givin' it to your Aunt Ida as a birthday present," he continues. Darcy's face is now mapped with horror. "But it'll probably just go in a place of honor on my wall at home."

"Duff," I interject. "I can't keep your money. It's just... not right, somehow."

"Bullshit, kid. What's the matter with my money? If you think this is a joke, then you're wrong. You kids need to come up to my place and *see* my collection." He looks up at the painting with obvious pride. "It's my painting. I paid good money for it. And I'm goddamn proud of you," he nods at me, "and you," and at Darcy. "And burgers are on the house."

• • •

On Wednesday evening, Darcy and I drive Sarge Waller and Jeannie out to see The Sharpsburg Hell. The days are getting longer and the valley of smoke is eerie in the glow of the waning sun. Darcy takes a side road and carefully follows its narrow track down into the middle of the fuming landscape. We park at a turn-around and hike up to a big rock that overlooks the valley.

Sarge and Jeannie are impressed by the sight. I open some Cokes and we sit there, watching as the sunset glow in the sky dims and the fierce orange of the burning fissures becomes more vivid.

"Would be a great place to have Hell Week, wouldn't it?" Sarge says in a soft voice. "I had pledge duty this afternoon and they were all really nice. It's not natural."

"How can you smoke here, Five?" Jeannie asks as I light up a Pall Mall. "Don't you know smoking isn't good for you?" We laugh at Jeannie's lame joke and enjoy the sight of the bowels of the earth displaying their fiery indigestion. But enjoyment is dimmed by the sorrowful thoughts of Joe Ransom.

• • •

Saturday morning's work party at the Ace house is as unnatural as The Sharpsburg Hell. The brothers treat us almost as humans. I help Mark Husted hammer, saw and paint our booth for the Greek Week Carnival in two weeks.

"My last project for Alpha Chi," he says as we work on the dunking booth. "You'll be in charge next year, Five."

"Yeah. I guess so. If we ever make it." This response is getting really tiresome.

"What're you guys doing tonight," he asks.

"Nothin' much. Going to see *The African Queen* at the MIA. You guys want to go with us?"

"Sure!" he responds. "I haven't seen it. Don't think Trish has." He pauses. "How 'bout we go out to the Thirty Three for a drink afterwards?"

• • •

The four of us sit in the gloom of the Club Thirty Three, probably the most notorious and racy night spot in Athens county. Darcy and Trish are sipping manhattans, Darcy amazed that she wasn't carded when we ordered.

"That's Brother Hepstal back there," Mark chuckles, "the bartender. Been out of school two years and he's worked all the way up to Saturday night bartender at the Thirty Three." He takes a sip of his beer. "Course, he had a natural talent for it. And... he treats the brothers right. And their dates."

Trish and Darcy have their heads together, whispering and giggling. Finally, Trish takes a big slug of her manhattan, fishes out the cherry and with its stem sticking between her lips, says, "I have an announcement to make." Mark and I look at her.

Darcy grins. "Yours truly has been accepted, on this day, May seventh, nineteen hunerd 'n fifty five, by the graduate school of the University of Cincinnati. Adjunct instructor and all."

We hug and kiss her and applaud, getting the attention of the nearby tables. Brother Hepstal comes over from behind the bar and Mark orders another round of drinks. The jukebox strikes up Kay Starr's *Wheel of Fortune* and we all get up to dance.

• • •

"To think of all the times I've driven by the Thirty Three," Darcy whispers into my shoulder, "and I've never know what a neat place it is."

We're lying in each other's arms, the Wonder Bar's light show playing on our glistening bodies. Darcy says she can't close her eyes because the room goes into a tailspin. I don't tell her but closing my eyes has the same effect.

"Five?" Little girl voice. "Isn't it great about Trish? She and Mark'll be in the same town… together."

"Yeah," I agree. "Mark's first rate. And Trish is one of the finest people I've ever met."

"Think I haven't noticed? I've seen you sneakin' looks down her dress." She giggles. Her fingers run down my chest toward my stomach. The Towne House lights snap off.

• • •

Torches burn in holders on the pillars flanking the Ace house front steps as we arrive for Monday's pledge meeting. The house is dark except for a single candle burning in the living room. The Tiler meets us in the darkened hallway and extends his arm toward the living room. Without a word, we file in and stand before our usual seats, couches, chairs, the padded bay window.

Tiler signals for us to be seated, then slowly looks at each of our twelve faces. Finally he speaks. "Pledges. This is the last time I'll call you by that title." We wait expectantly.

"Your initiation week begins tonight," he says in a solemn

voice. "Perhaps you think it's too soon … too soon after Joe Ransom's death. Personally, I think so. But the active chapter has voted and… it begins tonight."

We stir in our seats. Glances shoot around the gloomy living room. *Where do they keep the balloon?*

"When you leave here, return immediately to your rooms and pack your belongings. Except for class and study tours to the library, you will not leave the ACE house again until your initiation is completed.

"Now take careful notes. These are the things you must bring with you when you return at twelve o'clock." We sit with pencils poised.

"Each of you will bring a box of cigars. The brothers like different brands. Myself, I'm partial to Hav-A-Tampa's. The ones with the wooden tips." He gives us a wry smile. "And bring at least two packs of your favorite chewing tobacco."

"A large onion. If it's not large enough, you'll be sent back to get a bigger one.

"Toilet articles. And clean dress shirts. You will wear a coat and tie to class every day and each time you go out on campus.

"All your books and study materials. Five? Will you need any drawing materials?"

"Ahh, no sir," I respond, "my class projects are pretty much under control."

The Tiler continues, "Don't forget your shoeshine kits. Black and brown polish. The brothers like to have a really fine spit shine during Initiation Week.

"And a burlap sack. Each of you needs a one hundred pound burlap bag. Not the soft cotton kind. Burlap!" We scribble furiously. *Where in hell do you get a burlap bag in Athens on a Monday night?*

"One ten-penny nail. The big kind. Long ones. Each of you needs a nail. You might want to assign different people to try to round these things up." *Christ! It's a scavenger hunt.*

"Cigarettes. If you've got cigarettes with you now, leave 'em with me. You will be allowed occasional smoke breaks but the brothers will take your packs away from you. As your Tiler, I'll protect your cigarettes."

He pauses again to let us scribble our notes. "Any questions?" We heave a barrage of questions at him and he calmly answers each of them.

"For the next week, you will speak to no one outside the Ace house except for ACE brothers, your instructors, and any shopkeeper or person you come in contact with on a business basis." A stern look follows this announcement. "If you talk to anyone. Your girlfriends. Your classmates. We will find out. And! You! Will! Suffer! For It!

"Likewise, you will not sleep during your classes. We will find out. And you will not cut a class to go sleep somewhere. You will not return to your room for any reason." *I'm beginning to get the picture. It's going to be a long night. A long, long week!*

The Tiler looks at his watch. "It's now nine o'clock. If you follow my instructions, you should be able to do the things you have to do and be back here by midnight. If you can't find something on your list, be here at midnight anyway."

Once again he gives us his sternest glare. "If for any reason, you are not here by midnight… go on home. Don't bother to try to enter the house. The balloon will have gone up without you."

Dramatically, he walks to the door that leads to the hallway and stairs to the Keep. He flings it open and calls in a loud voice.

"Can you hear the leopard's roar?" A strange silence follows.

Once again, "Can you hear the leopard's roar?" We sit forward, wondering if there's a response we're supposed to make. Then, a third time.

"Can you hear the leopard's roar?"

From the depths of the house comes this unnatural sound. Reason tells us it is the combined voice of the active chapter.

But we have heard the leopard's roar.

"Go now. Quickly," Tiler says. "And return by midnight."

Chapter 25

Can A Leopard Change His Spots?

Our frantic three hours begin in the alleyway between the Engineering Building and the Delt house. Chet Husted hushes us and Benjo Kostic takes over. "Five, you run up to Begorra and tell Darcy the balloon's going up and to tell all our friends. She knows all the girlfriends, doesn't she?"

"I think so," I shrug. "Anyone here got a new girlfriend since Saturday night?" Their laughter eases the tension we feel. Down the alley, terrible cries and shouts emanate from the Ace house. Above us, similar noises tell us the Delt pledges may be starting their voyage as well.

"Don't worry about burlap bags," McClintock says. "I got a bunch of 'em stacked under my bed. My old man told me to have 'em ready." We smile at the advantage of having legacies in our midst.

"There's a produce stand out on the road to Coolville," I volunteer. "I'll try to get Darcy's car and see if I can get the onions. And that market out on State, it stays open 'til ten I think. I'll bet they carry chewing tobacco. Anyone here ever chew?"

"I have," the Martian responds, "get Red Man. And some Beech-Nut."

"Better get a couple dozen big onions, Five," Waller suggest. "I have an idea those fucks won't think the first ones we show up with are big enough."

"Take off, Five," Benjo says. As I jog away, I hear him barking orders. "Soos, get up to Quick's a pick up cigars. Hav-A-Tampa's. And some of those Marsh-Wheeling long jobbers..."

I jog up to Begorra and breathlessly tell Darcy my problem. She hands me the keys saying "Leave 'em under the first step at Duff's place. Will I see you in figure drawing in the morning?"

I nod yes and turn for the door. "No more Begorra orders this week, I guess."

"Take care, love," Darcy says as I go out the door.

• • •

We sit cross-legged on the floor of the living room in our underwear. Kong Thoreau paces as he instructs us in what to do.

"Cut a hole at the top of the bag. That's for your neck. And arm holes. Don't make 'em too big. We don't want your bags falling off you.

"You'll wear the bag and your underwear all the time you're in the house. Understand?" He doesn't wait for us to respond. "Now let's see your onions." Dutifully, we hold up our onions. He swats one from Simpson's hand. "Too damn small. Got another one?" I roll a bigger onion over to Simpson.

"Now take your nail and run it through the onion like this." He demonstrates. "Then tie a piece of this string onto each end. You'll wear the onions at all times while you're in the house." Kong places the strung onion around Shivers' neck.

"So," he leans back, "who's got cigarettes?" Without thinking, McClintock holds up a pack of Luckies. To Mac's horror, Kong snatches them away. "Thanks. I was out."

He produces some brown paper bags, the kind I used to carry my lunch in at Hockingport High. "Each of you will keep his belongings in a bag. Don't lose your bag or you're outta luck. Always have your chewing tobacco and cigars in the bag. "Who's got cigars."

Timidly, I reach down and extract a Hav-A-Tampa from its box and hold it up. "Not those pussy cigars," Kong growls. "I like a real cigar." Able holds up a long, black Marsh-Wheeling. "That's more like it. Light that fucker up, A.A." Able brings out his lighter, breaks the cellophane and lights the cigar. He grimaces and chokes as a puff of blue smoke erupts from around the cigar. Logan has a broad grin on his face. "Now… take a big bite out of your onion."

"Now listen good," Kong says, leaning forward with his hands on knees as if in a football huddle. "Tiler is your nurse maid. If you've got any problems, go to him. I mean problems! Real problems! Chickenshit problems like my girl didn't get the curse will just get your ass in trouble.

"And believe it or not, I may be your best friend for the rest of Hell Week. When you hear my voice, do as I say. Don't hesitate. Just do as I say." He pauses, swivels his head around our circle. "Understand?" We nod yes.

"Do not forget your lore. Believe me, you'll get rattled. But don't forget what you've learned." Again he pauses, then straightens up. "You have anything to add, Brother Tiler?"

The Tiler looks us over a last time. "I hope I've done the job I was supposed to do. I guess we'll find out before the week is out. Just keep in mind this one final thought. You are the Thirteen. The Thirteen is One! Keep your unity!"

"Well spoken," Kong Thoreau growls. "Now get your rotting asses down to the Keep. The Leopard's waiting and he's hungryyyy!"

• • •

In less than an hour, the Keep reeks of sweat, cigar smoke, raw onion, Red Man and vomit. Hard as we try to stay together, the Aces keep breaking us into ones and twos, screaming curses, questions and orders for push-ups, sit-ups.

"No Low-ree! How can you be so goddamn stupid?" A brother named Jim Cephus, who's never said more than two words to me before, screams in my face. "Take another bite of your onion and give me fifty sit-ups."

"You must not like Red Man, you spic dog-eater," someone screams. "Who's got some Beech-Nut. Give your pathetic barfbag pledge brother here some good chew." I hand the quivering Soos my packet of Beech-Nut and he takes a small pinch. "Not enough, Salazar, you queer. If you can't chew like a man, get your ass out of here. Right now. Get out!" The active grabs Soos and yanks him toward the door.

"Thirteen!" Kostic shouts, "don't let him go." And we leap to drag the pale brown Salazar away from his tormentor and back into the room.

Bile rises in my throat as I chew Beech-Nut, raw onion and take deep drags from the chewed wooden tip of a Hav-A-Tampa. Desperate, I recite for Cephus "...founded in 1849 as a debating society at Tusculum College, Greenville, Tennessee, by Winston Livy Gousha, Kendall Kirkwood and Garret Stowers Thur..."

Above the din we can hear the Martian shouting "sigma rho pi omicron xi nu mu lamdba kappa iota theta eta zeta epsilon..." The Aces seem entranced by his ability to recite the Greek alphabet in reverse.

• • •

The radium hands of my watch indicate five in the morning before Thoreau finally "puts us to bed" on the hard, worn rug of the living room. "Sleep, goddamnit. I know you've got eight o'clocks. So don't fuck around and think. Sleep!"

• • •

Andy Logan makes a face as I flop into the desk next to her in sociology. Even brushing my teeth for the full twenty seconds allotted, I can taste vile things and know how I must smell. She pats my arm and whispers, "My turn, Five." As soon as Gessler starts to drone, I lower my head on her White Shouldered white shoulder and drift away.

• • •

Walking into figure drawing, I whisper to Jan Dabny, "Professor Dabny, would you please tell the model that I am still alive and think about her constantly." Dabny recoils in instant disgust at my odor, then smiles and shakes her head.

At the first break, Darcy heads right for my easel where I stare at the nearly empty pad. She leans over and pecks a kiss on my ear. I jump, startled and stare around the room. *How will they know?* "Jeez, Five, but you stink. You OK?" I nod yes. "Don't suppose we've got a coffee date after class?" I turn and give her my most pathetic look. *Isn't it bad enough to have one*

334

tormentor during Hell Week?

• • •

By Wednesday night, we've had two full-fledged brawls — actives versus pledges — with one of the more timid brothers bring dragged off to the infirmary with a dislocated finger. But so far, the Thirteen has maintained its unity.

"Harder, harder!" I puff harder on my Marsh-Wheeling, a cigar that I've taken a liking to and admire for being the favorite of Winston Churchill. The only *real* pleasure from it, though, is puffing clouds of onion-tainted smoke into the purple face of Galen Curtis. Curtis, Gunner Schmidt and Jerome Mayhew have me "braced" in their room, shouting questions, calling me names, and watching in fascination as I chew onion and tobacco while obviously relishing the Marsh-Wheeling.

"Now you feather merchant pussy," Curtis growls, "I want you to watch carefully." He produces the now-familiar black marble. At the same time, his other hand brushes across my bag at my crotch.

Expelling a huge cloud of smoke into his face, I snarl, "Move your hand Mister Curtis. Don't you ever touch me there again."

Curtis goes ape-shit, grabs my throat and shoves me against the upper bunk. I raise my arm in defense, brushing the cigar tip across his arm. He howls in pain and leaps back.

"This sonofabitch burned me!" he screams. "That's it, fucker. You're gone. Out of here right now," he tugs at my shoulder and steers me toward the hall door where I lurch into J.E. Ehlers.

"Got a problem, Brother Curtis?" Ehlers asks calmly.

"Bastard cursed me. Burned me with his cigar, J.E. He's gone. I'm droppin' the ball on 'im right here." Ehlers raises his hand.

"Is this so, vermin?" he asks me. Even the good guys have dragged out their pet names during Hell Week.

"True, Mister Ehlers. I did burn him. But I did not curse him. I should have. I had cause." A jolt of pain shoots up from

335

my kidney where someone punches me. I lurch into Ehlers' chest.

"That's enough, Brothers," he says sternly. "Vermin, why don't you go downstairs to the library and take a cigarette break?"

• • •

We know it's Friday morning because the darkness of Thursday night has vanished. The clatter of kitchen activity wakens us from an hour or so sleep on the hard linoleum of the dining room floor. That's where we were doing our last exercise in unity, football log-rolls when someone tried to make Chet Husted and D.D. Smith do them by themselves.

"Shower time, you worthless turds," Thoreau growls amiably. "But keep it down. I'm sure you don't want to wake the brothers." For all his insane rantings during our pledge period, Kong Thoreau *has* proven to be our best friend in this land of the friendless.

He has broken up two genuine fights. First, Kostic sitting atop Gunner Schmidt's chest and pounding the active with furious fists. So much for unity among Korean vets. Then, the Martian with tears running down his cheeks, kicking his fellow band member D.D. Long in the ribs. In each case, we thought we were done for. And in each case, Kong soothed the waters and Hell Week rolled on.

"That's it Lowrey," Kong says mildly from the bathroom door. "I know you're not seeing your sweetie this morning so half a minute's long enough to brush your teeth."

• • •

Dicky Reb West, Soos, Pirate and I walk slowly toward our nine o'clocks. Walking to and from class is our only real time of freedom and we move lethargically, squeezing every delicious second away from Hell Week. We nod to fellow classmen but don't speak, except among ourselves.

"That 'you'll eat shit before you ever become an Ace' line

was new last night," Soos observes. "Have you guys gotten that?"

"Yeah," Dicky Reb rejoins, "it's almost as if they're working from a formula."

"Or a script," I add. "Except for CC running his hand over my jewels. I can't believe that bastard?"

Pirate smiles at a passing beauty, tips his imaginary hat. "Guys, I think we're gonna' make it. I really do. Didn't think that Monday night, or Tuesday. But this morning..."

"Yeah," Soos says, "I think you may be right. What else can they do to us? Make us pledge for another semester?"

"My only wish," the Reb says longingly, "is that Ransom was here with us." We walk on silently.

• • •

Friday night's a sort of recess. Kong sits and smokes in his chair while we sprawl around the dining room floor, studying. Studying on a Friday night is a first for most of us. And we suspect that the brothers need a break as much as we do and are now out TGIFing with their girls. *And with our girls, as they've so often claimed?*

Kong doesn't even seem to notice when Waller's head conks back against the wall. Nor does he mention Waller's drawn out snore. We all take a tip from this and try to catch a quick nap while still appearing to be studying.

But the respite is short. We snap to attention and when the first active rushes into the room, snorting for blood, we're deep in our books, lost in academia. Then the uproar is blanketed by an even more terrifying scream. Curtis storms into the room, holding a pair of shoes over his head.

"Which of you cocksuckers shined my shoes?" he rants. We *alleged cocksuckers* look at each other in great innocence. "Nooo! You bastards. One of you assholes shined my shoes. My good white bucks!" We look carefully and indeed, the red soles of formerly white bucks show beneath a glossy coat of black polish.

As one, twelve hands shoot up.

• • •

By five a.m., we're on our backs on the living room floor. Twelve recumbent bodies. No, thirteen. In our midst, a drunken Jim Cephus snores with bubbling noises.

The past hours are a blur of harassment and hazing. Surprisingly, all of us find our ability to do pushups is improving. There may be *some* benefit from Hell Week.

From the comfort of the forbidden couch, Kong Thoreau croons, "Go to sleep my little doggies... go to sleep now... for it's a long, long trail tomorrow..." *Good grief. Home on the range!*

• • •

Saturday morning brings us a full-fledged work party. The Greek Week carnival is only six days away. In informal clothes — other than the hated bags — for the first time, Waller, Kostic and I work outside in the courtyard with Husted and Dave Gamble — the Tiler — to assemble the elaborate frame of the dunking booth.

We've even allowed to sit on the steps during a smoke break. Such luxuries have become so rare that we feel uncomfortable doing so. It's a warm day and would feel so good to strip off my t-shirt but common sense tells me not to stretch my luck too far.

After a lunch of bologna sandwiches and Kool-Aid on the floor of the Keep, Kong lets us smoke our cigars at leisure as he conducts a long and thorough drill on the lore. This is followed by the most amazing thing! Permission to lie down and sleep. We nap like first-graders.

My sleep is punctured by a firm hand. It's Doak Phipps, my big brother. "Come with me, Vermin Lowrey," he says firmly. I look around the sun-dappled floor of the Keep and see that about half of my pledge brothers are missing. Looking to Kong for guidance and getting a nod, I follow Phipps up the stairs and to his room, one of three doubles in what's called The Tower.

"Sit on the bed there, Five," Phipps says. "It's OK. Really." He hands me a bottle of icy Coke. "Hell Week's not over yet, but this might taste good." I'm leery but the expression on his face tells me it's OK to take a sip.

"Five," he says sincerely, "you guys are about to start your last night of initiation. So far, you've made me very proud of you. As a pledge class. Especially as my little brother.

"But what's about to come will make the last six days look like some party. If you want, I can give you this pill to help calm your nerves. I would if I were you." He holds forth a fat, blue pill. It looks like one of those M&M candy things. Dutifully, I accept it and wash it down with a swallow of Coke.

The lower bunk is soft beneath my butt and the temptation to just lie back and let my eyes take over is so strong. As if reading my mind, Phipps says, "Five, you've done a really good job this week. Except for sleeping on Andy Logan's shoulder, I don't think you've broken any of the rules." *How in hell does he know about Andy Logan's shoulder?*

Doak continues, "In the next few hours, you're going to feel very much alone. Truly alone. And there'll be moments when you will have to make personal decisions. Decisions by yourself. Nothing you can talk over with your pledge brothers.

"Just remember the lessons you've learned as the Thirteen. Nothing is more important than your unity. The One. Every time you're faced with a decision, think about that unity." There's a soft knock on his door.

"It's time, Five. Keep cool. Keep your head. Listen carefully to everything that's said. I'll be close by." He looks at me with questioning eyes. *What the hell! Let's get it over with.* Doak rises. "It's time to go downstairs, Five. Follow me."

• • •

On the first floor, the house seems empty. We pause by the little hallway that houses the chapter telephone and leads to the small bathroom used by dates and girlfriends.

"You need to go, Five?" Doak asks. "You should probably void your bladder now. I doubt if you'll get another chance."

Suddenly my bladder tells me it needs voiding very badly.

In the closed bathroom, I lift the ragged hem of my bag and watch the trickle of blue urine splash into the bowl. *Blue urine? Oh holy shit!* Outside the bathroom, I look sheepishly at Doak. "I guess you didn't know, Five. All leopard cubs pee blue." He leads me into the pantry by the kitchen. There sits Kong Thoreau at a table covered with thick pads and rolls of tape. He directs me to sit.

"Five," he intones. "Like a leopard cub whose eyes have not yet opened, you will be in darkness for the coming hours. Don't be afraid. Brother Phipps here is going to apply Vaseline to your eyes and hair. It'll keep your eyes from becoming irritated... and the tape from sticking to your hair."

Gently, Doak smears each of my eyes with a thick coating of the jelly, then runs his hand around my head above my ears. Before me, Kong holds up one of the pads, as if measuring me. He takes a pair of scissors and cuts a small triangle out of one edge.

"You may not recognize this." I do but stay silent. "It's a Kotex. It'll serve as your blindfold so you may enter the darkness." Phipps places the pad against my eyes, then slowly winds some sort of tape around my head.

"Gauze. Too tight?" I nod no and he continues. I hear the *scrrrrrch* of adhesive tape being pulled from a roll. Then the bandaging continues.

• • •

Leopard cub or not, I *am* in the dark. Sitting on the floor in silence, I can sense the presence of others in the room with me. But I have been instructed to stay silent. Then a low voice begins speaking.

"Thus did the noble Templar lead his troops to the mole of Tyre. And there were met in fierce battle by the Saracens. But prayer and study of the Word convinced them of their rightful victory and they did assault the walls of Tyre.

"And before Tyre's gates, did the Noble's troops rejoice in celebration. Drinking and singing before the walls. While the terrible wrath of the Saracen within awaited.

"Then did the Noble, sick at heart at the sloth of his crusaders, travel into the desert. And become dizzy with thirst and hunger. And become lost as the darkness came upon him."

This soothing passage is broken by awful screams and cries. We're at once grabbed and jostled from wherever we were sitting on the floor roughly down the stairs and into what I can imagine is the Keep.

"Push-ups, vermin," a voice shouts. Is it a familiar voice? In this darkness, *none* has any familiar ring. "Count 'em out, you filth." I join the chant of my brothers as we start our push-ups. At least I am free of the odious onion bouncing below my chin. *This doesn't seem to bad!*

More calisthenics follow. Sit-ups. Running in place. Soon I can smell the rancid sweat of my fellow vermin. At a shouted order, we stop and stand in place.

"Remove your sacks, you filthy worms," orders another voice. "And that awful underwear." This sounds like Curtis. Reluctantly, I pull my bag over my shoulders and drop my drawers. "On the floor now. On your stomachs. Someone will guide you." Gentle hands on my shoulders direct me a couple of steps forward, then firmly down. The linoleum is cold and damp against the sweat on my bare skin.

"All right you naked bunch of assholes, let's do a few log rolls. To the left now, go!" *Football log rolls blindfolded? The fucker's out of his mind.* But I snap a push-up and whirl to my left, colliding with a slower body in the place that should be mine. Grunts. Groans. The smack of bare flesh against other bare flesh.

"Keep it up, shit eaters. Keep it up til you get it right," Curtis screams. "Right now, go!" We snap and roll to the right. Pain shoots through my elbow and someone grunts in agony.

341

After about six violent log-rolls, Curtis tells us to rest.

Then something warm hits my back. *Is one of these bastards pissing on me?* I hear muffled protestation from my pledge brothers. "Silence," Curtis rages. "Keep your goddamn mouths shut." The warm liquid dribbles on my head, then slides down toward my mouth. I can't help tasting it. *Sweet!* Some kind of syrup.

Then a rattling noise is followed by a shower of light, sharp objects upon us. "Now let's try a log-roll, you assholes," Curtis screams. *Cereal of some kind.* Slippery and slimy, we obey and roll ourselves in syrup and cereal.

"Looky here, brothers," Curtis cries jubilantly, "this one's got a boner!" *Well, I know it's not me.* "Isn't that cute. His little dick is all hard. Do you like this stuff, shithead? Does rolling around in this shit make you horny?"

Another voice chimes in, "Are you vermin going to lie there and let your worm brother get a hard-on all by himself? Let's see some unity! Let's see some boners!"

Even in the dark, I can recognize Kostic's hiss of outrage, "I'll show you a boner, you motherfucker." Try as I must, no results. Futilely, I lie there in exhaustion, refusing to think of anything except my poor exposed asshole and that bastard Curtis looking at me.

• • •

"And the Noble was visited by dreams during his chill night in the desert. Visions of a great beast. And his arm was in the jaws of this beast. His skin grew cold with fear. But the light of a new day awoke him from his sleep and he discovered the warmth of his body that was not an illusion.

"From the rays of the rising sun, he discerned the form of a beast. The creature of his dreams. A great leopard. And it spoke to him in a powerful voice and said, 'you have trusted the truth I bring you and accepted the warmth of my body. And now you must return to defeat

342

the devil Saracen."

"Call upon me in your hour of need and I shall be there. And you shall call me Acerbus. Seek out from their number the trusted Thirteen."

• • •

The gentle voice of Doak Phipps as he guides my crawling progress from place to place is my only link with sanity. We must crawl everywhere. Doak's hand on my shoulder halts me and I remain there, on all fours. In the dark.

"Vermin Lowrey?" This is a new voice. Soft. Reassuring. "Do you remember being told you'd have to eat shit before you ever could become an Ace?"

"Yes."

"Well, that time has come. You'll recall, your big brother, Denton Phipps, was just with you. Well, before he came to get you, he stopped here." Pause. "Crawl forward, vermin." Again, I dutifully obey, crawling across a threshold and onto a tile floor. "Stop," the voice orders. "Feel around you."

I rise on my knees and extend my arms to each side. My left hand touches some cold plumbing. *A sink?* On my right, a wall. Feeling in front of me, I encounter the lip of a commode. "One more crawl forward, vermin," the voice urges. "Now, reach into the bowl." My hand encounters water, then something solid, yet squishy.

"Now Lowrey, the time has come to prove your desire to become an Ace. Eat shit. Or die!" Gagging, I gingerly grasp the object, open my mouth and do it.

• • •

"Thus did the Noble return to his encampment beneath the walls of Tyre. And did he raise his thirteen bravest warriors in song and speech. Told them of his dream and vision. And roused them from their drunken torpor.

343

"And they sounded their horns. And clashed their swords and shields. And they did assault the walls of Tyre."

• • •

Each session of ACE lore is punctuated by individual harassment. More screaming and shouting. Much more terrifying coming at us out of the darkness.

"Lowrey, you shit-slurping river rat fuck," a voice whispers from nearby. "I'll bet you'd rather be in a nice warm bed with your little hamburger moose than right here. Wouldn't you?"

The darkness before my eyes is now fiery red. *Stay cool. Keep your temper.* "Whoever you are, you'll regret you said that. I swear. And in answer to your question… yes!"

I'm violently turned by a grip on my shoulder. "Then get the fuck out of here right now," Curtis screams. He drags me in some direction in the darkness.

Another voice intervenes, "Easy Curtis. Just take it easy. It's time for the tower. Let's let him prove himself."

A new set of hands turns my shoulders and a softer voice directs me to crawl forward. After some seconds, I encounter an obstacle. A step? "Rise now, Vermin Lowrey," the voice commands. My knees creak as I rise to my feet.

"We have steps to climb, Lowrey. Put your hand on my shoulder and I shall guide you." Slowly, I follow the body ahead of me up a set of steps. Ten steps. Then a landing. Another ten steps. We turn on another landing and walk forward slowly for five or six paces. Suddenly, I feel a chill blast against my bare skin. "Two steps, Lowrey. Careful now." The hand urges me up the two steps, one at a time.

Suddenly I feel a tightness around my balls! I try to jump back but firm hands hold me. "Don't be afraid," a voice cautions. "Don't be afraid of anything but your own decisions."

"Hold out your hands, Lowrey," a new, quiet voice instructs. "Closer. That's it. Now, I'm going to put something in your hand. It's heavy." I grasp a hard, heavy object. My fingers run around its edges. It feels like a brick. "Do you know what it is,

344

Lowrey?"

"A brick?"

"Yes, it's a brick from the courtyard below. And do you know where you are?"

"No?"

"You're standing on the ledge of the highest room in the tower. If you could see, you would see the lights of the asylum far across the valley." I can envision the sight in my mind, although I've never been to the tower's top room, off limits to pledges. "Don't worry," the voice continues, "we won't let you fall. Now feel the brick carefully. What do you feel?"

"A string? A string around the brick?"

"Yes. That's right. Now hold the brick very tightly in one hand. Carefully. And run your other hand down the string. What do you feel?"

"Ohmygod!"

"That's right." The voice pauses and a hand gently removes mine from my shrunken scrotum, attached to the brick by the string. My hand is placed back upon the brick. *I'm beginning to receive a picture, just like the snowy TV back home in Jack Gestner's living room.*

"Lowrey, you are the last of the Thirteen to face this test. You have to drop the brick. Do you wish to be the first of your class to fail it?"

"Nope!" My hands fly apart.

• • •

"And so they assaulted the battlements of Tyre. With book, word and deed. With song and faith. And the Saracen did flee back from the crushed gates and quiver in fear.

"The wrath of the Crusaders was terrible to see. From the Saracen coffers they seized the precious relics of Christendom. With their torches, they put the evil works of the Saracen to flame."

• • •

My time in darkness is endless. Intact in all parts, I revel in the knowledge that I have outwitted one of their meanest tricks. But my joy is short-lived as new assaults upon my ears and my person come from every direction.

We're back together somehow in a big room. The floor isn't sticky like the Keep. But the smell is strange. Rank. And weird noises create an eerie background for the shouted deprecations of the Aces. Growls. Howls.

Part of the smell is smoke; something burning? A sudden warmth swishes by my ass and I jerk away from it. *Are they going to burn us alive?*

Again, a pair of hands on my shoulders firmly but gently directs my crawl away from this noisy melee. A threshold goes beneath my hands and knees. I feel another presence. And the smell is even stronger. Rank. An animal's den?

"Lowrey. You have met every test." This is a new voice, somehow familiar. Yet strange. "Are you ready to meet the Leopard?" At that, a terrible snarl from close by makes me jump back. *Man alive! They wouldn't! Would they?*

Numbly, I nod yes. "Extend your hand, Lowrey," the voice instructs. "Slowly." As I do, another lower snarl tells me that I'm indeed in close contact with a fierce creature. "Extend your fingers." I spread the fingers of my hand and my fingertips come in touch with the soft fur of a pulsating, living animal. *How do they do this shit, anyway?*

"Now Lowrey, the Noble trusted in his vision. Do you have that vision, Lowrey? Does your wish to become an Ace give you the courage to trust that vision? Are you willing to meet the Leopard?"

Again, struck silent, I nod affirmatively. "Then slowly. Carefully. Move your arm forward. Into the Leopard's jaws." I do as instructed and can feel the hot breath of the cat on my arm. the fetid odor of its breath assails me through. *Can this be happening? In Athens, Ohio?*

Once more, a fierce snarl makes me jerk back, and as I do, my arm is scraped by sharp teeth. "Don't be afraid, Thomsen

346

Lowrey. You have nothing to fear but that in your mind," the soft voice intones. Reluctantly, I move my hand forward. I can feel warm breath, and something wet and hot, and with my fingers I reach out and touch the Leopard's tongue!

• • •

Again, I feel the presence of my brothers. We're lying, face down, on some smooth, cool surface. For minutes... is it hours?... we've been left in silence to rest... to recover? There are so many questions I want to ask? But to whom to ask them? Most of my senses are alert. A few are not. I drift off.

I'm awake. But am I still dreaming? An urgent shake brings me into the darkness of Hell Week wakefulness. Around me, I hear soft but urgent voices. *Awake. Awake.*

"Here, Five. Here's a new sack. Put it on." Doak's voice is some grand prize from a past of darkness. *How can I have won such a prize?* Gently, I pull the cloth over my head, his hands helping me guide it down over the sticky mess.

"Stand now, Five," Doak urges gently. "It's time. You've met the Leopard. Now you shall see the light... and learn the truth."

• • •

We shuffle along in our new sacks, cool and smooth against our tacky and crusted skins. Certainly not burlap. I say 'we' because I can hear the scuffling footsteps of... surely my brothers.

Once more, cool air wafts across my forehead and shoulders. But as we stand, somewhere in the darkness, I realize that it is a really very warm night. My mind flashes to a week ago when Darcy and I lay entangled on her sheets, watching the magenta reflections on our slick bodies.

Sure hands once more direct our steps. Then we come to a shuffling halt. Three strong noises report and echo against our ears. Our noses, assailed by many odors do not register. Our sight is gone. Our ears take in the sound of three sharp metallic

347

knocks against something heavy, something solid.

"Tiler!" a far-off voice booms and echoes. "How goes the night?"

"Noble Acerbus, the night is clear and cold," the voice of the Tiler responds, his words echoing around us. *We must be in the courtyard.*

"Why seek you entrance to the Temple Bar?" the ghostly voice rings out.

"I bring you supplicants, Noble Acerbus. Thirteen candidates who seek admittance across the Temple Bar."

"Are they qualified, Tiler?"

"Yes sire. They have proven themselves."

"Then admit them."

• • •

Senses reawaken. We climb four steps, then shuffle to a threshold where careful hands guide our steps. We stop. New odors become apparent. As I'm guided forward, I feel the warmth of a new experience before me. I pause and hear a door close to my front. It closes with a terrible finality.

After hours — or minutes? — I'm again guided forward. This time, I'm stopped by those same hands which gently push me to my knees. A voice, Doak Phipps' I recognize, whispers softly in my ear, "Quiet now, close your eyes. And keep them closed. I'm going to remove your blindfold."

I do as ordered as the hard snip of a scissors blade clicks against my skull. *I've never cared much about my hair. Why should I now?*

"Keep them closed now, Five. Wait quietly." Against his orders and my most fervent desire, I squinch my sticky eyes open. Nothing. Blackness. *God! I'm blind!*

"Tiler! Who kneels before the bar?" the hollow voice rings from somewhere ahead. I close my eyes tightly, feeling their lids plastered by a coating of good ole' reliable Vaseline.

"The supplicant Thomsen Lowrey the Fifth," comes the familiar voice of the Tiler.

"Is he truly qualified?" the voice asks.

"Aye sir, truly and readily qualified."

"Then bring him forth."

As I rise, a door opens to reveal a flickering room. Slight light, perhaps starlight, illumines the tall, strange figures of wraiths standing before me. Two long candles flank a strange tableau… a big dog's skull with a silver cup implanted in its top. At a squeeze from Doak's hand, I remain silent as the ritual progresses.

"The supplicant Lewis Alfredo Jesus Salazar…" the Tiler responds, pronouncing Hey-soos correctly.

"Then bring him forth."

This is repeated six more times but as we stand there, our eyes do not accustom to the dim light. Finally, the Tiler announces the Martian and he is brought forth. If my count is right, all twelve of us are here.

But once more, the tall figure calls, "Tiler, who kneels before the bar?"

And the Tiler's hollow voice responds from behind us. "The supplicant Joseph Eric Ransom."

"Is he truly qualified?" the booming voice inquires.

"Verily, sire. None could be more qualified."

"Then bring him forth."

• • •

There's a long moment of silence before the door behind us closes with a hollow slam. Then the room echoes with three sharp raps. "My task is finished, sire," the Tiler proclaims. "I bequeath these supplicants to you."

Somehow, maybe magically, the light of the two candles increases and we can see the features of the tall figure in the center. His robe is white but for a leopard's arm and claw extending across one shoulder and the snarling face of a leopard hanging down before his own.

At his flanks are six giant figures, all in black, the tall cones of their hoods casting pointed shadows against the ceiling.

The tallest figure steps forward and in the voice from a cave, says slowly to us. "You have come from the darkness of a newborn's innocence. And from that state, you have heard the last lessons of the lore of Acerbus."

He lifts the animal skull before him. We can see its long fangs. "You have met Acerbus and he has approved of your dedication to his cause." The skull is raised higher and its shadow shimmers across the ceiling.

"At his order, and at his bidding, I fulfill my duty to end your journey of darkness. You have learned the truth. You have seen the light..." whereupon a great wall of flames erupts from behind the shadowy figures, throwing them into stark profile.

"Go now, and gather in this place on the waning of the day so that we may welcome you into our order." There's a silence. The billowing flames slowly subside to a strange orange glow.

"Go in peace, my brothers."

• • •

Suds and hot water. Screaming in joy. Sheer madness at seeing electric light again. To have to the prickle of something clean, hot, nourishing beating upon one's skin. We luxuriate in the freedom of the Ace house showers.

"Is that an erection, I see?" Waller chortles. "Do you think this shower is sexy? You blithering piece of maggot shit?" We goose each other and splash loudly. Really. I *can* feel the beginnings of something stirring in my groin.

Out of the shower, drying off, I'm led away by Doak Phipps to his room. "Your stuff is packed, Five. Go home now. There's no place else to go. It's five in the morning."

I grin insanely as I crawl into my khakis. The stiff, smelly chinos that Mamma Wolfe bought me and I've worn to class for five stinking days.

Doak smiles at me. "I know how you feel, Ace. But go home. You've got to be back here in twelve hours. I'll be down to get you..."

No idea what inspires me but I burst into song, *"...in a taxi, honey! Now... don't be late."*

Chapter 26

The Thirteen Is No More

Our hunger for sleep is overwhelmed by the euphoria of freedom. I want to run up and pound Darcy's door until I can bury myself in her sleepy arms. But my brothers counsel against that, pointing out that even a shower hasn't erased the tang of a week's diet of cigars, onions and Beech Nut.

So we settle for another raid on the East Green Cafeteria kitchen where Chris brews an urn of coffee. Since the cafeteria doesn't open until ten on Sundays, we have a few hours of privacy before the cooks arrive.

"It was *too* shit!" Clark McClintock says vehemently. "I could *smell* it!"

"There's no way they would make us eat real shit," Waller argues. "I think it was raw hamburger."

"That's what I thought after I got done barfing," Kostic says.

"I never thought about it," I venture. "Someone told me once to keep my sense of humor when they start feeding you shit." The brothers chuckle.

"Man, I stood there on that damned window ledge holding that brick, must've been fifteen minutes," Soos proclaims. "I mean, that's a dirty thing to do, especially to a Latino! I hope those bastards got as cold as I did."

"Aw Soos, they *had* to cut the string somehow. Otherwise, the whole house would be singing soprano," Mac observes.

"What I can't figure out is the leopard," D.D. Smith drawls, "just where'n hell do you keep a damn leopard, anyway?"

"What got to me, though," the Martian says softly, "was when they presented Joe Ransom as the thirteenth candidate. I mean…" He sniffs, removes his glasses and wipes his eyes. We all wipe our eyes in silence.

• • •

I brush my teeth before bed, again in the middle of the day when I get up to pee, and once more at four in the afternoon. The onion flavor lingers but seems to be getting weaker. I also call Darcy at the Begorra and tell her how lucky she was not to be assaulted at five a.m. by an onion-breathing alumnus of Hell Week.

"You better believe it," she tells me. "Just giving you a hug in drawing class was a big challenge to my devotion." I hear her familiar giggle. "So… are you coming up tonight for burgers?"

"I doubt it. Doak Phipps picks me up at five and then we have initiation. God knows how long that goes. So, don't count on seeing me. I'll try to get by there tomorrow… tomorrow night after *fraternity* meeting for sure."

"Aw, Five. You're gonna be a fraternity man. Isn't that sweet?"

• • •

The ACE house is sparkling clean. We stare at the waxed floor of the kitchen, the smooth nap of the living room rug, and wonder where all of the Hell Week action *really* took place.

Kong Thoreau and the Tiler shake each hand as we enter the house. But they are the only actives present. Tiler leads us down the stairs and past the Keep, where a shining coat of wax denies the disgusting things that happened there just hours before. On the big sun porch, we each take a chair and stare out at the late afternoon sun in the west.

"Beautiful day for an initiation, gentlemen," Thoreau comments softly.

"How come you're not screaming at us, Mister Thoreau?" Dicky Reb West asks.

"Ahh, Reb. That's one of the secrets you'll learn in time." Kong's chimp features are even more contorted when he smiles. He checks his watch and calls over to the Tiler, "Brother Gamble, I think it's about time to go."

We leave the big sun porch in a single file, passing through another narrow doorway much like my *secret passage* on the last

352

night of rush. The narrow steps down are lighted by fake candle bulbs and the shadows our figures throw are long and spooky. Two landings and turns lead to more steps until we must be well below the level of the courtyard.

A long tunnel leads to a massive door made of heavy timbers and braced with black iron straps and angles. The Tiler grasps the knocker — a leopard's head in black iron — and gives three sharp raps. The door opens instantly on the third blow. Soundlessly, unlike the creak I subconsciously awaited from listening to *The Inner Sanctum* too many times.

We follow the Tiler into another passage, this one lighted with real flickering torches overhead. The now familiar hollow voices halts us in our tracks.

"Tiler! Who approaches the Temple Bar?"

"Noble Acerbus. I present thirteen candidates for brotherhood."

"Are they qualified, Tiler?"

"Yes, Noble Acerbus. They are well and truly qualified."

"Then bring them forward."

• • •

The room is even darker, gloomier than it was at the crack of dawn when we first saw it. The candles flank the leopard's skull, reflections from its silver cup kicking across the shadows. The candlelight barely illuminates the tall figure of the Acer, clad this time in a black robe but still wearing the familiar leopard skin and head that extends down over his forehead. Beneath it, we can recognize the features of J.E. Ehlers.

Spreading his arms, he says, "Brothers, we are gathered in conclave to examine the pleas of these thirteen candidates for entry unto our Order. Are you prepared to vote?" *Vote? Is this where the blackball falls?*

"Do you accept the supplications of these candidates without qualm nor reservation."

"Aye," comes the mass answer from many voices behind us.

"So say the all of you?" the Acer asks.

"So say we all!" the shouted answer returns.

"Candidates before the Temple Bar. Do you seek entry unto our Order without qualm nor reservation?" *This is the 'speak now or forever' part I've heard at weddings.*

"Aye," we answer.

Ehlers pauses, reaches up to adjust the leopard's fangs that cover his dark hair, then proceeds.

"Then did Acerbus, upon victory at Tyre, seek to return to his homeland with spoils and prizes. But his return was met with scorn, for a wise and kindly priest said unto him, 'These sparkling baubles are but dust. Your victory is in learning the power of the Truth against the edge of the Saracen blade.'

"And did Acerbus then turn to his men at arms and tell them, 'Be your lives guided by the Light of Truth and never stray in search of earthly goods.' And his men at arms spoke."

"Acerbus! So Say We All!" the roar booms across the hall.

The twelve initiates leap back, startled, as the wall of flame erupts behind Ehlers with a *whoosh.* We squint our eyes against the brightness of the dancing fire. From each side, two trios of hooded figures march up steps before the flames to create the tableau we first witnessed this morning.

In the outstretched hands of the three on the left side, a large sword is suspended horizontally. The others carry a silver chain with huge links.

The ritual continues. The sword is presented to Acerbus who places it point down in a stand before the podium. Accepting the chain, he holds it in one hand and covers part of it with the other. When he removes the covering hand, one of the links in the chain is broken! The chain is draped across the pommel of the sword and onto the podium.

• • •

We sway dizzily in our file before the endless ritual.

354

Acerbus asks questions and the brothers chant back the answers. A bell rings somewhere. A knight's helmet is presented and its visor lifted to reveal a human skull.

There's a small stir and interruption in the ceremony as Perry Shivers makes a small sighing sound and two brothers catch him as he faints. Shivers coughs as smelling salts are brought from somewhere, then sheepishly rejoins our line.

● ● ●

Finally, we seem to be nearing a point of climax. *At least I hope.* Ehlers raises the leopard's skull holding the silver cup and says in a priestly voice, "You have heard the truth and understood. You have seen the light of the truth and have sworn fealty to follow that light. Drink now and join our order. Drink of the blood of brotherhood."

He moves down the line to my right, holding the cup in such a manner that each drinker must look right into the eye sockets of the leopard. One small sip each. Leopard's blood has some proof to it and has a slightly sweet tang.

"Tiler," Ehlers calls, "introduce the candidates and escort them across the bar."

"Brother Acerbus. Brothers. I bring before you Clark Sims McClintock." Tiler holds Mac's hand and formally leads him in a minuet-like step across the ridge of marble that runs between us and the podium. "I introduce to you, Brother Clark Sims McClintock."

"Badge number seven fifty four," a voice intones. An older man, a stranger to me, steps forward and pins Mac's badge upon his shirt. Then he gives Mac a huge embrace. It must be his dad. I realize that we're being initiated in the same order we pledged. Almost.

"Brother Acerbus. Brothers. I bring before you Thomsen Lowrey the Fifth." I am led, hand high, in the same stylized step across the bar. "I introduce to you, Brother Thomsen Lowrey the Fifth."

"Badge number seven fifty five," a voice intones. Kong's grin makes me think he's about to roar at us when he pins my badge. I can feel its weight tug at the fabric of my shirt.

Ten more times the ritual is repeated. The Martian is last and when the Tiler calls "I introduce to you, Brother Christopher Watson Cobb," the Martian's apparent twin steps forward. Maybe a few years older but what a spooky effect he and his father present! The Cobbs sparkle the room with matching tombstone grins.

There's a quiet second or two. Behind us, feet scuffle and voices are cleared.

"Brother Acerbus, I bring you Joseph Eric Ransom. It is my honor to present Brother Gerald Watney Ransom, badge number four forty three, who will honor Brother Joseph Eric Ransom."

Mr. Ransom steps forward quietly but dignified. He holds the ACE badge in his fingers. The voice calls out, "Brother Joseph Eric Ransom, badge number seven fifty three. May his memory live forever in our minds and in the light and truth." Brother Ransom steps forward and accepts a square of black velvet, pins the badge upon it, then places the cloth so that the badge covers the pommel of the sword. He steps back and bows his head.

Acerbus steps forward and lifts the leopard's skull to his mouth, then drinks a sip and holds the cup even higher.

"Call for Pater Gousha!" a voice rings in the rear and we're suddenly singing the hymn...

"In ancient days did Acerbus strike at the walls of Tyre,

to smite the mighty Saracen and end his reign of fire.

With book and sword they fought to bring the word of common good,

and treat their foes with the light of Acer brotherhood.

As the last verse of the hymn begins, the flames suddenly fade to a few inches, then whoosh back up, then slowly die completely.

Ehlers raises his arms to each side as the music stops and

says, "Go brothers. Go in peace, and truth, and light."

• • •

In the gloom of the two candles, we can see little but are turned by grips on our arms. Doak Phipps grins in front of me, takes my hand in a peculiar manner, and clasps my left arm with his other hand. "Truth and light, Brother Lowrey. Welcome to our Order."

Slowly the room lights are raised to reveal more of the Temple's interior. The room is filled with the brothers, all shaking our hands in the same strange grip. "Truth and light" fills the room.

"Truth and light, Brother Five," says a voice and I turn to see Professor Logan... *Brother Logan, I guess.*

"Truth and light, Brother Logan. Thank you so much for coming."

"Wouldn't have missed it for the world, Five. I'm very proud of you, my boy."

• • •

"Now don't get me wrong, Brother Thoreau," Brother Soos Salazar says, flicking the ashes of his *Something Rey* cigar from Cuba into an ashtray and peering over his brandy glass, "but I didn't understand but about a third of all that freakin' stuff that went on."

"Me too," I add. "It was impressive as all get out, but I had trouble putting it all together with the lore we learned."

Kong grins and blows a soft blue cloud across his brandy snifter. "Don't worry about it guys. You'll go through three or four more of these initiations and it'll seem familiar. But you won't have to learn the ritual by heart unless you become an officer."

"Particularly Acer. Or Templar. Tiler also. Or King of Arms," Brother Dave Gamble adds. "And you don't call me Tiler anymore. There'll be another Tiler with the next pledge class."

"Well, I'm glad to be an Ace," Salazar declares in a cloud of Cuban smoke, "but I'll be damned if I know what I'm doing except having a good time right now.

Chapter 27

The Curtain Falls For The First Time

Our third visit finds the ACE temple once more transformed. Gone are the podium, the hanging banners, all the regalia of our initiation. Tonight, it's a rather plain room filled with folding chairs for our first meeting as brothers of Alpha Chi Epsilon.

Based on hints we've gleaned from big brothers and friends, we new initiates take our seats in a group at the rear of the room. A lot of regular handshaking goes on... not the peculiar grip. Laughter and joking fill the room. At seven sharp, Ehlers enters the room and stands behind the table at the front. He whacks the table with what looks like the handle of a sword and calls "Order." The room quiets.

"Scribe, call the roll," he says.

Jim Cephus begins calling names and each brother answers with his badge number. We quickly realize the roll is being called by seniority. I proudly sing out "Ten fifty five" when my name is called.

Chris Cobb answers with "Ten sixty five" and Cephus snaps his book shut.

"All present, Acer, or accounted for." In the rear, we exchange puzzled glances. Evidently, the memory of Brother Ransom is burned into *our* minds but not the books of the chapter. Chet Husted shrugs and we silently agree not to question it. *For now.*

The meeting moves swiftly along. Kong Thoreau presents his report as Initiation Chairman and another secret is revealed. His almost insane demeanor was only a role for our pledge period.

Brother Dave Gamble is commended for his job as Tiler and we join the enthusiastic applause. The senior brothers, including Ehlers, Mark Husted, Gamble, Chester Lee and others are recognized and thanked for their service. I'm disappointed to see that Galen Curtis is not among those seniors. *Or am I?*

Under new business, Ehlers announces the slate of officers nominated for the coming year. As vice president, J.L. Simmons is nominated to assume the presidency. "Are there any nominations from the floor?"

"Brother Acer, I would like to nominate for president Brother Galen Curtis," Gunner Schmidt says in his hoarse baritone. Mayhew seconds and there is a murmur throughout the room. I can see the back of Curtis' head, unmoving.

"Discussion of the nomination?" Ehlers asks. Immediately several of the Aces raise their hands. A lively debate follows and it appears that a small faction of the brotherhood is behind Curtis for the presidency. When a brief pause in the debate happens, I raise my hand. *What am I doing? I'll be the first new initiate to speak?* Ehlers recognizes me. "Brother Lowrey?"

"Brother Acer, I would like to ask of Brother Curtis… ah, what exactly was his relationship with the late Brother Joseph Ransom?" The room buzzes, most loudly from our rear row. Curtis leaps to his feet and glares at me.

"My relationship? He was a goddamned pledge," Curtis roars. Ehlers whacks the pommel on the table.

"Five dollars, Brother Curtis!" he intones.

"What kind of question is this green kid asking, Brother Acer?" Curtis is livid.

"Would you swear upon your honor as a member of this Order that you had no *relationship* of any kind with Brother Ransom?" I ask, looking Curtis directly in the eye. Curtis continues to stare at me, his jaw hanging. Again, the room is filled with whispered talk.

Ehlers raps for order again. "On your honor Brother Curtis? Before the fires of Acerbus. Do you swear?"

Curtis whirls to face the front of the room. "I so swear." As I take my seat, Benjo Kostic gives me a thumbs up. *We've got him!*

• • •

We can't claim sole credit for J.L. Simmons' election as

Acer since Curtis was outvoted by more than the number of our bloc. After the election, Ehlers hands Simmons the pommel of authority who uses it to adjourn the meeting. "Go in peace, brothers."

Peace breaks out in the courtyard as I'm smashed to the bricks with the weight of Curtis on my shoulders. "What kinda wiseass bullshit was that in there, you asshole?" he growls into my ear. Other voices are yelling and I can see feet out of the corner of my eye, moving in to help me. "I shoulda blackballed your ass when I had the chance!" Curtis screams.

Curtis is dragged off of me. I get up slowly, feeling a trickle of blood on my chin. My white shirt is dirty and torn. Benjo and Waller are among the brothers who hold Curtis by the arms.

"Just truth bullshit, Curtis," I say through a film of tears. "And you didn't tell it. On your oath, you didn't tell the truth and you know it." Looking down at my torn shirt, I see the ACE badge dangling from a shred. I grasp it in my fist and tear it away from the shirt.

"Here Curtis, let me do it right." I hold the badge out to him. "Take the goddamn thing. I want no part of *your* brotherhood." He doesn't move. Nor do I. Finally, I turn and hurl the pin to the ground in front of a shocked J.L. Simmons.

• • •

Tears streaming down my face, I half walk, half run away from the Ace house. By the time I reach the head of the alley by the Delt house, I'm surrounded by my eleven pledge brothers.

"Hold up. Slow down, Five. We're with ya' brother," Mark Husted cries. I stop and they gather around me. Through my tears, I can see Husted's shirt is torn and all of them are minus the Ace badges.

"We're the fuckin' Thirteen, Five," Kostic says. "And we're sticking with you. All the way." I wipe my running nose and streaming eyes with the back of my hand.

"Are you guys sure?" I ask. "You're dumping everything. Everything we've worked so hard for." They nod their heads with grim enthusiasm. Just then, Dave Gamble and J.E. Ehlers

361

come running up.

"What's this all about, Five?" Ehlers asks panting. "What got into you guys?"

"It's him or us, Mister Ehlers," Husted replies. "That cocksucker has gone too far."

"Brother Curtis?" Ehlers doesn't look half as puzzled as his voice sounds.

"That's the cocksucker we mean," I say bitterly.

"Perhaps we should go back to the house and talk this over," Gamble says. He may not be the Tiler any more but he looks with concern at the faces peering from the Delt house windows.

"There's nothing to talk about," Waller says. "If you guys don't do something about Curtis, we don't have anything to talk about."

Ehlers gently takes my arm and steers me back down the alley. "Listen, guys. Brothers. Curtis is sort of a hothead…"

"He's a cocksucker," Soos blurts, "plain and simple."

"Call him what you want," Ehlers responds, "but I'm sure we can work out the problem." Slowly, reluctantly, we follow him back down the alley toward the Ace house.

• • •

It's a serious conclave in the main hall of the Temple: Ehlers, Gamble and the Thirteen. Curtis is nowhere to be seen as we enter the house. A few of the other brothers look at us but no one speaks as we march through the hall, out into the court and up the Temple steps.

"He swore on his oath before Acerbus," Ehlers says with great sincerity, "we can't ask more of a brother." So far, we've kept our silence as to exactly what caused my question in the meeting and Curtis' attack on me.

"What's the oath mean, Mister Ehlers?" Chet Husted asks. "Exactly what does it mean?"

"Simply, if he wasn't telling the truth, he'll burn in hell. Alpha Chi Epsilon isn't a religion," Ehlers pauses, "but its oath is just as strong. Now, would you like to tell me what it's all about?"

362

Everyone looks at me. I stare at the thin strip of marble over which I stepped just a few hours ago. "I made a promise to Brother Ransom," I begin, "a promise that I tried tonight to keep."

"It was a deathbed promise," Benjo Kostic says. "Five was the last one to ever talk to Ransom."

"And it concerns Brother Curtis?" Ehlers asks quietly. "Can you tell me what it is?"

"Mister Ehlers," I reply slowly, hoping my thoughts will catch up with my tongue, "I'm afraid if I bring it before the chapter, any more than I tried to do tonight, it's a matter that may ruin the ACE house."

Chet Husted says, "Perhaps it's something we should keep among ourselves. It is serious, Mister Ehlers. But it's something we can't prove and Curtis will just deny... on his oath!"

"Well," Ehlers speaks again ever so quietly, "Brother Curtis has told me he doesn't plan to live in the house next year. Would that be of any help to you?" He pauses. "And won't you please call me Brother Ehlers? Will you brothers please consider taking back your badges?"

I nod my head yes slowly. *We'll get him, Joe. The Thirteen is One.* "Yes, Brother Ehlers. I'll take back my badge." *Pause.* "If my brothers will." Grim smiles surround me.

"Five," Ehlers says, "I'm glad you made that decision. Brother Gamble, the badges, please?"

We all stand and slowly Ehlers moves around our circle, pinning each badge upon the chests of my brothers. He comes to me. "Five, I'm afraid your badge got kind of smashed in the tussle out there. I hope you'll do me the honor of wearing this one until we can get another Ten Fifty Five for you." He removes his badge, about the size of a walnut, from his chest and pins it above the rip in my shirt.

We all stand there in tears and shake each other's hands with the peculiar grip.

• • •

"Who is it?" Darcy's soft voice comes from behind her door.

It's past midnight but I just had to stop and see her.

"It's me. Five." She opens the door a crack.

"I thought I'd see you earlier than this, Five." She looks at my face, at my torn shirt. "Oh God! What's the matter?" She drags me into the apartment and steers me to the rumpled bed.

"Nothin... nothing much. I just had a little scuffle with one of my *fraternity brothers*," I say calmly but feel tears welling up again.

"Curtis? Or Mayhew?"

"Curtis. It's not anything I can talk about."

"Even to me?"

"Even to you, Darce. It's something we've got to work out among ourselves."

"Five! You're crying!" She takes the sleeve of her big nightgown and wipes my eyes and nose. "Are you sure you're OK?"

"I'm OK, Darce," I return, more testy than I intend. "I just came by to tell you that..." Then I really break down. "I can't talk about it and I can't do anything about it... and I'm so goddamned frustrated," I blurb. She holds me in her arms and rocks me like a little baby.

"It's OK, Five. It's OK. Really it is," she croons. "Do you want to clean up? Spend the night?"

"I can't Darce," I snuffle. "I'd love to but I've got that damned sociology in the morning and I'll probably flunk if I cut one more." She kisses my wet eyes.

"All right," she whispers, "I'll see you in figure drawing in the morning?" I nod yes. "And we'll have coffee afterward?" I nod yes.

● ● ●

"Jesus? Is that your Ace pin?" Andy Logan hisses at me in sociology. I nod yes and grin. She kisses me quickly on the cheek. "Congratulations." Fingering the pin, she says, "I've never really examined one before but this looks bigger than my dad's."

"It is. It's J.E. Ehlers' president badge and I'm wearing it 'cause mine got broken somehow."

"It surely is elaborate." With that statement, Andy slowly lets her head drift down to my shoulder as Gessler begins his lecture.

In figure drawing, Darcy gives me an eyebrow of concern before she starts her first pose. I return with a thumbs up and a smile and the day is off to a good start. At the break, she leans over my shoulder and teases, "Hmm! *White Shoulders?* Been makin' out with Andy Logan in sosh again?"

• • •

"What a glorious morning!" Darcy exclaims, walking hand-in-hand with me toward the Frontier Room. "Why can't it be spring all year around?"

It *is* a glorious morning. The grass on the College Green is thick and bright with new life. Gray-green buds have burst into juvenile leaves on the elms and maples. The year's newest fashion trend — Bermuda shorts — cover a few pale white legs as students stroll and play around the Green.

While I get our coffees, Darcy claims a pair of chairs on the deck outside and we bask in the sun, watching kids hurrying to their eleven o'clocks. She props her legs up on the wall, tilts the chair back and stretches. "Five? Do we have to go to the Greek Week stuff this weekend?"

"Well, I have to be at the carnival Friday night," I respond.

"And I've got to work anyway," she says. "I was thinking more of the dance."

"You don't want to go to the dance? You don't like Sammy Kaye?" I ask in mock surprise.

"Sammy Kaye's music sounds like the noise a cow makes when it has colic and can't get the wind out."

"Jeez, Darce! I didn't even know you were in 4-H," She grins back at me.

"There are a lot of things you don't know about me."

"Well, what'd you want to do if we don't go to the dance?"

"I don't know for sure. Just something different. Let's think about it." She leans over and squeezes my arm. "Ohh, look at your fraternity pin. I haven't even noticed it. I feel so bad.

"And it's cute, too. Look at the little knight's hat." She flicks the visor on the helmet with her fingernail. "And it's… kinda gruesome, too." I have spent many minutes examining the tiny skull in the helmet behind the visor.

"It's not my badge, Darce. It's J.E.'s, the president's badge. I'm just wearing it til' mine is fixed. The regular ones don't have the helmet on them."

"Five? You want to talk to me about Curtis?" she asks softly.

"No Darcy. I can't talk about it."

In a huffy tone, she answers, "Well… you have *your* secrets. I have *mine.*"

• • •

At Thursday's figure drawing class, the students give Darcy a big round of applause as the last session ends. She goes around, primly wrapped in the kimono and shakes each student's hand.

On Friday, Professor Logan finishes his Fine Arts Appreciation lecture and I find, to my surprise, that I truly have an appreciation for art. A whole year and I've learned something important.

Friday night, I work behind the scenes of our dunking booth at the Greek Week Carnival, helping Mark Husted, Waller and Kostic keep the rickety contraption from collapsing and drowning one of the dunkees. The carnival features several kissing booths, mostly sororities, and they bring in more money for charity than our *Ace In The Hole* offering.

The carnival's nearly over when Gunner Schmidt sidles up to me. "Brother Lowrey, can we talk for a second?" I walk to one of the exits with him. "Brother Curtis is feeling pretty bad about what happened Monday night. He asked me to ask you if you two can get along. Let bygones be bygones?"

I study my answer for a few seconds, then give a non-committal shrug. "What Curtis and I have between us is our business. If he keeps out of my way, I'll keep out of his."

"Sounds good to me," Schmidt says, shakes my hand and then turns to drift into the crowd.

• • •

Andy Logan and I make what must be maybe our fifth Saturday morning sociology eight o'clock and we're surprised to find Gessler behind the podium, ready to send everyone off to dreamland. We both fight sleep and giggle as the class nears its end. Our notes are silly scrawls of pencil across crumpled pages.

Gessler throws one last surprise at us. "I'm afraid that we're going to end this class with some more bad news," he says with a grimace. "My schedule's just filled for next week so our final examination will be held at eight a.m. next Friday." The groan that has become our class's sociology battle cry echoes across the room. Friday is the last day of final exams.

• • •

Something different for Darcy and me is a picnic lunch and a drive out to Lake Hope on Saturday afternoon. It's a beautiful sunny day and the area around the lodge and swimming beach is packed with students, throwing frisbees and balls, lounging on the hillsides, even some swimming in the lake.

"Hey, swimming!" Darcy shouts. "I wish I'd thought about that, brought a suit."

"Doesn't bother me at all," I return, watching the people bobbing up and down in the swimming area. "That water looks like the ice just broke up a few days ago."

We drive along the curving road that leads to the far end of the park. Where it turns, we can see the lake continuing off into the deep valley. All the picnic tables are taken by big groups and we don't see anyone we know well enough to join. "How about seeing if we can rent a boat?" I ask. Darcy grins as if I'd just invented something really marvelous.

At the boat house, we luck out, arriving just as a group of rather drunken Theta Chi's returns a skiff. I take the oars and Darcy sits in the stern, bailing a mixture of lake water and beer over the side.

"You're a good rower, Five," she comments as I make the aluminum skiff glide up the lake.

"Oarsman, maam, and I should be. Grew up on a river, you know."

"Can I try?"

At the oars, Darcy giggles, then finally bursts into uncontrollable laughter as she cuts an abstract circle around the lake. "This is harder than it looks," she says, blowing her hair away from her forehead. After about ten minutes, she gladly returns the oars to me and I row us on up the lake, past the last of the picnic areas. The lake slowly curves and the shouts and babble of picnickers are absorbed by the deep woods on each side.

Along one shore, I spot a small cove and head for it. Gliding into its narrow neck, we discover a larger pool where a flat sun-dappled rock slopes down into the water.

"There, Five. Perfect. That's exactly the place," Darcy directs. I aim the bow for the bank beside the rock and Darcy hops out to tie the painter to a nearby sapling. We pull out a blanket and spread it on the rock, then assemble the picnic.

Our picnic is great. A thermos of iced tea with mint. Sandwiches made on long rolls which Darcy calls *grinders* and I argue are called *hoagies*. Regardless, they're good. She completes the surprise with a batch of homemade cookies. "Duff made 'em," she grins. "I couldn't have done it on a hot plate."

After lunch, we stretch on the warm rock and look up at the trees surrounding us, small clouds scudding across the blue sky. Pretty quickly I hear a little snore from my companion. Then, I too succumb to a nap.

A squeal from Darcy awakens me. She's standing on the rock, her calves in the water. "What're you doing?" I ask sleepily.

"I just wanted to see how cold it is," she says. "It's not too bad once you get used to it." Then she spins and does a frog-like dive into the deeper water. I jump back from the icy drops of her splash. "Hooo, it's *cold* but I'll get used to it," she gasps as her head pops out of the black water. "And deep too. You coming in?"

"No way! You're supposed to wait an hour…"

"Aw crap, you're a chickennnn," she jeers, swimming toward me and then sliding up onto the submerged rock. Slowly she stands, her dripping white t-shirt and shorts nearly transparent.

"Darce! You don't have any… underwear on!" Her nipples stand stiffly against the cloth. The triangle at her legs is inviting.

"Of course not, silly. I'd have to dry them out. C'mon in! You're chicken!"

"No I'm not, but I'm not going skinny-dipping. What if someone comes along?"

"Go in your underwear, then." I stand and peel off my shirt and shorts. The shape of my underwear betrays my true feelings. With a couple of steps, I do the Hockingport racing dive into the water, creating a huge splash. Darcy swims away as I try to catch her legs beneath the water.

I swim to her where she's treading water. She twirls and reaches for me. "Oh my, it's *so little!*" She grins and gives me a watery kiss. "But not for long." Treading water, we shuck out of our clothes and toss the sopping garments on the rock. Then we embrace.

• • •

Part two of our something different day is my surprise. Darcy's in a strapless sundress. I'm in my lightest tweed sport coat. *Got to get something besides tweed if I'm going to dress up in the summer.* And we're driving out West Union with the top down.

I pull into the parking lot of the Sportsman's Grill and Darcy coos with pleasure. "About time we spend a little of that prize money," I say with a grin. A pretty hostess whom I recognize as an ADPi welcomes us and leads us to a secluded booth where my *reserved* sign sits.

Darcy has a giggling fit when I'm asked for ID and she isn't after we order manhattans. The window lets us watch the setting sun through a screen of hazy trees. The perfect ending to a really fine day.

I order filet mignons and when the waiter leaves, we shyly admit that neither has ever had one before. Darcy's appetizers of snails — of all things — arrives and she dangles one of the disgusting things toward me on a little fork.

"Better eat one, Five, or you'll regret it later. They're really garlicky."

"If you think I'm going to kiss a woman who's swallowed a snail, you're crazier than hell." But I surrender and swallow the ugly creature whole, savoring only the flavor of garlic.

Picking at the last of her steak, Darcy looks up and asks, "Do you know what you're going to do this summer, Five?"

"Think so. Captain says he's got me a berth on a big towboat, if I want it. And Professor Logan introduced me to a man named Easley at initiation. He owns Athens Outdoor Sign and I can go to work there, learning sign painting."

Darcy looks up with raised eyebrows. "And?"

"Well, the boat job would pay better. But if I work in Athens, we can be together all summer. And I could probably live in the Ace house for next to nothing and get some painting done."

"I think you ought to take the job on the river," she says in a serious tone.

"Why? Don't you want to be near me this summer?"

"Sure I do," she responds, "but I won't. I won't be in Athens this summer." The look on my face prods her to keep talking. "Trish asked me to come to Cincinnati for the summer, stay with her. Her dad is pretty sure I can get a job as a waitress at a restaurant owned by a friend of his."

"Cincinnati?" *Mars? The Soviet Union?*

"Oh, Five. It would be so much fun. Trish wants to get a place on one of those hills. And Duff can't keep me busy at Begorra. I'd just be taking his money like a gift. So…"

"You're going to Cincinnati?"

"Yes, Five. I'm going to Cincinnati."

Somehow our perfect day is ending differently than I'd anticipated.

Chapter 28

Solace Discovered In A Solstice

Athens undergoes an eerie transformation when the last week of spring semester begins. Umbrellas unfurl once more as an all-day shower sends Sunday's sun-worshipers under roof and to — God forbid — study for finals. The Sunday night sold-out MIA movie turns people away and they walk through the drizzle to the Frontier Room just to find people standing, talking in the crowded hallways.

On Monday the campus seems deserted. Class bells jangle twice and their clangor echoes off Cutler Hall and around the College Green. Small groups of students trudge their reluctant ways to finals. Monday afternoon, I join Andy Logan in the cavern of Mem Aud for our fine arts final. On the stage, officious Pat Trevayne supervises the crew of proctors preparing to hand out tests.

Professor Logan stands resolutely in the rear of the hall watching the process, looking content with the result of his work of two semesters.

"Andy, I've got to study for the sosh final," I whisper as we await the tests being passed down the row.

"Me too," she answers. "I look at my book and *our* notes and it's like seeing them for the first time. What a bore!" She looks up, accepting the test forms as they reach us. "Why don't you give me a call Wednesday afternoon? We can get together…"

"No talking. You have one half hour for part one," Trevayne's voice booms through the P.A. system. We answer the questions as fast as we can. I skip over ones I'm not sure about, to return later and puzzle over my uncertainties. "Time. Please turn to part two." *Trevayne had to be announcer for gladiator battles in another life.*

Part two is simply a page of blank lines, each headed by a

number. Sixty blank lines. "We will project each slide for thirty seconds," Trevayne announces. "That's all the time you have to identify the work, and the artist. Half score for only the name of the work or only the name of the artist." She chuckles. "Don't worry about spelling, except we have to be able to read it enough to understand your answer."

Andy grinds her teeth. "Dad didn't tell me *this* was coming. I'll bet this is that bitch's idea," she mutters.

A half hour later, we're smoking on the portico of the auditorium. Professor Logan walks up and Andy tries to get rid of her cigarette. "Andrea? What have I said about smoking in a public place?"

"Yeah dad, and what have I said about hitting your students with a cute wrinkle in an exam and not telling about it? That slide show was really a wonderful surprise." She spins on her heel and heads off toward sorority row. Over her shoulder she calls, "Give me a ring Wednesday, Five, and we'll study for sosh."

• • •

The last ACE meeting of the year has a couple more surprises. Simmons, now the Acer, announces that there will be nine vacancies in the house for the fall semester. From what Husted has told me, living in the house would be about twenty dollars a month cheaper than living on the East Green. I surprise myself by volunteering to move into the Ace house.

Doak Phipps rises as rush chairman to tell us of the fall's plans. "Rush committee, you know who you are. You'll be back here Monday night, August 22. Everyone will be back by six p.m. Friday, August 26. That's our first rush meeting and fines will be levied for absence. Rush starts Monday, September 12.

"Don't forget, if you meet a good candidate for rush during the summer, drop his name and address to me. Now here's my address…"

Later, Curtis rises and turns to the rear of the room. His mumbled statement contains an apology for losing his temper and starting the fracas of the week before. When he's done, I

372

rise and mumble back a meaningless acceptance. We meet halfway and shake hands; not the peculiar grip. The brothers respond with light applause.

• • •

Stopping at the Begorra on my way home the meeting, I'm surprised to find Duff handling the place by himself. "I sent her home. She wasn't doing us any good here, moping around and blowing her nose."

"What's the matter?" I ask.

"You're one of the things that matter," he says with a wry smile. "I think she's sorry about goin' to Cincinnati, in a way. She told me about your job at Athens Sign. Jack Easley's a good fella. I told Darcy she could stay and work here for the summer."

"She's too proud, Duff," I comment. "And I think she's really excited about going to Cincinnati."

"So do I," he returns. "And she'll get over her fling with the young painter once she sees the bright lights."

"I hope you're kiddin' me, Duff. I really hope you are."

• • •

Darcy comes to her door with all but her eyes hidden behind a wadded t-shirt. I think it's the Lake Hope model. "Wudd'you want?" she snuffles.

"I want to come in and hold you in my arms and comfort you and dry your tears. How's that for a start?"

"Well... you *can* come in." She opens the door wider and retreats to the bed, flouncing into a huge mound of wrinkled clothes, magazines and other artifacts from the apartment. "I'm packing," she sniffles. "Don't mess up my piles."

I sit gingerly beside her and put my arm around her shoulder, pulling her tightly to me. "What's the matter, Darce? Why are you upset?"

"Five, I am scared to death. Cincinnati's such a big place," she snuffles into my shoulder. "Did you decide about your job for the summer?"

"Yep. No use hanging around here with you gone. I'm going on the river. I called mom this afternoon and told her to have the Captain fix it up." This statement is met with a new outburst of tears. She pulls away and flops face down on the pile of clothes.

"Oh Goddd!," she wails. "Now I *have* to go to Cincinnati." I lean against her shaking shoulders and kiss the back of her neck. "Duff said he'd really *like for me to stay* and I'd just about made up my mind to do it." Big sobs wrack her body. "I'm gonna miss you so much, Five!"

"Aw Darce, c'mon. It's just for three months. And I'm going to miss you too." I stroke her shoulders gently. "If you want, I'll call home and tell mom I've changed my mind."

She sits up and turns around. "No. I don't think so. You'll make more money on the river. And…" she gives me sad little smile, "maybe being apart will be better for us." Then she flings her arms around my neck and bursts into tears again. "But I'm gonna miss you so!"

•••

I spend Tuesday morning at Darcy's, studying for western civ while she putters with her packing. For a girl with such a small apartment, she seems to make packing her belongings an amazingly huge chore. Every ten minutes or so, she comes over to give me a hug and kiss, activities that don't help my concentration on England's 1640 invasion of Scotland to crush the Presbyterians. *What in hell is English liturgy, anyway?*

The western civ final itself is a pleasant experience. Right there on the second page is England's invasion of Scotland and I'm amazed that I can remember the date. Handing in my test, I cringe at the thought of two more semesters of this stuff.

Walking down the Bryan steps, I encounter Dense; the first time I've seen him since my initiation. "Where you going, Bear? Another final?"

"Shit no, man. I'm done. Finished. Ready to do some serious celebrating."

"When are you going home?" I ask.

"Not til' after graduation Saturday. Page gets to lead the

374

College of Education in and wants me to hang around to see it. I think she thinks it may be the only graduation I'll ever see in this place," he grins. "How about you?"

"Ah, I've got a Friday final, then I guess I'll catch the train and thumb my way down from Coolville."

"Shit, Five. Why don't you stick around and ride home with me Saturday? We'll drain some Strohs and you and Darcy and Page and I'll go out and raise hell."

"Darcy'll be gone, Dense. She's leaving tomorrow afternoon with Trish Spotswood for Cincinnati."

Dense's broad face draws into a scowl, then a big grin. "Hell, you'll be a free man then. All the better! Will you stay?"

What's another 24 hours? "Sure will. But you'll have to help me get that big fucker footlocker up to the Ace house. OK?" He grabs my hand in his big paw and shakes it with what might be Sigma Nu's *peculiar* grip.

"Done and did, brother."

• • •

Wednesday's English lit final is pretty daunting. I muddle through five hundred words on an 18th Century proverb *The first faults are theirs that commit them, the second theirs that permit them.* Somehow, I feel there may be a lesson here.

Trish's last final is done at two o'clock so Darcy and I eat lunch at the Towne House. She refuses a beer. "I've got a long way to drive." And looks as if she'll break into tears any second. Sitting side by side in the booth, we hold hands gently.

When I finish my burger, she squeezes my hand and gives me a little push toward the edge of the booth. Silently, I leave money on the table for our bill and we go out into Union Street, a few steps down to the green door and our last time together. For three months.

• • •

"I still can't understand why you're not staying for graduation," I tell Trish as Darcy pulls and shoves her piles of clothing into the rumble seat. *Doesn't the girl own a suitcase?*

"Aw, Five. I've marched in one ceremony. And my folks are in California. They're the ones who would get a thrill out of seeing me in a hood." She smiles. "It's not a big deal. Besides, we've got to find an apartment and look for jobs."

"I thought you had a job at UC?"

"Not until fall semester," she responds. "So I guess I'll be waiting tables or selling garter belts until then."

"Come on you guys, let's get this show on the road," Darcy calls. "Just one more load, Five." I follow her up the stairs to the nearly bare apartment. She stands there, arms akimbo, looking at a few pairs of shoes and the framed sketch lying on the kitchen table. "You get the shoes, will you Five?"

"Why should I have to carry your smelly shoes?" I joke but she's already out the door.

On the curb below, Trish is already in the car. "Five, we'll drop you a line as soon as we have an address and phone number, OK?" I nod OK and move to the driver's side where Darcy stands with the sketch clutched against her chest. A tear dangles from the edge of one eye.

"Take care of yourself, Five." She throws herself in my arms. "I'll miss you so much. Don't forget me, now. You hear?"

"I hear, Darce. I'll never forget you." Then she's into the car and slams the door.

"You go that way," she nods toward the campus. "And we'll go this way. Otherwise, I'll just drive around the block for hours." She starts the Ford and leans out for one last kiss. I feel a terrible pain in my throat and tears begin to form as I watch them drive off down Union Street.

• • •

When I arrive back at Biddle, 205 is half empty. That's another strange aspect of finals week. One minute, friends are there. The next, they're not. Toby has left me a note.

Five buddy. It's been a great year. Thanks for holding my head over the wastebasket... and all the other stuff!!!

Give me a holler if you get to Ashtabula this summer.
See you this fall and we'll raise some hell. Your Greek
buddy. The Grey Wolfe.

As the afternoon sun dips westward, I sit in the lonely room
with thoughts of Darcy and Trish driving into that same glare in
a '35 Ford on Route 50. The tears won't go away.

Leaving the silent dorm, I wander over to the cafeteria
where I find the Martian sitting in the nearly empty hall, glumly
drinking coffee and smoking. He gives me a little wave and
beckons for me to join him.

"If you came to eat, Brother Five, it's peanut butter
sandwiches and jello salad. Last meal of the year in the ole'
barfeteria." His grin exposes the funny little teeth but the
expression isn't a happy one. "What's the matter, you look about
as low as I feel?" he asks.

"Aw, Chris. Just down in the dumps a little. Darcy left a
couple of hours ago for Cincinnati."

"Yeah. I know how you feel. Dawn took off this morning for
Chicago. And she's going to work in some park in New Mexico
all summer." He gets up and takes my arm. "Come on, get some
jello and peanut butter. Sure cure for love-sickness."

• • •

My footsteps echo in the stairwell as I return to the deserted
dorm. I can hear the second floor phone ringing. *If a phone rings
in an empty forest...?* When I open the fire door, it's still ringing
with no one in sight so I pick up the receiver. "Biddle two. But
no one's here but me."

"Five? Is that you?" a girl's voice asks, familiar, yet strange.

"It's me, all right. Who's this?" Then I realize. "Andy? Is
that you?"

"Yes, Five. It's me all right. And you were going to call me
so we could study for sociology. Weren't you?"

"God, Andy. I'm sorry. I just forgot."

"Well, it's only six o'clock so there's still lots of time left...
and all day tomorrow. Want to come over?"

"Aw, Andy. I don't know. That's a long walk."

"I won't take no for an answer. Bring your invaluable notes and meet me outside Biddle in ten minutes."

• • •

Andy picks me up in her mother's car and we drive back to her house on Townsend Avenue. As we walk through the house, she says "The folks are gone for a week in Canada. So I've got the place all to myself." We stop in the kitchen where she offers me something to drink. "Beer? Iced tea?" I opt for tea if we're going to get anything out of this study session.

In the back yard, a tall familiar-looking girl is lounging in the swing.

"Five, this Fantasia Putnam, a sorority sister and... believe it or not, an honest-to-gawd sociology major." I shake the Fantasia's hand and inspect her carefully. She's pretty, alert looking. Has on shorts with sandals. Not what I'd think of in picturing a sosh major.

"Tase, this guy is Five Lowrey, my buddy in sosh class. We've been sleeping together all this semester," she laughs. Tase Putnam raises her eyebrows in exaggerated amazement. "In sosh class. Remember, I told you we have Gessler?"

"Jesus!" Tase's voice is husky and low. "What an ordeal that must've been. At least his final will be a snap." She looks at our sociology text. "Where do we want to start reviewing?"

I shrug. Andy shrugs. "The last thing I remember," I say, scratching my head as if for a lost fact, "is this bunch of pygmies trying to cross a river on a log..."

"Oh, for God's sake," Tase groans. "Andy. I think I *will* have a beer."

• • •

Fantasia Putnam turns out to be a wonderfully good sociology teacher. The three of us meet on Thursday afternoon at the library and spend a couple of hours going over Tase's notes from her freshman year. She certainly stayed awake in that

378

class.

Then we walk over to the Towne House for some kind of dinner, Fantasia still chatting about the effects of urban living on rural personalities and the work of Helen Keller and the Hull House programs. Some of the stuff is even seeming to sound familiar. On Union, I look up at the windows above the Wonder Bar but all I can see is reflections from the afternoon sun.

But I know they conceal an emptiness that I feel in my chest as familiar pain.

After the girls leave, I sit in my booth and nurse another beer. Before long, I'm joined by the Bear, Page and Judy Graham. Judy slides right into my side of the booth and gives my arm a squeeze as if we hadn't been apart more than a few hours. A couple of beers later and the memories of Darcy take on a beer-smudged haze.

Before I'm completely smashed, I say goodnight and walk across the quiet campus toward the hill that overlooks East Green.

• • •

"Little hung over this morning, babe?" Andy asks as I slide into my desk for the final.

"Naw, ready for anything," I boast, "even *mores, folkways* and *conjugal memory.*"

"That's *communal memory*, fool," she laughs. "Five. I do believe I'm going to beat this sucker. Pull my grade up... oh, all the way to a big D."

Gessler's test isn't any snap, regardless of Fantasia's opinion. But it *does* ask for an essay answer comparing folkways and mores. I try to dredge my brain for bullshit phrases and attack the essay with vigor.

In the Frontier Room, we giggle with our fellow sosh students about the final, Gessler's hypnotic lecture delivery, and the general uselessness of sociology as an academic subject. One guy in a plaid wool shirt *in nearly June* takes exception. *I wonder what kind of a pair he and Tase Putnam would make?*

Then I walk Andy back to the Pi Phi house. On their porch,

we sit in the chain-hung swing and smoke, not talking, just watching the sisters come and go. Pris Pitts, one of the senior Pi Phi's, stops on her way out of the house. "Hey guys, big TGIF party tonight. We've got the Esquire basement reserved. Come on over. The seniors are buying!"

• • •

The scene in the Esky basement reminds me how little I've been exposed to sorority life in the past year. The sight of Pris Pitts, her glasses fogged and her hair streaming beer, dancing on the table and flapping her unbuttoned shirt to flash her boobs makes me think this might not be the typical Pi Phi social do.

Andy turns out to be the champion chugger of our table, then goes off to barf before moving on to the semi-finals.

Fantasia Putnam, who's a descendent of General Rufus Putnam — who helped found the university or something — recites a really wonderful limerick about a pederast from Belfast and everyone roars. *I'll have to look up 'pederast' some day.*

We sing, shout, chug beer and generally have a great old time. Dense shows up without Page and the Pi Phi's welcome him as if he'd helped found their chapter. With a senior under each arm, he joins the singing, teaching them the Billboard Song.

"Erect a billboard upon a hill, because a billboard gives me such a thrill.

When I was younger and just a child, a sexy billboard drove me wiiiiiiillllllldddd!"

"Where's Page?" I yell over the din. He laughs, finishes off another mug of beer.

"Went home. Got sick. Sicka me, too, I guess. Who needs her when you got these lovely Pi Phi's?"

Two of the sisters are locked in a soggy embrace, sobbing loudly and proclaiming how much they'll miss each other. Andy pokes me in the ribs and leers, "They hated each other's guts for four years and look at 'em now."

Everyone squeals, then boos loudly when the bartender flashes the lights for closing time. *Closing time? It's two in the morning!* Singing *The Liquor Was Spilled On The Barroom Floor...,* we stagger in a big mob down Lash Alley. Guys and girls who've never exchanged ten words in four years are in lustful embraces. Andy keeps ricocheting off the wall of the Center and back across the bumpy alley into my grasp.

"You gonna sleep at the house?" I ask her as she rebounds from the wall another time.

"No way, gotta get the car back home, clean up the house tomorrow. The folks'll be back on Sunday. And these fools will keep drinking til' the sun comes up."

As Andy fumbles for her keys, I realize she probably won't make it to Townsend without arrest or a sudden meeting with a tree. "You sure you can drive that thing?"

"I dunno..." she slurs. "Just get behind wheel. Put in the ole' key. And vrrrooom." She looks up at me with bleary eyes. "Can you do a better job?"

"Don't know. I can walk pretty good." I demonstrate by mincing a few steps across the sidewalk before I encounter the low wall.

"OK, then you drive," she says and plunks the key into my hand. She gets into the passenger seat and lets her head roll back. "Oh, shittt, Five. Did I really win the chugging contest? Of all of Pi Beta Phi?"

• • •

Andy's sound asleep in a ball against the door when I pull cautiously into the Logan driveway. I slam my door loudly but she doesn't stir. Opening her door gingerly, I catch her by the armpits as she slumps out of the seat.

"C'mon Andy. You're home. Gotta' wake up and go to sleep."

"Mmmff," she snorts. "Back door. Key's to the back door." With one of her arms over my shoulder, I managed to stagger-drag her around the side of the house and to the back porch

381

steps. As we prepare to start up the steps, she wobbles away from me and does a disjointed dance across the yard. Falls onto the yard swing without breaking any bones.

"Andy. Damnit. Come on. You can't sleep out here."

"Can to. Done it before." She raises her arms and grabs my shoulders, pulling me down to her. "Five. Stay here. Sleep with me. I've been tellin' people all semester we've been sleeping together. Now let's do it."

"Joke, Andy. Funny little joke." She holds on for dear life. I can feel her taut nipples against my arms. Darcy wouldn't like the way I'm reacting to this. *Who's Darcy?*

"No joke, Five. Mean it." Raising her head, she offers her lips. Then, "Ohhh my gawd, watch out! Watch out, Five." I roll away and sit there on the ground as Andy Logan barfs in a most lady-like way.

• • •

Dense and I perch on the Cutler wall to watch the long lines of black clad graduates march across the Green to their seats in front of Mem Aud. The strains of Elgar's *Pomp and Circumstance* ring through the elms in full leaf. Despite my terrible headache, it's a beautiful sight. Stirring.

"Page wasn't really pissed," Dense says. "She had to be in at midnight. But also… she didn't know about the Pi Phi's party. Goddamn! That Pris Pitts is a pistol, isn't she?"

"Well, she certainly was last night," I say. "Wonder if she's down there right now?"

"Probably. Hope she doesn't flap her tits out there as she walks across the stage. Man, she sure was some fun to be with last night."

• • •

On our way out of town, I have Dense drive the Bearmobile by Townsend. I'm relieved to see Andy washing windows on the Logan's' front porch.

"Hey guys, how's it going?" she calls. If the girl has a

hangover, she's certainly hidden it somewhere. We get out and walk up to the porch.

"How you feeling, Andy? Got a little bit of a head this morning?" She grins and mocks a splitting headache, arm thrown dramatically over her forehead.

"I did this morning but dad's formula worked like a charm. Two raw eggs, a shot of Tabasco, and a double shot of vodka." I feel as if I may lose the lunch I haven't had. "And I woke up in the strangest place? Five? Do you know how I got there?"

"Well, if it was on your back porch glider, I carried your ass up there," I say. "And you might want to run the hose under the yard swing before your folks get home."

"Aw Five. That's really gallant. Did I? Ah, do anything I shouldn't have?"

"Can't remember a thing, Andy. You were a perfect lady."

• • •

"Break out the apple pies, mamma! The Bear's comin' home," Dense chortles as he drives the Bearmobile down 144 from Coolville toward Hockingport. Even though I've been home four or five times in the past nine months, the woods and hills that I grew up in have a strange, foreign feel to them.

"You gonna help out your dad this summer?" I ask Dense.

"Hell's bells, haven't I told you? No way. I'm staying about three days, then heading over to Middletown. The Martian's dad has me a job in Armco's mill there. Open hearth helper. Wonder what an open hearth is?"

I shrug in ignorance. "Sounds warm and comfortable, at least. Maybe you can see ole' Jackie Adamson while you're there."

"And have Page tear my balls off? No way, ace. How about you? You going to work at Emmit's fruit stand? Run up to Athens and help put that little Andy girl to bed from time to time?"

"Nope," I respond with a grin. "Darcy and Page could get together and compare their testicle collections. No, I'm going on the river. Captain's got me a berth on some towboat. I may even find out which one tonight."

The Hocking River reappears from its screen of trees and we roll into the old home town, Hockingport. It too looks familiar, yet new and different.

· · ·

The Lowrey household is also a nest of changes and surprises. Mom welcomes me with a hug, then leads me into the living room where *The Window* hangs over the mantle. Where most families would display their grandfathers, mine shows off my girl's tits.

"God mom, what's the Captain think of that?"

"He loves it, Five," she says with a broad smile. "Looks at it all the time. Perhaps a little too much?" Then to dispel the look of doubt on my face. "You'll see. He really does and he'll be home any minute to tell you himself."

"He's gonna be home? That's great!"

"Called from Parkersburg about forty five minutes ago. The *Princess* is laying over for the night so he thought he'd run down and have dinner with us."

"How's he getting here? What's he driving?"

"He borrowed Chet Hederick's old car. That wreck Chet keeps in Parkersburg so he can run up to see his momma in Mineral Wells."

· · ·

"Fine lookin' young woman," the Captain says at the dinner table. "Your mom says she's really quite a nice person. I'll be looking forward to meeting her myself." Compliments such as these are rare from the Captain under any circumstances. When they concern my half naked girlfriend, I find them absolutely amazing.

"Five! Tell mom that I don't have to wear a brassiere *all* the time," Sissie Eileen chimes in. "I mean, if Darcy doesn't…"

"Eileen Esther Lowrey," mom breaks in. "That'll be just enough of that kind of talk at the dinner table." *Yes. Things have*

384

changed at the Lowrey household in the past nine months.
"Thom?" she looks at the Captain. "When are you going to tell us about Five's berth?"

The Captain leans back from his cleaned plate, lights a Camel and exhales slowly toward the ceiling. I reach for my Pall Malls, another first for me at home.

"Five, I was pleased to hear you wanted to work on a tow," he says, "though I don't expect you to make a career of it. Still, it's good, honest work and you'll meet some fine people. See some interesting places."

"You don't have to sell me, Captain. I'm already sold."

"Yep. And I reckoned you wouldn't want to be on the *Princess,* even though it looks like I'll be getting her master's hat back before too long."

"Oh, Thom, that's wonderful!" Obviously this is news to mom as well as the rest of us.

"Yep. But I wouldn't want the crew to think I was playin' favorites. So... if it's all right with you, you'll go aboard the *Aspinwall Victory* as a deckhand."

"Aspinwall Victory! Sound's fine, Captain. What is she?"

"Barge Line's newest, biggest vessel," he says with pride. "Twin diesels, three thousand horses. Fine skipper, Lowell Manders."

"Lowell Manders is a good person, Five," mom contributes. "Will Five get home much, Thom?"

"Oh, about like me, I reckon. She operates mostly between Ashland and Pittsburgh. Mostly dry chemicals, specialty ores, that kind of cargo. All pretty safe."

"Sounds good to me, Captain. When do I start?" I ask, thinking of a couple of leisurely days hanging around Hockingport.

"Now that's the other thing. I talked with Captain Manders a couple of hours ago. He's heading down river and estimates making Lock 19 at about five in the morning. Can you be ready? That'll save us driving up to Parkersburg at three, especially since I don't have to be back until noon."

Sissie Eileen gets the last word as usual. "Five? Now can I move into your room?"

385

Chapter 29

Mark Twain Got It Right

Standing on the lock wall at Dam 19, the Captain and I see the beam of the *Aspinwall Victory's* searchlight long before she rounds the bend upriver. Early light of day paints the eastern horizon as the *Victory* aims her tow at the locks on our side of the river. We can feel the vibration of her big diesels, make out the soft red of the pilot house lights.

"There she is, Five," Captain says with a bit of awe in his voice. "One fine boat, a good skipper. I know you'll do well on her, son."

"Gosh, I hope so, Captain." We watch as the first barges nose between the lock fenders and the tow slows to a bare crawl. "Captain. This fall, when you get some time off, I'd sure like it if you could come up to OU. Maybe for a football weekend? Or something?"

"That would be fun, Five. Your mom and I'll talk about it. See if we can make some plans. Yep. That'd be fine."

Dark figures hustle along the barges, holding hawsers ready to loop over the lock wall bollards. As soon as the boat's stern clears the rear gates, a bell rings and the lines are secured. Captain touches my shoulder gently and we walk toward the deck of the *Victory* nearly flush with the lock wall. The wall trembles as hydraulics start pushing the rear lock gate closed.

"Permission to come aboard, Captain?" my father calls up to the pilot house. *Gee! Two captains on one boat. How do I handle this?*

"Come on aboard, Thom," a voice rings down. "You know I don't hold with that navy crap." We jump the two foot gap between wall and deck, me clutching the faithful gladstone bag. Mom has promised a laundry box will be waiting the next time we make Lock 19 coming up river.

We climb the ladder to the top of the second deck and stand

at the foot of the steps that lead to the *Victory's* pilot tower. Its door opens and a short, round man emerges and comes down the steps.

"Good to see you, Thom. I heard about your good news. Congratulations."

"Thanks Captain Manders. I want you to meet my son, Thomsen Lowrey V. But you'd better call him Five. He doesn't seem to answer to anything else." Captain Manders extends his hand and I shake it.

"Glad to meet you, Five. Welcome aboard the *Victory.*"

"Glad to meet you, Captain Manders. Thanks for giving me the opportunity."

"I'd better get going, fellers. Don't want to have to climb a wet ladder out of the lock." The Captain turns, takes my hand. "Good luck, Five. We'll see each other up and down the river. I'm sure."

A lump comes in my throat. I reach over and hug him tightly. "Thanks a million for everything. Dad. Thanks for everything and take care."

He turns and trots down the ladder, making a short jump from the lowering deck up to the dockwall. Turns and waves. I wave back to my dad! It's the first time I've ever called him anything but "Captain."

• • •

Holding a steaming cup of coffee, I sit back in the "catbird seat" and watch Captain Manders and his first mate, work the tow downstream from Lock 19. "Not too many rules aboard this vessel, Five," Manders says between puffs on his long-stemmed corncob pipe. "No beards aboard. You can grow a mustache if you've a mind to."

"Thanks Captain," I respond. "But I think I'd look pretty silly in a mustache." I can see his grin beneath a thick mustache reflected in the pilot house window. It's only later, when I've met the rest of the crew, that I realize that Ilsa, the cook, is the only member without a mustache.

"Hands work four hours on, four off. Then four on, four off

again. A full eight hours off every second night." I shuffle the figures in my head and realize I'll probably get more sleep on the *Victory* than I did in college.

"We'll run a fire drill and a boat drill, this afternoon," he continues. "Jeff here will show you your post and duties at general quarters.

"General quarters rings for any emergency. Three bells and the siren. Whatever you're doing, drop it and haul ass for your post. Is that clear?"

"Yessir, Captain. That's clear."

"You'll wear a PFD, that's a Personal Flotation Device, or life jacket, any time you're working the deck. Only place you don't need one is on the aft deck when you're off duty or on any deck behind railings."

The captain keeps reciting and I wish for my pad to make notes. For a boat with not too many rules, the *Victory* and her routines quickly fill my mind. About a half hour after leaving the lock, we make Hockingport on the starboard, the windows of its small homes and buildings shimmering against the rising sun through their screen of trees.

I can see our house and mom, the Captain, and Sissie Eileen, standing in the yard and waving. "Give 'em a wave, Five. Out on the fly bridge, there." I step to the open catwalk outside the pilot house and wave, about jumping out of my skin when Captain Manders lets go with a long, mighty blast of the *Victory's* horn. Then they, Hockingport, and another part of my life, are behind me.

• • •

In everything he wrote about being in the river, Mark Twain pretty much got it right. You can't grow up in Captain Thomsen Lowrey's household without knowing something about towboats. Even Sissie Eileen can tie a bowline and talk knowledgeably about warping a bollard.

My experience on the *Ernie M.* proves me capable of handling casual deckhand duties on the first afternoon. By the time we make Ashland, Kentucky, I've settled into the routine and find it comfortable, even enjoyable.

As the lowest hand on the roster, my duties include peeling spuds and onions for Ilsa Kleber, a pretty blonde woman in her early thirties and an excellent cook. Her thick German accent leads me to ask about her homeland.

"Ach, Five. Cincinnati. I never been to Germany. But ah, Cincinnati. It's a wonderful place." When I tell her my girlfriend is living in her wonderful place, my summer education about Cincinnati begins.

• • •

My duties are simple. Helping work the tows through the many locks that keep the Ohio navigable. This is more of a challenge when the tow is large and the string of barges must be broken to "double through" the locks. On weekends in the busy pools, I sit on the bow barge with a life-ring buoy, line and boat hook, ready to try to rescue fallen water-skiers.

Captain Manders has a strong dislike for water-skiers who seem to love to flirt with destiny before tons of moving mass that take nearly a mile to come to a dead halt in the water.

I sweep and scrub. Squeegee the pilot house windows after every rain. Check the tautness of the lashings on the barge bollards, lending my back to the ratchet handle when a lashing needs tightened.

My forearms and hands scab over with the first of "bargeman's rash," the many tiny cuts that result from brushing against the thorny surface of rusty steel cables. A vial of iodine is my constant companion.

And like Twain and his heroes, I sit in the catbird seat and listen to the pilot's constant chant of river lore, learning the names of cities, towns, bridges and bends, the locations of constantly shifting sandbars, the power of riffles and eddies.

By July, I'm handling the wheel on straight stretches of river, always aware of the watchful eye of Captain Manders or Jeff Clardy.

• • •

Dear Five,

Thanks for the cards and the great little drawings. I'm saving them in a scrapbook. It sounds like you're enjoying life on the Victory. We're finally settled in the apartment... a neat old place on Mount Adams with a super view of the river. Trish and I covered ourselves with filth pulling down the wallpaper, then again when we painted. It was so hot we took off all our clothes to work. You should've been here to see it. (Ha!)

My job at the Pilamar Restaurant is wonderful. Some nights I make as much as $20 in tips, although the salary isn't very good. But the boss is nice and it's a very swanky restaurant. Right on Fountain Square! Mark and Trish are still seeing each other a lot. She's stayed overnight at his place a few times!! He says he likes his job.

Every afternoon, I sit on our porch and watch the river. So many towboats and so much traffic. I wonder if you're on one of them. But I know you're not. Just wishing, I guess. I miss you. Love, Darce

P.S. Our phone finally got put in. The number is Eden 2-3456. Isn't that neat?

• • •

But the best part of being on the river is that, even at your most alert and watchful, the panorama of towns and cities, other vessels, of life upon the shore, passes at just the right pace to take it all in. And love every minute of it.

I gasp at my first sight of a steel mill at night, great whooshes of orange glare reflected from flickering black walls and through huge multi-paned windows as we plow upstream past Weirton. The towns of the upper Ohio — Wheeling,

Martins Ferry, Steubenville, East Liverpool — are jumbles of uniformly gray frame houses and brick buildings clinging to steep hillsides wreathed in smoke.

And my first view of Pittsburgh! The Triangle where two rivers become one beneath a ceiling of smoke and gasses. I hear of talk in Pittsburgh about eliminating the smoke and dust but when I walk up Smithfield Street, I also overhear people speaking of the airborne filth as money in their pockets.

Small towns glide by on lazy summer afternoons. Often, I'll sketch a group of kids swimming from rock perches or swinging from a rope hung precariously high over the river. Once I glimpse a group of teenage girls, naked as the day they were born, standing thigh deep in the river and waving merrily to us as we rumble by. I wave back and think of Darcy at Lake Hope.

The bridges are marvels. The Silver Bridge at Gallipolis is one of the most beautiful, as is the huge railroad span at Sciotoville. It's a giant black humpbacked monster where great locomotives leave long plumes of black smoke and white steam as they haul loads of coal from Kentucky to the lake ports in Ohio.

On our second trip to Pittsburgh, I find a marvelous art supply store where I buy several new sketch pads. Also a small watercolor kit and a Rapidograph pen, a mechanical wonder that eliminates the flat, always tipping bottles of Fisher's India Ink. The pen creates a fine, thin line and for the first time, I try sketching in ink without a pencil rough.

My sketch pads fill quickly for there was never a better studio than the deck of a towboat during four hours off. Ilsa scrubbing corn on the aft deck, letting the husks and silk fly into our churning wake. "The catfish love 'em," she says with a grin.

Captain Manders, stoic behind the wheel and the long stem of his General McArthur corncob pipe. I try to capture in watercolor the glistening barge decks ahead of us on a rainy night, illumined by fantastic spider webs of lightning playing across our watery horizon.

I draw the bum boaters who pull out from every town of any size, often rowing but usually steering a john boat powered by a smoking outboard. Their wares are various: fresh vegetables and fruit, paperback books, items of clothing, candy bars, overpriced cigarettes, and often, away from the watchful eye of the skipper or mate, illicit six packs of beer at exorbitant prices.

Once I see a lonely fisherman, running his trot-line at dawn, the dripping line sparkling with catfish, carp and gar. The image I try to sketch reminds me of Chinese paintings I've seen in Fine Arts appreciation.

• • •

Every time we go through Lock 19, mom has a laundry box, tin of cookies, and stack of mail for me. Twice, she meets me in Parkersburg or Pomeroy to drive rapidly home, where I catch a quick shower and hot meal, before rejoining the *Victory* at Lock 19.

From Dense I learn what an open hearth is:

...big mother of a furnace, filled full of molten iron from the blast furnace, then limestone, scrap metal and other shit. We cook this stuff at three thousand degrees for a few hours and it's hotter than a sailor's bunghole all the time. Guys I work with say you freeze your ass off in the winter, though. Whatever part's turned away from the furnace freezes and falls off. Don't I wish?

My job is to shovel limestone, and aluminum shot, and other weird shit into the mouth of this bitch for about two hours. Then I stand at the other end with a long rod and help pull clinkers and stuff out of the steel when they tap the furnace. The best part is drinking a cold six pack at the tavern across the street when the shift is over. Hope it's nice and cool where you are. Your friend from Hell. The Bear.

• • •

On July Fourth, we see the fireworks in Ashland on one side and Ironton on the other shore as we work downstream for

Maysville, Kentucky. Maysville marks the furthest downstream I've reached since joining the *Victory*. But as Ilsa points out, "it's still a hell of a long svim to Cincinnati."

My time on the Ohio isn't marked by a calendar. Rather by events. The big storm on the night we meet two downstream tows in the narrow channel by Blennerhassett Island. Sparks flying from barge gunwales as someone else's northbound tow scrapes the huge stone abutments of the Bellaire bridge. I watch this from a half mile away and find my mind stirring the memories of Captain's demotion due to a similar event.

Two whole days of freedom in Pittsburgh while the *Victory* has a prop replaced. We've plowed across too many sandbars in the curving stretch Captain Manders calls *The Gut,* ten miles from Long Bottom to Pomeroy by car, forty miles by boat. I go with the rest of the crew to Forbes Field for an afternoon game between the Pirates and the Reds. Ilsa and I cheer for Cincinnati, much to the consternation of the fans around us.

Countless scenes. Dozens of sketches. Hours of sunburn. Frenzied snatches of hard work. Before I know it, July has turned to August and my time on the river grows short.

• • •

The squawk and scratch of the pilot house radio is familiar background noise any time you're working near the bow of the *Victory*. I've used the radio several times to say hello to the Captain as we pass each other on divergent courses. But the pace and tenor of today's radio traffic indicates something is happening. Something important. On the river.

As soon as my watch is relieved, I head for the galley where Ilsa is always the first to hear and pass on scuttlebutt. Her big smile when I enter tells me whatever the news is, it's not bad.

"Oh, Five. Is truly wonderful," she beams. "The *Veirton Defender* collided with a string of barges and lost most of her towing brow. No one hurt, thank Gott!" Ilsa's German accent becomes so pronounced when she's excited. "As soon 's we off load in Ashland, we're heading down river for Maysville to pick up the *Defender's* tow." She waves her arms jubilantly.

"And then we're shoving that tow down to Louis-ville!"

Louis-ville? Louisville! We're heading for beyond Cincinnati. Jah. The news is vunderful!

• • •

Ilsa and I lean on the aft deck rail and watch the lights of Cincinnati glide up the bank toward us. Her excitement is contagious and I have to agree, *it i*s a beautiful city. Car lights trace curving paths through the night up the steep hillsides .

"See Five, there! That's Mount Adams, where the car is coming down right now." I look at the steep hill, dappled with black spots where no houses are built, and wonder which of the lights represents Trish and Darcy.

A bell chimes and the squawk box calls out, "Lowrey to the pilot house. Lowrey to the pilot house." I go off at a trot, grabbing a PFD from its hanger as I head for the tower stairs.

The big green sweep of the radar shows the river's curving path through Cincinnati. This *is* a busy pool with radar blips indicating other tows, lots of smaller river traffic. Eyes straight ahead, Captain Manders calls over his shoulder as I enter the pilot house, "Cook tells me your girlfriend lives in Cincinnati, Five. Do you know her phone number?"

"Yes sir, Captain."

"Then why don't you try giving her a ring on the ship-to-shore?"

I give the operator the number I'm calling, 'Eden 2-3456,' and after her mechanical 'Thank You,' I hear the buzz of a phone ringing somewhere out there on Mount Adams. Probably less than a half mile away. After maybe twenty rings, the operator comes back on the line. "Your party does not answer sir. Please try again later."

Sadly, I return the instrument to its hook and smile glumly at the skipper and steersman. "Maybe on the way upriver, Five," he tells me. "We'll see."

• • •

Our barge delivery in Louisville takes a half day and we hang around for another few hours before receiving orders to head upstream with a tow of empties at first light. By ten o'clock, Captain Manders once again squawks me to the pilot house.

"Five, I've wangled us a couple of loads out of Newport, right across the river from Cincinnati. Sounds like it'll take 'em until sometime tomorrow to get the last barge loaded. Kaolin... some kind of fine clay they use in paper making. Has to be dried and blown into the barges slowly."

I just look at the Captain slack-jawed. He grins. "So why don't you give your girl a toot on the ship-to-shore and see if she's free tonight? I figure we ought to make dock between five thirty and six this evening."

"You're serious, Captain? I mean...?"

"Serious as can be, Five. I had a girl once." He nods toward the phone on its hook. "Go on, give her a call. Tell her we'll be at Kentucky C & K dock by six o'clock. It's almost under the Butler Street bridge."

Waiting for the operator to complete my call, I hope against hope that Darcy or Trish will be home. I hear it ring once, twice, again. My heart sinks. But on the fourth ring, a husky voice answers, "H'lo?"

"Trish, is that you?" I shout into the handset. "It's Five!"

"Five, godalmighty, don't shout and do you know what time it is?"

"Sorry. Yeah, it's ten a.m.. Is Darcy there?"

"Of course she's here. But she's sound asleep. We work until the wee hours, you know. Why don't you call back later?" Her voice drifts off with those last words and I shout into the phone.

"Trish, don't hang up!"

"Why? Is there something wrong, Five?"

"Nothing wrong. It's just that I'm calling from the *Victory* on the ship-to-shore and we're heading for Cincinnati..."

"Ohh! Ohmygod. Hang on, I'll wake her up."

Seconds that seem like hours tick away. Manders and the steersman are both grinning broadly. Manders gives me a

396

thumbs-up.

"H'lo, Five. Is it really you? Where are you?"

"Hi, Darce. It's really me and right now, we're north of Louisville and running light for Cincinnati. Should be in there about six tonight. Can you get off work?"

"Really, Five?" She squeals to Trish in the background, 'He's stopping tonight!' "Five! I'll sleep all day and call in sick. Tell me where to meet you." I give her the directions with the Captain nodding in agreement.

"What's your boat look like?" she asks. Excitement bubbles in her once sleepy voice.

"It's big, about as big as anything on the river. And white. Two decks and a tall tower for the pilot house. And the pilot house has an orange roof."

"Well, I'll start watching for it, when? About five? We can see from our porch all the way down to Mount Echo Park."

"OK," I say. "We've got six barges in tow, high out of the water. They're empties and they all have silver covers on them. See you tonight."

"Six o'clock. Ohh, Five. I can't wait. I'm so excited!"

The day *seems* to drag on, although I'm surprised when we pass Mount Echo Park on our starboard just before five o'clock. Ilsa has spent the afternoon telling me more about the wonders of Cincinnati. And she's called her brother and arranged for a dinner for Darcy and me at the restaurant he runs.

As we ease against the Kentucky Clay & Kaolin dock beneath the Butler Street bridge, Clardy points at the far end of the terminal. "Comes someone in a hell of a hurry," he chuckles. The black Ford convertible swerves around a corner and skids to a dusty stop by the chain link gate. A security guard comes out of his shack to question the wild driver. Clardy aims the pilot's spotlight at the gate and gives *Victory's* horn a small toot. When the guard turns, Clardy winks "OK" in Morse as I wave my arms from the fly bridge.

We see the guard shake his head and wave Darcy into the terminal yard where she skids to another halt by the bollard we'll tie off to. Yep. Everything's OK in Newport.

Chapter 30

Vas You Effer In Zin-zin-nati?

Darcy stands there beaming while I loop a hawser over the bollard and wave my arm to the pilot house. Clardy's voice booms down from the speaker, "Tow's secured! Boat's secured! Mister Lowrey, you are relieved."

I turn and she comes running toward me. I raise my grease and rust-stained hands and take a step back. "Oh hell, Five, it's just stuff that'll wash out," as she leaps for my neck. Holding my hands out at my sides, I swing her around from my neck as we exchange a huge kiss. Applause and a snort of the *Victory's* whistle recognize our performance.

"God Darce, you look so great," I exclaim. A tiny spot of rust smudges the top of her yellow sundress. "And your hair? It's longer!" She pirouettes to make the longer dark hair swirl.

"And you! Look at you," she exclaims. "You are SO brown! And where'd these muscles come from?" she asks, squeezing my bicep. She wrinkles her nose, "but this orange thing smells pretty bad. I hope it's not you."

"C'mon. Come meet the crew. I've got to dump this PFD, get my bag and wash up. I shouldn't smell too bad. Haven't done anything all day but think about you."

• • •

"Yahooo, free at last," I scream into the wind, my head thrown back against the seat as we drive across the Butler Street bridge. "That's Mount Adams right there," I add, pointing up at the clustered houses on the green hillside. "Which one is yours?"

"You'll see in a minute. This road makes the old Ford huff and puff but we always get to the top." She swerves onto a curving road that weaves its way up a short valley beside some streetcar tracks, then hairpins around a shelf carved out of the side of the mountain. After two more hairpin curves, we hit a steep section, then the summit where nothing shows but sky and the distant Kentucky hills.

"Now take a look," Darcy exclaims. She pulls to a stop by a gray clapboard house, taller than it is wide. Its front door sits right on the sidewalk. "Grab your bag. I won't try to park in the garage for right now. C'mon," she urges, taking my hand.

Darcy leads me down a steep set of stairs between the gray house and its neighbor. At the bottom, a narrow door opens into the kitchen of a tidy basement apartment. "Here you are, the buzzards' roost!," Darcy chortles. I walk through the kitchen, then into a wide room that looks out upon a porch. To the left is a tiny dining table with four chairs. On the far wall is a fireplace with a long bookshelf mantle.

"Come on Five, look out here." On the porch, I can understand the name the girls have given the place. The river winds off in each direction for miles. And directly below us sits *Aspinwall Victory*, seemingly close enough to toss a baseball onto her aft deck. She can't be any more than a mile away.

Darcy shoves me into a cushion-covered glider and leaps onto me, straddling my lap. "All right, Five, we've got lost time to make up for." My hands slide up her smooth legs past her hips!

"Darcy!" I mumble through her pressing lips. "Whur's Trisss?"

She breaks off her kiss with a smack and leans back, attacking the buttons of my shirt with gusto. "Trish is a working girl with a great sense of dignity. I recall her saying she thought she would spend the night with Mark."

• • •

Rubbing my back with a thick towel, Darcy reaches over and sneaks a sip out of my drink... The Perfect Manhattan... which they've been working all summer to perfect. Below us, the lights of Cincinnati are beginning to twinkle on. The last rays of the sun glimmer from behind Mount Echo.

"Do you know where Over The Rhine is, Darce?" I roll my shoulders with the sheer pleasure her fingers and the scratchy towel are creating.

"Yeah! Mark took Trish and me down there one night, drinking beer and dancing to oom-pa music. It's real German."

"Well... I have a place for us to eat there tonight. If you like German food?"

"I think I love German food," she says, easing up with the towel, "but don't you want to eat at *my* restaurant?"

"You said it was pretty swanky?" She nods yes. "And my wardrobe is very much jeans and sport shirts. Swanky enough?" She nods no. "And don't you eat there about every night?" Darcy grins, nods yes and squeezes me in another hug.

"You're right. I think I do love German food."

• • •

Over The Rhine is a cluster of older German houses and stores perched on a hill overlooking Mill Creek and the railroad yards. It takes us several minutes of searching the narrow streets before we find *Der Munchen Garten,* not as pretentious looking as some of the other restaurants we've passed, but welcoming just the same.

Ilsa's brother, Joachin, could be no other than Ilsa's brother. I laugh and ask, "Are you twins?" as he welcomes us in the oak walled foyer.

"Nein," he laughs back. "Ilsa is a twin, but not mine. Her twin is Siggy, my younger brother. But you should see all of us. We all look like twins. All seven of us!"

Joachin brings us his *purfecttt* manhattans and a bowl of some kind of hearty soup. This is followed by thin strips of beef swimming in a thick, luscious gravy and surrounded by little yellow noodles. Darcy eats with enthusiasm, all the time wiggling her toes between my legs under the booth. I sit back as far as I can to avoid their contact. *After all, I am hungry. So is she.*

A trout in vinegar sauce with red cabbage and dumplings is the main course, accompanied by a 'Rhine wine from the Bass

Islands on Lake Erie.' The wine is made from the Kleber's own grapes.

Darcy's foot finally makes contact during coffee and strudel, very nearly causing me embarrassment. I finally have to chastise her firmly by running my hand up her bare leg as far as it can go.

We have to argue firmly with Joachin when he refuses to bring us a bill. "Nonsense, my young friends. Ilsa says you are the best cook's helper she's ever known and there is only one payment she hopes for." My eyebrows shoot up. "I, we, would like to have a painting of her, in German national dress, for the restaurant. Does that sound like fair payment?"

• • •

"Exactly what does this Ilsa girl look like?" Darcy murmurs into my bare chest. We're back on the porch, big goose pimples rising from our sweating bodies as the night air turns cooler. "I mean, that Joachin guy looked *pretty good* to me," she whispers.

"Pretty much like him," I lie. "Her mustache is perhaps a little heavier than his. And she never shaves her legs or under her arms."

"Five, that is disgusting! And how do you know, anyway?" She rears back and hits me with one of the glider pillows.

"And she has the cutest little mole right about here..." I tease, aiming a finger just above her exposed lower rib cage.

• • •

Huddled naked in our blanket, feet propped on the banister, we watch and listen to the light traffic on the streets below us. Except for her dock lights, the *Victory* is totally dark. Off in the east, up river, the first rays of pre-dawn begin to send the stars away.

It seems impossible that we've been awake the whole night through, talking, loving, holding each other, just marveling at the warmth we've missed in each other. And yet, here comes the sun. We've been talking about Trish Spotswood and Mark Husted.

"Darce. You know, we're going to miss them next month when they aren't back in Athens."

"Mmm," she murmurs through closed lips. Darcy turns and squeezes herself into a tight ball beneath my arm, cuddled as close as she can get. Against the faint morning light, I can see her eyes are filmed. She shudders in my arms.

"Is there something wrong, babe? Are you going to miss them that much?"

"Five, it's been such a wonderful time together. I've never had such a great time."

"Yeah, and in just twenty-some days, we'll be back together."

"No we won't Five!"

I look at her sharply, not sure of what I've just heard. She squeezes me harder. "I'm not coming back to Athens, Five. Not this fall."

"You're not? Why? Is it something I've...?" She hushes me with a finger to my lips.

"Noo, silly. Nothing you've done. It's just that... my life here is so incredible! Even without you... and God knows I miss you every minute of every day. But Five..." she hesitates and sniffs into the blanket.

"But Darcy," I protest. "I love you!" The words burst out unbidden. "I'm in love with you!"

"And I've been in love with you, Five, ever since that first night you came into Begorra." She kisses me soft but long. "And I know I'll always love you, no matter what happens."

"But that doesn't matter?" I ask incredulously.

"Sure it matters but, hon. Here, I'm a real person. Not just a hamburger slinger in some college town. Not just a girl who poses nude and people joke about and call dirty names." I watch her silently, realizing these words are pouring out from a place they've been stored for a long time.

"I'm just a waitress, sure. But some nights I make as much in tips as I could at Begorra in a whole week.

"And Mark's gotten me some modeling work. Nothing big yet. But real modeling for pretty good money and no one has asked me to take my clothes off... yet!" I start to protest.

"No. You're right. You never asked me to... and I never wanted to be asked... but Five, I'm alive here. I feel different about myself."

"And about me, I guess," I say morosely.

"Yes!" She looks at me through shimmering eyes. "I feel differently about you because I want you so much. But neither of us is ready... to get married... or anything like that."

I feel something shudder and lurch deep in my body. Is it my stomach? Or my soul?

"I would love to have a little Six and his brothers and sisters running around... someday," she says with a smile. "But first, I want us both have a lot of fun out of life. I want to do significant things myself. Can you understand?"

I can feel her speech has reached its peak, that no more words will follow, only tears. "Yeah, Darcy. I think I can understand. But I want you to realize... whatever I've accomplished... and will accomplish... is because of you. You are the *Light Show*. It's you that made it possible for me. And I'll always love you for it."

Our tears mingle on our cheeks as we kiss long and hard, holding each other as tightly as if a whisp of breeze might snatch the other away forever.

"Ahh, Five. Thank you for loving me. I wish you'd maybe told me a lot earlier. But I'll always be here for you... ready to pose... no matter what." Her face gleams through its sheen of tears. "And if you ever find anyone else to pose for you, remember, she's just a naked woman."

• • •

By nine o'clock we've showered for a third or so time and I've shaved cleanly, dressed and look pretty respectable. Darcy and I smoke and drink our coffee on the porch, listening for Trish's footfalls on the steps.

But it's Trish and Mark who arrive. And our breakfast turns into a celebratory brunch. They have hot cinnamon rolls and berries with thick cream. I hug and kiss Trish firmly, shake Mark's hand in genuine pleasure at seeing him again.

"Has Darcy showed you her portfolio, Five?" Mark asks. I look at Darcy who shrugs with a faint grin.

"Uh, well, we've talked about it... sort of... but I haven't seen it."

He and Trish share a smile but don't really seem surprised. "Go get it Darcy," Trish urges. "Don't be shy." Darcy returns with a pair of loose leaf binders.

"This is my scrapbook," she says proudly, sitting on the arm of my chair and opening the book to an array of my hand-made post cards with scenes from the river. "It'll be really valuable some day, I know.

"And this," she says with a dramatic flourish of the other book, "is what I've been doing on my summer vacation."

Glossy black and white prints, one to a page, show a new and different Darcy. She looks gorgeous in sophisticated clothing, stockings and heels, a pillbox hat with a veil casting intricate shadows on the planes of her face.

In another, she's a cute little housewife, spotless and shining in the modern kitchen of the Fifties. She looks as if she's never seen a spot of dust in her life, but if she ever does, she'll kick its ass.

There are a number of head and shoulders poses, in dresses and in drapes. Beautiful work. A beautiful woman.

Each photograph captures the quality I saw that first night in the rainy glow of her apartment, her smile that betrays an inner radiance.

"And here's the high point of the day," Trish says. "Even Darcy doesn't know this." She looks at Mark.

"Darce, we've got you a shoot with Arthur Drekken tomorrow for P & G." Darcy's eyes get round and wide. She gives Mark, then Trish, and finally me a huge hug. My face must display my ignorance because Mark touches my arm. "Proctor and Gamble, Five. Ivory Soap." He grins at Darcy. "The kid's on the verge of the big time."

I ruefully grin at Darcy. *And the kid'll never come back to Athens again.*

Chapter 31

A New Thirteen Is Born

As rivers go, the Hocking is pretty piddly. Even near its mouth where I grew up, it's not much more than a wide creek, rambunctious only in the heavy rains of spring. As the Bear and I head back to Athens this late August afternoon, the still surface of the Hocking wears a velvet blanket of dust, pollen and the debris of a dying summer.

"Damned glad we're done with two-a-days," he says. "And we've got the entire weekend off from practice. I've lost ten pounds since we started two weeks ago."

"You don't look like you've lost anything." His huge arms now ripple with muscles, stretching the fabric of the OU Athletic Department t-shirt he wears.

"Oh hell yes! 'Course, I did come back from Middletown with twenty new pounds but most of it was muscle. Damn, Five, but I've never worked so hard in my life. Still, it was neat not having to study after you were done."

"So what happened to your eyebrows?" I ask. His eyes sit in circles of pale skin and just little tufts of his once bushy black brows show through.

"Left 'em on the open hearth. We wore goggles most of the time but my eyebrows stuck out. Just got singed away," I guess.

Rolling along, we talk of my months on the river and Darcy's decision not to return to Athens. Strangely enough, each day away from her has lifted some of the pain from my gut or wherever... but I still ache with missing her.

"Well, shit," Bear observes, "you'll find a new girl. It's not like you guys were pinned... or engaged or anything."

Heat waves shimmer up from the brick streets of Athens, a ghost town at six in the evening. The Bearmobile, with its Sigma Nu markings and Armco stickers, draws hoots and jeers from the brothers as we pull into the courtyard of the ACE house.

• • •

Sarge Waller and Benjo Kostic have asked me to room with them and I'm pleased to find out they've chosen the "tower suite," the smaller of the two triples available. But we agree that living in the little sun porch where Curtis first attacked Ransom would be a hard thing to do.

I'm also pleased to find our room is neat and tidy. All three beds are made and Waller points to the lower bunk of a tier. "If you want the upper, I'll give it up," he says, "but I've spent my entire life sleeping in an upper bunk and'd just as soon not change now." I tell him the lower is fine. "I also took your sheets 'n stuff home and washed them. Figured you might get in late."

It's going to be nice living with a refugee from a military family. A faint chirping noise interrupts us.

"What's that?" I ask. Waller reaches into the top shelf of an orange crate and produces a telephone handset.

"Here in the big city, we call it a telephone."

"Yeah, but we can't afford a private phone," I protest.

"This one we can. Phone set's courtesy of ROTC surplus and the line's a boost on the house line, courtesy of Ohio Bell and yours truly, Bell's trusted lineman. And you've already had a call or two from that Andy Logan girl."

Benjo bursts into the room and shakes my hand vigorously. "Welcome back, Five. Whadda you think? Sarge's showing off his new toy?"

"The number's kind of unlisted. Actually, it's the house number but ends in seven instead of six. Be very careful who you give it to," Sarge says with a smile. "Although I did give it to Andy, in case she wants to give *me* a call."

"And we can call out without having to go down to the first floor," Benjo adds.

"Just can't make any long distance calls. Only collect because the operator will think we're calling from the house phone."

As I unpack, they fill me in on more news. "I had my dad check with a buddy at Fort Jefferson in St. Louis. You can't

408

believe how these old riff'ed officers stick together. Anyway, looky here." He holds up a crinkled sheet of brown Thermofax paper.

"None other than our asshole brother's service record," Benjo gloats. He hands me the copy of Galen Curtis 201 form.

"And record is right. Just look at this shit," Waller says in a low tone. "Two Article Fifteens. Two court martials for assault. Six months in the Schofield Barracks stockade... that's in Hawaii."

"Yeah," I reply, "I read *From Here To Eternity* this summer."

"And six months in the stockade in Pusan," Benjo says in awe. "That's a rough mother of a place."

"The sonofabitch spent more time behind bars than he did dodgin' Chinese bullets," Waller says.

"If he dodged anything at all," Benjo adds sarcastically. "Anyway, it tells us he's one mean bastard."

"Can we use this in any way?" I ask. "Take it to the Acer?"

"Not yet," Waller cautions, slipping the sheet beneath the cover of his dictionary. "Let's hold onto it and see what happens."

• • •

"Settle down, brothers," Acer Simmons raps the pommel for order. "Let's get to work. We've got nearly a hundred recs to go through and I have some committee appointments. We'll do those first."

We Aces slump in our chairs. Even with all the windows thrown open, the Temple is hot and stuffy. We'll have some snoring before too long, especially since many of the brothers have been celebrating TGIF.

J.L. Simmons starts with committee assignments: of the newest Thirteen, he names Shivers as athletic chairman, the Martian as music chairman, Chet Husted as assistant social chairman.

"Brother Five, it'll come as no surprise to you but you're going to be Homecoming and J-Prom float chairman. And you

409

may want to keep an eye peeled next week for a rushee art major. You're the only artist we have now." He pauses, then looks back at me. "And sometime next week check in with Jan Leonard at the *Athena*. She's the editor this year and I told her you'd be glad to help on the art staff."

"Brother Salazar. I want to have an assistant Tiler for the next pledge class. Will you take the job? It'll mean helping Brother Doak at all the pledge meetings, work parties, the like. And missing some of the active meetings but, I feel it's important." Soos grins as he accepts a role of importance.

"Brother Waller. I like what we talked about. So you're going to be the ACE dog-robber. You know what your duties are?" Sarge nods his head yes and the rest of the chapter turns to stare at him in wonder. *What in hell's a dog-robber?*

"Brothers Kostic and Simpson will run for sophomore class office. We'll talk about that more in the coming weeks." Simmons looks around. "And I want the rest of you brothers to look for activities in which you can take part. ACE needs people in leadership posts on campus... all kinds of leadership. Even Brother Five, painting his naked ladies, is doing more for leadership than many of you." His smile tells me he's kidding, a little, and serious a lot.

"Now, let's get down to these rush recommendations. First, I've got six letters here on this one and he's not even a legacy." Boos and hisses from the legacy Aces scattered around the room. "John Sickles Bell. Has a 3.5 from Columbus East. Good jock. Great personality. Anyone know him?"

"Is he white?"

"Sounds like a Civil War general to me."

"Vote yes on Sickles, let's get on with it," someone roars.

"Any no's?" Simmons asks. "Brother Thoreau. Yes on Sickles."

The names roll on, each accompanied by wise-ass questions, some serious queries. The next two are legacies: Clark Spindale, a prof's kid from Athens, and Daniel Goforth, also from Columbus. After resounding no votes on each — big joke — their names are added to the rush list.

By three in the morning, we've gone through the entire list

of ninety-six names and voted yes on each. An honest no vote would mean we turn the fire hose on the kid when he shows up at the door.

• • •

On Saturday night, the house is thrown open for an unplanned, impromptu party. Girlfriends, pinmates, and hangers-on, including O-Annie Oxburn, show up for free beer and easy atmosphere. I keep an eye open for Andy Logan but knowing I haven't invited her, I'd be surprised if she showed up.

A couple of strange guys turn out to be Dan Goforth, our legacy with many recs, and Wally Armistead, his buddy from Columbus. Having rushees in the house before rush starts is strictly illegal but no one seems to be terribly nervous about it. Least of all, the self-assured Goforth and Armistead.

"Gosh Five, I'm sorry to hear Darcy isn't coming back," O-Annie says to me as we sit on the wall outside the sun porch. "She's a neat girl. Are you going to have her up for football weekends, anything?"

"Yeah, I've already written her to come for homecoming," I say. "She's working full-time and doing some modeling so I doubt she'll be able to come, say every weekend. But homecoming? I'm sure she'll make it."

"Guess what I'm gonna do, Five?" Annie asks with a sly grin. "I'm going to rush again."

"I thought you pledged Chi O last year, Annie?"

"Oh, I did, but I never went active. I just wasn't the Chi Omega type, I guess. But this year, I'm going to really work at being a good pledge. Everyone will like me this year!"

• • •

Benjo Kostic leaves Sunday night for the East Green where he'll hold the first of his rush meetings. He and Jim Cephus are our IFC guides and "bird dogs" for likely rushee candidates. His report back that night from Gamersfelder Hall is pretty funny.

"I cannot believe we looked like this bunch of geeks, just

411

last year," he moans. "I mean, guys with hair greased back to points you could punch a beer can with. This one guy's sittin' all by himself, big space around him at least five feet. Get near and you find out why. He farts like a rhino.

"Five, I did run into a kid named Ken Easton. Says he's going to major in art. From Pomeroy, that's down by you somewhere isn't it?"

"And then, there's this unbelievable gangster guy, talks like Edward G. Robinson. F.X. something or other. You'll recognize him when he comes through. Probably be carrying a violin case."

• • •

When the first rushees come up the steps Monday night, some of us realize with a pang that we're missing out on the *grand parade* of sorority rush over on College Avenue. Tonight, for the first time in many years, rushees of *both* sexes are wandering around Athens on the same nights. I joke that if we get lucky, maybe some lost sorority rushees will show up on our doorstep.

Rush from the other side of the door is quite different from the bewildering experience of the year before. Doak Phipps is the "spotter" and makes sure he hears each name as a new guy is introduced. If that name is on our "want list," Doak intercepts him and sends him to a "handler."

Brother Frank Blaisdell is in charge of the handlers and makes sure a kid on our list is never left by himself to maybe wander off to another house. For the stars of our list, rush begins on the first night. The highly-recommended Jake Sickles, "Goofer" Goforth and Wally Armistead get first-class treatment every night they appear at the Ace house.

A thin guy from Jackson with a mop of black hair over his forehead makes our rush list by standing at the piano and banging out and singing the hit *Behind The Green Door*. My stomach does a flop at the thought of what *used to go on* behind the green door.

Kenny Easton from Pomeroy turns out to be a nice kid with

an earnest desire to major and do well in art. Blaisdell steers him to me and gives my shoulder two discreet taps, my appointment as a handler.

• • •

By Wednesday night, I can see the pledge class begin to jell. Goforth and Armistead are sure bids and certainly seem friendly and sociable. But I've heard from Toby that Goforth and Armistead are pulling the same country club bullshit at the Phi Delt house.

Ken Easton brings along a few sketches and I'm pleased at how good they are. If only I had gone to Pomeroy High or some other big high school where they had art classes.

F.X. Costellano — Francis Xavier — turns out to be the New York hood that Benjo told us about. The guy is a riot. But after talking with him for a while, I realize that he's not putting on an act. He *really is* afraid of cows and doesn't trust trees in groups of more than three.

The seriousness of rushing is broken by the appearance of three cute little blondes in high heels and fancy hair-dos who totter up the steps and then rattle the windows with their giggles. "How could we have possibly made such a mistake?" one shrieks. Mayhew makes a note of their names on his little pad.

The Martian starts getting punchy and leading guaranteed losers on a tour of the house that includes the furnace and its piping system, the broom closet under the stairs, and ends with the side door that leads back to High Street. When asked about it, he replies, "It's a technique I learned last year."

• • •

Thursday is a day of rest. Doak, Blaisdell, Cephus and Kostic spend the afternoon at the dining room table, shuffling their index cards and making meaningful marks on their endless lists.

Our Thursday night meeting is a riot in many ways. It doesn't start until ten p.m. so the brothers can get home from

413

their dates, full of beer and oversexed. Gunner Schmidt starts a shouting match when someone drops a no vote on an army vet rushee: a little blowhard of a guy whose conversation is liberally sprinkled with *frauleins* and *schatzes*.

In turn, Curtis waits until a long discussion is nearly over about a man that many like. His praises have been sung and we're ready to vote. "No!" Curtis booms. A great roar of outrage results. Brothers shout for him to explain his reasons. "I don't have to have a reason. I just don't like the fucker..."

"Five dollars, Brother Curtis," J.L. knocks down another cursing fine.

"Motherfucker, then Brother Simmons. Is that one word or two?" Curtis retorts. "My vote is still no. I don't want him as a brother."

By four o'clock, we have our list pretty well wrapped up. Thirteen prime candidates including Kenny Easton, the artist, and the piano-playing kid from Jackson, the two legacies, the socialites from Columbus, and more. They're followed by the B list which is followed by the C list.

I hit my bunk with the question of what list I came from lurking in my head.

• • •

Friday's big push is on. Everyone on his best behavior. Most of us wishing Curtis were in Korea or Hell. Tonight, we'll make our moves to offer positive invitations to each of the guys on the first list. And try to get from them a commitment... or at least an indication of the way they're leaning. It's a true minuet of duplicity. Except no one wears a white wig.

At the same time, we need to keep the pressure on and interest of our B and C list rushees. The experienced Aces tell us repeatedly that a kid left alone for a few minutes on Friday night is as good as gone to someone else's house. The illegal keg of beer in the Keep helps with a party atmosphere that holds many rushees around, some long after they should have left.

I'm brought in by Doak and Blaisdell for a long talk with Ken Easton and am pleased that he seems positive about ACE. I take him up to the tower suite and show him some of my drawings, careful not to give him the impression I'm hot-boxing him.

By ten o'clock, we're exhausted but the real work of the night begins with the last rush meeting.

A heated argument arises over a rushee from Kentucky named Dale Lemley. Curtis wants to no vote him and everyone is threatening him with dire consequences if he does. Finally, Curtis calls for a secret vote. The ballot box is passed around and we each write our vote on a tiny slip.

J.L. Simmons' face is flushed with anger. Doak has just emptied the box on the podium and among the white slips, a black marble rolls out. "Is this someone's idea of a goddamn joke?" he hisses.

"Five dollars, Brother Acer," we roar. Waller and I exchange glances. The blackball is only symbolic. And who does it belong to?

"I'm going to treat this as a bad joke," Simmons says firmly. "Lemley is a yes and we'll bid him tomorrow night." Curtis scowls around the room. Then he gets up and leaves.

• • •

Saturday is relatively relaxed. I am assigned to bird-dog Ken Easton and I pick him up at Tiffin Hall, where I *might have* lived if I had not pledged. We walk up to the Fine Arts building and I show him around the studios and classrooms.

At Begorra we each buy our own hamburgers as I introduce Easton to Duff. Duff shows me a card from Darcy but it doesn't say much except how hard she is working, how much she likes Cincinnati.

The Martian sneaks me into East Green Cafeteria where Easton and I garbage down hot dogs and sauerkraut. *Sauerkraut on the last night of rush? Some GDI's idea of a good joke on the Greeks.*

By the time I get back to the Ace house, I can tell Doak that I think Easton will go ACE if we give him the bid.

• • •

"Ken! It's an honor… and a pleasure for me… to be the one to ask you to tender your pledge to Alpha Chi Epsilon," I repeat the words I heard just eight months ago. "I'm asking you to join me in this order, Ken, as a pledge and to follow the path and light to our brotherhood."

J.L. Simmons looks on as Easton, pale and frightened looking, shakes his head up and down. His lower lip quivers. "Gosh, Five. I was kind of afraid you guys wouldn't ask me. Yes. I'll pledge."

"Good man, Ken. Welcome aboard. Come on, I have some folks I want you to meet," J.L. says shaking the bewildered Easton's hand. I walk with them down the stairs to the Keep and then to the anteroom where we already have eight accepted pledges waiting.

J.L. opens the door and I lead Ken into the smoky room and announce in my best drill-field voice, "Gentlemen, may I introduce this man as the ninth member of The Thirteen? Kenneth Easton. Ken's agreed to become one of your number."

• • •

Phipps and Simmons rattle around the house at five in the morning, pounding doors and rousting the handlers. "C'mon brothers, up and at 'em. You've got a half hour to be on the East Green. Have your men at the top of the Bryan steps at six o'clock." Simmons has his tux on and pounds the doors with the foot of the drum major's baton.

Doak Phipps looks pretty strange in the gondolier's hat and his boxer shorts but he assures us he'll be there fully dressed at six.

I warned Easton the night before to be dressed in some sort of clothes so I'm not surprised when he answers his door at Tiffin in a pair of jeans and a Pomeroy Purple Panther jersey. *Just like he's going out for a game of touch football.*

"How's your head, Kenneth my man?" I ask. His smile emerges from a gray face and we leave the room. I give him a

416

cigarette as we walk up the Bryan steps, joining other handlers and their charges. Only ACE pledges its rushees in this manner and you can see the freshmen marveling at the weirdness of the event.

We line them up in single file and J.L. gives a silent wag of his baton to start the parade. Doak, the complete Tiler in his red-ribboned hat and a pair of red spats, follows to make sure none of his new pledge class passes out on the march across the campus.

We handlers drift our way across the wet grass. And as the first rays of dawn break across the lintel of the main gate, J.L. lifts his baton and a new Thirteen is born.

• • •

"Pretty good bunch of pledges," Soos Salazar comments to the rest of the group sitting on the Ace front porch. It's Sunday afternoon and naps are over. It's time to confront the new semester. "I hated to see that piano player go Beta but what the hell?"

"That Castellano guy may make a pretty good Ace some day," Doak Phipps adds. "There's one guy who'll know how to take actives for a ride." We hoot at the idea of our *gangster* pledge taking someone for a ride. A one-way ride.

"Two guineas and a mick," Blaisdell grins. "What a bunch! And that hillbilly Lemley. What a crew."

He's talking about the New Yorker Castellano, Dante DeLucia, an all-state football player from Cleveland, and Sean Fallon O'Hara, a red-haired Irishman from Pennsylvania. We also got Jake Sickles, Goforth and Wally Armistead. All told, ACE's newest Thirteen looks pretty good. Eight from the first list, three from the second and the rest from the third.

Chapter 32

Finding My Page In The Social Register

After the unreal pace of rush week, class registration seems like a relief. I miss Trish Spotswood's counsel and our after-registration coffee. But somehow, I make it through the process with no eight o'clocks nor Saturday classes. I even remember to put nineteen thirty-three down as my birthdate for a new ID card.

Professor Logan hails me as I'm leaving registration. "Good to see you back, Five. How was your summer? I enjoyed seeing the card you sent to Andy. Those are nice little sketches."

"Thanks professor. Summer was pretty nice. I really enjoyed being on the river. But I lost my girlfriend — and my model — to the big city."

"Yes, I heard. Well, there'll be other models." He pauses with a smile. "Other girlfriends, too, I'd wager. But I have some news for you."

"News? After a week of rush, I can stand some news, especially if it's good."

"Oh this is good," he says. "First, as a winner in last year's Student Art Show, you're automatically qualified to hang a work in the University's fall faculty-student exhibition. I believe you'll be the youngest student to ever do so."

"Man, that's great professor. But I really don't have anything ready. When's the show?"

"Not until early December. And I'm sure you'll have some things done by then. You're taking advanced painting, plus media and materials, isn't that right?" I nod affirmatively.

"And… your lofty status as a student show winner entitles you to a private studio in the fine arts building. I think you'll have to share it with one other student but at least you'll have a place where you can leave your work without having it tampered with."

"That's great, Professor Logan. My gosh, I've never had a studio, public or private."

"Well, see Miss Trevayne about a key. She'll get you fixed up. And come by and see us sometime, will you?"

• • •

Good news continues, at least at first glance, when I get back to the Ace house and discover a letter from Darcy in my mailbox. It's long and chatty, full of news about waitressing, her increasing modeling jobs, our brief togetherness of a few weeks ago, Trish's excitement at leaving waitressing for academia. Then comes the last page:

Five, thanks so much for inviting me to homecoming. I really would love to come but... the modeling assignments have been coming so fast that I don't dare try to get into U.C. full-time. So I've been taking adult ed courses there on Saturday and won't have a day off all fall. It breaks my heart to have to say no. So this is an invitation from me for you to come here for Thanksgiving. Please say you will. Your love, Darcy

• • •

With almost no experience at asking girls out, I find the task of getting a date for our *Kick Off A New Season* party a challenge. So I take the easy path and call Andy Logan at home. But Mrs. Logan, cheerful and friendly as ever, tells me Andy's living at the Pi Phi house. First I'm surprised when I actually get through to the Pi Phi house. And second, I'm surprised when Andy comes to the phone.

"Hey Five, it's good to hear from you. I was hoping you would call last week but... rush 'n all. I guess you were pretty busy. We sure were."

"Hi, Andy. Well, yeah. We were pretty hectic. I guess it's all worth it but I'm glad I don't have anything else to do with the pledge class. Did you all get a good pledge class?"

"Oh, the greatest," she laughs, "as usual. Pretty and smart. Talented young things. Makes me feel old and discarded, all the attention they're getting."

"Well, I'll give you some attention. How about coming with me to our *Kick Off* party Saturday night?"

"Aw, Five. That's nice and I would really like to. But I already have a date."

"Serves me right," I respond glumly. "Should've called you earlier. Well, maybe you'd go with me to the first football game next week?"

"Oh Five. I can't. You see… I'm ah, dating someone right now."

"Dating someone? Going steady? Pinned?"

"No, nothing like that. He's just a nice guy and… well, you know!"

"Yeah. I know. Well, thanks anyway."

"Five. I know someone here I'm sure would like to go out with you. Do you remember Tase Putnam?"

"The *sociologist?*"

"Yes, the sociologist. Don't run her down, though. She helped me get my D. I'd be glad to talk to her, if you want."

"Yeah, I got my D too. But I guess I'd just as soon not get involved with anyone in the Pi Phi house."

"Are you sure? We've got some really neat pledges, too. I could get you fixed up for a coffee date with one of them."

• • •

After hanging up from my disappointing conversation with Andy, I leaf through the other two names in my faded mental black book. Judy Graham? *No. For some reason, I don't think so.* I contemplate for a few seconds more then dial Howard Hall, where I'm sure O-Annie still lives.

• • •

Pat Trevayne looks up from her cubby-holed desk in the fine arts building. "Oh yes, you're Andrea Logan's friend, aren't you?" she says with an arch smile. "And you're our prize who earned his very own private studio. As a sophomore." This is my first encounter with the girl Andy refers to as "the bitch," and she's not as gaunt and stern as she appeared on the Mem Aud stage.

Light brown hair in disarray, strong facial planes. When she stands, she's as tall as me. As she walks by me to a box on the wall, I get a whiff of some light perfume mixed with turpentine, perhaps linseed oil. She opens the box and produces a brass key and beckons for me to follow her down the hall to the basement stairs.

"You'll have to share the studio, of course," Trevayne says with an air of dismissal, "but you two should get along. Culden has some strong opinions about art but don't we all?" I don't answer this question, obviously rhetorical. After all, my opinions about art are largely unformed.

The studio is gloomy and smells of mold and media. A thin window near the ceiling shows this to be a basement room, about twelve feet square. Two large wooden studio easels, a pair of lockers, one taboret and a couple of hard chairs are its only furniture.

Trevayne blows hair away from her nose and she looks around the studio. "If you're good with your hands, there's an old taboret down in the storeroom that could probably be put back together. Culden's already claimed this one, obviously." She holds out the key and plunks it firmly into my outstretched palm.

"Well, good luck. Call on me if I can be of any help," she says earnestly. "And I did enjoy your painting. Rather representational but I could see that you were an inspired young man."

• • •

O-Annie shows up in the Bryan lobby in a dark green OU football jersey, about three sizes too big for her. The contrast between jersey and her aurora of red hair is striking. On her left breast is a pledge pin.

"You pledged, Annie! Congratulations!" She thrusts the pin toward me with a big smile.

"It's Zeta, Five. And they're really neat girls. I don't know why I didn't see that last year." We head around the corner and down the hill toward the Ace house. "Also," she chatters, "I don't have far to go to pledge meetings 'cause they're right next door to the dorm."

The Ace *Kick Off* party has a football theme, although the OU season doesn't start for another week. So everyone's in some sort of jock garb. Mine is an old gray athletic department shirt from the Bear, stretched way out of shape by his muscles and barely filled by mine.

The Martian has "The Starting Five" going full blast. D.D. Smith is on drums, replacing the graduating drummer, and one of the pledges, Otis Lever, is playing the piano. O-Annie is a good dancer who gets progressively better with drinks. So we drink and dance and enjoy ourselves.

The Wonder Bar gang, Curtis, Schmidt and Mayhew, show up with their usual assortment of scaggy women and display the fact that they've been warming up somewhere else. Mayhew quickly abandons his date to hang over the piano while he goes off to hustle sorority pledges.

Sarge Waller and Jeannie Cavallero sit with us for a while, but Jeannie moves off when she realizes I don't really want to talk about what a great gal Darcy is... and how much I must miss her.

In the Bryan lounge just before eleven, O-Annie leans me against a pillar with her arms around my neck, her forehead against mine. She smells like bourbon, sweat and the remainder of her perfume.

"Was fun, Five, wasn't it," she whispers. "But you aren't the same old Five, are you?" She tilts her chin up and we kiss gently. Her wide lips are firm, then yield a little as we hold the kiss. She breaks the kiss and leans back. "You kissed me better than that last year when we were just friends." A small shrug. "But then, what the hell. Things take time."

• • •

423

Monday night's meeting is relatively routine. That is, a lot of pep talks about leadership and student elections, some house business, questions of the various chairman. And then the bitching lamp is lit. This is the time when we brothers are encouraged to bring forth anything on our minds. Emphasis is on constructive criticism.

"I would like to mention to Brother Mayhew," Kostic says, "that while I can accept flirting with someone's date as a natural, say even normal, thing, what he was doing with my date was just out-and-out bird-dogging. And frankly, I resent it."

Mayhew, Curtis and Schmidt huddle their heads and giggle. *A few brews at the Wonder Bar before the meeting, perhaps?*

Soos Salazar, in from the pledge meeting, holds up his hand. "I'll second that, Brother Kostic. Pledge Spindale has already complained about Brother Mayhew bird-dogging his date."

"You have anything to say about that, Brother Mayhew?" J.L. asks from the chair.

"Naw. Haven't you guys ever heard the saying about all's fair in love and war?" he asks with his arms spread wide.

"These pussies wouldn't last a minute in war," Schmidt grumbles.

"Five dollars, Brother Schmidt!" J.L. admonishes.

"And they obviously don't know how to handle themselves in love," Mayhew adds to the manifesto.

"Handle themselves," Curtis guffaws. "That's what they know about women. How to handle themselves."

"Brother secretary?" Jim Cephus rises. "Put me down for five bucks. Brother Curtis, I think you and your buddies are ignorant assholes most of the time. And I, for one, will appreciate your cleaning up your conduct when you're at the house." Applause rings out. The VFW trio glares around the room at all of our laughing faces.

• • •

My studio door unexpectedly swings open as I try to insert the key in the lock. Inside, a hunched figure jumps in alarm. I

424

believe it's a woman but look more carefully to be sure.

"Fuck, man. You scared the shit out of me," she mutters, reaching for a cigarette smoldering in the ashtray on the floor by her feet.

"Sorry," I say sheepishly. "I didn't realize you were in here."

"So?" she growls. "Who'n the fuck're you?"

"I'm Five Lowrey. And you're?"

"Culden." Culden has mid-length hair that hangs down all around her head in snarls. She's wearing a gray man's undershirt. At least it looks gray but I suspect it just hasn't been washed recently. Paint spattered jeans and sandals complete her wardrobe.

"Culden? That's it, just Culden?"

"Culden Ellis." She looks up from her crouch on the floor. She appears to be gluing sheets of newspaper together on a piece of plywood. As she works, I glimpse her breasts through the gaping armholes of her shirt.

"So we're ah, studio-mates? I guess?"

"That's what Trevayne told me," she says gruffly. "I don't know how I got so goddamned lucky."

"Hey Culden, look at it from my eyes. Maybe it's a two-way street." I watch her as she smoothes a rag soaked in white stuff across the newspapers. "What're you doing there?"

"Applying gesso, of course. Shit, Six. Is that it? Six? Are you that green?"

I raise my hands in innocent supplication. "It's Five and forgive me. I'm just a poor dumb sophomore. But I am taking media and materials this semester. Perhaps I'll learn about gesso."

• • •

My first hour in the studio seems worth two semesters of art education. I know where Zanesville is. I've even been there. And I find it hard to comprehend how a pretty little town famous only for its Y-bridge could produce a piece of work like Culden Ellis.

"I'm pissed off 'cause Jackson's dead, don't you know anything?"

425

"Jackson?"

"Jackson Pollock, you dumb shit. He's been dead for a month now and you don't even know? The greatest American artist who ever lived?"

"Damn, I'm sorry Culden. Course I know who Pollock is. I just didn't realize he was dead. What did he die of?"

"God love a duck! Where in hell have you been, you farmer? He was killed in an auto wreck. At least that's what *they* say."

"Look, I'm not going to keep apologizing to you. But I spent the damned summer on a riverboat and we didn't get all the latest news from the world of art."

Later, she looks over my shoulder as I leaf through my summer's sketches.

"Not bad. Kind of Grandma Moses-y looking crap. But old man Logan'll probably go for that, give you an A. He eats that primitive representational shit up."

As I'm getting ready to screw L-brackets to assemble an canvas frame, she stands, scratches her breast with a gessoed hand, and grabs the hardware away from me.

"Not galvanized, you poor simple fool. Galvanized stuff'll rust and turn the whole canvas to shit in five months. Go get some brass hardware and screws. And better get a couple of one by twos to brace this thing. What're you building, a goddamn coffin?"

• • •

It's the fourth quarter and Ohio Stadium is two-thirds empty. O-Annie is stretched out on the sunny bleacher beside me, her sleeping head in my lap. The Bobcats are rolling to an easy victory over Western Reserve and most of the Aces have beat it up the hill to refresh themselves after a hard day of drinking at the game.

We new guys discover that sitting in a fraternity bloc is vastly different from our old dormitory days as fans. The pledges arrive early with big coolers of ice and mix to stake out and protect our turf. Everyone buys one drink, either 7-Up or Coke, from a vendor just to get the waxed cup. Then the cups pass up and down the rows from the ice chest to the brothers and their dates. Discreet amounts of booze are poured from sport-coated flasks at each passing.

By the fourth quarter, everyone either goes home or passes out. Football at OU seems to be a quaint diversion on the field for the entertainment of the cocktail party. Still, to have the Bobcats ahead is a thrilling departure and several of us stay to cheer on our hero, the Bear.

With rules switching to two-platoon this year, the Bear gets to play more as a strictly defensive end. And his summer at the open-hearth has given him the tools to play better as well. He spends the afternoon in the Reserve backfield, looking for heads and arms to rip off.

• • •

We march up the hill behind the backward-hatted band playing *Stand Up and Cheer* at the top of their horns and reeds. O-Annie sort of drags along, one arm over my shoulder, one of my arms around her waist. She is what you might call slightly slack.

Crossing the bridge, I wave at the brothers standing on the sun porch. They return my greeting with upraised glasses. Waller lifts O-Annie's trailing arm in mock salute and a cheer comes from the ACE house.

I deposit O-Annie on a porch chair and go up to the room to get my bottle for our drinks. When I return, she's sound asleep, her little Zeta pledge pin shining against her black sweater. Cute as she looks, I decide to leave her be and join some others on the steps where I smoke and drink both our drinks.

"Check out Brother Curtis," Waller says. "He's a regular life of the party." In the courtyard, Curtis and one of the pledges toss a frisbee with their dates. Their fun is obvious by shrieks and laughter.

"I just can't figure that guy out," Salazar sighs. "Sometimes he really can seem like a pretty nice person and then…"

"Yeah. Wish Joe Ransom was here to tell us more about him," Kostic says.

"Nice going, Benjo," Dicky Reb groans. "Just when I've got enough booze in me to forget about Joe, you stir the ole' black stuff up all over again."

We silently agree and sit glumly on the sun-splashed steps, watching the frisbee players and sharing our silent memories of Ransom.

O-Annie's definitely not ready for the post-game party Saturday night so I steer her back to Howard, then walk over to Begorra for some burgers. The after-game crowd has thinned out, giving Duff some time to shoot the breeze. But this is depressing, since most of our talk is about Darcy.

I walk back to the house, change into shorts and a t-shirt and leave the frivolity for the fine arts building. The studio door is locked but when I open it, I'm stunned at the sight of Culden, naked as the day she was born, standing at the top of a small ladder.

A big grin of relief wipes across her face. "Oh shit, Five. You scared the ass off me. I thought it was Trevayne."

"Naw! You've still got your ass. That I can plainly see. But what in hell are you doing?"

"Painting, naturally." She holds up a cup dripping with pure yellow latex. Beneath her is the gessoed board and already it holds tracks and splotches. Culden's doing her Jackson Pollock thing. She starts down from the ladder.

"Oh keep it up," I say. "I'll just watch, if you don't mind." I take a folding chair and ask, "and why were you afraid I was Trevayne."

"That bitch! She's always on my ass. I like my privacy when I paint. But it's too fuckin' hot to paint in here with the door closed and clothes on. And she'd kick my can right out of here if she could find a reason, like this." She grins and wipes her forehead, leaving a smear of yellow across it.

I glance up at the darkened window, half expecting to find Trevayne's curious face peering through. Of course, she'd have to crawl on her stomach under a hedge to get there.

As I watch, Culden continues to dribble her yellow paint. Then she climbs down and picks up a brush and a cup of black. Back on the ladder, she loads the brush, then whacks it on the ladder's edge to create a spray of black drops. Fine drops spatter her stomach except where the ladder leg masks a stripe of white skin. I reach for a sketch pad and my Rapidograph.

"Do you mind if I sketch you while you work? Will that bother you?"

"Shit, no. Nothing bothers me." She stares down at me like a paint-speckled vulture from her height on the ladder. "Does *this* bother you?" she asks, nodding her head down toward her gleaming, dotted body.

"No! Not at all," I respond hoarsely, crossing my legs.

"Hah! I can *see it doesn't.* Do you want to screw around a little?"

"No, Culden. Thanks a lot. I'll just sketch if it's OK with you."

"OK by me," she answers, scratching an unshaved armpit. "You're not queer, are you?"

• • •

Back in the tower suite, I find Waller, Benjo and Soos Salazar sitting on the beds in deep discussion.

"Five man, where ya' been? You missed all the shit!" Waller exclaims.

"What shit? What now?"

Soos looks at me with a pained expression. "Oh man, Five. We got a problem again."

"Curtis?" The three nod yes at me solemnly.

"One of the pledges, that Zigler guy from Salt Lake," Soos relates. "He's in the living room, all dark 'n everything, makin' out with his date. Some little sorority pledge chick."

He pauses for a drag on his cigarette. I light up in sympathy. "He thinks they're really gettin' somewhere. Kissin' hot and heavy. Then he feels her hand on his leg, on his tool, you know?"

"So he grabs her by the boob," Waller breaks in, "and she lets out this screech and swats him one. With her free hand."

"But the hand on his leg doesn't move for a second," Benjo says. "And guess who was next to him, supposedly makin' out

429

with his bitch from the Wonder Bar?"

"So how'd you find this shit out?" I ask.

"Zigler told me," Soos says, "after he takes this poor babe home and gets his face slapped about four times. He was really shook up."

"Soos told us," Benjo adds, "and we figured out the rest."

"Oh shit, brothers," I whisper. "We do have a problem. And how's it going to end?"

Chapter 33

Tunder And Lightning And Everything Nice

The quandary of Galen Curtis isn't solved in the next few weeks. The three of us try a circumspect talk with Brother Cephus, whose outburst at the meeting gives us cause to think he might understand the problem. Perhaps he does, but we come away without having told him of our suspicions simply because they seem so unbelievable.

Soos Salazar and I meet for coffee one morning with Doak Phipps but the new Tiler also seems unbelieving of our veiled problem. Soos blurts out his frustration. "C'mon Tiler, just suppose that there's this fraternity and one of the brothers is, ah, molesting the other brothers. What would they do?"

"Molesting?" Doak asks. "You mean homosexually?"

"Yeah," Soos responds. "That's what we mean."

"Are you talking about Alpha Chi?" Doak asks. "Is this more than hypothetical?"

"I'm afraid it is," Soos says. I nod in agreement.

"Then it's simple. We go talk to the Acer. Prove it's true and get the guy kicked out of the chapter."

"We can't really prove anything," I add morosely. "We know. But we can't prove anything."

"Well crap," the Tiler says, "is it one of the new pledges?"

"No," Salazar responds. "But it *could* affect the pledge class."

"Damn. We can't very well have sex education lessons and warn them about keeping out of the way of some phantom queer in the Ace house," he says. "And you guys won't tell me who it is?"

"I don't think we should until we can prove something," I say. "And we have to trust you now, to keep it quiet as well."

• • •

ACE and Theta Chi are playing intramural tag football. I sit on the sidelines, making quick action sketches. Brothers, pledges, dates and others line both sides of the field.

Suddenly, I'm blind as a pair of hands cups over my eyes. "Goooo, Aces. Guess who?" a girl's voice whispers.

"If it's not Mater Gousha, you'd better not go around whispering our secret cheer," I laugh. "I give up. Who?" The hands fly away and Andy Logan hops in front of me.

"Hey, Five. I'm glad that was you. I don't usually go around grabbing strange men. At least when I'm not drinking."

"Hey Andy. Great to see you. What are you doing down here? What's that outfit?" She wears a white blouse and a shortish green and black plaid skirt, dark green knee socks and shoes with cleats. Her blonde hair is pulled into a ponytail.

"Field hockey, Five. That's where the real action is." She points over my shoulder to a field behind me. "I played when I went off to a private school for a year. It's fun and someday it's going to be the first varsity sport for women at OU."

Twenty two players and an referee scurry around the grassy field. The OU girls, in uniforms like Andy's, seem to be getting swept off the field by the team in red jerseys.

"Dennison," Andy says. "They're really tough but we should tire 'em out by the third period. Come and watch. Your Aces ought to beat the Theta Chi's without you."

The field hockey game *is* interesting. The women swirl back and forth across the field in relatively graceful pursuit of the ball and after a few minutes, I see offensive patterns develop, defensive schemes to stop the attack.

"See the big girl there, the blonde with the pigtail," Andy says. The girl she points to *is* big, a beautiful creature with long legs that cover a lot of yards with each stride. "Isn't she magnificent?" I nod that I think so too. "Now, look at our goalie. The one with the big pads on her shins." There is the same girl, it seems.

"Twins?" The two look identical.

"Yep. The Braswell twins. Sigurd and Signe. They're from up in northern Michigan. You should hear them talk. Great accents. We call them Tunder and Lightning."

"They're really something," I exclaim as the goalie flicks her stick out to stop a Dennison shot. She scoops up the ball and with a fluid motion rifles a pass to the edge of the field where her sister rolls it down her stick and heads down the field.

"I tried to get them to pledge Pi Phi in the worst way," Andy says wistfully. "Thank heavens, they didn't pledge at all. Maybe we can get them next semester."

The game whirls on and just as the whistle ends the second period, one of the Braswells pops a pass to a short dark OU girl who hooks a shot into the Dennison nets. We leap up with the official's whistle.

"I've got to get back to the huddle," Andy says. "Are you going to stick around? Only twelve more minutes to play. We've tied 'em now. Got them where we want them."

I watch the final quarter. Andy's pretty good, playing defense in front of the goal and frustrating several Dennison attacks. The short dark girl tries three shots on goal for OU but Dennison's goalie makes fantastic saves and the game ends in a one-one tie. Grabbing a towel, Andy waves me over. Why I go, I'm not sure. There aren't any other guys around.

Andy comes over and puts an arm around my waist. She's warm and damp and feels desirable. My mind flashes back to the yard swing last June.

The Braswell twins, as tall as I am, come over and Andy introduces me to them. Sigurd or "Tunder," and Signe or "Lightning." Their smiles are wonderful and blonde hair frames flushed, beautiful faces.

"And this is Annalise Hechter," Andy says, grabbing the short dark girl by the arm. "Annalise's from Denmark, Five, and she's our best player." All three of the girls speak in charming accents, Norwegian *and* Danish as it turns out.

"And this is Five Lowrey, the guy I slept with all last semester," Andy brings out her tired joke with a giggle. The three girls look amazed. "In sociology class," she adds. "If you have to take sosh, find a neat guy with a soft shoulder to sit next to." Andy squeezes my arm and looks up. "He's also the best damned artist on the campus, except maybe for my father."

Walking across the field with Andy toward the footbridge, I

forget that the Aces and Theta Chi's are still locked in battle. "So how's your boyfriend, Andy?"

"Oh! I guess we're not dating any more. He was kind of rushing things, you know?"

"Yeah, I guess I know. Gee! That's too bad. I'm really sorry," I say with mock sincerity. "But now I'm glad I didn't get involved with anyone else at the Pi Phi house."

"I can tell how sorry you are, Five," she responds. "And I'm glad you didn't get involved with some Pi Phi too."

• • •

Crashing thunder and almost constant lightning make it virtually impossible for Waller and me to study one evening. Rain hits the window of our tower room in sheets, each new blast causing us to look up and stare out at the foul night.

The door bursts open and there stands Benjo Kostic, peering from a dripping olive drab poncho. "Saddle up, you guys," he says breathlessly. "There's something you've got to see. Gotta hear."

Waller hands me one of his army ponchos and dons another. We follow Kostic off into the storm. On Union Street, the lights from the bars are the only signals that life exists. We cross the empty street and enter the Wonder Bar.

"Just be cool," Kostic says. "Order a beer and then we'll drift to the back. Our vet brothers are back there in a good old fashioned drunken bull session and I thought some of the stuff Curtis was spouting was pretty interesting."

As usual the Wonder Bar is crowded with vets, jocks and their women, and noisy from the consumption of lots of beer. At the rear of the room, we sidle to the edge of a crowd standing around the big round table with a poker light hanging above it. In the gloom, I catch a glimpse of Gunner Schmidt standing across the circle. He gives us a strange smile.

Seated in front of Gunner, Curtis is indeed holding forth. "Then the fuckin' gooks and chinks start stirrin' themselves up to try it again. I mean, man, all down the hill in front of us, they're stacked up and groaning. Their bodies smoldering with willy peter shrapnel. We shoot into the bodies just to get 'em to shut up." Heads nod around the table and everyone uses Curtis' pause to grab a swig of beer.

"So they got their goddamn bugles blowin' and those fuckin' record players playin... you know what I'm talkin about. And we got guys pissin' on their machine gun barrels to cool 'em off... and guys prayin' and shittin' themselves..."

"Yeah, man, Pork Chop Hill was the worst," a voice solemnly pronounces from the gloom.

"Fuckin' A," Curtis agrees. "But we ragged-assed sonsabitches hung in there and drove the gooks off one more time."

A new voice cuts through the smoky gloom, "Pork Chop Hill, Curtis? I thought I'd heard you were gettin' some R&R down around Pusan while that was going on." Kostic's face is just a gray mask at the edge of the crowd. Curtis' head snaps up. The group is instantly silent.

Curtis glares at Kostic. "What the fuck you talkin' about, you stupid Polack?" Kostic doesn't reply. Just continues to gaze steadily at Curtis. Then he nods and the three of us leave the Wonder Bar, gunslingers in a strange town escaping with their asses.

• • •

Nearly two hours later, our door shakes with a loud knock. Kostic nods and Waller gets up to open the door. Curtis, soaking and bombed, staggers into the room. Gunner and Mayhew remain in the hallway outside.

"You fuck!" Curtis shouts at Kostic. "You Polack asshole. What is this Pusan bullshit, anyway?" He clenches a fist, doubles his arm and stares down at Kostic.

"No bullshit, you blowhard!" Kostic replies calmly. "You weren't on Pork Chop Hill. I was with the 17th Infantry on April 17th when we went in to relieve those guys. I'll always remember every one of those fifty-five poor bastard's faces. And yours wasn't one of them.

"Lying asshole!" Curtis retorts. "You're just trying to

impress your little pansy boyfriends here."

"You're the liar, Curtis," Kostic says. "You weren't even in the 7th Division, or the 31st Infantry. You were in the 25th Division and I can prove it!"

Curtis is so angry that he sweeps Waller's books from his desk. From the opened covers of the dictionary, the Thermofax of Curtis' army record flutters to the floor. Waller shoves it with his foot, trying to scoot it under his chair.

"Say what you want to, Curtis," Kostic stays calm, "but I know where you spent the battle of Pork Chop Hill. And you know it's the truth."

"And we know the truth about..." Waller says but stops when Kostic shoots him a warning look.

"Schofield Barracks, also," Kostic finishes. "Are there any other things we should know the truth about, Curtis?"

Curtis spins so fast that raindrops fly off his coat. Schmidt and Mayhew jump back as he storms out of our room.

"I think you guys just made a bad enemy," Schmidt says and they turn to follow their buddy.

• • •

Culden is heaping ridicule upon my efforts at painting a riverscape. Ridicule seems to be her favorite form of constructive criticism.

"Jesus, Five. Look at 'em. Cute little people standing and waving. Aren't they sweet? And these little naked girlies?"

"Up yours, Culden. That's how it looked," I reply. "You weren't there. I was."

"I didn't have to be there, Lowrey." She throws a wadded piece of gessoed newsprint at my head. "I've already seen all this shit on Hallmark's finest."

Ruefully, I look at my painting. Just over a foot high, it's nearly five feet long and its strange format contains my effort to show all the scenes of my river experience in a single panoramic sweep. The dissatisfaction that I've felt about this work bubbles up under the heat of Culden's criticism.

"Come on in," she yells in answer to the knock at the studio door. The door swings open and Galen Curtis stands in the threshold.

"Out bitch," he gestures to Culden. "I've got some things to say to your asshole friend here." Culden stands her ground and Curtis grabs her arm and spins her through the door. "Goddamn cunt! Can't you understand English?" He pushes the door closed behind him.

"Now then, Lowrey. Tell me exactly what the fuck it is you guys are trying to do to me?"

"I think you should have the picture by now, Curtis," I reply, trying to emulate Kostic's calmness of the other night.

"You asshole!" he screams, leaping at me and hitting me in the chest. I stagger backward and lose my footing. My hand hits something solid that gives way as I crash through my canvas. Curtis hovers over me, his face a torment of rage, his fists clinched.

"What was that bullshit in the meeting… about Ransom?"

"I know, Curtis. We all know," I mutter. *Is there something I can club this bastard with?* "Ransom told us. We know everything…"

Curtis leans forward to hit me, then stops still. A strange expression crosses his face as Culden's voice hisses. "Don't move. Not one hair, you bastard." Curtis doesn't move. "I mean it. Now turn around slowly or I'll run this ice pick right through your ugly neck."

Curtis shuffles around in slow little steps, Culden moving to stay behind him. In her hand is the thin handle of a long sable brush.

"Now get out of here and don't ever come back," she says menacingly. "If I ever see you again, I'll stick this thing in your balls." She shoves Curtis with her free hand and slams the door, snapping the dead bolt.

"Jesus, who was that?" she asks, leaning against the door.

"That, believe it or not, was one of my fraternity brothers."

"Goddamn, what an animal. Remind me never to go to an Ace party. Must be a zoo over there."

Another knock interrupts us. "Who is it?" I call.

"Me! Dicky Reb. Are you OK in there, Five?"

Culden opens the door to reveal Dicky Reb West there in a long rubber apron. He glances at Culden, then at me sprawled against my crushed painting.

"What in hell's going on? I just came out of the darkroom and Curtis went flying by like someone had lit a fire to him."

"I'll tell you later. Everything's OK, though. Thanks to Culden here. Culden Ellis, this is one of my other, my good, fraternity brothers. Dicky Reb West."

"Well, I'm meetin' the whole fuckin' crew," Culden says, appraising West in his apron. "What do you do, work in the Betty Crocker kitchen?"

She and West watch as I try to reassemble the torn and twisted canvas. It's ripped where my hand punched through and the tear runs half its length. The frame is broken and twisted.

"Aw," Culden says, "your pretty painting. It's all ruined." I shoot her a black look. "Just as well," she adds. "It was piece of shit anyway."

• • •

The anti-Curtis forces gather in the Esquire basement where I relate the latest events and we fill the other members of the Thirteen in on the Wonder Bar incident and confrontation in our room.

"So he knows we know," A.A. Able says, sipping his beer. "Now let me get this clear. He knows *we all* know about Ransom? Or does he know Ransom just talked to Five?"

"Shit, I don't know for sure," I say. "My guess is he thinks we all know. At least that's what I told him. I said 'we all know, Curtis. Ransom told us everything.' At least that's what I think I said."

"I'm pretty sure he's got the picture," Benjo Kostic says. "Big thing is to watch our asses. Everyone be alert. I think this bastard is dangerous. That stunt at the art studio this afternoon shows us that much."

The discussion goes around the table. Once more, we can't make a decision as to what action to take about Curtis. "We just bide our time," Waller says. "I think he'll make the wrong move

438

and we'll know how to react then."

On the way out of the Esky, Dicky Reb takes me aside. "What's with that Culden girl? Give her a good wash and clean up her mouth and she's kind of cute."

"And she's a fast thinker, Dicky Reb. Keep that in mind if you ever get her in your darkroom."

• • •

As Darcy's letters get shorter in length and longer between arrivals, Andy and I drift into becoming a couple. We're comfortable dating, going to movies, to a concert, and a couple of informal parties. She's affectionate but I find it awfully hard to completely blank the image of Darcy from my mind.

On this gray Friday afternoon, I'm standing beneath my umbrella watching the OU Bobcats battle Capital University in field hockey. With two ties and a close loss, they're still fighting for their first victory. And they refuse to be nicknamed "Bobkittens."

Late in the game, Lightning Braswell tramples a Cap player in a battle for the ball and when no whistle blows, she sprints down the field with everyone in pursuit. The Capital goalie slowly edges out of her crease as Lightning moves to the right. She lifts her stick back for a slap shot and follows through!

But leaves the ball rolling in the grass where Annalise Hechter picks it up on her blade. When the Capital goalie lunges for Lightning's fake, Annalise taps the ball in for the winning goal. Soaked and muddy, scratched and grass-stained, the women leap and hug each other in the joy of their first win.

I'm engulfed by one of the Braswells. "Five, you're our good luck charm!" she screams, lifting me off the ground in a bear hug. The next thing I know, I'm flat on the ground with this big pile of muddy femininity on top of me.

I trudge with them and the Capital players back toward the equipment building. The OU girls store their pads and sticks and say good-bye to the other women who must ride wet and muddy on a bus back to Columbus.

"Come on, everyone. It's time for a celebration," Jackie

Guswaite, the club president yells. "Everyone up to the Esquire!"

"That includes you, Five," Andy says, grabbing my soaked arm and stretching the sweater sleeve about three extra feet.

• • •

For TGIF, the Esquire basement is always a mob scene but the Bobcats soon clear a space in the crowd for themselves in the back. Seems no one wants to sit close to these muddy, sweaty and delirious girls who order pitcher after pitcher of beer.

"God, you guys were terrific," I say to my table mates. "I'd love to paint you, just as you are right now."

"A team picture! All wet and slimy," Signe Braswell says with a laugh.

"And bloody too," Andy adds, displaying her forearm where a long scratch still seeps blood.

"One of those old-timey pictures like football teams," Tunder Braswell adds. At least I think she's Sigurd. "With Jackie reclining in the front on one elbow."

"Or in the locker room," Andy says enthusiastically. "If we had a locker room."

"You should paint us in the nude," Annalise Hechter adds, "perhaps like we're interrupted while undressing." The other women giggle and coo in fake shock. Annalise looks around in disapproval. "You guys. In Denmark, we feel no disgrace to display our bodies. We are proud of our bodies."

"Oh Five knows how to handle nudes," Andy grins. She nudges me in the ribs. "He has lots of experience."

• • •

Curtis goes to ground for the entire weekend and doesn't show up Monday night's meeting. Mayhew and Schmidt are remarkably quiet and well-behaved when they're around the house.

On Tuesday afternoon, Culden and I are finishing the frame

for my new canvas. It's pretty big, maybe three by four feet, but Culden is happy with it. "At least it's not that long Valentine thing you were working on."

She grabs a pair of scissors from her taboret when a knock sounds on our studio door. "Who is it?" she calls to the door.

"It's Andy Logan. Is Five Lowrey in there?"

I open the door, thanking my stars that Culden has a sort-of full set of clothes on, and introduce the two. Amazingly, these two women from opposite poles of the universe seem to get along.

"I just wanted to stop and see your studio, Five," she says, "and Culden. It's pretty nice but not a lot of natural light, eh?" The three of us grin at the basement window.

"And Five. We've got the Pi Phi sweetheart dance coming a week from Saturday. I wondered if you'd be my date?" Culden's eyebrows pop up.

"Sure Andy. Do I need a tux? I think I can borrow one." A few more minutes of chatter and Andy says good-bye.

"So that's your sweetie, uh?" Culden asks. "She seems nice. Doc Logan's daughter, isn't she?" I shake my head yes. "Well, it's as good a way to get an A as any." By now I can tell when Culden's acid sense of humor is turned on.

"You gettin' anything else besides an A?" she asks with a leer.

"For Chrissakes, Culden! What kind of a question is that?"

"Well, you oughtta be. I can tell that from the way she looks at you."

• • •

Andy picks me up at the studio with the Braswells in tow. We're going down for a field hockey match with Marietta. Culden's eyebrows arc again at the sight of the towering twins.

Tunder and Lightning peer around the studio. Two curious Norwegian pines in an alien environment. My blank canvas stares back at them from its easel.

"Is this what you're going to paint us on, Five?" Lightning asks. My questioning look says it all.

"I haven't said anything to him yet, Signe," Andy says quickly. "We'll talk about it later.

• • •

Andy limps off in the first quarter, a lump swelling on her ankle where "that Marietta bitch whacked me." With her foot in my lap, I rub ice cubes on the ankle as we watch the match. The Bobcats are cleaning up on Marietta's hapless Pioneerettes. *Pioneerettes?*

"So what's this Signe was saying about a painting, Andy?" I ask.

"Aw, you remember Friday afternoon at the Esky? Well, Annalise and the Braswells got to talking more about it. They'd like for you to paint us as a team."

"Yeah. And in the nude, I suppose?"

"Well. As a matter of fact, that's what they have in mind."

"Everyone? The whole team? Nude?"

"Nah, I don't think everyone would do it. Some of these girls are pretty shy and pretty square. But those three are serious about it. And so am I."

"Right. Four, five pretty girls in the nude. And what's the department chairman going to think of that?"

"No, Five. Not just standing there, posed. A team picture like we were talking about. Wet, sweaty. Covered with dirt and blood. In a locker room."

"Ah. Now it's all clear. We just come down here every afternoon. You get all sweaty and stuff. Then we go, where? Over under the stadium and you pose for a couple of hours? I'm sure no one would notice."

"Five, damnit," she gives me a cross look. "Don't be sarcastic. It could be an interesting painting. We'll figure a way. If you'll just think about it. And talk to us about it. Will you?"

• • •

"Strangest damned thing I've ever heard of," Culden says. She, Andy and I are sitting on the wall outside the fine arts

442

building, smoking and talking about the field hockey painting. "But you can't pose in our studio. It's too damned small for that kind of crowd."

"Culden? You think it's a good idea?"

"Why not, Five? Better than your river thing, at least. Done right, it could be a damned good painting. And I know you can do it right. I remember the work that beat me in the student show."

Andy leans forward, blows smoke through the grass. "Just thinking out loud but... how about a photograph?"

"You mean like pornography?" Culden snorts. "One negative and ten thousand nudie prints of OU's first women's varsity team all over Athens County. Hah!"

"It's not a varsity team yet," Andy says defensively. "It's just a club and we don't even have a university charter. One picture. One print for Five to work from. Could that be done?"

For the first time since this absurd scheme was hatched in the Esky basement, I have an inkling of a positive idea. "I think it maybe *just could* be done. But we'd have to get one other guy involved."

• • •

"Ohmygawd, Five," Dicky Reb chortles, "I know there was a reason I wanted to major in photography. You're not bullshitting me, are you?"

"Naw, Reb. It's for real. But you've got to keep it quiet. Discreet. Understand?"

"Yeah, sure. But Culden already knows about it some. She talked to me this morning."

"Well, Culden's got a big mouth... as well as a dirty mouth," I observe, "but I guess she's part of the crew also."

"How many again?" Dicky Reb wants to know. "Five? Six? Should use a view camera, I guess."

"OK, whatever it takes. But I need just one good print to work from. No others. And the negatives get destroyed. Is that clear?"

· · ·

Andy manages to recruit six others of her field hockey club to pose. Along with the twins and Miss Denmark, she's actually enthusiastic about the project.

"Why not, Five? Our house is covered with paintings and sketches of my mom and she's nude in most of them. I'd like to have something to help me remember what I looked like now when I'm old and saggy." I work hard to envision round, pleasant little Mrs. Logan posing in the nude but the image won't materialize.

"We'll see, Andy. It's just not right, somehow," I mutter lamely.

"What'd you mean, not right? It was all right for Darcy to pose for you, wasn't it?"

"Yeah, but it's that's not the same."

"Crap! I've got everything Darcy has. Maybe even a little more. You'll see."

When we get to the fine arts building, Dicky Reb, Culden and six field hockey players are waiting in our studio. The Rebel has a sheepish expression on his face. "C'mon ladies, right down the hall. This way." Culden leads them to the photo studio we've reserved.

"Jesus, Five. I can't believe this. My gosh," West whispers, "I shoulda worn a jockstrap." He locks the studio door behind us, then knocks on another door, opening it when there's no answer. "OK. This is a bathroom, You can get ready in there but keep it down. There may be someone in the next studio. I've got that door locked."

"Just get good and wet," Andy instructs. "I've got dirt here." She grins at me and holds up a brown paper bag. "And we didn't wash the skirts and socks after the last match." The hockey players vanish into the bathroom.

West busies himself with lights on tall stands, adjusts the roll of gray seamless background paper, checks his view camera. "I'm only going to make two exposures. That's all the sheet film I've got, so we've got to get it right," he says, more to reassure himself than anything else.

The girls emerge from the bathroom, hair dripping, their t-shirts soaked and smeared with mud. Several of them have smeared mud across their foreheads and cheeks. One has a pair of soot-black stripes under her eyes. I've arranged two benches on the seamless paper.

"OK, we're ready. Jackie? Are you going to recline in front of the group?" Andy asks.

"Yeah, fine," the player-coach responds, "but I'm keeping all my clothes on." She lies down on the paper, propped up on one elbow. And smiles broadly. I arrange the other girls around behind her, Andy and another girl sitting on the front bench, the twins standing behind with a leg up on the second bench.

"I didn't wear no brassiere," Lightning Braswell announces as she pulls her t-shirt over her head. "It causes marks on my boobs."

"I *never* wear a brassiere," the Danish girl responds.

From beneath his black hood behind the camera, West moans "Oh Jesus!" Then we're confronted with seven soggy girls including three naked chests and Andy Logan pulling her t-shirt toward her head.

"Stop Andy!" I say. "Hold that right there. That's perfect." Her stomach and the bottoms of her breasts are exposed.

"Five!" she mutters warningly.

"Believe me," I say. "Really, that's terrific!"

West reappears from behind the camera and moves a couple of lights. I turn Tunder so that her back is partially to the camera. "You want I should drop these shorts off?" she asks. I gulp and nod yes, handing her a towel to hold as if she's just out of the shower.

"I feel naked," Lightning Braswell comments. "Not sexy. Just naked." She certainly does look naked. "Wait a second. I've got an idea." She pulls her soaking t-shirt back over her head, then grasps its neckline and pulls hard. The resulting rip exposes a one breast and she grins. "There! *That's* sexy."

Culden smirks in the shadows behind the lights as Dicky Reb moves around the girls, gingerly holding his light meter as close to the bare flesh as he dares. "Be sure you get the right exposure, Dicky!" Culden giggles.

He pops back behind the black cloth. "OK. Here goes the first shot. Now everyone hold really still." We hear the dark slide being pulled out. "All right. Now." There's the whick of the shutter going off.

The girls relax. Andy finishes pulling her shirt over her head. She *does* have everything Darcy had… and a little more. She glares at me, daring me to make a comment.

I modify the pose slightly, have Andy rest her forearms on her knees and look up at the camera. I walk over and sweep her ponytail over her shoulder. "You can't hide me, Five. I swear you can't," she whispers.

Dicky Reb calls them to attention again, pops behind his cloth and pulls the slide. Again the shutter whirs. I hear his moan. "Ohmygawd. Who'd ever believe this?"

• • •

The four of us stand in the orange glow of the printing darkroom. Andy says she can stay out past ten. Culden says she doesn't give a shit. West developed the two sheets of film and we waited impatiently until they were dry enough to print. Now he slides one into the enlarger, focuses and we can see the negative image of the field hockey team appear on the easel.

"Eight by tens. That's all the paper I've got. What I wouldn't give for some bigger paper," he mutters. He adjusts the aperture and then sets the timer, turns the enlarger light off. Then he slips a sheet of paper into the easel and pushes the timer button.

We gather around the developing sink and watch the print rock back in forth in the tray. Slowly the image appears. I can feel Andy's breasts through the damp t-shirt against me as she holds my arm tightly. "Ohh, isn't that neat?" she whispers.

The print goes into the fixer tray and we wait for about a minute. Then Dicky Reb turns on the white lights and we can see the result. Big grins spread around our quartet as we witness the birth of *The Players*.

"Lordy, lordy," West says. "Now I know what little girls are made of."

Chapter 34

We Must Live In Interesting Times

"Did you say I've got a lot to learnnnn…" Andy croons into my ear as we slow dance under blue lights at the Pi Phi Sweetheart Ball. The local vocalist is pretty good — not quite Kay Starr — but her rendition of *Teach Me Tonight* has couples all over the floor gliding in slow embrace.

The Pi Phi Sweetheart dance is a far cry from our Queen Of Hearts Ball. Decorous almost, with very little drinking and almost no loud noises. Vodka sneaks into glasses from hidden flasks but only a couple of the sisters show any effects.

As the band plays *Good Night Sweetheart,* we take to the floor for one last dance. In a long velveteen cocktail dress, Andy is a picture of sophistication in blue. As we slide around the floor, she whispers, "Five, the seniors have five rooms booked at the Sunset Motel. They're going to party 'til dawn. We're going aren't we?"

I can feel her body tense as I hesitate. "Ah, no Andy. I can't. Much as I'd like to. But I've got to be back at the house by one thirty."

"One thirty! But we've all got overnights," she protests. "Why do you have to be in?"

"Our pledge class is going for a little walk tonight," I whisper. "And I have to be there."

"No you don't," she whispers. "You're not the pledge master." She squeezes my hand and pulls me tighter to her. "C'mon. It'll be fun and no one will miss you at the ole' Ace house."

"Andy… believe me. Please? I can't explain it. But I do have to be there."

The ride back from the Athens Country Club is quiet. We're in the back seat of someone else's car and although she snuggled against my arm when we got in, Andy hasn't said a word since she announced we're going back to the Pi Phi house instead of the motel.

On the porch of the Pi Phi house, Andy gives it one last try as she pulls out her key. "Come in for a little while, Five. It's only ten after one. Mother Exner's probably going out to party with some of her housemother buddies and we'll have the living room all to ourselves."

Her goodnight kiss has some cool reserve after I refuse.

"Andy. Please believe me. I wouldn't leave except that I *have to*. It's really important." She looks at me with doubt written on her face. "Maybe someday I can explain it. But right now I can't." I pause and look at her. A soft little smile appears. "So thanks again and I'm sorry if I ruined your evening." She leans up and kisses me again. "Good night, Andy."

• • •

I peer into the Keep before going up to change. The sweat party is well underway. The brothers hurl loud jeers my way for showing up in a tux. By the time I'm in jeans and a sweater, the pledges are pretty well worked over.

"Any of 'em drunk?" I ask Waller who's standing at the edge of the room.

"Not bad. That Zigler guy may have had a few too many. He's the one I'm keeping an eye on. Your little brother knows his stuff pretty good," he adds. I watch as Easton chants out his lore, even running through the Greek alphabet without a stumble.

Doak Phipps whistles a halt to the harassment and herds the pledges back upstairs. We follow along and shrug into our jackets. "Curtis is here," Kostic whispers. "Looks like he's got his car out there. All three of us if we can handle it. Just Waller and me if there's a fuss."

The pledges rush out of the living room looking scared and wild-eyed, searching for their jackets. I sidle up to Easton and slip a book of matches and a pack of Chesterfields into his jacket pocket. He looks up. I wink.

Outside, the brothers are herding hooded pledges into a car. Three to a car and then there's one left over. Pledge Don Zigler, the kid from Utah. Curtis walks over and gently takes the hooded pledge by the shoulders. "I'll take this one," he says to no one in general. Kostic nods and we move in.

"We'll ride along and keep you company," Kostic tells Curtis without mentioning names. Curtis looks startled, shakes his head no and starts to move Zigler toward the car. Kostic follows right along with Waller and me in the trail.

Curtis opens the back door and shoves Zigler into the car. I open the opposite door and get in the back seat. Waller follows Zigler in on the other side and Kostic slips into the front seat. I can see Curtis' eyes in the rearview mirror. They are angry eyes.

● ● ●

After forty minutes or so of winding around, we reach the rendezvous point on a gravel road between Albany and Shade. If the pledges head toward Albany, their walk home will be about twelve miles. By Shade, it'll be less than ten. Either way, the tiny towns will be locked up tight at two-thirty in the morning.

We get back into Curtis' car. He gets in and looks over at Kostic. "I'm planning to go out to the Thirty Three, brothers. Are you sure you don't want to ride back with someone else?"

"That's OK, Brother Curtis," Waller says in a soft voice. "You'll be going right by the house so dropping us off won't be out of your way." Curtis starts the car and we roar off down the gravel road toward Shade. Out the back windows, we can see car lights following, taillights leaving in the other direction.

"You always take pledges out by yourself, Curtis?" Kostic asks softly.

"What the fuck's that mean?" Curtis growls.

"Oh, just a thought. Nothing special. Just thought I'd ask." We ride back to Athens in silence.

● ● ●

It's nearly midnight Tuesday and I'm studying for a midterm in western civ. At least we've made it to the 1730's and I'm reading about stuff I can understand. French fur traders have just founded a place called St. Genevieve, the first permanent white settlement west of the Mississippi, when the phone chirps.

I have to search around for it since Waller and Kostic constantly hide it under something to keep our convenience a secret. It chirps again, from beneath Waller's dirty clothes.

"Hello, tower suite," I answer.

"Five? Is that you?"

"Darcy? What're you doing calling? Are you all right? Where are you?" *No one calls long distance unless someone is hurt or dead.*

"Yes, I'm all right," she giggles. "And I'm in Cincinnati. But I'd rather be there with you. What are you doing?"

"Studying. Boring stuff but has to be done. Why're you calling?"

"Oh Five, it's about Thanksgiving." My heart lurches. "The most exciting things are happening," she bubbles. "But I can't be here for Thanksgiving. That's why I thought I'd better call."

"Where are you going to be? Coming to Athens?"

"Oh no! I'm going with three other models, and a couple of agency people. We're going to New York City!"

"New York?" *All I know about New York is that it's big and it's at the very end of the B&O.* "That's really something!" I enthuse, hoping the false echo in my voice doesn't go over the wire.

"Oh yes. We've got a studio shoot and then, we'll get to see the Macy parade. And on Friday and Saturday, we're going to shoot on location. Isn't that great?"

"God yes, Darcy. It's really great." My false enthusiasm must squeeze through the phone wires.

"Aw Five, I am sorry," she says. "I want to see you also. In the worst way. But this is such a great chance. I just couldn't turn it down. Maybe Christmas?"

"Yeah, Darce. Maybe Christmas."

"OK. I'll send you a card. And get some real New York pizza. Save you a slice. Love you, Five. Gotta go now."

"Yep, Darce. Have a great trip. G'nite." I stare at the disconnected phone and realize one more line tying me to Darcy has been cast off.

As work progresses on *The Players,* Culden Ellis assumes her role as muse, conscience, and pain-in-the-ass nag. After our midnight session in the darkroom, my high-minded determination gave way to everyone's desire to have *just one* of the prints.

So Dicky West made a total of four; two from each negative. I work from my favorite pose, the one where Andy's raising her shirt, but Culden constantly brandishes her copy in helpful criticism. As is often the case, Dicky West sits astride a backward chair taking it all in. *A free movie with the world's weirdest cast.*

"Christ, Five. Don't draw her *that* way," Culden rants, examining the last of my preliminary pencil work. "You're making her tits look like grapefruit." The subject of her observation is one of the Braswell twins.

"Sorry Culden, but her tits *do* look like grapefruit. Look at the picture," I retort, waving my glossy print of the girls in her face.

"You're missing the goddamn point," she comes back. "What are you doing, creating a painting, or just copying a crummy photograph?" The creator of the crummy photograph clears his throat. "Sorry, Dicky Dove," Culden says. "Nothing personal."

She turns back to me. "But the point is, she will hate you for it, whichever she is, Tunder or Lightning, because I'm sure she doesn't think her breasts look like grapefruit." Little flecks of blue and silver latex paint fly off her lips as she shouts into my face.

I shrug. "OK, what do you suggest?"

"Here, look at this!" Culden shouts, raising her sweatshirt up to her chin. "Look at this breast. I'm sure as hell not one of those Norwegian babes but the lines are the same." Dicky Reb has his chair leaned up on its front feet and is in danger of collapsing onto the floor.

"Draw the curve. Feel the curve in your heart. Not just the

curve down but the curve up," Culden traces her finger across the contours of her pear-shaped breast. She grabs my hand. "Here, goddamnit. Feel for yourself. If you can't feel in your heart what you can feel with your fingers, then you fucking well ought to be painting houses."

With kneaded eraser, I turn to the canvas and begin the chore of rearranging one of the Braswell grapefruits. Once more, Culden has made a point in her own rather dramatic way.

"Culden honey?" Dicky Reb drawls. "Just what is it you're going to do when you graduate from this place."

"Shit babe, I don't know. Probably go to some elementary school and teach little kids to finger paint."

• • •

While I'm going forward with *The Players,* progress on the Ace homecoming float seems in reverse. The basic idea — *Roll Over Miami* — is not too bad. A big steamroller that moves forward over a flattened Miami football player. A manic bobcat will be at the wheel.

The animation is fairly simple but the concept is mired in boredom. I assign Waller *the dog robber* the task of coming up with a gimmick that will make the float a contender. It all comes together one afternoon in a pawn shop on North Court Street.

Waller proudly leads the Martian and me into the dim, cluttered store. The pawnbroker, a balding little man with a jeweler's loupe on his forehead, greets Waller like an old friend. After locking the front door, he leads us to a room in the back.

"There she is, brothers," Waller exclaims. "Chris, do you think you could play that?" A short dusty keyboard extends from the battered cabinet of a familiar-looking instrument.

"A calliope?" I ask. "You've found a calliope?"

"Actually a baby calliope," the pawnbroker interjects. "Just two octaves and very low steam pressure. I've had it for years."

The Martian's face lights up as he pushes the wide keys. "What's it run on, steam?"

"Yes," the pawnbroker answers. "A carnival went bust back before the war, the second war, and the fellow who owned the shebang sold everything on the spot. I picked up a few items but this little calliope's all that's left. You can have it for twenty-five bucks."

"If I can get an air compressor, can we try it out?" Waller asks.

"Sure," The pawnbroker grins, "but somewhere outside."

• • •

Once we figure out how it works, the calliope is an instant success, much to the chagrin of the Delt house and our other neighbors. The Martian pounds out traditional calliope classics such as *Over The Waves* and rattles windows with his rendition of *Rock Around The Clock.* The canine population of Athens county joins in the chorus.

The idea of a steamroller outfitted with a calliope catches on and we attack the float project with new enthusiasm. The float truck is moved to the Beasley-Matthews garage to start construction on the framework.

With Kostic, Waller, and a couple of pledges, we're trying to get the piece of linoleum that will be the Miami player to cooperate one evening when Culden bursts through the door.

"Jesus guys, get out here quick" she shouts. "Dicky's hurt." We run across the lot and up State Street following the sprinting girl. In the middle of the next block, we find Dicky Reb West sitting on the curb, clutching his shin. Blood streams from his scalp.

"You OK, Reb?" I ask. He looks up with a pained grin and nods yes. Kostic strips off his t-shirt and uses it to swab West's bleeding scalp.

"Some bastard tried to kill us," Culden says calmly. We look at West. He slowly nods assent.

"We'd just walked across from Congress Street, starting toward the garage," he says, wincing as I roll up the leg of his pants. "I heard a car but didn't see any lights, didn't think anything about it."

"Then there was this big thump," Culden adds. "I turned a little and out of the corner of my eye saw this car half up on the sidewalk, coming at us."

"What kind of car?" Waller asks.

"Shit, I don't know. It's dark and there weren't any lights. I pulled Dicky and jumped but the fucker somehow managed to hit him," she says breathlessly.

"Fender just grazed me," Dicky adds through clenched teeth. "On the shin. Hurts like a mother but I don't think anything's broken. I hit my head when I landed."

Except for a bruise on his shin and the scraped scalp, Dicky *doesn't* appear to be hurt and we walk slowly and silently toward the garage to call it a night. No one seems to want to ask the obvious question. Finally, I do. "Do you guys think it could've been Curtis?"

"Shit, I don't know," Dicky Reb groans. "And we can't call the cops. No description. No nothing."

"Maybe it was just some drunk miner trying to get home," Waller suggests.

"Yeah, maybe?" Kostic says, "but my money's on Curtis."

• • •

Someday when I'm an alumnus, I'll go to the Friday night bonfire and pep rally. But as usual, we're putting the finishing touches on the steamroller float. Brothers, pledges, girlfriends and dates are all helping with the chores that can't be done until the last minute; cutting paper, stuffing chicken wire, painting trim.

The Martian chafes that he can't rehearse with the calliope but in the confinement of the garage, we vote against this unanimously. Dawn Morgan and some of her sorority sisters gather around him, tucking and sewing the Bobcat costume he'll wear on the float in the morning.

Inside the float, Andy Logan holds the rope that pulls up the linoleum cutout of the Miami player. As the steam roller moves forward, the flat curls back to reveal the Redskin in all his agony. Culden paints wonderful comic-book tears flying from his eyes.

Somewhere near midnight, Waller cranks up the Reo and

circles slowly around the parking lot. The pledges inside make the roller turn realistically and move forward. The Miami player writhes in his flattened agony. Dressed in all but his Bobcat head, Chris Cobb tootles out *Over The Waves.* In the distance, a police siren adds to the howls of neighboring dogs.

"Call for Pater Gousha…" someone yells. We hurry the float back inside, turn off the lights, and head for the Tavern.

• • •

"She lost her honor at Miami…an Acer done her wrong…" we sing the parody of Miami's fight song as the Martian bangs out the tune on the calliope. We've lost our early position in the parade after Charlie Minelli, director of the OU band, complained that we were drowning out his musicians. Brother drum major D.D. Smith surreptitiously shoots his boss the finger and gives us the high sign.

But even bringing up the rear, everyone will remember *Roll Over Miami.* The Martian plays *Stand Up And Cheer, Love And Honor For Miami,* and the strangest version I've ever heard of *Green Door.* For once, I don't get a lump in my throat. Compressed air spurts dry ice clouds out of the calliope's pipes as realistically as steam ever would. The crowd gives us a great hand as we roll past.

• • •

We're still standing after the *National Anthem* and the OU band plays the opening chords of *Alma Mater, Ohio.* The choked emotions that I feel at the start of every football game return once more as I sing the corny words.

With three wins and two losses, the Bobcats are heavy underdogs against unbeaten Miami but we cheer wildly when they come on the field in their green pants, white jerseys and helmets. Behind the south end zone, the Martian hoots along on the calliope with *Stand Up And Cheer,* earning a nasty scowl from Bandmaster Minelli.

Miami takes the opening kickoff and the crowd groans as the

Redskin receiver breaks free and skirts the sideline. A white jersey shoves him out of bounds at our three yard line. The crowd stands as our defensive platoon takes the field. The Bear is matched up against Miami's all-conference tackle, a hulk who weighs three hundred thirty pounds.

I scream "Come on Bear, knock him on his fat ass!" It's one of those magical moments when my voice is the only noise in the hushed stadium. I sit down quickly, hoping mom, Captain and Sissie Eileen in the east stands didn't recognize my voice. A ripple of laughter rolls into a great cheer which the Bear acknowledges with a bob of his helmet.

Andy squeezes my arm and grins. "Five, I do believe you're blushing."

Miami runs a sweep right at him and the Bear throws himself beneath the stampede, helping push the Miami runner out of bounds for a yard loss. On the next play, the sweep comes at him again but this time it's a naked reverse and the Miami ball carrier skips into the end zone untouched. Miami seven. OU nothing.

Our offense runs three ineffective plays and punts away to the Redskins. But the defensive unit holds, with the Bear fighting mightily against the rotund Miami tackle. Late in the second quarter, Miami fair-catches a punt on their own fifteen.

On the first play from scrimmage, the quarterback throws a short pass to the flat and a big green arm reaches up to magically snatch the ball away. The Bear breaks for the goal line but is pulled down by a mob of red jerseys on the three. OU's offense can't punch it in and we settle for a field goal. Miami seven. OU three. We cheer madly as the Bobcats leave the field at the half.

$$\bullet \ \bullet \ \bullet$$

"And the winner… winner… winner… of the float competition is… the loudest float in the history of the university…" In the Ace block we jump to our feet and our cheer masks the PA announcement. "…pha Chi Epsilon!"

I race down the steps and hop across the wall that separates the stands from the field. Kostic already has the steamroller on the move with the Martian playing a wild version of *Aces High*. The Ace block cheers again when I accept the big trophy and wave it over my head. Then I run for the float, climbing on the front and riding a victory lap around the track.

Past the east stands, I wave the trophy and am tickled to see the Captain, mom and Sissie Eileen waving back.

• • •

The second half is a reprise of the first. Only Miami doesn't score again. OU doesn't threaten on offense and our punter helps the defense keep Miami in the hole.

Bear causes a Miami fumble late in the fourth quarter and OU recovers on the Miami nine.

"Poosh 'em back, poosh 'em back, poosh 'em back in the booshes," we roar as Wesley DeVon takes a hand-off, hurdles a Miami tackler and scoots across the green turf for the goal. A mass groan erupts as he's smacked flat on the two. DeVon staggers around and is led off the field between two trainers.

Another run into the line gains maybe a foot and the Bobcats face a third and goal. Another groan as a Miami defender snatches the attempted pass to Len Stolski away, then watches his sure touchdown interception slip through his fingers. Fourth and goal.

A cheer goes up when Wesley DeVon runs back on the field buckling his chin strap. Miami digs in. The Bobcats snap the ball and Stolski leaps at the rising Miami line. Our cheers hush for a second as the Redskin wall shoves him back but then pandemonium erupts as the officials signal a touchdown. DeVon has taken a direct snap and bootlegged the ball around the end undetected. We convert and lead the Redskins ten to seven.

Minutes later, the Bear and his buddies have stopped Miami one more time and October 29 goes down as one of the great victories in OU history.

• • •

I paint a big *10-7* on the front of the steamroller and we

follow the OU band up President Street toward the bridge. Chris Cobb has punched eye holes in the back of the Bobcat mask so he can wear his hat backward as well. One hundred plus band instruments and a single calliope make *Stand Up And Cheer* ring across the Hocking Valley.

Andy and I sit against the rolled up linoleum Redskin and ride in victory, waving and accepting congratulations from the marching throng. A mighty cheer comes from the ACE house as we cross the President Street bridge.

Beside us sit Dicky Reb and Culden Ellis, another surprise of the day, all cleaned up and dressed almost normally. Looking pretty good. However, I flinch when she flips a bird to someone in the crowd.

Mom, Captain and Sissie Eileen are standing on the bridge so Andy and I hop off the float and walk with them down the path past the Delt house. The Delts have won a second place in house decorations so they're getting a celebration started as well. In a green sweater and white skirt, Sissie Eileen carries our trophy as if she'd just won it as homecoming queen.

• • •

On the sun porch, the party is in full swing. Even Curtis breaks a scowl to grin and say congratulations. I break away from my parents, Professor and Mrs. Logan, and Andy to walk over to Mayhew, who's leaning against a wall in deep conversation with my little sister.

He turns when I tap him on the shoulder. "Watch yourself there, Brother Mayhew. She's only fifteen and she's my little sister. And the big guy over there is our father." Mayhew turns gray and Sissie Eileen gives me her dirtiest look.

I walk everyone over to Begorra for a dinner surprise. At my request, Duff has re-hung *Light Show* in the diner so that the Captain can see it for himself. Thankfully, Duff refrains from asking me if I've heard from Darcy. Captain studies the painting over his coffee cup for a long time, then turns to me and winks. Then the Lowreys and Logans pile into the family cars and go out to the Sportsman for dinner.

• • •

Captain and mom surprise me at the homecoming dance by tearing up the floor. "I wouldn't miss it for anything," mom said when she heard Woody Herman and the Herd was the band.

"Holy shit, Five, look at the old folks dance!" Sissie Eileen elbows me as they swing and twirl to *Big Noise From Winnetka.* "Mom taught me to dance but not *like that!*" Still in her sweater and skirt, Eileen, as she's told us she'll now be called, is underdressed but still gets several offers to dance.

Soaked, Andy and I stroll off the floor after *Shaker Heights Stomp* and join our crowd. Captain grasps my hand and gives me a hug. "Five. It's time for us to head on down the road. But we've had a great time."

"Oh, Captain Lowrey," Andy says. "You've got to stay until intermission and see Five get his trophy once again."

"And I've got to dance with the Bear," Eileen chimes in. "He just got here with Page and said he'd give me the second dance. After he dances one with Page."

• • •

I keep from making an ass of myself, falling down, or otherwise embarrassing my family at intermission. Now we're back at the courtyard of the ACE house saying goodnight to the rest of the Lowrey clan. Mom gives me a big hug and whispers, "Thanks so much, Five. It's been one terrific day. And I like Andy a lot. She's a really nice person." She grins and whispers "I think she's even taken Captain's mind off of Darcy."

Captain has his arms around Andy and Eileen who's still clutching the trophy. "You take care of this girl now son. She's a keeper." He winks again. I've never noticed my father's lewd wink before.

"And can I come up pretty soon and stay over in the Pi Phi house?" Eileen asks Andy as she gives her a good-bye hug.

"Sure you can, Eileen. We'll have a pledge pin on you before you know it."

· · ·

In the Keep the Martian and Four Aces are wailing away, helped by several inebriated but talented alumni musicians. One floor down, Andy and I sit with our feet on the railing of the sun porch. Beside us, Culden and the Rebel are in a similar pose.

"I didn't realize you fraternity guys had so much fun," Culden says in general. "Shit, if I'd known this, I would've joined a fraternity a long time ago."

"Culden, honey. You cannot join a fraternity. You're the wrong sex," Dicky Reb chides jokingly.

"Aw Dicky Dove, I think I'm just the *right sex* to join a fraternity, don't you Andy?"

Andy giggles. "I don't think I want to touch that one, Culden. But I have a feeling if you did, the pledge period would be pretty easy."

Culden's feet suddenly fly up in the air and she's on her back, exposing most of her charms. Someone has pulled her chair out from beneath her.

"If it isn't the slut with the little ice pick," Curtis slurs. Mayhew leers over his shoulder. Dicky Reb leaps out of his chair and smashes his fist across Curtis' jaw. The vet staggers back and falls. Someone in the crowd screams.

I'm on my feet and have my arms around Curtis as he tries to get up. "Easy Curtis. Do you always have to be the asshole in a crowd?"

"Fuck off, you artist queer," he growls. But he's too drunk to break out of my grasp.

I turn to Mayhew. "Get this drunken prick out of here right now. I'm sick and tired of him ruining every good time we have in this house." Mayhew nods and takes Curtis by the arm, dragging him through the parting crowd. Boo's and hisses follow them out.

Culden is dusting herself off. "Jesus Christ," she mutters. "I think I've changed my mind about joining a fraternity. If I want to meet guys like that, I'll join the fuckin' foreign legion.

Chapter 35

For Some Of These Things, We Give Thanks

The interval between homecoming and Thanksgiving break is a blur of activities. Studying for mid-terms. Working on *The Players* for mid-term review. A couple of dispirited parties at the Ace house but no more run-ins with Curtis. The Bobcats continue their winning ways on the football field, running their record to six and three for the last game of the season.

It snows the night before the game. Big fluffy flakes that wrap Athens in a soft white blanket. On Saturday morning, WOUB puts out a call for all students to gather at Ohio Stadium to help clear the field.

We go down as a group, brothers and dates, to roll huge balls of snow to the sidelines. At one thirty, the public address system booms another call for help and the student side empties as hundreds of us go down to roll snowballs.

All to no avail. Marshall's Thundering Herd scores once in each quarter and holds the Bobcats scoreless. OU finishes its season with a respectable six and four but the parade through the snow up President Street is damp and cold.

• • •

Thanksgiving break begins at noon on Wednesday the twenty-third but many students risk careful roll-taking and skip their last classes for an early start home. Among them are Dicky Reb West who is spending the weekend with Kostic at his folks' house in Portsmouth.

After my Wednesday morning English class, I walk over to the studio to work on the painting. Professor Logan has scheduled a studio visit for after Thanksgiving to review my progress. But I need to have it finished by then, not for the grade, but to hang in the Faculty-Student Show.

My key works in the studio lock but the door won't budge. I try shoving it but no luck. Then I pound on the door with my fist. "Culden? Are you in there?" I can hear the noise of movement inside the studio. Then something moves behind the door and Culden peers out, looking like death warmed over.

"Ohh, Five. Thank God it's you," she says. As I enter, I can see she's had a chair propped against the door handle.

"What's wrong, Culden? Why the barricade?"

"Five. I was scared. Too scared to go out. So I stayed here."

"What do you mean, stayed here? Since when?"

Tears roll down her cheeks as she plops onto a chair. "Since last night. I finally fell asleep sometime this morning."

I put my arm around her quivering shoulders. "You slept all night here? Why in God's name?"

"Ohh man. I was just scared shitless. Someone jumped me out there last night."

"What do you mean, jumped you?"

"Well, Dicky Reb and Benjo had just stopped by the dorm last night to say good-bye. Then I decided to come over here to work. About nine o'clock," she chokes back the sobs.

"In that courtyard back there. I'd just walked down the steps... then someone jumped out and pulled that over my head." Culden points to a black cloth lying in the corner. It's a familiar looking black cloth. I step over and pick up the hood with its drawstring.

"He dragged me over by the dumpster, I guess," she cries, "and pushed me down... down on my knees." Her shoulders are shaking. Sitting on the chair beside her, I hold her tightly in my arms.

"Then he pulled that thing up," she nods toward the hood, "and tried to make me..." tears, sobs and shaking increase, "make me, suck him!"

"Jesus, Culden!"

Through the tears she looks up and gives me a very Culden-like grin. "I tried to bite him. Bite the bastard's cock off. But he hit me across the head. And when he did, I slipped." She pauses for a breath. "I grabbed out and got his chest with one hand.

"Then I grabbed his balls. And twisted for all I was worth."

Tears, mucus, streaks of paint cover Culden's face as she cries and smiles at the memory.

"Five, I wanted to tear his balls off. I mean it. Just rip 'em right off. But he screamed and pulled away. I could hear him running across the bricks. Jesus! You shoulda heard him scream."

"Then what happened?" I ask, holding her trembling body tightly.

"I snatched that bag thing off my head and ran in here. I didn't see anyone. So I unlocked the door and then locked myself in."

"Later, I heard noises outside the window but I didn't see anyone," she says. "But I was too afraid to go outside and go home. So I propped a chair against the door and sat here in the dark. Then I laid down and I guess I finally went to sleep."

She buries her head in my chest but the tears have eased a bit. "Oh Five. I was so scared." She looks up at me again. "But I almost got the sonofabitch's nuts. And I did get... this."

Culden opens a fist to reveal an ACE badge. "I must've torn it off his chest when I pushed him away."

With two fingers, I take the badge from her palm and turn it so I can see its reverse side. The engraving is tiny but clear.

"G. Curtis. 726. 4-53"

• • •

In the toilet, I use a wet towel to wash Culden's face. She has a green bruise on her temple but otherwise, she seems unharmed. In the studio, she rummages for a hairbrush and runs it through her tangled strands.

"Culden. You've got to go to the police. I mean we know who it was that tried to rape you," I insist.

She just smiles wanly, looking as if she might burst into tears again. "Bullshit, Five. Do you have any idea what the campus cops would say if I came in and said I'd been raped? I mean, *that's* got to be more humiliating than the act itself."

"But we know who it is!" I feel like screaming.

"Yeah! And what would an asshole like that tell the cops? He was out with his buddies from the Wonder Bar and five of 'em would back him up." Culden pauses and sniffs. "Besides, it wasn't even really rape. I mean, he didn't even get his ugly little dick in my mouth. And he's hurtin' a lot more than I am this morning."

"Damnit Culden, that's beside the point."

"No it isn't Five. I'm not going to the police. That's it." Her tears are gone now and her lips are white with determination. "We have this," she says, holding the ACE badge. "And somehow, I'll find a way to use it on the cocksucker."

"OK, Culden. Maybe you're right. But I want you to hold onto the badge. Hide it somewhere safe. We will find a way to use it against him. And cocksucker is the appropriate term, believe me."

"You guys... Benjo, Sarge, Dicky Reb, you... you've got something going with this guy. Don't you?" I nod yes but don't say a word. "Well, I want in. Whatever it is, I want to be a part of it."

• • •

Culden refuses my offer of breakfast at Quick's so I walk her back to her dorm. She leans up and hugs me and kisses me firmly, right on the steps of Boyd Hall in broad daylight.

"Thanks a million, Five. I'll see you next week. Some kids from Zanesville are picking me up in a little while to go home. And I'll be OK." I rub my finger across the corners of her eyes.

"You'll be OK, Culden. I know damn well you will. Happy Thanksgiving."

• • •

I've heard the word *despondent* before but never known the true feeling of the word until now. The ACE house is nearly empty and the kitchen is closed so I walk over to Begorra. Duff's behind the counter by himself.

"You're looking pretty low, Low-ree," he quips his favorite play on my name. "Missing your girlfriend?"

"That's just one of many things, Duff," I say, chewing on my third Begorra burger. "Every time a B&O eastbound goes through, I wonder if Darcy's on it with her model buddies and her agency friends."

"Well, Five, I've known Darcy for a long time and she's always been kind of a heartbreaker." He looks up at the painting. "I mean, she breaks guys' hearts every day when they come in here at look at *Light Show*. And she's a tough little girl. She'll get what she wants."

"I know that, Duff. I don't begrudge her doing well for herself. God knows she's had some pretty hard stuff dealt to her. It just hurts to be standing by the tracks as she whizzes by."

"But she's a loyal kid, Five," he says earnestly. "Whatever she's felt for you, she'll always feel. Regardless of new boyfriends... or new lovers." He gives me a sympathetic look. "But knowing Darcy, maybe it's best to be standing by the tracks instead of getting run over by the train."

• • •

I put on my best face for Thanksgiving because I'm not going home. Just out to Townsend Avenue where the Logans have invited the Lowreys for Thanksgiving dinner. It'll just be mom and Eileen driving up from Hockingport since Captain's on the river somewhere once again in command of the *Point Princess*.

And our Thanksgiving *is* festive. A big turkey dinner with oyster and chestnut dressing, mashed potatoes and giblet gravy. Right out of Norman Rockwell. Even though I've been to the Logans' before, I keep my eyes peeled and discover a number of paintings and sketches with the nude Mrs. Logan as the model. *Good grief! She was a honey!*

After dinner, Andy takes Eileen uptown to show her the Pi Phi house. Mom and Mrs. Logan move to the kitchen to clean up the mess while Professor Logan and I settle down to watch the Lions play the Packers on television.

"Andrea's told me some about your project for advanced painting, Five," Dr. Logan says calmly. "It sounds quite interesting."

"Ahh, exactly *how much* has she told you, Professor?"

"Ohhh," he pauses, "that it's a sporting portrait. And that she's one of the models."

"Oh?" I respond.

"That she's ah, in a state of dishabille, shall we say."

Dees-ha-beel?

He leans back and smiles. "Ah well, the sporting motif's very respected. Eakins, one of our most noted American portraitists, is actually best remembered for his sporting works."

"Friday Night At Sharkey's!" My God, I'm exchanging artistic chit-chat with the chairman of the department!

Logan smiles. "Actually, I think it's Saturday, but… that's very good, Five. Of course, Eakins did get into some contretemps with his students and his models." This is a part of art appreciation I didn't hear.

"But as I've told Andrea many times, she's a grown woman and capable of making her own decisions."

"Well professor, you'll get to see it next week. And if you feel that it will bring an embarrassment to…"

"Nonsense, Five. I'm sure Andy wouldn't do anything like a Varga or Petty calendar and I'm confident of your skills and judgment. Besides, when Michelle and I were students at the Art League of Chicago, posing for one's lover or friend was quite common. Of course, that's from an old dog who remembers those years with fondness."

He's on a roll and I'm happy to listen to him reminisce. "When I first came here in the thirties, they still taught the first four weeks of figure drawing using plaster casts. Imagine! Right out the last century. Thank God this is a more enlightened university today."

• • •

Later that afternoon mom and Eileen leave for Hockingport. Andy drops me off at the ACE house and continues on her way to a Pi Phi alumnae Thanksgiving party where they'll take baskets of food to needy families. I'm surprised to find Sarge Waller in our room.

"Hey Five, thought you'd be down on the river burping

466

turkey right now."

"Same to you. No, we were invited to Logans.' It was great. But what're you doing here?"

"Aw, Dad had a bunch of those ROTC folks in. I find it pretty hard to take, especially knowing it galls him so to be socializing with enlisted personnel these days."

"Really? I've met your father, you know. He seems like a great guy to me." I relate to him how Sgt. Waller helped me escape the clutches of ROTC and the drill field.

"That's dad, all right. I think he hates ROTC as much as he loves the Army."

"Not quite changing the subject," I say, "but our old army buddy Curtis has taken *that one* step too far."

"What do you mean?" Sarge asks, looking up at me with new intensity.

So I tell him of Culden's experience at the Fine Arts Building, about her twisting her assailant's genitals, and the trophy of Curtis' ACE badge.

"You're sure it's his? No doubt about it?" Waller has a pained grimace.

"G. Curtis. 726. 4-53" I read from my note. "Plain as day. Wrote it down and told Culden to put the badge in a safe place."

"Well shit, that about cuts it. Doesn't it?" Sarge whacks his fist into his other hand. "I'd love to get a look at Curtis' balls right now."

"I'd love to see 'em on the floor," I reply, "right here. With Curtis somewhere far away."

"Yeah! Listen, Benjo and Dicky Reb'll be back from Portsmouth about four Sunday afternoon. You're going to be here all weekend?" I nod yes. "Then get the rest of the Thirteen the word. We need to have a meeting Sunday night."

"Right. We've got to do something. I have the feeling Ransom's ghost may be getting impatient."

• • •

Saturday is gray and rainy. Wisps of fog or clouds float through the trees. This is Athens at its most gloomy, especially with the campus empty of people. After a toasted roll and coffee at Quick's, I go to the studio and spend the morning working on *The Players.*

Once more I have that feeling of completion mixed with the urge to do more. I add highlights onto hard edges, then use grays to tone them down. The seven figures look exhausted but exulted in their pose of *dishabille.* I'm happy with the way I've captured Andy's quizzical expression as she lifts the shirt toward her head.

The Braswells are monuments to feminine beauty although Lightning's breast peeking through her torn shirt still has a certain grapefruit quality. I'm having trouble with shading and *my soul* is having problems with what my fingertips haven't encountered. *Thanks a lot, Culden.*

The setting itself is one of gloom. Dark walls, almost mossy green, make the backdrop. The girls who weren't such enthusiastic models hover in shadows just lighter than the walls. Banners of light angle from above to illumine the central figures. A dirty skylight, perhaps.

Wherever these women change for their hockey match, it's not a plush locker room.

• • •

When I return to my room late in the afternoon, it's almost dark. I call Andy's house but no one answers. So I settle into my bunk with the reading light on and open a worn copy of poems and short stories by the beatniks. Allen Ginsberg's *Howl* and an essay by a guy named Kerouac are pretty weird. But the stuff serves to keep my mind off the other subjects I find so morose: Curtis, Culden, Darcy.

I must have dozed because I jump at the soft knock on the door jamb. There in the open door is Andy, dressed in jeans and a sweatshirt under a yellow slicker like little girls wear to school.

"Hey," she says. "Want some company? I've driven by here three or four times today and finally saw your light on and…"

"Company! What a great idea!" I smile. Before I can

scrunch out of the lower bunk, Andy tosses her slicker on the floor, kicks off her shoes and squeezes in beside me.

"This is cozy, Five. Mmm. You smell like spirit gum. How come you've never invited me up to your room before?"

"Ah, I didn't exactly invite you up this time," I answer softly as she snuggles under my arm, "but I'm glad you're here."

She picks up my book, "Whatcha reading?" She riffles the pages, looks at the cover. "Ohh, weird. Y'know, I think it would be fun to be a beatnik. Never take a bath. Never shave your legs."

"Andy, I don't shave *my* legs." She giggles and punches me with a soft fist. The punch turns into an embrace and we kiss long and hard.

"Five," she murmurs, "why won't you paint me?"

"Well," I look up at the springs of Kostic's bunk above me, "a wise artist told me that it's not a good idea for an artist to get, ah, involved with his model." She gives me a puzzled look. "He told me about Thomas Eakins. You remember Eakins?"

"Dad talked to you?" she says in an amazed tone. "He's nutty about that old homo Eakins." The word *homo* is like an icicle across my heart. "Dad told you that you shouldn't let me pose for you?"

"Ahh, not exactly, Andy. But…" I have a painful lump in my throat and tears threaten to brim over. *Culden. Curtis. Darcy.* My Thanksgiving ghosts have come back into my warm room.

"What's the matter, Five?" Andy runs her finger across the corner of my eye and looks at the tear it wipes away. "What's bothering you?"

"Andy. I can't really talk about it. It's well, it's something I *can't* talk about."

"If it's Darcy," she says in a soft voice, "I know about your Thanksgiving trip being washed out and all. Sarge and Benjo told me. Don't be mad at them, though. Please?"

"Naw, it's not just Darcy." *Please God. If I can't talk to this girl, who can I talk to?* "It's more than that. Darcy's the least important of my worries."

Andy's lips are soft on my cheek. "You can tell me, Five, if you want to. Maybe it'll do some good to share it with someone

469

else."

And so I do. Everything!

• • •

Now I'm snuggled against Andy's chest and she softly runs her hand across my hair. I can feel her heart pounding.

"Five, it's just awful. And you can't really prove anything except that he tried to rape Culden?"

"Right! And Culden won't go to the police."

"Well, I can understand that, but still. Ohh, poor Culden. But what are you going to do?"

I take a deep breath. I do feel relief at having told the tale of Curtis to this gentle girl. But I still don't know what to do.

"I don't know Andy. We're going to have a meeting. The Thirteen. All twelve of us. And we're going to do something."

We huddle there in my bunk as gray afternoon turns to black evening. The rain and mist outside the window throw the nearby streetlight into crazy patterns across the glass. Andy has turned off my bunk light.

"Five? If you had to make a choice?"

"A choice?"

"Yeah. If you had to make a choice between painting a person you really like or sleeping with her, what would you choose?"

"Jesus, Andy. That's some choice. It's something I'll have to think about."

"OK," she says in a small voice. "You think about it."

Minutes of silence pass. We just lie there comfortable in each other's warmth, listening to the rain spit against the window.

"Andy, have you got your mom's car?"

"Yeah. The folks think I'm staying at the Pi Phi house tonight."

"Can we take a ride? I'll buy the gas."

"Pretty awful night for a ride, but sure. Don't worry about gas either."

"Well then, I'll buy us some dinner out at the Linger Longer.

How does that sound?"

"God Five, that's wonderful! I haven't been to the Linger Longer since high school."

• • •

In the little diner we eat spaghetti and deep-fried rolls. A scrumptious, fattening dinner that sets me back nearly four bucks.

"Do you know where The Sharpsburg Hell is?" I ask her.

"Sure! We rode by it in the school bus once when our chorus went up to Marietta. What an awful road. Everyone was sick by the time we got there. Why?"

"Well, I'd like to drive out and take a look at The Sharpsburg Hell. If you're willing."

• • •

Steam and smoke pour out of the fissures, which crackle and pop as the icy raindrops hit the open flames. We've parked at the top of the hills and walked down the dirt road among the cracks in the earth. They glow brightly even in the hazy rain.

"God, it's beautiful," Andy whispers. She clutches my hand tightly as we look into the hollow filled with orange cracks and red smoking puddles. "And it's awful, too!"

"Yep, they named it right. C'mon. I want to go this way. I shine the beam of the flashlight I pilfered from Sarge's drawer to light our way down the trail. We climb a short rise and discover another vista of glowing cracks, smoldering coal burning for eternity.

"Are you looking for something, Five?"

"Yes. In a way. I'm looking for something." I pause and put my arm around her waist. "I'm not exactly sure what but I think I've found it."

• • •

I drive leisurely with one hand, the other arm around Andy's shoulder. She's snugged up against me. The drizzle has let up. We both smell of smoke and sulfur.

As we turn onto Court Street, I look down at her face smiling at mine. She has a smudge on her chin.

"Andy? You know that choice you asked me about?"

"Yes Five. I remember."

"Well... I've made my choice. I'm not going to paint you." She wriggles closer to me.

"OK then," she says in a low, matter-of-fact voice, "we'll just park this car somewhere near the train station. Mother Exner will think I stayed at home. And we'll walk up to your room from there."

Chapter 36

The Fires Of Acerbus

One by one the brothers of the Thirteen file into the East Green Cafeteria at midnight. The Martian has conned the cooks into letting us use the kitchen where he has coffee brewed. We sit around the long, familiar table, smoking and waiting for everyone to arrive.

Dicky Reb West is the last to arrive, his arm wrapped tightly around Culden's shoulders.

"What's she doing here?" Chet Husted asks.

"She has every right and reason to be here," I say firmly, "as you'll find out in a few minutes."

With everyone seated with coffee and cigarettes, Benjo Kostic takes over. "Something new has happened with Curtis," he says softly. "And it's just about as serious as anything else so far." He pauses to look at the tight-lipped Culden. "Culden here is going to tell us the story and I, for one, think she's a very brave woman to do so."

Quietly, calmly, Culden relates the attack by Curtis at the Fine Arts Building. She tells it in the same detail that I heard that Wednesday morning when she was near hysterics. Twelve solemn faces watch her solemnly as she speaks. When she finishes, she leans back against Dicky West's chest and wipes her hand across her face.

"Sonofabitch!" Kostic screams as he crashes his fist against the table.

"Listen up," I get their attention. "Culden does not want to take this to the police and I don't blame her. It's just another case of her word against Curtis' and you can bet he'll have guys who'll say they were with him, drinking somewhere."

"So what do we do, Five?" Soos Salazar asks.

"We either make him confess. Confess so it'll stand up in court. Confess to everything. Or we do something else," I say as

473

ominously as I can.

"If you guys will hold him, I'll cut his nuts off," Culden volunteers with a grim smile. I can almost hear twelve scrotums shriveling around the table. I hold my hand up for attention.

"I've been thinking about this one hell of a lot. Listen and tell me what you think of this as a plan…"

After I outline my thoughts, the faces around the table show grim resolve.

Waller speaks up. "I've been there. I think it'll work."

"But we've got to pull it off without a hitch," Kostic says. "Even better than the ride we took him on. Everyone has to do his job. Right?" Heads nod.

As we leave, Culden takes my arm. "Five. Please don't ever get angry with me. Because you can be one evil-minded, scary sonofabitch."

• • •

On Tuesday before Pearl Harbor Day, Professor Logan appears at the studio door. Culden butts her cigarette and starts to leave.

"No, stay here Culden," I say, "if that's OK with you Professor Logan? Culden's played a big role in my getting this painting finished."

"Fine by me, Five," he says. "So let's see the work."

Without any drama, I pull the muslin drape off the now-dry canvas of *The Players*, watching Logan's face for any sign of reaction. There is none. *God, I'll bet this guy's a whale of a poker player!* He stands there, hands folded in front of him, looking at the painting. The image of his daughter, all but the nipples of her breasts showing, looks out at him from the greenish gloom. So do the likenesses of the remarkable Braswells and the stunning nakedness of Annalise Hechter, brazenly proud of holding nothing but a hockey stick.

"Hmmm," Logan makes a sound in his throat. He steps closer to examine the brush work… or his daughter's exposed charms? "That's quite a painting." *Now there's a commitment, I think.*

"Where is this place, Five?" he asks, never moving his eyes from the canvas.

"It's in my head, Professor Logan. I guess it's a fantasy locker room."

"But these young women have posed, haven't they? I mean, you didn't get them all in here?" He glances around at our cell-like studio.

His eyebrows shoot up in reaction when I say, "I, uh, painted it from a photograph."

"A photograph? My word!"

"The negatives have been destroyed, Professor Logan. Culden was there when the photographer cut them into little pieces." Culden nods affirmation.

"And these young women? They all posed willingly?"

"Yes sir," I respond.

"It was really their idea, Doctor Logan," Culden interjects her first statement. "Really!"

"And *they are* students? Right?"

"Yes sir," I respond. *Am I in trouble?* "They're all members of the field hockey club."

"Quite remarkable specimens," he muses. *Specimens? We're in a biology lab, looking through a microscope?* "These two," he nods toward the canvas, "they must be the Braswell twins Andrea's spoken of?"

"Yes sir." *With tits like grapefruit.* Culden grins as if reading my mind.

"And this little woman?" This time he extends a finger at Annalise. "She has a certain... quality." For the first time I breath easier as a smile cracks his face. "I'm not sure I would care to meet up with her under the, ah, *wrong* circumstances." He grins broadly. Culden does as well. I just stand there.

"It's quite a painting, Five. You may get some heat from the Dean, perhaps. But I have a certain amount of pull with the show committee. In my opinion, this painting should hang." I let a long sigh of relief escape my lips. "Get it framed and matted, Five. It will not only hang, but I have an idea it might sell as well."

Without further words, he turns and opens the studio door.

475

There in the hall stands Andy, a sheepish, anxious grin on her face. "Well dad?"

"Quite remarkable, Andrea. Quite remarkable, indeed."

• • •

The Saturday night reception for the Faculty-Student Show is another extremely civilized event. Andy has pressured her father to let us invite the six other models. Tunder and Lightning attract a lot of attention in white cocktail dresses that could barely hold at least four grapefruit.

Annalise has on some Danish creation, burgundy velvet scooped deeply in the front. Many of the taller men in the crowd make an effort to converse with the short hockey player. '*I never wear a brassiere' comes to mind.*

Andy and I are talking with Jackie Guswaite who seems in total awe at seeing her image on the wall. "It's fantastic, Five. Oh, I want a copy for myself."

"It's a painting, Jackie. Five can't just whack out copies like a…" Andy pauses, "like a photograph." She grins at me. "But someone will want to buy it, I'll bet anything."

A touch at my arm alerts me to another presence in our group. I turn to look directly into the face of the Dean, holding a martini and smiling his wonderful executioner's smile.

"Well, Mister Lowrey. We meet again."

"Good evening, Dean. Do you know these ladies? Miss Logan. Miss Guswaite." The dean acknowledges them and returns his attention to me.

"Professor Logan assures me that your, ah, work here, ah, possesses every integrity that is required in art." His smile is truly terrible.

"Dean Fundt," Andy says in her most charming rush voice, "you know the old saying 'art is in the eyes of the beholder,' don't you?"

"Yes Miss Logan. I've heard that adage. And I don't dispute the value of this piece. I find it quite charming, myself." *Tons of lead leave my shoulders.*

"Other members of the university community may not, of

course. But then, that's what a university is, correct? A community of opinions all in search of the truth?"

I smile blandly at the Dean. *If only you knew of our search for the truth, Dean. If only you knew.*

"And Miss Logan, I've been honored at seeing likenesses of your mother in your very own home. I must say, you share her grace and beauty." Leaving Andy standing slack-jawed, he smiles and moves off to another knot of conversationalists.

Tunder and Lightning Braswell sandwich me and shower me with kisses. "Ah, Five. It's wonderful. You *will* want to paint me again?" one of them asks.

"Us," the other Braswell interrupts. "Not one but two. Or none at all."

"We'll see ladies," Andy says with a sly smile. "I'm not sure I want you two alone with my buddy here."

As we leave the party, Andy takes my arm and guides me back by *The Players* one more time. "Look," she says. There, on the corner of the frame, is a tiny orange *Sold* sticker.

• • •

Saturday it snows and on that evening, the Aces and their dates go caroling. Other groups are out as well and the streets of Athens ring with Christmas songs. Halos of candlelight mark the passage of each group.

Back at the house the mood continues. Doak Phipps plays Santa Claus and hands out mostly joke gifts to brothers and their dates. My gift to Andy is an envelope full of tiny shards of black and white emulsion; the negatives that cause Dicky West to burst into tears every time he thinks about them.

My real gift to Andy is a lavaliere on a fine gold chain. "Will you wear this Andy? If I really give it to you?"

"Oh, Five. It's lovely." She holds the chain on her fingertips to let the tiny ACE Greek letters sparkle in the candlelight. "Of course I will." She leans up on tiptoes and we kiss.

"Merry Christmas, Andy."

"Merry Christmas, Five. And…" she bites my earlobe, "does this mean you'll paint me now?"

After Monday's chapter meeting, we convene again at midnight in the cafeteria to go over the plan once more.

Everyone recites his assignment quietly. Kostic checks a list in his small notebook. I've seen it and it's written in a mysterious code. Pirate Simpson, who plans to go to med school, proudly displays a pint of vodka.

"Schmirnoff. Hundred proof. My girl thought Midol would do the job but I was afraid they'd color it blue. So I've dissolved four Phenobarbitals in it. Looks pretty good, doesn't it?" Indeed, the bottle looks as clear as... vodka."

"That won't knock him out? Or kill him?" Soos Salazar asks.

"How I wish," Culden mutters.

"Naw. I don't think so. We won't let him drink the whole thing. Don't want him totally smashed," Simpson laughs. "By my reckoning, four of these babies will just keep him woozy and out to lunch."

Chet Husted, the broadcasting major, gives his report. "There's this Nagra tape recorder at WOUB. No one ever uses it so I think I can sneak it out without anyone noticing. It's a little brute but I've got to buy some batteries for it tomorrow. They're expensive." We nod approval.

"How about you, Brother Able?" Kostic asks.

A.A. smiles. "I'll have the stuff. Tried out a couple at the lab today and they should work." The mad chemist looks at me. "Did your buddy come through with that aluminum shot, Five?" I nod. The Bear has donated a small bag of the stuff he used to shovel into the open hearths.

"I got the key to the regalia room. No problem with the clothing," McClintock adds.

"Reb? You'll sneak Culden into the house by the courtyard door. Right?" Kostic checks.

Dicky Reb nods yes. "And up the passage stairs to your room. Think eleven o'clock is early enough."

"Yeah. Should be. He's never left the Wonder Bar before

midnight on a Tuesday before. How about you, Culden? Your job is probably the toughest," Kostic comments.

We all look at my studio-mate. She smiles and nods her head. "But are you guys sure I can't bring my straight razor?"

• • •

Kostic, Waller, Dicky Reb West, Culden and I sit quietly in the tower suite and watch the clock move slowly from Tuesday into Wednesday. It's nearly one o'clock before the phone chirps. I pick up the handset.

"He's home," Perry Shivers says quietly. "Just pulled in to his apartment. By himself, too."

"OK," I respond. "Let's set it for one thirty. Make sure everyone's in his place." I turn to Culden. "Ready Culden, honey?" She slowly nods. "Here's the number."

Culden slowly dials Curtis' number and waits while it rings. Once. Twice. Three times. Then she smiles.

"Hello! Is this Galen Curtis?

"Oh good. This is Culden Ellis. Do you remember me?" She looks intense as the holds the set to her ear.

"Yeah, that's me. Listen, I've been thinking and… well." Her expression is exasperated. Curtis is obviously talking.

"Uh huh. Yeah. Well, I do have something of yours that I thought you might like to have back and…" Another pause and *oh my God* expression.

"Well, perhaps? Yeah. I'd be willing to talk about it…

"Yeah? Why not right now? I can sneak out of the dorm." She grins and nods yes with enthusiasm.

"Uh huh. Yeah, I'll think about that too. Why don't you meet me at the east door of Boyd Hall? You know where that is?" Another pause.

"Well of course. Come by yourself, though. I don't want to meet any of your friends.

"OK. How about one thirty? It's one now. Yeah. That's good. I'll see you."

She hangs the handset up and grabs Dicky West in a hug.

"Can you believe this fucking idiot?" she asks. "He actually

479

thinks I want to finish what he started?"

• • •

Kostic and I crouch beside a sloping brick wall in the courtyard at the east end of Boyd Hall, a brick women's dorm on Park Place. Benjo has unscrewed the bulb over the exit door where Culden waits in darkness, not ten feet away. Over by the Fine Arts Building, Soos Salazar hides near a big tree to warn us in case a suspicious Curtis arrives by foot.

Benjo nudges me and whispers, "One more time. You be quick with the hood. And I tap him one. Just get your arm out of the way quickly or you won't feel anything with it 'til morning." I was amazed when the veteran produced a homemade blackjack... a sock filled with bird shot.

A shrill whistle echoes across the campus. It has to be one of the lookouts signaling Curtis' car has come past. I see Culden's shadowy form stiffen at the sound. Then Curtis' car appears on Park Place, only its parking lights showing. We're at the jumping off place. So many things can go wrong. But we can't go backward.

A single figure leaves the parked car and moves slowly up the walkway toward the east side of the dorm. Culden stands there calmly.

"Culden? Where are you?" Curtis hisses.

"Here!" her whisper sounds like a gun shot. She moves slightly away from the door so she's facing our direction. Curtis walks confidently up to her.

"So! You decided you'd like a little taste of what I offered you after all? And you like to play rough, huh?" Culden stays silent, looking into his face. Benjo touches my hand and we move forward. One step. Two. Three!

I slide the hood over his head and my left hand over his mouth. Benjo Kostic whacks Curtis on the temple with the shot-filled sock. His only sound is a muffled *whompf* but I have to hang on for dear life as he jerks forward violently. Culden has kicked him in the groin!

Soos arrives and takes the keys to Curtis' car from Kostic

who's rifling the prone form on the ground. "See you at the depot," he hisses to Soos who hurries off.

I produce black electrical tape and bind Curtis' hands in front of him and tape them to his belt. As Kostic and I drag him to his feet, Culden pulls the drawstring of the hood tight. Really tight.

Right on schedule, Waller pulls his car up with no lights as we cross the sidewalk. Shoving Curtis in the back seat, Kostic and I join him on each side. Culden hops into the front seat.

"Goddamnit Culden! No ad-libbing," I growl. "Are we going to have to search you for hidden weapons?"

"Shit! I'm sorry, Five. I just lost it there and let 'im have it." Her tone of voice betrays how *really* sorry she is. As we pull out, I put my fingers to my lips. I can feel Curtis' body shake. He groans. At least Kostic didn't kill him with the sap.

Curtis groans again. Culden holds the pint of vodka over the seat. I accept it as Kostic whispers into Curtis' ear. "Easy Brother Curtis. You're OK now. This damn pledge class really plays rough. You're lucky we just happened along and saw the whole thing."

Our victim mumbles something unintelligible. Kostic nods to me. I unscrew the vodka.

"I'm going to slip your hood up a little bit now," Kostic tells him. "Don't struggle. You'll be all right. I'll bet a little sip of vodka would help that headache though." Curtis tries to lift his arms, then sucks on the Schmirnoff gratefully.

"That's enough. Now just relax. We're just going to take a little ride."

• • •

It's nearly two thirty by the time we hit the dirt road outside of New Marshfield. We drive well within the speed limit with decent intervals between the three cars. Curtis sits there without a word, awake, probably trying to figure out where he's going. I've made sure the hood — the same one he used on Culden — is light-tight.

We pass the Benquist farm and then continue on up the

ridge. The car behind us stops at the farm for a moment, then follows. That will be Husted picking up the key from the Benquist mailbox. Without asking too many questions, Mr. Benquist allowed us to use his "far barn, if you promise not to burn it down or make too much noise."

We park along the familiar ridge that we first saw more than eight months ago. Kostic and I pull Curtis out of the car. Kostic offers him another swig of vodka which Curtis accepts. Then we march him through the dark up the little embankment and down into the abandoned strip mine.

• • •

With his hood off, Curtis stares through the dark at the twelve of us with glazed, groggy eyes. At this point, it's not important if he sees our faces. We're committed and the thing can only go one way.

"Curtis?" Kostic asks softly. "Do you know where you are?" Curtis shakes his head no. "Are you sure? You've been here before, you know. A Saturday night last May."

"Fuck you," Curtis mumbles. "Never been here befo'."

"Oh yes you have," Kostic continues. "Don't you remember? You dragged a pledge named Ransom out of your car. After you buggered him. And you dragged him up here and left him down there in the mud."

Curtis trembles. Again, he turns his head as if he's waiting for the cavalry to arrive. No bugles sound.

"We haven't made our minds up yet, Curtis," Benjo continues. "Whether to throw your ass down there in the mud to die? Or to go on with our little ride? What do you think we should do?"

"Fuck you."

• • •

Back in the cars, we drive for twenty minutes or so, finally circling around to the Benquist barn about a half mile down the hill from the farmer's house. Soos works the padlock and opens the door. Frank Able enters with a single battery light.

Solemnly, we march the hooded Curtis into the barn. Able sets the lamp so that it reflects up the wall behind us. Curtis has another nip of Schmirnoff and we make him sit on a straw bale in the middle of the room. Shivers, the wrestler, and Able, the swimmer, stand behind him ready to rip an arm off if he moves.

Again the hood comes off. Curtis looks around the room with frantic eyes, taking in each of our twelve faces. Kostic nods and the door opens again. Culden's long shadow is cast across the wall before she appears in front of Curtis.

"Hello, Curtis," she says in a soft voice. "Remember me?" Curtis nods, gulps and looks at her grim face. For the first time, we see a hint of fright in his features.

"I remember you," she says. "Maybe you can still smell me when you have that hood on. It's the one you used on me." Curtis continues to stare, a tiny drop of drool appears at the corner of his mouth.

"I can still smell you, Curtis. I can still smell your rotten cock," Culden's voice remains steady. We all hold our breath. "You wanted to show me your little cock again, didn't you Curtis? Well… why don't we take a look at it?"

Shivers drops the hood over Curtis' head again and pulls the string tightly. Curtis jerks but his guards hold him steady. Now we have a brother on each foot. Culden kneels and unbuttons the fly of his khakis.

"Why look at it!" she exclaims. "It's just a little bitty thing. Isn't that silly? I remember it being all hard and ready to go." We grin at her performance. She gives me a questioning look. I nod yes and hand her the dullest butter knife from the Ace kitchen.

"Do you suppose it would get hard, Curtis, if I *suckedddd on it a little bit?"* she asks in a sexy voice. We watch but the flaccid penis just shrinks a bit more.

"Or maybe you'd like it if I did this," she lays the cold side of the knife blade against his penis. An involuntary stream of urine squirts down Curtis' leg. Culden jumps back. Wiping her hand on his leg, Culden leans back forward and cups her hand around Curtis' scrotum.

"What I'd like to do is *thissss,*" she hisses, again running the cold flat steel across his balls. Curtis lets out a shriek. Culden grins and stands up. I nod to Shivers who lifts the hood.

"But what I want you to see Galen Curtis, is this." Before his dilated pupils, she shoves the Ace badge in his face. "I've had it in my hand ever since that night I ripped it off your chest. And before this night is over, I'll have your balls in my hand also."

Culden moves through the door, slamming it behind her. It's all we can do to keep from applauding.

Curtis weeps.

• • •

The session in the barn goes on for another hour. I confront him with the incident of his erect penis in his room. So does Waller. Mark Husted questions him repeatedly about the night he dumped Ransom in the ditch. McClintock repeats to him what we know about the first assault on Ransom in Curtis' room. How he dumped Ransom in his dorm with a bleeding anus.

Curtis' initial silence to our questions is now broken. He argues back. Denies. Contradicts himself. All the time, the little Nagra tape recorder winds away.

It's my turn again as we near the end of the second phase.

"Curtis. I was at Ransom's bed the night he died. I was the last one he talked to. Do you know what he told me?"

"No. And the lying little faggot… he just fucked up… " Curtis blubbers into meaningless sounds.

"He told me, 'Five. It was Curtis. He did it to me again. Get him for me.'" I hiss. I swing my open hand across the side of his head, a lot harder than I've always thought about. Spittle flies from his mouth and beads of sweat from his hair.

"You fucked him in the ass, didn't you Curtis? Right there in the car? Then you dragged his unconscious body up that slope and dumped him in the mud of that strip mine. Didn't you?" I scream. Curtis flinches. The whites of his eyes wall around toward me.

"Then… you butt-fucking pervert pederast! You stood there

484

and smoked a cigarette!!!" The brothers lean forward with looks of surprise. Am I carrying my act too far? "You smoked a cigarette and then you ground it out beside him and you left him there to die."

I slap his head again, this time with a partially closed fist. Tears fill my eyes. Curtis sobs loudly as the hood is pulled over his head again.

• • •

In the car, I continue to rant and rave. It's not hard now because it's no longer an act. We've moved Culden to another car so Mark Husted can be there to record any statement Curtis is ready to make. But so far, he doesn't confess to anything. Just blubbers and argues.

Perhaps the vodka is working too well.

We're into the last stage. Kostic and Waller continue to shout at him, badger him. Over and over with the same questions. In his hood, Curtis moans and gags and utters meaningless disconnected words.

We drive east, bypassing Athens, and hit the Sharpsburg hill past Amesville. It's nearly six and the eastern sky is beginning to lighten ever so slightly. At the top of the hill, we turn onto the dirt road into The Sharpsburg Hell.

The pre-dawn sky is clear and each fissure stands out like a burning open sore. Wisps of smoke and steam rise up a foot or so, then swirl away in the light breeze. The car ahead of us pulls off the track and lets us pass. Kostic drives on down the track another fifty yards or so. Then we stop.

"This is it, Curtis," Kostic says coldly. "You've taken our test and you've failed. If you have anything to say to us, you'd better say it now because you don't have any more chances."

"Whatta you want me to say?" he mumbles. "That I screwed that dumb Ransom fairy? So what?" He mumbles, then. "And you, Lowrey. I know you would've sucked my cock. I can tell your kind. Recognized your fag ass the first night you walked in the house."

"Keep going, Brother Curtis," I encourage softly. "What

about Culden Ellis?"

"Filthy little bitch had it coming. Flaunting her tits around. Wanna cut her tits right off her, stuff 'em up her..." his head yanks sideways as Waller clubs him across the jaw.

"That's it!" Waller opens the door and drags Curtis out. Kostic and I are out of our doors just as fast. "Come on you worthless cocksucker. It's time to meet your maker. Or the scum that's about to inherit your worthless soul," Waller screams.

The words we've rehearsed have flown out of our minds. This is no longer an act.

"Drink! Wanna drink," Curtis mumbles through the hood, slimy with spit and mucus. I lift the hood and he drinks energetically. Waller knocks my hand away.

"No more, Five. This mean bastard's had enough to drink. I want him awake and alert when the flames start eating at his ass."

"Let's go, brothers," Kostic says in a battlefield voice. We drag the stumbling, sobbing Curtis down the trail, then across a narrow stretch between two yawning fissures. Our path follows a maze of sharp turns and switchbacks, each bounded by its own infernal holocaust.

Finally we reach the spot I've chosen. To the east, I can see the brothers silhouetted against the ridge, only forty to fifty feet away. We make Curtis kneel on a patch of rocky ground about four feet wide between two long fissures. Smoke and steam roll out of them. Between us and the ridge, another huge fissure boils with burning coal, smoke and gasses.

Kostic and Waller nod, then leave by the trail we arrived on. I'm left there with Curtis and for long seconds, I fight the terrible urge to just shove his quaking body into one of the fiery holes. But then I lean over and cut the strips of tape that bind his hands. I'm ready to leap back if he attacks. Or stab him. But he just kneels there and trembles.

I take my leave.

• • •

The path is even more twisting than I realized as I make my

486

way back to the others. By the time I get to the ridge, I'm out of breath and wheezing from the smoke and gasses. Waller and Kostic are there, clad in their long black robes and high peaked conical hoods. Kostic throws my robe over my shoulders. I can hear him sobbing. Waller hands me some small bags. We climb to the top of the ridge. Culden stands in *her* robe and hood just beneath the ridge line.

The twelve of us stand in a line with the sun rising behind us. Below us, Curtis still kneels on the rocky ledge.

"Curtis," Kostic cries out. We join the chorus. "Curtisssss. Curtisss." Our call is like the moan of birds of prey. Buzzards. Vultures waiting on a nearby limb.

"Curtissssss!"

The figure below us moves, still on his knees. As he realizes his hands are free, fumbles with the hood and drags it from his head. One of us tosses the first bag into the big fissure between Curtis and us.

The magnesium chip explodes with white and silvery sparks and a cloud of white smoke. Another bag is tossed. Burning sulfur lends its yellow smoke to the eerie scene.

Curtis scoots around on his knees and looks up at us. The aluminum shot creates another sparkling explosion, different but just as dramatic. He scuttles back from the flames.

"What do you wannntttt?" Curtis screams. It's a pained, pitiful cry.

Kostic's voice calls out. "Curtis, you have violated your oath of brotherhood and now you face the fires of Acerbus." Curtis shrieks in despair.

My voice, wrung in tears, joins the indictment. "You have violated the rights of your fellow man and he has come to make sure you face the fires of Acerbus. Brother Ransom. Join us! Witness!" Like a wraith, Culden's robed and hooded form appears to join our line. Again, Curtis gives out another horrible shriek.

Waller finishes. "These are the fires of Acerbus. Upon your oath you swore you would face them would that you violated that oath. Let these fires burn in your memory throughout eternity." Waller raises his arms in a wide vee against the dawn.

We follow his example.

Then we chant, "So say we all!" and turn down the hill away from the screaming Curtis.

• • •

Tears stream down my face. Not from the smoke and gasses, though. My brothers and Culden are all in tears. We stand by the cars in our robes, clutching our hoods, ashen-faced, and listen to the horrible sounds Curtis makes beyond the ridge.

"So say we all," Kostic intones. He puts his arms around me, then embraces Waller. I can't stop crying. None of us can.

"No!" I wipe my running nose. "We can't do this."

"We have to, Five. We've gone too far. We cannot go back," Kostic says wiping his face. Tears streak his ash-smeared skin and the stubble of his beard.

"If we leave him, we're no better than he is," I argue. "We'll be murderers, too. I can't do it."

"We have to, Five. We're the Thirteen," Soos Salazar cries.

"Fuck the Thirteen," I shout. "I'm going back for him. I'll never tell… don't worry. But I can't leave that pathetic bastard down there to die. Joe Ransom wouldn't leave him."

"You really mean that, don't you Five?" Kostic grabs my shoulders and looks into my eyes. I think he's about to hit me.

"Yes I do. I really mean it and I'm going back."

"No, *you're not.*" Kostic shouts. "We're the Thirteen. We are the One! *We're* going back. All of us."

"But it'll fuck everything up," McClintock screams. "What about Ransom? What about our promise to him?"

"Come on, Mac," I say, giving my hand and the peculiar grip. "We are the Thirteen. We are the One. And I think Joe Ransom knows we've kept our promise him."

Culden stands there in her robe, a small funereal figure holding a funny black hood, and watches the twelve of us as we strip our the robes and start back down the hill.

• • •

488

When we reach him, Curtis is no longer screaming. He just makes strange blubbering noises. One leg of his pants is charred and smoldering. As the others watch, I reach down and grasp his arm.

"Come on, Curtis. It's time to go."

"Going home?"

"No Curtis. We're going to see the sheriff."

Epilogue

It's January now and the memories of the past few weeks are etched in my mind like the frosted designs of a Christmas ornament.

Before the month is out, Galen Curtis will be sentenced for manslaughter, assault and assault with intent to rape. As we drove from The Sharpsburg Hell that morning, Curtis turned mean and truculent again. But when he heard the tape recordings of the things he'd admitted to, his mood changed and he volunteered everything to the sheriff.

Yet, I cannot gather my thoughts about Galen Curtis. As surely as he went to the mouth of Hell that morning, so did I. So did we all. The Thirteen.

The brothers of Alpha Chi Epsilon astonished us as well. We returned to the house and asked J.L. Simmons to call an emergency chapter meeting. By three that afternoon, the brotherhood was gathered before the Temple Bar where I offered a brief summary of the events and my resignation as an Ace. My resignation was followed by my eleven brothers.

Not only did they not accept our badges but overwhelmingly voted to take the situation before the Interfraternity Council and the Dean's office.

So Alpha Chi Epsilon is on probation for the rest of the year. Pending the final hearing from the Dean's office, we *may* get to keep our charter and stay an active fraternity at Ohio University. The Dean assured me that he would give it serious thought and as well as I've come to know him, I respect him as a serious man.

Darcy has come back into my life by way of the cover of *Seventeen* magazine. Her smiling face and pixie figure beam against the shadows of a lonely Wall Street. Ticker tape and confetti strew the empty street behind her. I have the cover framed and on my desk. Duff has his framed version on the wall of the Begorra beside the *Light Show*.

Probation means the Ace house will be silent of parties for a while. We will be allowed to initiate our pledge class but I have a feeling it'll be a subdued Hell Week. Our only social allowance is serenades for newly-pinned brothers and their girls.

That's something I've been thinking about for Andy and me in the months to come. If I remain an Ace.

Andy has been my rock through the Curtis episode and the strange Christmas vacation that followed. I must admit, she does have a way with me.

Culden has come through the whole thing with her sharp wit and even sharper tongue. She even seemed disappointed that Curtis' confession of his assault would relieve her of having to testify against him. That would have been a scene!

Culden continues to be my beatnik muse. Take for instance today. I'm working on a sketch and when my model asks for a break, Culden looks from her easel and grunts.

"Damn it to hell, Five. You're doing it again. Look at that. Her tits look like eggplants."

She takes my hand and lifts my fingertips to Andy's breast. "Feel this, Five. Feel the curves. The lines. If you paint from your heart what you feel in your fingertips…"

THE END

About the Author

James Patterson is a writer, photographer and graphic designer. A former industrial editor, his magazines have won international awards. His travel stories and photos have been widely published in newspapers and magazines.

Patterson is a contributing writer for *Mac Today* and *Photoshop User* magazines, specializing in digital photography. He has taught Macintosh graphics applications at the college level for the past 10 years.

A 1958 graduate of Ohio University, Patterson served as a special agent in the US Army Counterintelligence Corps.

He and his wife Betty live in Largo, Florida.

Printed in the United States
18954LVS00001B/4

9 781585 004782